dangerous TRUTHS

KRIS BUTLER

DARK CONFESSIONS SERIES

BOOK ONE

dangerous TRUTHS

KRIS BUTLER

FOREWORD

This is a why choose novel, meaning the main female character doesn't have to choose between love interests.

This is a dark contemporary romance that deals with depression, grief, and child loss. And while it is also a mafia romance, it's different than any mafia romance you've probably read before. The story is mostly focused on Loren, her job as a therapist, and the men she meets. She gets pulled into things and the mafia will come more into play later. And while it is a depiction of a therapist, it is not meant to reflect a self help book or follow any ethical boundaries. It is a work of fiction.

This is a medium-high burn with a slow-build harem. The characters are adults with most being 30 and above. This story deals with some themes that may be triggering through Loren's job, and the clients she sees. It deals with past abuse, kidnapping, sexual exploitation, and murder. Please be mindful of this moving forward and make sure to take care of yourself if things become too much.

This is an adult romance and is intended for readers 18+ due to language and content. Cuss words are used throughout, and sexual scenes are explicit. This series will contain MM though not in book one.

The journey begins on the next page....

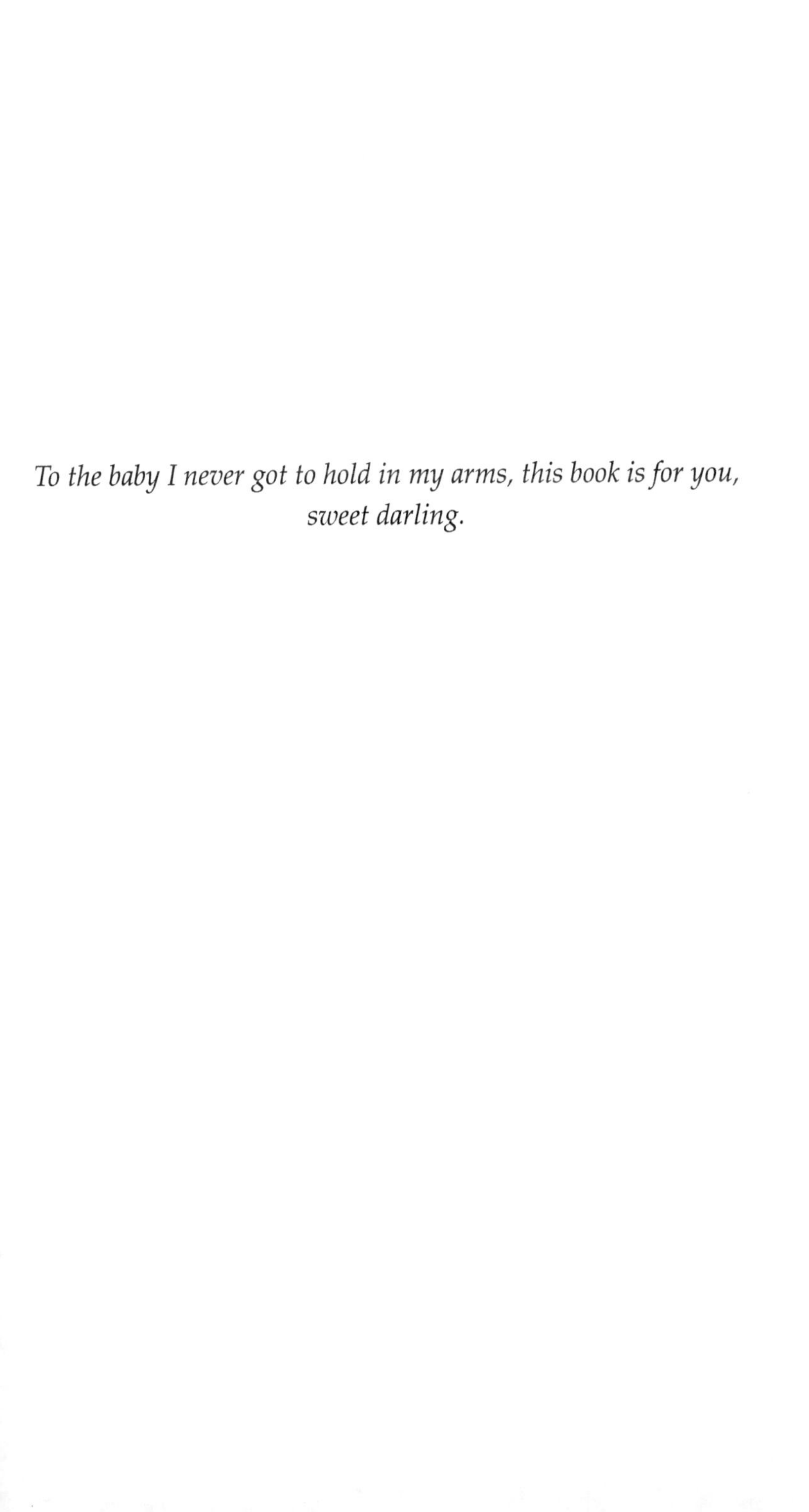

To the baby I never got to hold in my arms, this book is for you, sweet darling.

PROLOGUE

LOREN

The slamming of the door reverberated throughout the house, shaking the walls and windowpanes. I sat on the corner of the bed, my arms wrapped tightly around my knees as my head rested there. Sound ricocheted around me, my body tensed as I waited for it to end.

He was angry. *Again.*

Though, he was always angry these days. It didn't matter if I did everything right. There was always a reason for his ire.

I didn't put the dishes in the dishwasher correctly.

The dog barked too much.

That car intentionally cut him off.

His boss had singled him out.

His family didn't care.

None of his friends called to hang out.

The restaurant got his order wrong.

They, they, they—never the one at fault, always the victim. *It was exhausting always being wrong.*

As a therapist, I worked with irrational thoughts,

deluded thinking, and a victim stance mentality daily with my clients. They paid me to help them and listened to what I had to teach them. Motivated clients even used those lessons to make positive changes in their lives. I took pride in my job and had a very successful practice. It was something I excelled at. So, I should be able to handle this too, right?

Apparently, husbands made horrible clients.

The house finally quieted as the echo died down, my body starting to relax in the wake of this new peace. Barkley nudged me, making me lift my arm so she could nose her way under it. Crossing my legs, she laid her head in my lap, looking up at me with her big eyes, and I melted. Petting my dog, I calmed even more as her soothing energy penetrated my senses. Barkley had been my saving grace this past year. My life hadn't always been this way. In fact, at one time it had been damn near perfect.

Or so I'd thought.

Brian and I were high school sweethearts living the ideal life. Until one day, it just wasn't. The before times had become a mere memory now.

We'd been together for over fifteen years and married for ten of those. Married young and full of hope, we thought we'd breeze through life. Why wouldn't we? Everything else in our lives had been so easy. The biggest farce you discovered as an adult was that *good things* didn't always happen to *good people*.

The past five years taught me that lesson.

Somewhere during that time, I quit feeling like a person, much less a wife. Once life started shitting on us, it didn't let up until we were covered in it. From toxic jobs, family conflict, and loss of loved ones, everything piled up until I could no longer see a way out.

Every day, the darkness grew, and I felt more and more alone. Numbness surrounded my heart, and it felt like I had to wade through molasses just to breathe. I thought marriage meant I'd have a partner through it all, but instead, I carried the burden for both of us as he checked out, leaving me alone to handle it.

I was sick of handling it.

Laying back on the bed, I curled into the fetal position as the tears fell. Barkley snuggled up close and licked my face trying to offer me comfort. Eventually, I fell asleep, hoping tomorrow would be better. Hope was all I had left at this point.

Life didn't work that way though, did it?

In what felt like quick succession, the last of my hope fled as the dominoes fell, successfully crumbling the makeshift structure my life had become.

The first domino was a debilitating gut-punch leaving me breathless as I tried to recover from the hardest thing any woman had to. *Losing a child.*

I grieved and suffered alone, and a lot of that time was a fog now, a haze of memories barely accessible. Maybe, it was the cause of the second domino to fall, or perhaps it was inevitable regardless. Either way, it broke something in me, and I didn't know if it would ever heal from it.

The second domino was discovering my *husband*, my *high school sweetheart*, my so-called *protector*, the *man* who'd vowed to love me above all others was having an affair. It struck true, hitting me the hardest. I lost all trust in the world. It cemented the fact that it didn't matter in the end what kind of person you were. The bad went unpunished, and the good were screwed over; no one was safe from heartbreak.

The final domino shattered my belief in the goodness of people. I was served divorce papers at work. *At. Fucking. Work.* It was a stranger who told me my husband was divorcing me in front of my colleagues and clients. The real kicker, Brian kept the house and Barkley.

Three hits left me splintered all over the floor and I didn't have the energy anymore to get up. I was officially out—out of luck, out of hope, and out of caring. I dreaded every day and felt less of a person than I had the day before.

Yet, no one knew my pain, or the sadness I hid behind my eyes. I displayed the face people wanted to see. *Perfect Loren.* The mask was firmly in place, the illusion strong as I suffered in silence. But I no longer recognized the reflection staring back at me in the mirror. The person I'd once been a far cry from the woman staring back. I was lost with no direction to go.

The dangerous truth of it all? I was without hope, love, and relationships. What was the point in caring when nothing mattered in the end?

Soon, I would fade away into nothing, just a vacant memory lost in the breeze.

ONE

LOREN

The liquid sputtered loudly as it dripped from the coffee machine at an agonizing rate. I contemplated whether it was even worth the wait as I stared longingly at the liquid. Not like it did much for me these days anyway. Coffee was not the elixir of life people said it was. *No, coffee was just coffee.* It couldn't solve my problems as much as I wished it would. Of course, I was still addicted to the stuff. Plus, there was something oddly satisfying about the routine each morning as I drank it.

Finally, the drip stopped, and I could pull my mug from under the spout. It was odd, but watching it dribble into my cup had become my daily curiosity. Every morning, I stood at the counter and watched the coffee trickle slowly into the cup, hoping it would magically fill me with something. Only problem, I didn't know what the 'something' was.

Shuffling over to the couch, I plopped down on the seat, careful not to spill anything. Before, I'd been one of those fancy coffee drinkers taking pleasure in the fancy foam and flavors, but now, I drank it black. Just like my soul.

Sipping the scalding liquid did nothing to warm my insides as I stared out the large window of my high-rise condo. The view from here was the best thing about this place, even if I didn't always appreciate it. My window looked out over the cityscape and there was a dog park below. Often, I would get lost watching the owners and their dogs as they chased balls together. It was a bitter-sweet thing making me—

Better to not go down that line of thought, I scolded myself.

Today, it was winter and *nothing* could make it look appealing. The outside was barren, desolate, and dead, accurately reflecting the state of my life. A few remaining leaves scattered across the grass on their journey to find a better resting place. My thoughts should concern me, but these days, they were par for the course. When you lived in a constant state of despair, you got comfortable with the shadows.

The only sound in the room was the sipping of my coffee and the second hand of the clock. If I weren't already depressed, the absence of sound would send me there. According to Robert Blakesly though, "Silence is not the absence of sound, but the absence of self."

So, here in the silence, I was no one.

When I lifted my mug, and nothing poured out, I realized I'd already drunk it all. Shrugging to myself about the empty cup, I got up and shuffled back into the kitchen. Picking up my feet required too much effort, and at home, I had the freedom to be this way. Lethargy was my friend here.

In the safety of my condo, I could wallow alone without having to pretend I was okay. The moment I took a step out of my building, I had to transform into 'The Loren Carter' the one who had it all together.

Quite frankly, she was fucking exhausting. *I exhausted myself.* What did that say about me? How people didn't hate me, I wasn't sure. They probably did, but were too polite to say anything.

Two years ago, my life had seemed as perfect as every girl dreamed it could be. Married to my high school sweetheart, successful in our careers, and living the white picket fence dream in the 'right' neighborhood in Chicago about to start a family. Everything was at our fingertips ready for us to grasp it.

Brian was VP of a successful real estate firm, and, rightfully so, it was stressful. He complained about his job, but I thought it was typical job stress. We'd both been raised to believe if you worked hard, you would be rewarded. *Well, that had turned out to be a crock of shit.*

What had seemed manageable stress became a ticking time bomb. It was impressive how easily the house of cards collapsed at the first real presence of wind. When true tragedy struck, we discovered what we were really made of, which, unfortunately, wasn't enough to withstand it. My life crumbled, along with my belief things could be better.

The only thing I had now was my job, my practice.

Dressing for the day, I debated if I wanted to go work out this morning. In an attempt to curb my depression, I'd signed up for one of those barre classes. It was something to take my mind off things, but it wasn't as physically exhausting as I'd hoped. Most of the ladies in my class were nice enough, but they were just more people I had to be fake around. At least they didn't know me or my history, offering me a semblance of anonymity.

Smiling was exhausting when all I wanted to do was scream.

Grabbing my bag, I decided today was as good as any to make changes. I was a *fucking therapist*, I should be able to shake this depression, for crying out loud. But no one ever expected the therapist to be depressed. Jokes on them.

Just because I knew good coping skills didn't mean I was any better at using them. Knowledge, *unfortunately*, didn't make you immune to pain. In fact, perhaps therapists made the second worst type of client.

Locking the door, I headed down the hall toward the elevator. Being on the eighteenth floor, I was thankful for it. Having to climb that many stairs in heels would be murder on my feet. Bet my ass would look amazing, though, not that anyone saw it these days.

My neighbor in 18D exited his door right as I passed. I could time my mornings by where we were in relation to the elevator and one another. Today, based on my distance, I was running ahead of schedule and would reach it first. Getting there first was one of those minute things I took pleasure in each morning.

Besides, whoever got there first had the prime spot inside to avoid the stinky guy a few floors below. I wouldn't lie, the simple act of winning at something was a huge draw for me too.

My smirk must've been obvious today as I hit the down arrow because I heard him chuckle behind me. It was odd hearing him laugh and the deep rumble it produced took me by surprise. In the year I'd lived here, we'd never spoken actual words with one another, only exchanging the courteous head nod in greeting. Turning, the shock evident on my face, caused him to chuckle even more.

"I know, I know," he started, his voice hitting me even more head-on. "That's not part of our whole repertoire thing we have going on, but your smirk was just too cute and it erupted out of me unconsciously. I promise to swallow my laugh and return back to ignoring you, offering only the occasional nod."

I stared, even more stunned at his words. As I processed them, I wasn't sure how I felt. Taking the opportunity to truly look at him for the first time, I verified his smoky voice accurately reflected his classic rugged looks. His dark blonde hair was lightly tousled, shrouding his pale green eyes, and a light beard covered his face. He was probably a few inches taller than me, around 5'11" or 6 ft to my 5'9" height. The difference was hard to tell in heels. He smelled of clean cotton and soap. It was... nice.

My silent racing companion was dressed well in a navy suit and grey vest that fitted him snugly, emphasizing his build. It had to be tailored due to the exceptional fit emphasizing his body. 18D noticed me assessing him, and smiled wider, enjoying my perusal.

He wasn't cocky, despite his handsomeness. In fact, I didn't detect any arrogance. It was more that he was enjoying me observing him.

The ding of the elevator pulled me from my assessment, causing me to jump a little at the sound. My momentary distraction resulted in losing the prime spot in the elevator as he zoomed in when the doors opened. Grumbling under my breath, I stomped in, causing Mr. Sexy Voice to chuckle louder. *So glad* he was delighted by my annoyance.

"I haven't been purposely ignoring you, you know. It's just, I tend to be oblivious, and besides our morning race to the elevator, I doubt I would've been able to pick you out of a line-up," I grumbled in defiance. He irritated me and I didn't know why.

"Well, let's remedy that, shall we, *neighbor*?"

He seemed sincere even if he was poking fun at me, so I let go of my annoyance and offered my hand in politeness to shake his proffered one.

"Loren."

"Nice to meet you, Loren. I'm Monroe."

His name rolled around in my brain, and I liked it, it fit him. Awareness of feelings I was unaccustomed to slammed into my mind, reminding me I *couldn't* like him. People required effort, and I had none to give. My walls slammed back up. Acquaintances were better anyway. This way, I didn't have to care. Caring had only ever led to pain.

"You too... Monroe," I stumbled, my walls preventing it from sticking. "Though, if you really wanted to be 'neighborly', you could trade me spots and save me from Stinky Steve."

"Ha! Sorry." He fake pouted, touching his chest. "I'm nice, but I'm not *that nice.* You'll have to suffer the torture and be quicker next time," he quipped, a small smile replacing his pout.

Narrowing my eyes, I wasn't happy with this development. He could at least follow the unspoken rules of elevator courtesies if he was going to make me talk to him. The quiet descended around us and my upbringing had my ingrained politeness kick in, asking a follow-up question.

"So… " I started until I realized I'd already forgotten his name. Quickly, I tried to make it less obvious, "how long have you lived here?"

I leaned against the wall facing him, my arms crossed with a frown in place. If he wasn't going to help me out with the stinkfest, then I didn't have to be *that polite,* I decided. It was the first time in months I'd felt anything other than numbness or sadness, and I was grasping hold of it.

Chuckling again, he shook his head before answering, "Just a little longer than you, I believe, about a year and a half now."

I nodded, not sure what else to say. His stupid laugh kept disarming me, and it was throwing me off my internal brooding. Turning back to the front, I surprised myself when I asked another damn question.

"Um, so what do you do?" stuttered out of me.

His demeanor made me feel relaxed with the ease of

how he took things, but annoyed it was at my expense. Everything in my life had always been dissected or calculated. The situation was odd but not necessarily unpleasant. I hadn't been prepared to navigate this on an elevator ride, allowing him to lower my guard one laugh at a time. My neighbor was more dangerous than I'd given him credit for.

"I'm an attorney for a pharmaceutical company. What about you?"

"I'm a trauma therapist."

Silence descended upon us as we watched the numbers decrease. I despised telling people my job. They either began to tell me all their life problems or acted extremely uncomfortable, like I could somehow read their minds and knew all their secrets.

Newsflash, I didn't, nor did I want to unless you were paying me for an hour. Hate to break it to you, but I was as self-absorbed as the next person when I was outside my office. I only had time to think about my own problems.

He cleared his throat around the fifth floor, Stinky Steve's floor, and we both held our breath to see if he would be joining us today. A sigh of relief flowed from us both when it didn't. However, I was still pissed he hadn't given me *my spot.*

"That sounds intense," he finally uttered.

"It can be."

Wow, I broke our cordial agreement for the world's most boring conversation. Go me, I sure knew how to pick them!

The ding of the elevator reaching the ground floor echoed in the close quarters, and we both breathed another sigh of relief. Awkwardly, I smiled goodbye and hoped this meant we could return to our anticlimactic races to the elevator with no more chatting. I was convinced small talk would slowly kill us all in a vat of niceness.

The blistering cold hit my skin as I exited the condominiums. One of the best things about living in downtown Chicago was the commute. With the variety in public transportation available, it made getting anywhere simple. I hadn't driven my car in months, and it mostly sat unused in the parking garage, only taken out when I had to deal with my parents.

I wondered if I should make sure gasoline didn't go bad or something. It would be my luck that the one moment I needed my car, it wouldn't start. These were the types of things Brian had taken care of for me. He might've been a shitty man in the end, but he'd been a good husband for most of our marriage. Some days, I felt utterly helpless when I had to take care of something like this, something he was so good at just doing.

Grief was a funny thing that way, making me miss him for just a minute before I remembered the raging asshole he'd been in the end. Pulling up the collar of my coat, I hedged my way through the crowd, getting lost in the sea of bodies. It was comforting being just one of many.

The coffee shop loomed ahead, and like a true addict, I was already craving my fix. Coffee might not be the elixir of life, but it was my drug of choice. Getting coffee before work was part of my new normal, and as small as it was, it was something that kept me going some days.

The ding of the bell over the door announced my arrival as I trudged forward to join the line. Immediately, the heat of the place hit me, and I began to swelter. Buildings needed to figure out how to regulate temperatures from outside to inside better. There was nothing worse than overheating, then removing all of your articles of winter warmth, only to add them back a few minutes later to face the weather. *Especially* while jostling cups of coffee.

I liked Bean Paradise because it had excellent coffee and didn't ever have a long wait. It wasn't overpriced, making it easy to indulge multiple times a day. The fact it was adjacent to my practice, New Horizons, didn't hurt either. Ordering my usuals, I quickly redressed myself in my winter apparel before grabbing my tray of hot beverages. It was game face time.

Putting my mask into place, my escape was officially over. I wondered how long I could keep this up before it ultimately splintered me? My smile seemed to slip a millimeter each day, and before long, I wouldn't even be able to force it, my muscles revolting against me as well. I just hoped I had something figured out before then.

TWO

LOREN

Sipping my coffee, I glanced over my schedule for the day, trying to prepare for the sessions I had. My job was the only thing I still enjoyed. It was an escape from my own sadness in some weird way, and instead, I could help other people hold those feelings and find their way out. It was a bit delusional on my part, but it was working for me at the moment, so I had no desire to change.

I hid behind my mask to shield my pain, to protect me from the prying eyes of the world. It was both a blessing and a hindrance. At some point, I was going to have to drop it in order to heal. Nothing ever grew when contained.

"Knock, knock," Doris, our receptionist, chimed as she stopped in my doorway.

"Hey. How's it going this morning?"

"Not too bad, thanks for the coffee you placed on my desk. I see you have a full day, and a new one. I'll let you know when your client's here."

"Thanks, Doris," I smiled, "and you're welcome."

Doris was my lifesaver. She took care of all the scheduling, billing, and managing the files, leaving the other therapists and me to concentrate only on clients. They should really make therapists take business classes as part of their degree program. It wasn't a skill that came naturally to a lot of us empathetic people. Thankfully, we had Doris to keep our heads straight.

Finishing my responses to all my emails, I scrolled aimlessly on Pinterest, lost in a haze of aesthetically pleasing boards. I mostly pinned things I pretended I would do, but never actually did anything with them. It was a habitual thing, it seemed. Dreaming of a life I could never have, not anymore. At one time, it had been as picture perfect as a Pinterest board.

Shaking away the moroseness, I put my barriers in place to shut everything out of my mind for a few hours. While useful and necessary, it was exhausting by the end of the day, leaving me emotionally and mentally drained. Compassion fatigue was a real thing.

While I liked all my clients, some were always easier to like, making those sessions richer. Therapy was effective even without a natural connection, but when you felt that click, it was magic. The sessions transformed into these places where anything could happen. I lived for those sessions.

My first few clients this morning were long-term ones I'd been working with for a few years. Knowing their histories well, and the goals they were working on, made it less prep work beforehand. It was an incredible experience to maintain some clients long-term because you got to witness different levels of growth from them throughout their lives. When they celebrated, you celebrated with them and watching those clients make positive choices or use their coping skills, it made the fatigue worth it.

And when all you had was your job, *it had to be worth it.*

"It sounds like you're at a place in your life where you're ready for some change but unsure what direction to start."

"Yeah… that sounds about right. I just don't know where to start."

"How about this week, you focus on visualizing where you want to be and identify different plans to get there? We can review them together in your next session."

"Yeah, I can do that. Thanks, Loren."

"You're welcome, but you did the work. I just got to witness it. Good job sharing today. I'll see you next week, okay?"

"Yep. Bye."

Walking my fourth client out the door, I hurried back to finish my documentation on the session. A 'therapist hour' was fifty minutes, leaving you a precious ten to document and do anything else necessary, like pee. It was often a mad dash to do that in an office full of women. Never failed, no matter where you were, there was always a line for the bathroom.

One more client before lunch, and it was my new

intake. Reviewing the form, I was able to give myself an idea of what to expect.

Client I.M.:

Teenage girl with a history of trauma.

Suffering from panic attacks, anxiety, depression, and potential PTSD.

Will be accompanied by her father.

Trauma clients were tricky and had to be handled with care. So many clients didn't return after the initial session because of this. Coming to therapy for the first time was difficult enough. Making them feel bad only led them to have a bad association with treatment and never want to try again. I strove to make it as comfortable as possible because I hated losing people who had bravely taken that first step to healing.

Especially, when it was something I currently failed at.

Opening the door to the waiting room, I became momentarily stunned by a man standing against the wall. His head was downcast, hands in his pockets, and one foot crossed over the other. His obsidian hair covered his face hiding his eyes as dark stubble lightly peppered his face. He had a presence about him that drew my attention, and I really wanted to see what he was hiding.

This reaction to him shocked me. I hadn't been affected by a man in years. Regaining my composure, I reminded myself I was in a place of business, *my place of business.* Pulling my shoulders back, I turned to address the teenage girl, trying to ignore the alluring man in the corner. I hadn't even seen his face, but I couldn't quit staring at him. I wasn't used to feeling this way. It unnerved me, and I didn't like it. Clearing my throat, I hoped I wouldn't sound as wanton as I was feeling.

"Imogen."

The teen girl lifted her head, anxiety written all over her face. Her long brunette hair had been covering her face, and now, I could see her pale blue eyes and freckles as she looked up. At the sound of her name, the man had glanced over as well. Looked like he was with her. That wouldn't be distracting in session. *Nope, not at all,* I thought.

Focusing on what I needed to, I kept my gaze directed toward the girl in front of me and avoided looking in the other direction. Professional mask in place, I smiled encouragingly at her while keeping *him* in my peripheral.

"If you're ready, you can come back."

She nervously stood up, glancing at the man I assumed was her father. Upon closer inspection, he seemed relatively young to be a teenager's father, but that didn't mean it wasn't possible. He looked mid-thir-ties, just a few years older than me. A baby at eighteen wouldn't be out of the realm of possibilities.

"Me as well?" The masculine voice rolled over my body, and it took everything in me not to visibly react to him. The sound was sin personified.

"If Imogen is comfortable, then yes, you may both come back. If she's not, then I would like to meet with the parent and youth for the first 15 minutes to go over history, but after, I can just meet with the client."

I glanced at Imogen to gauge her preference. She was

standing with her arms crossed at her wrists. At my glance, she shrugged her shoulders in indifference.

"It's fine," she eventually mumbled.

My empathy meter started to rise, allowing me to block out the seductive man and I gestured for her to follow me to my office.

"Feel free to sit wherever you're comfortable. I'll be sitting over here where the computer is," I gestured.

Imogen took the couch across from me, and her petite frame became engulfed by the cushions. I watched as she visibly turned inward, almost trying to make herself even smaller. Her dad chose the chair next to the couch, close but giving her space. In my experience, that was a good indication of their connection. Body language told you a lot about people's relationships, if you paid enough attention.

"I'm Loren, and I get the pleasure of learning about you while asking a million and one questions. Today's focus is to learn about your history, identify the symptoms, and figure out a plan to address them. If there is something you don't feel like talking about, then we don't have to go there today. Just share with me what you can, okay?"

Her nod was a clear sign this was going to be me digging for answers today. Hopefully, her father would be more open, or it would be a quiet and challenging hour.

"Are there any questions you have for me before we get started?" I hadn't really expected any, so I was surprised when the deep voice rolled over my body again.

"Could you give us your background and credentials?" the mysterious man asked. It took me a minute to respond due to the unexpected nature of the question.

His masculine voice urged my body to give in to the shiver with the authority he wielded. I glanced up to respond, which was an immediate mistake. Golden umber eyes, both dark and light, stared right back at me. In this enclosed space, his smell of expensive cologne intensified the moment. *It smelled of seduction and secrets and I wanted to roll around in it.*

Snared in his gaze, I lost my words.

My mouth hung half opened with what I was going to say forgotten on my tongue. Blinking, it helped reset my brain and focus back on the present. Closing my mouth, I swallowed, trying to remember what I had looked up for in the first place.

"Yes, absolutely. As the website states, I've been in the field for over ten years. I own this practice with two colleagues, and we started it three years ago. Before that, I worked in residential facilities, outpatient clinics, and the VA. I have a masters in Counseling from Northwestern, and I'm a Licensed Mental Health Counselor with special certifications in both sexual abuse and trauma-informed treatment. I work primarily with women and teens dealing with anxiety, depression, and trauma."

I stopped before I kept going and gave him my blood type and Social Security number. Something about him called to my need to please, and I wanted him to like me. *It was weird.* I shouldn't be having these thoughts about my client's father, but he had this air about him that demanded your attention. When he didn't say anything to my answer, I turned back to Imogen, hoping I could forget him. Unlikely, with his magnetic energy filling the room, but I was determined to try.

"Thank you, that's satisfactory. I'd also like to ensure that confidentiality is upheld with the highest standard. No one has permission outside of *me* to know she's here. *No one.*"

As he spoke, I sat stunned for a moment, not understanding what he was implying. Of course, I would keep things confidential! That was a foundation of my job.

"Okay, well, I guess I meet your standards, and yes, of course, confidentiality is very important to me, and is something we go over as part of the intake." Clearing my throat, I attempted to regain my composure, his questions had thrown me out of my normal routine and caused me to forget. Focusing back on my client, I tried to start again. "Alright, let's start with your name, age, and who's with you today."

"Um, well, I'm Imogen... Mas… ters, and I'm 17, and this is my brother, Attie."

I was surprised at her admittance as the paperwork had clearly stated father. Something weird was going on here. I began to type up the information, focusing on keeping my face clear except for my encouraging smile. A throat clearing brought me out of my train of thought.

"It's Atticus, or Mr. Masters. Only, Immy is allowed to call me Attie."

His voice had me turning back to him again and each time I did, it was like being hit with his seductive spell anew. This was going to be a problem if I couldn't quit getting lost each time I glanced at him. He watched me with a domineering look in his eyes, melting my insides.

Atticus didn't appear to be an intimidating person, but something about his presence screamed *danger*, while also making me want to kneel in respect. I wanted to give in to whatever he was demanding with those dark golden eyes whispering to me. Blinking again, I found the words I'd been trying to utter.

"I will make sure not to call you that. I'm confused though, the paperwork I received stated that Imogen would be accompanied by her father?"

My words had Atticus's face shutting down, and Imogen withdrawing. Well, that hadn't been the right question. *Shit.*

"He's not involved in Imogen's life. I have legal guardianship."

"Of course, I will correct the forms."

"Please do. Thank you."

"Right, so Imogen, can you tell me what grade you're in? The school you attend…"

The next thirty minutes were filled with Imogen giving short answers to my probing questions, but she was at least answering them. She seemed to be isolated, socially withdrawn, and had no pro-social activities. No clubs, job, or afterschool events. She didn't even attend public school since she was homeschooled by a tutor.

Imogen's hobbies and leisure activities were limited, indicating her range of coping skills to be small. We hadn't even gotten to symptoms or what brought her in yet, but I didn't have a good feeling. She wasn't adequately prepared to deal with regular teenage drama, much less a traumatic one.

"Can you share some of the symptoms you've been experiencing and for how long?" My question was met by silence, not surprising—tactic two time.

"How about if I ask you some things and then you can just answer yes or no? Would that be better?"

"Yes," she answered, a smile of relief.

Smiling to remind her I was safe to share with, I relaxed my face as I started my list, pausing briefly between each one to see if she nodded or not.

"Anxiety? Depression? Poor Sleep? Flashbacks? Appetite change? Impulsive behavior? Poor decision-making? Inability to focus on tasks or schoolwork? Isolation? Withdrawing from others? Feelings of helplessness? Feelings of worthlessness? Self-harming behavior? Any thoughts of wanting to hurt yourself? Others?"

When we were finished, it was fairly obvious she was experiencing PTSD. Never wanting to assume, I also gave her a PTSD scale. As she filled it in, I glanced at the clock, realizing I only had five minutes left.

I started to formulate my diagnostic conclusion while she finished the criteria. Somehow, I'd been able to block Atticus throughout most of the interview. He hadn't needed to share too much, only a few things on family history and some addition to her behavior he'd observed. He'd been supportive and allowed her to talk, even if she struggled, only stepping in when she looked to him for help. I admired him for that. I didn't know their whole story yet, but their dynamic intrigued me.

"Just a few more things to cover, but I wanted to

thank you, Imogen, for sharing with me today, and Mr. Masters for being here to support her. I know it's a difficult decision to come here and tell a stranger the scary things in your life, but I want you to look at it as a step toward finding a solution, and you're no longer walking the path alone. I'm here to walk along with you, if you let me."

Imogen gave a tiny smile, but she appeared to accept what I'd said. I covered the aforementioned informed consent and confidentiality, ensuring them both I took it very seriously and ethically, I could only break it for three reasons—abuse, homicide, and suicide. Mr. Masters appeared appeased by the answer for once and I gained a little of my confidence back he'd shaken loose. We scheduled for the following week, and I was hopeful she'd return. It was always hit or miss after the first one before the rapport was built.

"I always offer a treat at the end because I feel like therapy can be like dementors at times, and the best way to treat a dementor attack is chocolate. Hopefully, you're familiar with Harry Potter. Otherwise, I'll probably sound weird."

"I love Harry Potter," she beamed, and I watched the first genuine smile spread across Imogen's face. Doing a victory dance in my head, I felt confident she'd return now. I always found if you had one thing to connect with them on, it increased the odds they would.

It also meant I would get to see more of the seductive man as well. Though, I wasn't sure if that was good or bad. My behavior was throwing me off, but every time he spoke or directed those umber eyes to me, I forgot why I shouldn't be melting into a puddle.

Atticus stood up, smoothing down his three-piece suit that looked expensive, but fit him well. *Very well, in fact.* Forcibly pulling my gaze back to Imogen, I walked out with her chatting about Harry Potter houses.

Atticus trailed behind us quietly and a stray thought crossed my mind, continuing to surprise me. Please, let nothing be on my ass.

I think I needed to check my brand of coffee when I got home because something was off with me today.

THREE

ATTICUS

The swish of her pants drew my attention as it stretched over her ass and the subtle smell of coconuts drifted to me. I'd been dreading this appointment but knew I needed to be here for Immy. I owed her that much. More actually. She was mine to protect now, and I vowed to her and myself that I would do better, *be better* than the man who'd raised us.

Imogen was my half-sister, the product of my father's second marriage. She hadn't been around a lot when I was a teenager, or perhaps as a seventeen-year-old, I just didn't care to be around. But when she was about four or five, I'd returned from college one summer, and she captured my heart. Immy had this light about her that always pulled me in. She was so different from the world we lived in, and I think a part of me had always wanted the escape she offered before I'd even admitted it to myself.

Our *father* was none other than, Dayton "the Grim Reaper" Mascro, head of the Mascro family, boss of the criminal underground, and an overall *jackass*. There was a time when I'd respected my father, idolized him even, but that changed over time as I saw the corruption and deceit he weaved.

It sounded ironic to be upset with a mafia boss for corruption, but there was truth to the saying, honor among thieves. The family might lie to the world, steal what they wanted, and use any means necessary to get things done, *but there was a line.* You didn't cheat your own family. If there was no honor amongst the family, how could any trust be sowed amongst murder and mayhem? Simple. You couldn't.

I was so lost in my thoughts and fixated on the scrumptious ass in front of me that I hadn't realized she'd stopped and asked me a question. The realization that I'd let my guard down in this place was sobering. I couldn't afford to be complacent now.

"Mr. Masters?" Mrs. Carter asked again, a hint of irritation in her tone clueing me in that it wasn't the first time she said my name. The name took me off guard for a moment until I remembered she didn't know our real last name. Shit! I couldn't afford to be distracted by a nice ass.

This wouldn't do. I didn't care if she thought I was staring at her ass, but my guard couldn't be this relaxed around her. Something about her disarmed me, made me feel safe, and while that might be a good thing for her job, it was a death sentence for mine. Irritation bubbled up in me toward her for making me forget who I was for a moment.

I'd wanted to be here for Immy, but to protect her the best, I needed to be the boss—cold, calculated, and in control. My moniker in the family was "The Suit," not only for my well-known attire, but because I would take you to the cleaners before you even knew what was happening. So, I stared at her blankly, waiting for her to become uncomfortable and explain herself. I didn't want her to be comfortable around me. This wasn't about me; It was for Immy, and Immy alone.

"Attie, don't be rude. She's not—" Immy stopped herself abruptly, remembering the rule, *you don't mention the family to outsiders.*

"Um, well, I was just asking if you wanted my card or needed anything else?"

It was oddly amusing seeing her flustered now. Mrs. Carter had seemed so put together in her space, self-assured even, but out here, I could see some of the cracks in her facade. I was an expert at reading people, after all. She was meek and would crumble under any pressure I'd put on her. I ignored how excited that made my cock feel.

Nodding, I turned and looked out the window dismissively. At least, that was what I told myself, not that I didn't want to stare at her any longer.

"Mr. Masters?"

At the sound of her voice, I scolded myself for the mistake I'd made. Every time she said Mr. Masters, a sensation snaked down my spine. Turning, I held out my hand, needing to get out of this waiting room. I'd faced mobsters and gangs numerous times, but this woman was the one bringing me to my knees. I couldn't come here again. It was a weakness I couldn't allow.

Mrs. Carter handed me the business card, grazing my

hand with her fingertips as she did. I was surprised at her touch. Most people didn't dare touch me unless it was on my terms. This simple act surprised me and made me realize how little human contact I have if her simple hand graze created an inferno within me. It ignited me, reinforcing my decision to stay away.

I shoved my hand, along with her card, in my pocket and headed out the lobby door without even a backward glance. Immy snickered at me, clearly amused by my reaction, being able to read me better than anyone. Her expression didn't bother me, though, because it was the most expression I'd seen from her in months. Guess this therapy thing might be helping already. I wanted to feel pleased, but any emotion outside the cold numbness was too risky at the moment.

As we walked out the door, I caught sight of my bodyguard, Sax, and a few other men who'd been spread throughout the building. Sax gave me a discreet nod as I passed, his tall and domineering frame often being enough to scare most people away. His nod communicated everything was clear, and we could proceed to the vehicle without any trouble. It might seem like overkill, but it was better than being killed.

Sax had been my guard for several years and my best friend long before that. We grew up in the family together. Our shared history was an asset, allowing us to communicate simply through looks, most of the time, due to knowing one another so well. It also meant I undoubtedly trusted him with everything. He was the one person who knew the absolute truth about my father and what had happened that night with Immy.

The door of our waiting SUV opened as we approached, and I waited for Immy to slide in before following her. I scanned the area in my brief wait but didn't notice anything out of the ordinary. This was what I was meant to do. Constant surveillance.

The divider in the back was up, so I took the opportunity to talk openly with Immy and get her evaluation of the session. She'd been hesitant to attend at all, but after six months of waking up from nightmares, Immy had finally agreed and asked for help. She saw my look but rolled her eyes at me. *Only she could get away with that.* Sighing, I dropped my boss mask and genuinely looked at her, allowing concern to show this time.

"Do you want to keep going? Was it helpful?"

Immy took a few moments, hopefully, to only ponder her response and not to be stubborn. There was only so much defiance I would allow, even from my sister. Shrugging before she spoke, I was relieved when she finally answered.

"I think so. She seemed okay, I guess. Nice and didn't seem like she was trying too hard. She even passed your stupid test." Immy rolled her eyes, but I caught her smile.

That was practically five stars from a teenager, in my experience. I liked Mrs. Carter too, not that I could voice that, but I was glad Immy was willing to see it through. Settling back in my seat now that Immy had reassured me, I started to scroll through the messages I'd missed while in her office. The underground network never slept.

There were a few troubling messages from one of my guys I would need to deal with, but first, I needed to check out a restaurant to see if it would be a prosperous place to set up a business.

"Do you want to stop for lunch at a place I need to check out? Or do you want to be dropped at the house?"

"What kind of food?"

It might seem odd to take my baby sister to a mafia business meeting, but it was our way of life. From birth, we were taught to respect the mafia and its organization. The minute you forgot what it was, was the minute it killed you. Immy's mother was an unfortunate example of that. She'd trusted the wrong person.

"Would you believe me if I said sushi?" Immy turned, looking at me with speculation and trying to determine whether I was joking or not.

"Sushi," Immy said as a statement, disbelief dripped from her words.

"Mmhm."

Inside, I was holding back my laughter as she tried to work it out. Immy was a sucker for sushi, but we rarely had it because there weren't many great ones around us, and well, I was a sushi snob. So, if I was offering, she assumed it was a good one but wouldn't want to get her hopes up.

"I guess I could eat."

Nonchalance was not her strong suit, but I let her believe she'd pulled it off. I didn't get to indulge her often, so I couldn't miss the opportunity when it presented itself, even if only under the guise of something else. Quite frankly, I was just as excited about lunch as her.

A few minutes later, we pulled around back to the

entrance. As the car rolled to a stop, the doors were immediately opened by some of our guards from outside. There were some odd perks to being the boss.

Nodding at the one holding my door, I stepped out and offered Immy my hand. She stepped out like the princess she was and placed her arm in mine. We might not always like our titles, but we knew when to wear them. Heading toward the back entrance, I saw the owner waiting there as we approached.

"Mr. Mascro, we're so happy to have you. Please, follow me to the private dining booth we have for you."

Nodding was my only response. My boss mask was firmly back in place, so I didn't offer him anything else. He hadn't earned it yet. The man shuffled on his feet, clearly feeling some of the tension I was intentionally building. After a moment, the owner turned and led us to the private booth.

The restaurant had a unique setup where it was mostly VIP booths with private curtains, some private rooms, and the main customer area had small tables with intimate lighting, so no matter where you sat, you felt as if you were alone. It was a profitable business and marketing concept, which was how it'd landed on my radar.

Nodding again as I passed him, I slid into the booth after Immy. Ignoring the owner even more, I turned to Immy to see what she was in the mood for today.

"What do you want to try today?"

She rolled her eyes at me, knowing what I was doing, but went along with it. She knew the score.

"Not sure. I want to see what the specials are."

"Hmph," I answered, still ignoring the man. With a huff, he turned and walked away and a tiny smirk lifted at the corners of my mouth.

A waitress arrived just then, bringing with her some menus and appetizers. So far, I was impressed with the place despite my disinterested facial expression. We both perused the menu, and I saw the different combinations offered. It looked like it would be a wise investment if the food tasted as good as the atmosphere promised.

After we ordered, the curtains were drawn closed, offering us privacy—or some semblance of it. I knew Sax was outside the booth, and being privy to everything in my life meant I could talk openly with Immy. It was the only comfort I had some days.

"Thoughts?"

I was curious about her interpretation of things, both because I valued her opinion but also to see how she weighed things in a business sense as part of her training. Everything was a business decision in the mafia. *Everything.*

"I like it. It has a good vibe, private, and seems to have a good business plan. If the food tastes good, then I think it would be a good investment."

"Agreed." Sitting back, I placed my hands in my lap, relaxing. "Now, how are your studies with your tutor going? Have you picked up your language more?" Another eye roll. It must be a two-for-one deal today.

"Ugh, it's fine. Mr. Wheeler is so boring, though. He's the absolute worst," Immy whined. Chuckling at her reaction, I nudged her with my elbow.

"That's the point. He's a tutor. He's not supposed to

make it easy on you. I know I asked you earlier, but I just wanted to check in again. Are you feeling okay after opening up about it?"

Immy started to fidget, and I knew it was hard for her to talk about this, but I needed her to know she could. I wanted things to be different with us. It could be better between us now and not how our father had ruled.

"It's never fun remembering it, but it does seem to get a little easier each time. As much as I don't want to admit it, I think it is best for me. Thank you for going with me."

"Of course, I'm here for you, squirt. I want things to be different in the family, and that means that you're a priority to me."

Her nose scrunched up at her childhood nickname, but her blush showed me she was at least pleased, if not embarrassed, at my statement. A knock on the wood alerted us to someone returning, Sax's way of giving us a heads up so no eavesdroppers heard our conversation. We both straightened for the waitress to deliver our food.

Once it was plated in front of us, we devoured it and tried several of the dishes. I was glad Immy seemed to be healing and enjoying the lunch we shared. As we were leaving, she nodded, indicating she approved of the place.

The owner shuffled on his feet as we drew close. Sax led Immy out the door back toward the car, leaving a few other guards behind with me. Stopping in front of the nervous owner, I slid my hands into my pockets as I assessed him with a domineering stance.

"Mr. Sanu, I'm impressed. I would like to offer you a

business arrangement. I will have my financial manager send over the paperwork."

He looked like he might pass out, and I wasn't sure if it was from happiness or nerves, but either way, he was no longer on my radar as I exited the restaurant. The day was still early, and there were still more meetings to attend as we headed back to our downtown condo.

I ignored the fact that Mrs. Carter's touch was still on my mind. Romantic entanglements weren't a reality I had. Besides, it wasn't like I had free time to date, even if I could.

As I said, the mafia never slept. Unless you were dead.

FOUR

LOREN

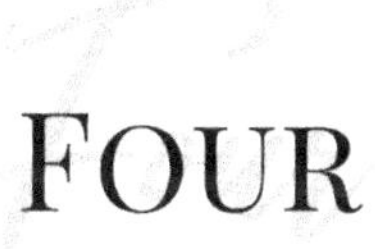

The day had been long, and the last place I wanted to be was the gym, but my mind hadn't stopped swirling since my new intake. As I walked to Windy City Gym, I hoped this class would be more challenging for once. Nighttime was the hardest part of the day for me. The more physically exhausted I was, the easier it was to sleep. Otherwise, I'd stay up for hours running everything over in my head. It had already been three tireless nights of this, and I just needed a fucking break.

Changing into my barre-approved gear, I slipped on the unique grip socks made for these classes. There was a lot of chatter around me, but I tuned it out. I was operating on autopilot by this time of the day, having used all of my energy in my sessions. I didn't know as many people in the night classes, which made it easier to fade into the crowd.

Stretching, I grabbed my water bottle and equipment before heading to my favorite spot on the barre. Just before I got there, I was elbowed out of the way as a redhead sauntered right up to my place. Bitch. On second thought, I remembered why I hated coming to class at this time. It was filled with the cliquey bitches who saw me as what not to become. *Divorced.* The early morning ladies were at least nice to my face.

Not having enough energy to care tonight, I turned to find a different place, but by the time I'd walked in and been shoved, all the best spots were taken. The only one left was on the short sidebar by the door. Fucking bitches, all of them.

Throwing my shit on the floor, I was debating if I even wanted to stay at this point. An uncommon feeling was starting to rise in me as well. *Anger.* When I stood up, I caught sight of the hot trainer I would often watch. There was something about his brashness that captivated me, even if I didn't understand why. He was working with someone on the bench press, so his back was turned to me. The barre instructor started listing off positions to begin over the speakers, so I returned my focus to the class.

"Squeeze, tuck, and hold. Higher on those toes, ladies."

Lifting up, I held the pose, my hands resting on the barre, as I breathed.

"Tuck and hold. Tuck and hold. Release."

Falling from the plank position, I was glad the class was almost over.

"Touch those toes, come on, you can do it!"

Finally, it was cool down. I was about to rip the microphone off her head and shove it up her ass if she said 'tuck and hold' one more damn time. I swear, only sadists became instructors. Ordinary people didn't get off on this shit! Of course, I paid for it, so what did that say about me? It was becoming increasingly obvious I had a lot more aggression coursing through me today than usual. This class had done nothing to calm it either.

"Deep breaths. Alright, ladies. Great job today! Way to tuck and hold!"

It was like she wanted me to hurt her! Grumbling under my breath, I commented how I wanted to tattoo 'tuck and hold' on her forehead causing the girl next to me to laugh. Oops, guess I wasn't as quiet as I thought. Grimacing, I turned to her expecting to get the bitchy girl treatment, but surprisingly, she had a friendly demeanor about her.

"Hi, I'm Katie. Sorry to eavesdrop, but I agree with you. Pain and torture should be rained down on the instructors. Do you think they send them to torture 101 before becoming an instructor?"

"Seems accurate," I replied, a brief smile pulling at my lips. Laughing together at our snark, I decided to try and be friendly. Couldn't hurt, right?

"I'm Loren. And you make a valid observation. I think I even saw her smirk on the last one. She definitely gets a sick pleasure from it."

We both laughed again as we disinfected our barre area and equipment. People assumed a barre class wouldn't be a workout, but I often sweated more in these than I did in aerobics. As we wiped down our things, the awkward pause after you had nothing else to say fell upon us.

"Well, I guess I'll see you around. Nice sharing the torture with you."

"You too," I responded to her back as she walked away. Well, I had tried to be sociable.

Heading to my locker, I ignored the chatter of the other women, their gazes heavy on me as I quickly changed into my warmer clothes. I could feel the weight of their stares pressing into me, a reminder that I wasn't whole. My mind whirled, and the need to get out of this locker room rose. The feeling of failure sat heavy on my chest, constricting my oxygen. Combined with the feeling of overwhelming judgment for stepping out of my comfort zone. The emotions crashed into me and all the memories flooded my brain.

"How stupid could you be, Loren?" A crash followed his words as he threw the pot into the sink. I'd mixed up the recipe, and dinner had been ruined. Brian was upset, and the fact I was a horrible wife was reinforced. Quietly, I curled into the corner of the couch and blocked out all the noise.

"Loren, no boys will ever want you if you dress like that. They'll only think you're good for one thing if you wear stuff like that," my mother scoffed as she berated me for my outfit. I had on a tank top, but apparently, it was too risqué. She continued as I stood at the base of the stairs, my arms crossed over my chest. "You can't be smarter than they are either. I saw how you were the other night with your science partner, and you have to stop that. You mustn't make them feel stupid..." her voice faded out as I picked at a scab on my arm.

"You're worthless and nothing, Loren. I thought you were a good fuck when we were seventeen, but you never grew beyond the same boring position. Always so scared to do anything other than what is expected of you. You're so fucking boring!" Brian shouted as he threw clothes into a bag. Quietly, I rocked myself as tears ran down my face. "And now, you can't even give me the life you promised when we got married. You're useless, and I'm done. I've been fucking women all over Chicago while you've been laying in bed eating bonbons, or whatever it is the fuck you do. I don't care."

My breaths began to pick up at a quicker pace as I fumbled with my belongings. *In and out, in and out.* Shoving my way out the door, I slid down the wall once I was clear of the locker room and all the perceived judgment I felt in there. Dropping my head between my legs, I slowly gathered my breath in slow, deep inhales and exhales.

The room stopped spinning just as the noise returned. Fearing that everyone was looking at me, I slowly raised my head. I was alone in the hallway, but I hadn't gone unnoticed. One pair of dark eyes watched me through the glass that separated the hallway and the training floor. It almost felt like I was staring into a mirror.

Blinking, I refocused, but when I looked again, the eyes were gone. Scanning the vicinity, I couldn't find the person they had belonged to, but I was confident it was the brash and hunky trainer from earlier. A rush of people exited the locker room a moment later and sound filled the hallway.

I gathered the stuff I'd dropped and got up as if everything was normal. The crowd offered me the opportunity to fall into the group, so no one had noticed me sitting on the ground. Buttoning my coat as I went, I stopped to pull out my gloves and hat. Something caught my eye on the edge of the bulletin board—an advertisement for a new class.

Now offering Kickboxing Lessons. Private sessions only. Must buy an additional package on top of the gym membership. See front desk for details. Must have potential to be accepted.

Kickboxing. Hmm. Now, *that* sounded interesting. Maybe it would give me the exhaustion I'd been looking for. Turning back around, I headed back toward the desk area. One of the peppy blonde girls was working the counter. I honestly tried not to be a bitter judgmental bitch, but these girls gave other women bad names. Completely plastic, tanned, and fake all over described it best. They only worked here to find their next meal ticket by hoping to steal away a rich sugar daddy. Good luck, ladies.

Bambi, or some other obnoxious sounding name, dismissed me with a look as I walked up to the counter and went back to chatting with the older man. See? Totally called it. He looked old enough to be her grandfather. A shiver of repulsion rolled through me. Ick. Tired of being ignored enough today, I started ringing the bell in front of me—obnoxiously.

Ding, ding, ding, ding, ding, ding, ding.

I didn't stop until she finally turned, glaring, mind you, and walked over.

"Can I help you, *ma'am*?" she asked, emphasizing the last word.

Ah, bitch, please. I could eat girls like you for breakfast. Try living with a man who made you second guess everything for ten years, and then we'll talk.

"Oh, I'm sorry to pull you away from your great-grandfather over there, but I'm sure his prune juice is kicking in any minute now. So, perhaps you could do your job and assist me, that would be great! I would like to inquire about the kickboxing lessons."

Her face scrunched up at my use of "great-grandfather," and I could tell she was about to rain down vengeance on me, the threat clear in her eyes. The mention of kickboxing had her stopping, and a maniacal grin spread across her face. *Creepy.*

"Of course, you have to get approval from the instructor. He's currently with a client, but you can interrupt him in one of the private gyms upstairs. He's in #5. He won't mind at all." Why didn't I trust her?

"Okay, great. Thanks. Make sure to ask your grandpappy for a Werther's Original before he leaves!"

Quickly, I backed away toward the stairs. My bravado faded and I was now afraid of her wrath for that final blow. She seemed like the type to try and throw something at me.

Had it been petty? Hell yes. But it'd felt fucking

amazing. So worth it after the toxic emotions I'd felt today.

Climbing the stairs, I felt rejuvenated at holding my ground for once. I even patted myself on the back for my quippy remarks. Typically, I was the one who thought of a response five minutes after the fact—so not helpful. Glancing at the door numbers, I started to think she sent me to a fake room until I reached the end of the hallway, and there it was gym #5. Knocking, I didn't hear anything, so I pulled open the door and peeked my head in. There in all his glory was Mr. Dark Eyes, brooding asshole extraordinaire, surly hotness himself, and none other than apparently, the kickboxing instructor.

And he did not look happy at my intrusion if the glare on his face was any indication. Well, hello to you too, jerk. Maybe it was how I wore my hair today? Why else were all these people suddenly talking to me and giving me attitude? Perhaps, it was just the first time I'd noticed. The blinders were off, and I was starting to see through the fog. Anxiety filled me at the thought that my world wasn't how I'd perceived it as.

I knew why the front desk girl was smiling all evil villain style, now. She'd known he wouldn't be pleased for my interruption and was excited about the torture I was about to experience. Well, screw her too. Deciding I was tired of being everyone's punching bag, I crossed my arms, leaned back against the wall, and glared back.

His chocolate brown hair was curled slightly from the sweat on his forehead and matched his dark pooling eyes that were glaring daggers at me. A short beard covered the bottom of his face but did nothing to hide his full lips. They were currently lifted in a sneer as he stared me down. From this close, I could gauge his height to around 6'2". The sweat that dripped down his toned chest wasn't distracting in the least. Besides, whatever curiosity I'd had about him previously evaporated as the stubborn aggression to stand my ground took over.

See, asshole, you aren't as scary as you thought you were. Bring it.

FIVE

WELLS

T he hot brunette with the sad eyes was staring at me fully for the first time, and I didn't like it. I'd seen her around numerous times before, but she always seemed to be in a daze. I recognized the haunted look in her eyes, and it drew me to her like a moth to a flame.

Earlier, I'd seen her hunched over at the wall, and for a brief moment, I'd thought about checking on her, but then I came to my senses and stalked off. Women were not something I spent my time on anymore. Too many strings to get tangled in. And this one had complicated written *all* over her.

Finishing my sessions for the day, I retreated to gym #5 for some last minute training. I had a fight tomorrow night, and the one perk I had here, free access to my own private gym. It just meant I had to get through the day dealing with trophy wives and trust fund brats who had way too much time on their hands before I could hide here.

And now, she was here, invading my sacred space. Glaring at her, I hoped my asshole tendencies would send her packing all on their own. She seemed like a wisp of a woman who would jump at the slightest provocation. To my surprise, she leaned against the wall and glared at me with what I assumed was meant to be an intimidating stare. That's cute. She was like a kitten, but I didn't think she had any claws.

"This gym is off-limits to guests. Leave."

"I was told to find you actually, so I think you'll find *I do* have permission."

I hadn't expected her to respond when I confronted her, her reaction causing my breathing to pick up at her dismissal.

"Well, *kitten*," I sneered, "you were told wrong. Now, go."

Turning back toward my punching bag, I soon lost myself in the rhythm of the one, two, punch, one, two, kick sequence. Hitting a hundred, I wiped the sweat from my brow before grabbing the water bottle from the bench. My heartbeat was ringing in my ears as I drank down my water, spilling some as I greedily inhaled it.

The quiet surrounded me, and I dropped my shoulders as I finally relaxed. Gathering up my towel and bag, I headed toward the private locker room off to the side.

"I want you to teach me that."

Stopping in my tracks, I was surprised to hear her voice. I'd honestly forgotten about her once I started hitting the bag. Keeping my back to her, I sighed loudly before answering.

"Fine. I only have Tuesday and Thursday evenings open. If that doesn't work, not my problem. If you miss, you still pay. Got it, *kitten*?"

I didn't wait for her answer as I didn't care one way or the other if she showed up. In fact, I hope she didn't. Just another fucking upper-class princess to remind me of where I didn't belong.

No need for that. I already knew. Besides, that had been made abundantly clear a year ago. The door slamming was the only indication she'd heard me as I stepped all the way into the locker room.

BANGING on the outside door alerted me I had fifteen minutes until I was up. Wrapping my hands, I clipped off the tape as I flexed them, testing the flexibility. It was fight night, and my blood was pumping, ready to create some destruction. Fighting gave me an outlet that I needed desperately, in addition to the financial gains. It was the perfect win-win scenario.

Doing some quick punches and kicks in the air, I finished my last bit of stretching before exiting the utility closet I used as a dressing room. It was an underground fighting ring—not some fancy Vegas show. The location was always different and unknown to anyone until the day of the fight. It was how the organizers kept ahead of the police trying to shut them down.

Several things went on behind the scenes here that most weren't even privy to, much less even knew occurred. While this was a Mascro venture, the other families were allowed to mingle as long as they kept the peace—Chicago underground's version of a consulate. Immunity was freely given unless you crossed the line.

The other families could then bet on the fights, sell their drugs, put up their fighters, and pimp out their sex. It was encouraged even, but you didn't disrespect the Mascros, and you didn't murder anyone on site. It was considered rude, and frankly, in poor taste. Say what you will about the mafia families, but they all had their codes.

If you lived by the code, you were good, but break it, and all of the families would be after you. I should know. I'd crossed one of them once. Now, I spend my days trying to escape the mistakes of my past and get out from under the crushing debt I'd incurred. Which usually entailed being pissed off most of the day. At least, it worked well for fighting.

"Crash! You're up, man. Make it rain, dude! I got money on you."

I ignored the idiot trainer and walked up to the makeshift ring in the middle of the warehouse. The place was packed as usual with various types of people. Several littered around the ring, wanting a front-row view of the violence, while others used the top floor railing to conduct business and watch the fight.

While the locations might change, they always had the same layout. It reminded me of a traveling circus with how quickly they could set up and break down these places. Bar areas, dance floors, bleachers, and the ring were standard pieces they always used. The VIP section was the only area that tended to change depending on location. The number of deals that went down during these things had to be astronomical.

Glancing around, I saw a few familiar faces who

always seemed to be at these things. Putting my mouth guard in, I climbed through the ropes into the ring and bounced on my feet. The thrill before a fight was the only time I truly felt alive now. Focusing on my opponent, I took in his build, gait, and arm width. He had more weight on him than me, but it wasn't all muscle. Inevitably, it would make his movements slower, though they would pack a solid punch. I'd need to be fast and hit him in places that would slow him down quickly.

"Tonight, we have Crash opposing Bounty. Last moment to place your bets, when the bell rings, all are final. Are... you... ready... !"

The bell rang, and my focus narrowed on my opponent. I cleared my head of all the noise so I could anticipate his movements. He leaned forward slightly on his right leg, giving away his attempt to make a left-handed punch. Ducking under his arm, I was able to punch him with two quick jabs in the ribs.

All the times during the day I'd held myself back flooded me and I used the forced down aggression to fuel my punches. Bounty stumbled back at the force, and I took it as an opportunity to kick and clip his chin. All the spoiled brats and flirty women I had to deal with became the opponent in front of me. I couldn't hit them, but I could hit him. Bounty was now disoriented and pissed. Everyone made mistakes when they were angry.

Charging me, he was no longer trying to be stealthy and forecasted his movements even louder. The calm taste of control began to settle on my tongue with each strike I landed. Dodging his right punch, I blocked his kick before bringing my knee to his ribs and punching him quickly in the head. He stepped back, off-kilter, and I was smug in knowing I'd just rung his bell.

I charged him this time using his distraction but changed direction at the last minute, initiating a kickflip and punching him in the same spot on his ribs with two jabs. The rhythm and movement of a fight was more sophisticated than people realized, and there had always been something about it that called to me. In the ring, I wasn't the screw-up. Instead, I was the master of this domain.

The last of my anger rushed to the surface as I prepared for my final takedown. I visibly winced for him as he held his ribs. Crowding him, I began to punch him repeatedly. Bounty got a lucky shot to my lip, but at this point, he was so far gone, he could barely stand. With one final uppercut, I sent him flying to the floor as the bell for the round rang. KO'd.

Wiping the blood off my lip, I spat it on the floor and made my way over to the corner. Grabbing the offered water bottle, I squirted some in my mouth and over my face to rinse the blood off. The crowd was cheering loudly outside the ring, and as I stepped under the rope, I found one of Mascro's guards waiting for me.

"You've been invited into the VIP section for the evening. Nicolai would like to offer you use of the shower and provide you with any clothes you may need."

What the fuck, this place had a shower? Sure beat the janitor's closet I'd been stuck in. I'd never met the man behind the fights in the year I'd been here, only hearing about him in name.

"Sure, why the hell not," I shrugged. It wasn't like I had anything else going on tonight with my active social calendar.

The guy apparently got a kick out of my answer based on his wide grin. Directing me toward the stairs, I followed him, hoping I wasn't about to be led to some weird sex thing.

Some of the crowd hollered at me as I passed, some were congratulating, and some yelled for knocking out Bounty so quickly. It wasn't my fault the guy was named after a paper towel brand. I tuned them all out. I didn't care. I wasn't here to fight for their entertainment. Fighting was the only thing that kept me sane.

We came to a stop in front of a portable shower stall I'd never noticed before. Wow, the mafia had everything in these warehouses. Stepping through the door, it was clean and had more room than I'd expected. There was room to change and a bench and shower portion. Stripping, I tossed my sweaty clothes on the ground before stepping under the water spray. I was surprised when hot water rained down on me. Fuck, it must be nice being these guys.

After a few minutes, I heard the door open and assumed it was the guard dude bringing me the clothes he'd mentioned. When the curtain moved, I glanced over, confused about what he wanted in my shower. Instead of the burly guy who'd led me here, a tall, picturesque blonde stood smiling at me. Oh, did I mention she was naked? Her tits were clearly fake with how perky they were. She looked young, too.

Sighing, I turned my back to her, hoping she'd take

the hint. I didn't want to deal with her, and the fact that my cock was still flaccid meant that part of me didn't either.

"A gift for you," she attempted seductively, touching my back.

What part of me turning away from her communicated, *'yes, bitch, please, invade my privacy?'* The media harped about consent for women, but did they ever consider consent for men? Hell no, we were always expected to want it, so we weren't given a choice. The belief we should be so lucky if a woman wanted to have sex with us. *Fucking insane.*

"Listen, I don't know who you are, but I'm not interested. Go." I threw it over my shoulder, not even wanting to see her.

"But Mr.—"

"I'm. Not. Interested."

Turning back around, I decided to just get out of here. Twisting the water off, I walked past her frozen form and grabbed the towel hanging there. Drying myself quickly, I threw back on my clothes in a hasty manner. I'd just leave. It wasn't worth it if I was going to be expected to do something for this dude. It had to be the only reason he was lavishing me with gifts now. He wanted something. They always did.

Unlucky for them, I no longer gave a shit about stuff and had nothing left to lose. *They'd already taken everything.* Walking out, I passed the confused bouncer and just nodded.

"I left her nice and wet for you, man. Better go check."

Ha, let him try to figure that one out. Maybe he

would go sex her up, and then the VIP guy would forget about me. He headed into the shower stall, allowing me to make a quick exit of my own.

Stepping outside, the cool air kissed my wet skin, but it was a welcomed relief after the hot insides of the fight ring. Walking over to my bike, I picked up my helmet from my handlebars and strapped it on. Straddling the one possession I still owned, I sat for a minute, taking time to relax.

I'd made it another night without being killed. How fucking sad was it that was how I measured my days?

Deciding to ignore the question, I revved my bike and pulled out of the lot. The vibrations and power under me relaxed me as I drove away. Some days I dreamt of driving and never stopping. But how far would I get before my troubles caught up with me? Not far enough.

SIX

NICCO

The fighter in the ring had fought in our club a few times now, and I was impressed with his skill level. I'd been running the fight club for the family for over three years. It was easy enough, and I enjoyed it for the most part. Plus, it had a level of freedom to spend my days as I wished.

Lately, my cousin was pressuring me to take on more of an upper-level role. The head of the family shift had left some open positions, but I wasn't interested in moving up. I liked my life the way it was, and I wanted more for myself.

Motioning toward my guard, I nodded for him to retrieve the fighter, Crash, after he won. It was clear he was the better man in the ring, and it was only a matter of time now before it was over. Just as I thought, he KO'd his opponent, proving my point.

At the ring of the bell announcing the end of the match, I glanced around the rest of the space. From my spot in the VIP section, I could see everything going on in the warehouse. There were other families doing business here, but it was neutral territory, and typically, there wasn't much trouble because of that.

Turning, I leaned back against the railing, eyeing who was in the VIP area tonight. Mandy, a bar girl, saw me looking and sauntered over, thinking she was hot shit. She was attractive by beauty standards, but she had no substance, and nothing about her was appealing to me.

"Nicolai, you're looking fine tonight. When are you going to tattoo me? I'll let you do *whatever* you want *wherever* you want," she purred, twisting her hair around her finger as she eyed me.

Did she think that was sexy? Because it screamed desperate to me.

"I'll have to check my schedule, doll. Excuse me, my cousin just entered, and I need to speak to him."

Thankfully, Atticus had shown up, offering me an excuse to leave her before she propositioned me a little less subtly next time.

"Cous! Did you catch any of the last fight?" I greeted.

Atticus and his guard, Sax, turned at my voice. I wasn't sure which of them looked more severe. I often wondered if they competed for who had the best resting asshole face. It would be a close call who'd win.

"Nicolai," Atticus nodded, "how's business tonight?"

"Good." I grinned wide. "The odds on the last fight were great, and we still have a few left to go. Should be a top-three night."

"That's good to hear. Any trouble?"

"Nah, man. Everyone is playing nice."

"Let's keep it that way. I met with a restaurant owner

today about taking over his business. It's a sushi place. I would like your help with the project."

"Sushi? No shit. I bet Imogen is excited." At the mention of his sister, his facade cracked a little, smiling at my comment.

"That she is. I know you don't want more responsibility, but I would be inclined to do you a favor if you helped me with this. There is another matter I have to see to, and I need someone I can trust to handle this. It would mean a lot to Immy, as well."

"Ah, fuck, man. You had to bring her into it, didn't you?"

Running my hand down my face, I stepped back to think for a minute. Atticus was six years older than me, but we'd always been close. He was more of an older brother in my life, and it was hard to say no to him. And Imogen was my little sister. We grew up in that house together, and I wanted the world for her. Being owed a favor and making that girl smile, though, might be worth the headache this may create for me. Dropping my hand, I looked up at him, and his smug smile indicated he knew he had me.

"Fine. *For a favor.* Send me the details."

Fuck, I had a feeling I was going to regret this. Atticus made his rounds before leaving with Sax an hour later. Grabbing a drink at the bar, I realized the fighter "Crash" had never made it up here. Interesting.

IT WAS FINALLY A SOCIALLY acceptable time for me to leave. Being the head of this club meant I had a certain expectation on how long I remained visible. It completely sucked when all I wanted to do was be anywhere else. Everything about this life I portrayed here was a facade; a trick made to have you think one thing. I was perceived as the fun-loving, careless cousin of the boss in the family.

Running the fighting rings to the underground was due to my 'perceived' level of status. I had just enough clout to be given respect, but not enough that I was a real threat. Despite Atticus holding me in high regard, I still hadn't proved myself enough for other members. So the pressure to do more, show more commitment, was always there underneath every veiled comment from others.

This restaurant would be the first time I'd said yes to Atticus. I hoped it wouldn't bite me in the ass because I had plans, plans that fell outside the life of the mafia. Jumping on my bike, I took off for my second home. I'd purchased a little storefront last year, and the business was going well. It was a quick ride through the city to my shop, Ignite Ink.

The lights shined bright from the street as I parked my bike. The sign hung in the front window casting its glow onto the sidewalk. I sat back on my bike, my helmet in my hands and looked upon my shop with pride. This place was mine. Every detail about it meant something to me.

When I entered a few minutes later, the chime above the door alerted my crew to my arrival. The buzz of the tattoo gun could be heard along with some hard-rock music Davis had blaring. The atmosphere at the shop was relaxed and carefree, and I felt it chip away at the facade with each step I took.

Since it was well after midnight, only two employees were present. The shop tended to be open more than it was closed. The mornings mainly consisted of scheduled appointments, and the evenings tended to be more walk-ins. But with the variety of shifts and the four other tattoo artists, and our one piercer who worked with me, we all stayed busy.

It was my haven outside the family. No one here was connected to any of the underground and were people I'd meet on my own through tattoo conventions and shared interests. This place was something I'd built on my own, and I was damn fucking proud of it. Atticus knew of it, and had so far, allowed me to keep it clean. I hoped it stayed that way. I lived in dread of the day he asked me to do something *for the family.*

"Hey, Davis!" I shouted over the noise as he worked on a heavily tattooed man.

"What up, boss man?" he greeted, head bent down as he worked.

Chuckling at him, it never got old being called that. Walking in further, I found Cassandra on the phone. She handled the front when she wasn't doing piercings since they didn't take as long to manage. Cassandra winked when she saw me, causing me to shake my head and smile. The woman was old enough to be my grandmother, but it never stopped her flirting.

"Right-o, I have you scheduled with Nicco for

Monday at 3 pm. Thank you for choosing Ignite Ink." She grinned wide at me as she hung up the phone. No one knew I was part of the Mascro crime family here since I used my mother's maiden name. So on nights I had fights, they always assumed I was on some illicit date I was keeping secret.

"So, what's her name this time? Do we get to meet her?"

"The only woman in my life is you, Cassandra. No one else can compare."

"Oh, you smooth talker. Just you wait. One day, she's going to walk in and knock you off your feet."

Laughing at her, I shook my head and headed the rest of the way to my office. Being around the people here was always an instant mood lifter. Shutting my door, I leaned back against it and took a breath, and for the first time in hours, I could drop the mask entirely. Feeling relieved, I shuffled over to my desk and booted up my laptop.

These nights at the shop had become my refuge. At first, it was a way to escape the pressure and expectations I'd been born into. But once Atticus had taken over, it seemed like a real possibility to have a life outside the family. I didn't dare talk about it, though. The surefire way to have your dreams destroyed was to hope and plan shit. Yet, I couldn't seem to help myself, and once the shop was going steady, I pushed for more.

I'd decided to enroll in online classes to get my teaching degree. I couldn't admit that one out loud, though. Not only would I be laughed at for wanting something different, but then it would be snatched away from me, trampled on, and destroyed before I could even walk into a school to teach.

It was risky, but if I didn't at least try, I was worried I would end up down the same path of drugs and despair my mother had, or worse, killed like my *supposed* father.

My mom had been one of the club girls for the family, and with her Pakistani and Italian heritage, her looks had drawn in the clientele, making her popular with the youngest Mascro. Naomi Collins hadn't been a bad mom. She just hadn't been completely there for me either. Even when she was alive, she'd been distant and sad, and I felt more like a burden to her than a son. I'd often been left on my own to fend for myself starting at the age of four and onward.

It was probably how I became good at art, though, and I owed her that much. She'd give me a coloring book and crayons and leave me in shitty places for hours while she "worked". Back then, I hadn't understood the fact she had sex for money. I didn't like what my mom had done to provide for us, selling her body, but I understood her need to survive and I would never begrudge her for that.

I didn't remember when the drugs had started, but I would often find her passed out with needles in her arm as I got older. When I was eight, I hadn't been surprised to learn she'd finally overdosed.

I went to live with the boss, Dayton "Grim Reaper" Mascro, after her death since my father had supposedly been the Reaper's little brother. According to him, my dad was shot and killed during a family crime fight years ago when I'd only been a baby. Mom would make vague comments about him, but nothing I could ever really glean any info from.

When I moved into the big house, I'd tried to find out more about Benny Mascro, but other than an old photograph, it was like he didn't exist. The story I was told never sat right with me, or the lack of information. But, at some point, I realized I had no one I could ask for the truth, so I left it alone.

Now, I just wanted my own life away from the Mascro name and to embrace Nicco Collins—the real me. And I wasn't just the fun guy who knew how to party, I was determined, and I had a plan.

Step one—the shop, Ignite Ink.

Step two—classes and a degree.

Step three—find a way to exit the family without having to die.

This favor would either be a win in my column or be the lynchpin that blew it all up in my face.

My online class started, and I zoned in on the professor's lesson about brush strokes. In this tiny room, in the back of my tattoo shop, I got to pretend I was a regular guy, living an everyday life with an ordinary dream.

Kind of fucking sad when you thought about it, but it was my dream, and I would hold onto it with everything I had.

SEVEN

LOREN

pathy was drowning me as I walked the dark streets of Chicago. It was dangerous to be out this late alone, but the danger was the only thing I allowed myself to feel. For some reason, the thought of staying in my apartment tonight had my skin crawling, and had driven me to do something for once. It was Saturday night and I hadn't left it since returning from my gym session Thursday night.

Getting dolled up, I slipped on a short silver dress, a pair of strappy high heels, and had on some skimpy lingerie underneath. Maybe if I dressed the part, I would feel it—it seemed to work in the movies. Plus, there was that whole concept of 'dress for the job you wanted'. To me, that meant our mood had to be connected to our clothes to some degree, right?

It seemed to be working because I felt exhilarated at the thrill of being reckless despite my exhaustion at having to go through that beauty routine. It should terrify me, and the fact it didn't was even more alarming.

Pushing that aside, I strode up to the mysterious club I had googled this afternoon.

There wasn't much information about it, just the allure and mystery of 'walk along the edge of the dark side' and 'awaken yourself'. Something about the 'awaken' and 'dark side' had drawn me in, and I found myself thinking it over for longer than I'd realized. As I approached, I spotted a line with a roped-off bouncer manning the door.

Wanting to try my luck with my new brazenness, I strode up like I belonged and nodded at the bouncer. He looked me over and seemed to accept that I passed inspection because he nodded to himself before lifting the rope and allowing me entry. Hiding the shock it had worked, I touched his arm as I walked by, smiling at him. I didn't know who I was at the moment, but I embraced it. Always leave them wanting more.

Once I was inside, I had no clue what I was doing. The interior was dark, and I could hear music playing in a central area. Flashing lights clued me on which direction to go at least. Following them and the thump of the bass, I made my way down the dark hallway. Two doors stood in front of me, at least answering my question of why the music was muted.

A girl was placed between the doors, almost like a hostess stand at a restaurant. She was dressed in a very tight, black cocktail dress, and it made me feel confident about my own outfit. Her heels were sky high, and laces wrapped up her legs, creating a remarkable effect. She smiled seductively at me as I reached her.

"Welcome to Climax, where you skirt the edge of darkness. Which side are you venturing into tonight?"

I had no clue what she was referring to, so I pointed to the door on the right with the music.

"Excellent choice. In Illusion, remember you must wear this mask at all times. Anonymity is key here, allowing our guests to experience a different side of themselves that the world inhibits. Any time you do not wish to engage with someone, just simply turn off the lights around the outside rim with a tap of your finger."

She demonstrated what she was referring to on the exquisite black lace mask. When tapped, it lit up with intricate tiny lights that had been woven through it. Pun aside, it was illuminating elegance. My heart raced with adrenaline, the knowledge I was doing this setting in.

She walked behind me and adjusted the mask as she tied the long strands into a secure bow. As the mask settled on my face, the lace felt soft against my skin. Her hands were gentle as she tied the knot and brushed my hair over my shoulder. Goosebumps erupted on my skin, and a shiver ran down my spine.

The mask and this place emboldened me and allowed me to cast away my fears and walk on the edge of darkness as described. I understood it now. They took away your inhibitions permitting you to use the mask as a shield to live out your fantasies—awakening your innermost desires.

Taking a deep breath, I walked through the door, ready to escape the heavy blanket of grief that was my constant companion. It was almost as if my subconscious agreed, and I felt lighter as I crossed the threshold. With each step, seduction grew within me, and I felt *powerful*. I stepped out through the corridor into the club area, and the music filled me. Part of me was curious about what was in the other section, but I also knew I wasn't ready for whatever was over there.

Men and women were scattered around the space, all with the masks attached to their faces. Most were lit, while others were not, as they sipped drinks at tables and booths. It was fairly equal in men and women. The women were dressed similar to me with short, sexy dresses and high heels. The men varied from classic suits to expensive jeans and dress shirts. Either way, everyone was attractive and exuding sex appeal. I felt my pulse race with desire at the thought of being with a stranger.

While I wasn't typically one to engage in such a fashion, the thrill of it excited me, and the no strings attached suited my needs. Most of the day, I was in a fog of pain and trying to make it from one part of my day to the next. But sometimes, at night, I would still get lonely… and, well, horny. I was a woman, and I still had needs. My vibrator was great, but it didn't make up for the feeling of being held, grabbed, and taken. *I wanted to be taken.*

Deciding some liquid courage wouldn't hurt, I sauntered over to the bar. Leaning against the bar top, my dress pooled around my cleavage in this position, putting it on display. My boobs in my thirties weren't as great as they used to be, but a great bra really was a girl's best friend. I wasn't one to typically display my body, but here, in this place, it felt natural. Almost as if my hidden desires had also been illuminated when I stepped through the door.

"Hello, gorgeous. What's your poison going to be tonight?" purred the attractive man in front of me.

While I couldn't make out his entire face, his dark eyes shone with amusement, and his smile promised sinful things. Maybe I would just stay right here with my panty-dropping bartender.

"Surprise me."

He winked and walked off at my words, and a momentary feeling of regret surged in me at being that bold. Hell, what was I thinking? I couldn't do this. I could pretend to be someone else on the outside all I wanted, but I was still damaged on the inside. The bartender returned and slid a drink to me, his eyes holding mine the entire time and grazing his fingers across the top of my hand as he walked off. He left me with another wink, and my knees felt weak at the indication.

Okay, *maybe* I wasn't as awkward as I thought. Picking up the drink, I wasn't sure what it was, but as I sipped it, I was introduced to a myriad of flavors as they spread over my tongue. Holy shit, that was amazing. I'd need to be careful and pace myself, because I would so be that girl who couldn't hold her liquor later if not.

Swirling around on the barstool, I crossed one leg over the other with the movement. The slit on the sides of the dress fell to my leg, exposing the length of my thigh. Just that simple show of skin alone made me feel like a sexy queen. The drink did its job, making me feel confident. So when a tall, dark, and handsome man walked by, I hopped up to follow.

Unfortunately, heels were not my forte, and I soon lost track of him as I weaved in and out of people to catch up with him. I made it to the second floor that appeared to be a balcony area that overlooked the dance floor below. There weren't as many people up here, so I meandered through until I found an open spot to people watch.

Leaning against the rail, I finished off my drink and placed it down at my feet. It was probably a bad idea as I was apt to kick it down below, but where else was I supposed to put it? Scooting over to put some space between me and the disastrous cup, I wasn't watching my surroundings, and I bumped into a man standing a few feet down the railing.

"Oh, I'm so sorry. I was just trying to get away from that cup."

"Did the cup offend you in some grievous way? Do we need to find a manager to talk to the cup?" Laughing because that was funny, I shook my head no.

"No, I think it's safe now. And it was more from me, so I didn't accidentally take out someone below."

"Hmph. Sounds ominous, and maybe a little fun."

"I guess it could be."

"Is this your first time here?" the man asked. His mask was lit up, and in the dark lighting, it made his eyes almost glow. I couldn't get their actual color, but they bore into me with a fierce intensity, setting my heart racing. He was tall and muscular, but his other features were hard to determine due to the darkness.

"Yes, it—" but before I could utter another word, he tilted his head, making eye contact with someone behind me.

"Excuse me."

He walked off, leaving me bereft as I turned to stare down at the pulsing bodies. It was oddly relaxing to watch them gyrating and swaying with one another as a neutral bystander. Two dancers were getting extra frisky on the floor, and as I watched them push the limits, I started to get turned on myself. Entranced by their display, I didn't realize I had started to rub my legs together, attempting to gain some friction.

"Do you like watching them, *Bellezza*?" a dark voice purred behind me.

It was gravelly and low, sending shivers through me. His body pressed against my back, trapping me against the bar in front of me. Surprisingly, I didn't feel scared, and excitement coursed through me. The mysterious man ran a finger down my arm, bringing all the goosebumps to the top of my skin. Sucking in a breath, I tried to find my words.

"Yes, I do," breathed out of me in a husky whisper.

"Do you like what I'm doing to you?"

"Yes," I stuttered as he ran his fingers down my other arm. His breath was on my neck as he tickled my skin with what I assumed was his stubble and sent a million naughty thoughts racing through me. *Where in the world did those come from?*

"Do you want me to stop, *Bellezza*?"

"No."

"Good girl. I will give you what you want, but you have to do something for me. Understand?"

"How do you know what I want?" I managed to ask.

"Because it's written all over your body. You're so responsive, *Bellezza*, I could read you with my eyes closed."

His gravelly voice had my toes curling as he called me *Bellezza* and the promise of what he could do to me. I wanted what he was offering at that moment, more than I had wanted anything in the past five years.

"Ye-e-s," whimpered out of me as I leaned into his body. He wasn't playing fair as he continued to only lightly touch me, keeping my arousal contained.

"Such a reactive good girl, *Bellezza*. I will give you such pleasure while you watch the couple below, but you have to remain facing toward the front. Under no circumstances are you to turn around. No seeing my face, no exchanging names. In order for this fantasy to work, you have to commit to it. Do you understand?"

"Yes," I breathed. I didn't understand his commands, but I would do almost anything to feel more of his hands on me. I needed him to touch me.

"Open your eyes, *Bellezza*, and watch them."

How he knew my eyes had closed was beyond me, but I pried them open as his hands made full contact with my body. He pulled my hips back firmly and rubbed his hard erection against my ass. Slowly, in the most tantalizing way, he trailed his hands over my skin, enticing me to move with him in some fluid dance we were making.

The couple below was just as seductive as I continued

to watch them, and I realized he was copying their moves. Mr. Seduction moved his hand around to my front and used the slit of my dress to slip under the hem. His hands skimmed the edge of my barely-there lace thong, and my knees almost gave out at the contact. Watching the couple below closely, I could make out the man's hand under his partner's skirt.

Taking a page out of their book, I rubbed my ass in the same motion as the woman below and reached back with my arm, wrapping it around his neck. I sank my hand into his thick locks as I moved to the music. Mystery man appeared to approve as he growled out a moan in my ear. His fingers started to run across the lace more firmly, and I knew he could feel my wetness already through the fabric.

"I knew you would be responsive. I can feel your desire already. Oh, the things I could do to you, *Bellezza*."

His voice almost sounded disappointed, like he wouldn't get to beyond this right here, and I didn't like it. I wanted this man to touch me all over and elicit cries of pleasure from me. I felt bold and reckless, and I tipped my head back slightly and licked up his jawbone as I ground my ass against his incredibly hard cock.

His fingers tensed on the insides of my thighs for a moment, but when I didn't push my head back any further, he relaxed and breached the lace of my panties. It had been so long since a man touched me there that I practically came from that one touch alone.

Mr. Seduction began to drag his fingers over my pussy lips as I rocked my hips against his cock. I spread my legs further apart, offering him more room to maneuver, and he took advantage of it by slipping a finger inside my tight walls.

"Oh, *Bellezza*, you're skirting the edge of danger right now. Are you watching them below? Do you want to be her?"

Shaking my head no, because from where I stood, I had the better deal. Her date was plunging his fingers in her as they danced, squeezing her breast with his other hand. It was very wanton and provocative, and despite being in the middle of the dance floor, it was unlikely anyone down there could see them all lost in their own bubble of seduction.

Up here, I reigned over it all, and I could push this as far as I was comfortable with while having the edge of danger to it. We could be seen, but in the darkness that surrounded us, it was unlikely. As he started to push his finger into me more, I tugged his hair harder as I rubbed against him. It was the most erotic moment of my life.

The mysterious stranger snaked his other hand up and pulled at the taut nipple he could feel through my dress. The fabric draped enough in the middle, offering him easy access to my breasts. He slid his fingers under the fabric and cupped my breasts in his hand, keeping tempo below as he finger fucked me.

My seductive stranger started to massage my breast as his finger became drenched with my wetness. Rolling my nipple over with his thumb, my breath hitched when he plunged two fingers deep in me. My arm around his neck was the only thing holding me up now as my legs became jello from his ministrations.

Biting my earlobe, he purred into my ear. "Are you

watching them, *Bellezza*? Do you think she's having a better time... or that you are?"

Without even having to think about it, I answered quickly. "I am." The word moaned out of me unbidden.

"Good girl, *Bellezza*." At his words, he plunged three fingers and began to rub circles on my clit with his thumb. How he was so good at this crossed my mind, but I decided not to think about that and just enjoy the moment. Before I knew it, he had me cumming so hard when he pinched my nipple and my clit in unison.

Moaning, I was glad the music covered my moan as I fell apart around him. In a surprising move, he lifted his hand from my breast and tipped my head back far. My eyes had closed as I came, so I didn't see his intention until his lips crashed into mine. His tongue swiped at the seam of my lips, and I opened greedily for his kiss. With one swirl of his tongue, he had me seeing stars as he kissed me.

As quickly as it started, he pulled away and stalked off before I could even catch my breath. As I came down from my orgasm, all I saw was the strong back decked entirely in black as he disappeared from sight. Grabbing the rail, I tried to center myself back in reality as my whole body tingled with tiny fireworks.

Longer than I'd admit, I stayed up on the railing until I could safely walk. I made my way back through the crowds and down the stairs. My mysterious man was nowhere to be found, not that I knew what he looked like, as I left the club. The attendant smiled and gave me a knowing smirk as I walked by, and I didn't even think to stop and ask her about the mask.

Fuck it. I was keeping it. She'd taken my card number earlier for the door fee, so they could charge me if they needed to. Unknotting the ribbon, I slid it off my face before I made it outside. Wrapping the ribbon gently around it, I hoped to keep it preserved until I made it home. This mask had made me feel free and was the only reminder I would get of the mind-blowing seduction I'd experienced.

In the morning, I would fall back into the grief and pain I wore daily, but maybe this mask would serve as a reminder of the electrifying emotions I felt here tonight. It had been dangerous and wild, and the ugly truth of it all was I didn't know if I was strong enough to stay away from feeling that again.

It had felt good to be bad, to be *naughty*, and I craved more.

EIGHT

LOREN

The water ran over my body as I started to wake up in the shower. I hated showering. It was time-consuming, and it seemed to be the place all my demons came out to play. Alone in that tiny square, I fought many mental battlefronts before I even brushed my teeth.

Unfortunately, it was one of the first signs for others to know when things were not okay, especially in my world. Between therapists I worked with, and the upper-class society I was forced to rub elbows with, neither tolerated greasy hair. It only took one rumor to start, and everyone would know the truth. I couldn't have that. Pretending to have all my shit together started with my appearance. From there, everything else snapped into place.

I sudsed up my coconut shampoo and lathered it in my hair as I tried to ignore the thoughts plaguing me this morning. The regret and shame were thick as I massaged my hair. Last night, I was a completely different person. In the light of day, I didn't know how to feel about it.

The only comforting thing about showering was the normalcy and routine of these acts. I didn't have to think about the process, the steps, or whether I was doing something wrong. I stepped into the shower, and my muscle memory did the rest. The mind-numbing movement through the motions opened the gate for everything else. I thought about everything and berated myself for all the mistakes I made the day before.

Finally, the torture ended, and I turned off the water. Stepping through the glass door of my shower, I toweled off with my warm towel and relished the heat from the towel warmer. Combined with the heated floors, my bathroom was paradise and had been one of the perks of this condo. At least I had that going for me if I ever started to enjoy showers again.

The rest of the morning dragged on as I dried my hair and put make-up on. Even my morning requisite of watching the coffee slowly drip into my cup hadn't shaken my mood. So, having to pick out an 'appropriate' lunch outfit for brunch at my parent's hoity-toity club was hellish.

It was Sunday, which meant my forced guilt lunch with my parents was upon me. I could only avoid a few of them a month, or the devil would take it upon herself to visit. I couldn't have that, so my time was up, and I had to attend this week. Lucky me.

Dressed in a pair of black slacks, a burgundy cashmere sweater, and black leather ankle boots, I was hopeful I'd pass my mother's inspection. I made my way to the elevator, and as I pushed the button down, I realized it had been a few days since I'd seen my neighbor from 18D. What was his name again? Monroe maybe? By the time the elevator dinged, I'd already forgotten again. I really was shit at life.

After realizing it had been sitting in the parking garage for about two months, I decided to drive my car since it probably needed to be started at this point. The drive to the restaurant was clear, no traffic in sight, meaning I made it there with plenty of time to spare. Go me, winning at something today. But I didn't want to be early and have to endure my mother any longer than necessary.

Waiting in my car until my requisite time, I scrolled through Facebook. Never give my mother more time than requested. She would only use it against you. The hour I had to spend in her presence was already enough, thank you very much.

Jacqueline Hanover was a hard woman to love. Cruel, cold, and distant, she only cared about her appearance and status. As an only child, I had been the sole focus of her attention. While that might sound like a good thing, it was, in fact, not. She constantly pushed me to be perfect, and whenever I failed, I would be the witness to her tantrums and the receiver of her wrath.

For the most part, I had lived up to her expectations. I had been a straight-A student, on the honor roll, a cheerleader, and involved in several clubs. I dated my high school sweetheart, who came from a respected family, and both of our career paths were acceptable. Our engagement and marriage were expected and provided my mother with the backdrop she needed to show off for her society friends. While I had hated most things I'd been forced into, I had at least accepted they were worth it—until they weren't.

Our relationship had never been the maternal loving one I had witnessed other girls my age have, and I didn't know why back then. Now, I understood that our relationship had always been more of a transactional relationship rather than a loving one. Sadly, it made a lot of sense.

The moment I stopped being her "shining star" of a daughter was the moment I truly saw my mother for the narcissistic bitch she was. Harsh, maybe, but it wasn't enough that I'd lost my baby and my husband. No, my mother had to ream me out for being a disgrace and embarrassing *her*.

Somehow, my life had become hers to wield, and when I didn't do as she wanted, she snapped. Our relationship hadn't been the same ever since. If it weren't for my father, I would've just walked away. How Kenneth Hanover ever married her and stayed for all these years, I would never understand. While I had a good relationship with my father, I'd also come to resent him. He never stood up to her, and allowed the treatment she bestowed upon me. He would simply sigh and dismiss it as 'that's your mother's territory'.

More like, 'I'm not going to stick my neck out for you'.

So once a month, I had to drag my sorry ass to these brunches and put on a fake face, a happy attitude, and smile like the perfect daughter I was known for in public. It was fucking exhausting. I was getting to the point where I'd almost rather endure her banishing me from high society. Steeling myself, I inhaled a large gulp of air before I expelled it through my lips. The vibration from the movement felt weird and at least made me laugh, which felt even odder.

Entering the lobby, the hostess welcomed me as I spotted my parents already seated at their regular table. My mother's chestnut brown hair was slicked back in an elegant chignon. Her eyebrows were plucked to perfection, and her pantsuit wouldn't dare have a wrinkle. She had on a similar outfit to myself, so while that inwardly made me cringe, at least I wouldn't get grief for not dressing appropriately.

My father's raven hair was similar to my own, though he was starting to grey around the edges, making him look distinguished. His beard was neatly trimmed, and he was dressed in a pair of pressed gray trousers, a light blue button-down shirt, and a matching lounge jacket. They were both looking over the menu and hadn't noticed me yet. I was debating making a run for it when the concierge spotted me and headed in my direction and led me to the table of doom. Doubtful the table was actually called that, but it seemed fitting.

"Mother," I stated as I kissed the woman on the cheek. I hated every minute of this, but especially that *one.* Turning, I addressed my father next, "Father." At least I enjoyed my father's hugs. Kenneth Hanover always smelled of expensive leather and spice, bringing me comfort in the form of his hugs.

"Loren, dear, you look well. Did you encounter traffic on your drive?" my mother inquired out of obligation.

It appeared she was being courteous and asking

about my drive, but actually she was making a slight dig at my arrival time. Sitting down, the clock chimed in the distance, indicating I had indeed arrived precisely at 11 am as stated. She was merely being a passive-aggressive bitch from the start. Oh, what fun this was going to be.

"Thank you, Mother. How have you both been?"

Ignoring her slight at my arrival time, I opened my menu to see what the specials were today. As much as I hated these brunches, the food at the club was superb. They changed their menu weekly, so there was always something new to try each time you came. They would rotate favorites in as well, so if you fell in love with something, there was a chance of it returning.

Both concepts created a frenzy amongst the elite, who always had to have what others did not. The waitlist here was months out, but my parents being the snobs they were, had a standing reservation each Sunday. Yeah, they were *that* level of rich.

Catching sight of my favorite dish, I found something to be excited about and ordered Eggs Benedict. Torture hour just might be bearable. Our usual waiter arrived, and I tried not to cringe at each condescending remark my mother made to the man. I always tried to counter-balance her horrendous behavior to hopefully save my food from the spit they had to put in hers.

People needed to learn not to disrespect their waitstaff.

The hour-long conversation of chit-chat was drawing to a close as we finished up our meals. Mine had been excellent, but it was hard to enjoy it with the side of micro-aggression I hadn't asked for. My mother found ways to take several snubs at me while we ate.

"*It's amazing how you can pull off that look,*" aka I was tacky despite being dressed similarly to her.

"*I couldn't eat another bite. I don't know how you do it,*" aka I was fat.

"*I couldn't imagine having enough time to workout that many times a week,*" aka I was lazy if I was using my time to work out. It was a double dig actually because if I did have time, then I wasn't spending it doing something she approved of, as well as a loser because I had nothing else to use my time for—*double whammy*.

And left for last was the crème de la crème of emotional bullshit.

"*Courtney and Frances announced their engagement the other day, isn't that wonderful?*" aka I was a sad loser and going to die alone.

Mostly, I tuned her out and "hmm'd" at her when it was appropriate. Unfortunately, I had tuned all the way out today and found myself agreeing to something I hadn't wanted to. Fucking hell.

"Wonderful! I will let them know you'll be stopping by this afternoon. Mitzi will be so happy to hear you're getting involved."

The smirk on my mother's face told me she'd known I wasn't paying attention and had asked me on purpose to do something she knew I would've said no to, and now, she had trapped me.

"This is a good opportunity for you, Loren. I think you'll enjoy it. I'm happy you've agreed to take some time for it," praised my father.

Kenneth Hanover, despite his faults, was a kind man. He regularly volunteered for organizations such as Habitat for Humanity and Relay for Life and was always willing to help out financially when needed.

My whole life, I'd grown up going to sites and walks with him and my mother used it as a means to show off to her society ladies that the Hanovers cared about the less fortunate. She used it as a tool to get more praise and accolades even when it wasn't even about her. She stayed home but somehow managed to get awarded best humanitarian three years in a row. I kid you not. Jacqueline knew no opportunity that she couldn't spin in her favor. When you thought about it that way, it was quite impressive, *sickening*, but impressive nonetheless.

I hadn't volunteered in about a year because I didn't feel I could appropriately give to an organization. It looked like that hiatus was up for whatever my mother had roped me into.

"They're having a fundraiser this afternoon. You should stop by and talk to Mitzi. I'll tell her to be expecting you and send over the details. Well, we really should be going, dear. We have tee times starting soon."

My mother was a vortex of disappointment and judgment. She was so fast that half the time, you weren't even aware she struck until you were staring at the destruction. Jacqueline quickly kissed my cheek as my father squeezed my shoulder, and they were both gone before I could even protest about this afternoon's mandate. Didn't she know I had an afternoon date with Netflix? I didn't have time to meet one of these busy body ladies who would only report back to my mom about me.

Unfortunately, my phone began to ping with the directions to the fundraiser, and I realized it didn't matter. I was going to this meeting whether I liked it or not. I suddenly felt like I was fifteen again. Too many social niceties were at play, and it would take more energy now to get out of this than just to attend. Bracing myself, I made a deal I'd only stay for an hour and then leave. I headed to my car with my plan at the forefront of my mind.

As I thought over the past ninety minutes, I wasn't even sure breakfast had been worth this torture.

NINE

LOREN

My phone was leading back toward downtown Chicago, and I realized quickly that the GPS was heading toward my office and condo. Well, at least I would be familiar with the area. There weren't many people out with it being Sunday, so I quickly found street parking a couple of blocks from my destination. Deciding to leave my purse in the car so I wouldn't have to keep up with it, I pocketed my phone, keys, and an ID wallet. I locked my purse in the trunk and followed my phone the rest of the way to the building.

A huge sign with a sun logo and the words *Ignite* greeted me as I approached. It was a nice building with shrubs, new paint, and a clean walkway. My apprehension eased a little, and then immediately, I felt bad for assuming the worst about this place because my mother was attached to it. When I entered, I headed to the counter, hoping they could point me in the right direction to Mitzi and I could get this over with. I had some hardcore Netflix binging to do tonight.

"Can I help you, ma'am?" the teenager at the desk

asked. Trying not to cringe at the use of ma'am, I smiled politely. Why was that word the absolute worst? It made my skin crawl every time someone referred to me with it. While I assumed she was being polite, unlike the Barbie wannabe at Windy City, it only made me feel old.

"Hello, I'm here to see Mrs. Hildebrand."

"I'll let her know you're here." She picked up the handset, and I walked away from the desk while she made the call. People hovering over me while I tried to do something was a pet peeve of mine, so I tried never to do it to others.

Looking around at the walls, I noticed photos of the center's various activities and was thoroughly surprised. The center appeared to work with homeless youths and kids in adverse living situations by helping them have a safe place. They offered numerous activities and support for teens, both educational and therapeutic. What drew my attention the most was the focus on STEM.

Science, Technology, Engineering, and Mathematics programs had become very popular, and I was excited to see them here. Girls and inner-city kids had the least amount of opportunities in these fields, so their focus on providing various fields of study was impressive. Whoever had designed their program had made it well balanced and advantageous for kids who might not always have those opportunities. While it was just a display wall, it seemed the center was doing well with several smiling and happy kids on it. I was kind of amazed.

"Loren, so good to see you again. Thank you for taking time to stop by. I'm so happy to have you."

Her voice caught me off guard, and I turned and took in the petite woman. She was a few years younger than my mother, had a kind smile, and dressed more casually than my mother would ever dare to with jeans and a sweater. Mitzi's hair was blonde and hit her shoulders, and as I stared at her, I recalled meeting her before at some function.

"Mitzi, so good to see you again. And I'm looking forward to learning more about this place. I have to admit, though, my mother didn't give me too many details, just that there was a fundraiser today and to stop by?"

"Ah, I see you got the Jacqueline hoodwinked approach," she laughed, and I admittedly liked her. Anyone who could see through my mother's manipulation was a winner in my book. "I talked with your mother over lunch last week about needing some new volunteers, and Jacqueline mentioned you would be interested. I have to confess myself, I thought she was committing you to something you wouldn't have the time for." She smiled, and I knew right then that this woman wasn't like the other ladies my mother socialized with. I was surprised they were in the same circles, quite frankly.

"Well, regardless of how you're here, I'm so happy that you are. Come, let's chat about the program and see if it's something you're interested in. No pressure just because of your mother, though, promise."

Despite the fact my mother conned me into this, I found myself liking Mitzi. She wasn't pretentious or elitist like most of the women in my mother's circle, and I remembered now that she had married into the 'neighborhood'. Jacqueline made it sound as if living in the North Shore zip code was as prestigious as getting into Harvard. I imagined it irritated my mother to no end that Mitzi lived in Kenilworth, which was the more impressive neighborhood of the area.

I imagined if Mitzi's husband wasn't as important as he was in their circles, no one would bother with her. She made them all feel inferior with her easy-going personality, younger looks, and the fact she worked. Her association with the non-profit suddenly made more sense with how I'd ended up here.

Jacqueline was using me to make herself look better in the eyes of her friends. I didn't know why it surprised me, but something about it stung a little more today.

Mitzi led me down a hallway to an office, and we took a seat at a small side table. I liked that she was making an effort to be open and not sitting behind a desk to talk with me. Her body language was inviting and accepting and helped relax me even more. Perhaps this wouldn't be so horrible.

"Can I get you anything to drink?

"I'm good. Thanks, though."

"Of course. So, let me ask if you've ever heard of our program before?"

"No, I haven't. Today is the first time I've heard of it, actually."

"Don't feel bad about that." She laughed, patting my hand playfully. "We changed our name last year and have been doing a whole rebranding thing. One of those reasons was a new benefactor, but the other was that our previous name wasn't very inclusive or empowering. Does the name *Privilege* ring any bells?"

"Oh," I answered, having heard that one before.

"Yeah. It was meant to be, 'it's a privilege to be part of your life'. But it didn't come across that way, and then after the *incident*, it was agreed to separate ourselves from that name and brand."

I remembered this now. It was all over the news how a board member was found to be manipulating teens to do things for him that were of a criminal nature. Then would give them extra "privileges" in exchange for certain things at the center. Yeah, it had been a wise decision to change that, not to mention the negative connotation the name had for anyone of a different race.

"Ignite works to help kids ignite their passions and strive for a future. We offer shelter, food, clothing, tutoring, counseling, and a safe place for kids to explore who they are. The STEM project has been very successful, as well as the arts and athletics. We get more referrals for teens every day, which means we are always in need of more volunteers. I was hoping we could persuade you to join us and maybe come on as a mentor for the teens? I know you're highly credentialed as a trauma therapist with an emphasis in sexual abuse, and well, I think you would make a huge impact helping these kids ignite their lives on a new course."

I was stunned. I stared at Mitzi for a second as everything processed through my mind. I had assumed they wanted me to donate or collect canned goods. Clearly, I needed to update my perception of what a not-for-profit did. My mother wasn't the most reliable resource either.

Mitzi waited for me patiently as I worked through it and offered me a comforting nod when I looked up to ask a question.

"What would that entail? I'm not saying no. I just want to have an idea what I'd be signing up for."

"Understandable and a good question to ask. In this situation, though, I think seeing for yourself would be a better option. The kids are hosting a fundraiser for their upcoming robotics competition and art fair. It's down in the courtyard. Come and join, meet some of the kids and other volunteers, and it might help give you a better picture of what we do here."

"Sure, that sounds fair."

I followed her out of the office and down a different hallway than the front reception area. I could hear music playing as we got closer and the sounds of laughter as it filtered through. Stepping through the door Mitzi held open for me, I found myself standing in the middle of an enclosed courtyard. She waved me off as she headed back into the center. The area was filled with teens and several adults. Various booths were lined up against a wall, and a huge cluster of people were in the middle section. A few booths held baked goods, handmade crafts, and a few games.

Deciding to stick to the edges, I started to make my way around. The first booth was operated by two young girls selling cookies. I pulled out some cash and snagged a few to eat as I walked around. The girls smiled shyly but seemed excited about the sale. I took a bite as I started to walk and almost moaned out loud at how delicious they were. The damn things were gone before I even made it to the next booth. Okay, I was going to have to get more before I left. Cookies were my weakness.

The next one had scarves and beanies that looked crocheted from yarn. There was a line for that one, so I moved on. Another booth looked to be run by a teenage boy. He was tall with a slim build and shaggy brown hair. His booth displayed black and white photos from around the city. The kid had an interesting way of seeing things.

He focused on the clutter in some of the images and blurred the background making trash or graffiti stand out. In others, he highlighted what looked to be compassion and kindness. One series in particular intrigued me. It was of a homeless man sharing his food with a dog and another where he was offering his blanket to a child.

For some reason, it spoke to me and kindled a tiny spark in me I hadn't felt in several years. When I was younger, before the expectations my mother demanded ruled my life, you couldn't find me without a Polaroid camera in my hand. I used to capture everything from my Barbie dolls to blades of grass. Something about seeing the world through a viewfinder had always excited me.

"How much for this set of pictures?" I glanced over at the boy, and he seemed shocked into stunned silence.

"Um, I hadn't really thought about it. I didn't think anyone would buy any, to be honest." He shrugged, his cheeks tinting red. Something about his demeanor made me want to hug him, and I wasn't typically a hugger.

"I tell you what," I started until I realized how rude I was being. "Actually, I'm sorry, what's your name?"

"Oh, um," he shuffled, "it's Jude." He stuck out his hand, and I smiled brightly at him. I liked this kid.

"Hi, Jude," I greeted, shaking his hand, "I'm Loren."

At my shake, he smiled, and I suddenly felt I'd done something significant by shaking his hand. Crap, Mitzi was good. She was reeling me in without even having to try.

"Well, Jude. If I were to find something like this at a gallery, it would typically be about $20 per print for this size. So, how about $60? Does that seem fair to you?"

He looked momentarily stunned as he slowly nodded his head yes.

"Perfect."

Luckily, I had cash on me and wouldn't need to hunt down an ATM.

"Uh, ahem, yeah, um, thank you," he professed after clearing his throat.

"Believe in yourself, Jude, and know your worth. I think you could go somewhere with this." I spoke with conviction, wanting to enthuse to him his potential. "Well, it was nice meeting you."

"Yeah, you too. Thanks again."

I smiled at him before I moved on and watched as he sat back in his chair, a look of wonder on his face, and damn, if that didn't make me feel good. A feeling so foreign I wasn't even sure what it was at first. Making my way around the rest of the booths, I looked on in a daze as I contemplated what this meant.

I was finally able to see what was going on in the middle and noticed some type of robot fight as the two sides battled. Huh, weird, but kind of cool. I guess this connected to the STEM part Mitzi was talking about.

Deciding I should head out, I made my way back toward the door I'd come through earlier. Out of the corner of my eye, I caught a glimpse of a very familiar man. Kneeling next to one of the robot teams was my neighbor, 18D.

The sight of him stopped me in my tracks, and I watched as he interacted with the kids. When he looked up a moment later, he caught sight of me standing awkwardly in the door. He turned his head quizzically, almost like he was trying to place me and then smiled with a little wave.

Realizing I'd had enough new things to deal with today, I did my own little wave before quickly turning and leaving. I'd text Mitzi later, no need to go to her office now. It wasn't until I arrived back at my car that I remembered I'd forgotten to grab more cookies. Damn.

TEN

LOREN

Monday was flying by, and I wasn't sure how I felt about it. Some days, it felt as if the world was barely turning, and every movement made was as difficult as walking through quicksand. Sinking lower and lower with each step toward a goal I no longer recognized. Hand outstretched and thinking, if I just, if I could, if I… but I never could grasp it.

Other moments felt as if everything was rushing by around me as I stood frozen in a singular moment. The world carried on impervious to my pain. Why didn't the world feel this crushing despair the same way I did? Wasn't it obvious? Life shouldn't continue for anyone else when my world had ended. It only seemed fair that everyone else waited, it was selfish actually for them to carry on.

Or maybe I was the selfish one for wanting others to feel this debilitating grief and sadness with me?

Some days, I could recognize it wasn't fair of me to expect that, and others, I couldn't care less as I floated adrift, lost in the sea of misery.

Today felt in-between. It was flying by, but I didn't feel as stuck in the same spot as usual. For once, I was moving forward, albeit slowly, but I was advancing. This new sensation, this foreign concept, it was the thing that had thrown me. Why now? What changed?

"Loren, your 4 pm is here," Doris pronounced, breaking me from the stare-off with the wall I was having.

"Thank you, Doris," I muttered, trying to ground myself back into the present. Her soft smile hinted at knowing I'd been far away but too kind to point it out. Such a sweetie that Doris.

Putting down the pen I was holding, I stood and straightened my dress. I wasn't sure what possessed me this morning to wear a dress, but something about it had called to me. Memories of the other night in the club flashed through my head, temporarily sending a rush of heat through my body. Now was not the time to be pulling those memories up. Shoving them down into the dark recess of my mind, I made my way to the lobby.

Opening the door, I found Imogen sitting in the same chair as last week, but she was alone this time. Well, alone was debatable, as I expected the massive man in a suit who stood in the exact corner her brother had was for her. I was becoming more and more curious about this family. The man eyed me, and something about him flitted across my mind in recognition, but Imogen stood and made her way toward me before I could think about it for too long.

"Hello, Imogen," I greeted, warmth filling my voice. Her posture relaxed some, and I felt assured, sensing she appeared comfortable in my presence at least. I could be a fuck-up in my own life, but I put everything I had into helping my clients. It might be a weird form of masochism, but at this point, it was all I had going for me. I wasn't sure if that was just sad or noble.

"You can call me Immy," her quiet voice replied.

Though her voice was low, I could hear the strength resonating in it this time, giving me hope. We made our way into my office, and she chose the same seat as the last time on the couch. Taking my seat across from her, I gauged how she was doing based on what she was presenting. Imogen was sitting back against the sofa this time, arms down by her side and picking at a piece of string on her jeans. Her hair wasn't as much in her face, and she was looking up from time to time instead of hiding herself completely. Overall, I'd say Imogen appeared more open and accepting based on her body language.

"How was your weekend, Immy? Did you do anything fun?"

"I, uh, I went to a new sushi place, Sushi Roll, with my brother."

"Oh, that sounds yummy. Was it good?"

"Yeah, it was, actually," she smiled, recalling the memory.

To help ease conversation, I proposed a game I had for therapy to present different conversation starters. Imogen was interested, so we took turns answering them. Rapport building was the hardest part of therapy at times. If people couldn't trust you, they would never tell you the things really going on or listen to what you had to offer.

If I started too intensely, or demanded answers too soon, it formed a barrier between us, or worse, causing them not to return. Creating a safe environment and therapeutic relationship made it possible to challenge clients later, allowing them to believe in the process. I'd found that the cards made them feel relaxed and not put on the spot, creating an organic conversation flow. People shared things more freely than if you were to ask a direct question.

"Have you ever wanted to go to public school?" I asked, lifting the card off the table.

"Not really. I mean, there are some things I wonder about, like the stuff I see in movies or read. But the flip side is I also see bullying, and I don't really stand for that, so I think that aspect would be hard for me. I'd end up in the principal's office all the time or worse, turn into a heinous mean girl cheerleader," she chuckled.

"Would you believe I was a high school cheerleader?"

She looked at me quizzically, trying to put two and two together. It was funny watching her as she worked this out for herself. There was a little fear, too, from her statement that I might take offense to her comment.

"Nope, don't see it. You're just so… *nice*."

Laughing, I thought to myself how easy it would be if we were all some archetype from a book or movie. At least then you knew your motivation and the choices to make—took out all the guessing.

"Well, thank you for that. But I was, in fact, a cheerleader," I chuckled, the shock on her face making me laugh even more. "I was also on the debate team and a hundred other clubs. I was what you call an *overachiever*."

"I can relate to that. My dad… well, he um," she swallowed and cast her eyes down, gathering herself before she continued. "He has, or *had*, very high expectations. He pushed me to do things that I loved, but it only caused me to hate doing them in the end. Does that make sense?" Immy asked hesitantly as she peered up at me.

"Total sense. Sometimes, the expectation of others can suck out all the pure joy from something. I realized only yesterday how true that was in my own life. I stopped doing something from my teen years because it didn't fit my mother's plan unless I became a prodigy at it. When there's that much pressure pushing down on you, it feels hard to breathe, much less enjoyable," I admitted more honestly than I meant.

"Yeah, that's it. I've always loved the piano. Ever since I can remember, I would sit down and just play. I would make up my own songs and stories, not really caring how it sounded. It was just fun. Once my father clued in and saw my 'potential', well, that's when it started to become something I hated. I haven't played in six months, but lately… lately, I've been wondering if it would be different now, you know." Immy searched my eyes, looking for an answer to absolve her of some pain.

"How would it be different?" I asked delicately. I had a feeling this was connected to whatever had happened.

"Because he's gone, and I won't *ever* let him hurt me again."

There was an edge of steel in her voice, and she stared at me head-on, no fear. Her strength radiated through her, and for the first time since I met her, Immy personified resiliency and determination. Something about this teenager embracing her fear and facing her big bad wolf resonated with me and bolstered my own resolve.

The spark I'd felt momentarily the day before grew a little stronger, almost as if I was re-igniting the passion within myself.

"I think that's the strongest I've heard you be. I can't wait to hear more about this. It's a powerful statement, Immy. The path to face that fear will be difficult and treacherous at times. I hope you allow me to come alongside you in this journey, in this fight for your freedom. Because even when the monster is physically gone, they don't always disappear mentally or emotionally, and that's where your battle will be fought. It will probably be the hardest thing you've ever done, but the strength I see in you right now tells me you can do this. You won't be alone, but you have to choose to fight."

She sat thinking for a minute, completely still in that moment. Her fidgeting had stopped a while ago, and now, she sat upright as she pondered my words. I could tell she was weighing everything and the cost. When it appeared she came to a conclusion, she looked me straight in the eyes and nodded.

"I would like that. I'm tired of feeling weak and scared. I'm tired of being less than. I want my future back, my hope, and my... innocence. I know I can't have it the way it was before, but I want whatever version I can if it means I don't have to feel this way anymore. *Anything but this.*"

At her last words, she moved her fist to her chest, pounding on her heart. She held eye contact with me throughout, and my empathy was screaming at me to comfort her. One of the most challenging things about being a therapist was having to maintain boundaries. *Get close, but not too close. Care, but don't care too much. Self-disclose, but don't share too much.*

I hated the *too much* part.

Because right now, at this moment, my heart was screaming to hug her, to offer her some comfort and show her she wasn't alone. Instead, I smiled and patted her hand like an eighty-year-old woman.

"You got this, girl, and I will fight alongside you, reminding you the whole way. Okay?"

"Okay."

As I held her gaze, I felt my watch buzz, alerting me time was up. A sign of an extraordinary session was when time passed without your notice, and you wished you had longer.

"You did really well today, Immy. Next session, we can go over some coping skills and talk more, if you would be okay with that?"

"Yeah, I'd like that. Thanks, Loren."

"Absolutely. Okay, hard question time. Are you ready?"

"Uh, sure."

"What candy are you picking today?" I asked with a smile.

"Hmm, you're right. That is a tough one," she chuck-led, and I relished in all the new emotions I was receiving from her. I loved these little moments when I got to witness her personality come through. I was fighting for more of those.

As she picked out what candy she wanted, I casually slipped the question I wanted to know. "Your brother isn't with you today? I didn't see him in the lobby."

"No, he had meetings or something. Sax brought me."

"Sax? Huh. Cool name, though."

"Yeah, he's like the coolest, though he won't show it. But I've worn him down over the years. I think he wanted to speak with you after actually, I just remembered. Sorry," she cringed.

"No problem, I'll walk you up and let him in. Are you okay to wait in the lobby by yourself?"

She nodded, but I could've sworn I heard her say, "I'm never really alone."

I wasn't sure what to make of that cryptic statement. When we exited the door, Sax was still standing against the wall. Man, I wouldn't survive in a job where I had to stand in one place forever. I'd be fired after five minutes.

I was guessing it was a job, anyway. Immy hadn't made their relationship clear other than she'd known him for years. I realized then that she was good at giving you only part of the answer, yet making you feel like you had the whole thing.

Hmm, interesting. I would need to watch for this and make sure she wasn't giving me the responses she only thought I wanted. The giant man looked up when we exited, capturing me in his crystal blue eyes. *Whoa.*

"Hi, um, Immy said you wanted to speak with me quickly. I have a few minutes before my next session if you want to come back with me?"

The man nodded and followed me back to my office. I felt a little subconscious and could feel his tall shadow looming over me. When I got to the door, I stood back until he passed me. I probably imagined it since his frame was so vast, but it felt like he grazed against me when he walked by. Shutting the door behind him, I tried to dislodge my wayward thoughts as I turned to him.

The giant didn't sit, so I didn't sit. It seemed like I would need to stay on the same level as him. It was quiet for a few seconds, so I took him in entirely. He was dressed in a nice black suit that seemed at odds with his beard and the severe facial expression he maintained. His dark blonde hair was coiffed up in the middle and short on the sides. I could make out a few tattoos that seemed to peek out from his collar and cuff links. His eyes were the thing that kept drawing me back with their clear blue depths.

His presence overall was disarming, making me both want to throw him down and equally run from him. Realizing I'd just thought about throwing him down, my cheeks flushed bright red. The giant man smirked and told me he knew exactly the effect he had on women. I wanted to hate him for it, but he made me feel things I couldn't be mad about. He still didn't say anything after a few minutes, so I decided to get this ball moving before doing something I'd regret.

"What did you want to talk with me about... *Mr. Sax?*"

Something inside of me had snapped, and I wanted to see what he did when I used his name. Shit, I was going mental. His smirk lifted a little more, and his nostrils flared, making me feel he'd liked the sound of his name a lot.

"Mr. Masters wanted me to ensure that Immy's files were confidential and what she talks about needs to stay out of the notes. It's important that the information stays contained. Mr. Masters is a powerful man, shall we say, and some of his *competitors* might try to use info on Immy to get the upper hand. We can't have that liability. Do we have an understanding?"

I swallowed, unsure what was happening or what kind of business would try to use a teenage girl's therapy notes. Stuttering out a breath, I found my voice to respond.

"Confidentiality and HIPAA for my clients are of the greatest concerns for me. You don't have to worry about that, and I'm actually offended you would assume I could be bought or bent to compromise my morals," I huffed out at the end. Crossing my arms, I glared at him with a stern look, no longer swayed by his hypnotizing eyes. The more I digested his words, the angrier I felt at being asked this *again*.

Clearing my throat, I raised my chin in defiance and faced off with the neanderthal, "You don't know me, Mr. Sax. So, I'll excuse your and Mr. Masters' behavior, *this time*. But for the future, *Sax*," I seethed, so angry I dropped the formality, "my clients' trust and safety are of the utmost importance to me. *Nothing* means more to me than protecting them. Nothing. *That* you can count on."

Unsurprisingly, I was breathing fast, my heart racing, and my face hot from the emotions I was feeling. *I was livid*. The realization that I hadn't felt mad in forever hit me like a ton of bricks, and the significance of that immediately sent a bucket of cold water over my head. My hands had moved to my hips in a power pose as I squared off with the dangerously gorgeous brute. Fucking hell, he was all the bad boy fantasies wrapped up in one expensive suit.

"Oh, *spitfire*," he purred. "I look forward to getting to know you then. I will convey your message to Mr. Masters."

He had inched forward with some sort of swagger I hadn't expected but stopped before he was too close, veering toward the door. Just as he passed me, he leaned down and whispered in a husky voice, "I bet your pussy is the same lovely red as your face right now. Next time you call me, *Mr. Sax*, I'll show you just how that makes me feel, spitfire. I'll be feasting on your hot cunt while your legs are wrapped around my face. *That's something you can count on from me.*"

My breath caught at his words, my heart returned to a marathon speed, and a hidden part of me wanted to test him on that promise. The arousal was intense, and I hated to admit how slick between my legs I was. Fuck, I needed to get it together.

Rushing to the bathroom, I tossed some water on my heated face trying to cool myself. That wasn't how I'd expected the meeting to go at all, and as my anxiety skyrocketed, I was glad it was over.

So, why did I secretly crave for it to happen again? Just to see if he would feast on me and what that would feel like? Brian had never made me feel this provocative before, and I couldn't remember a time he had looked at me with such unabashed lust.

This was bad, oh so bad, and it was going to blow up in my face. I could already see it. But maybe... just maybe, I was due for a little *bad*. What the fuck had being good ever gotten me anyway?

ELEVEN

ATTICUS

"It seems we have a *problem*," I snarled at the simpering fool shaking in front of me.

"I-i-i-t-t-t w-a-a-s-s—"

"Stop whimpering and speak, or this meeting will end only one way," I glowered.

Looking at my watch, I was already over this meeting. I had a strict schedule to adhere to, and this floundering idiot was putting me behind. I didn't like being late, and I especially didn't like it when it was because of traitors to our family.

"It... wasn't... what... you... think...," he finally managed to get out.

"Oh, is that the line we are going with? Well, then explain this to me," I started, shoving a photo under his nose. "Now, is my eyesight failing me, or is that *not* you meeting with Delgado?" His nod was imperceptible as his lip trembled, but it was there.

"Good, glad you're finally being honest, Marcus," I softened my tone some, wanting to lead him into a false sense of safety. "Now, is this your signature on a deposit that mysteriously never made it into our accounts?"

I tried to hold back my anger at the action, but rage was leaking out of me at his actions. Stealing from the family was the worst offense.

Again he barely nodded, and I wanted to smack him for having the gall to steal from us, but not the balls to admit it. He knew I had him at this point. Marcus was trapped, and there was no escape. Only my mercy would save him now. Walking around, I leaned back against the table and folded my arms as I prepared to hear his lame-ass excuse. Nothing would absolve him of his treachery.

"Please, fill us all in on how it's not what I think if the proof of your meeting with Delgado and your signature is, in fact, real. Hmm?"

"I was doing it to get an 'in' with Delgado, you know, to spy for you. Yeah, I wanted to prove my worth and show how I could be a good asset… a double agent," he stammered out, pleading his case. Sweat gathered on his brow as he awaited his fate.

"Oh, little ant, *tsk, tsk*. You overplayed your hand just then. Because the only person who gets to make that decision is the boss. Are you the boss, ant?"

He shook his head faster this time, visibly shaking as I approached him.

"No, you're not the boss. I'm the *fucking* boss," I growled, spitting some in his face as I got down to his level.

Uprighting myself, I walked the perimeter of the room, building the tension of his fate, and clasped my hands behind my back as I thought of the best approach to deal with him. He had betrayed the family, and that was an automatic death sentence.

But... while I didn't condone his extra activities, he did have an *in* now with Delgado. Would it be worth it to take advantage of that angle, or would it be seen as weak by the rest of the family?

My father would execute, no question. He was ruthless, but I wanted to be calculating and not always respond with violence. This could either blow up in my face or be the spark I needed. Deciding to take a chance, I turned back to the worthless man now bent in a prayer position. The fool, God wasn't going to save him, only I could, and I was *no saint.*

"Listen close, piss ant. From this moment forth, you answer to *me*, and me *alone*. You no longer think for yourself, and you especially don't try to do something big. You will follow the strategy I provide, and you will do it without getting caught. If you get caught, I will deny any knowledge and let them kill you. This is your one chance to redeem yourself to the family and live. Do we have an understanding, ant?"

His head was vigorously bobbing now, no longer giving me the bare minimum.

"I need to hear you say it."

"Yes, I understand. No plan, you tell me," he sputtered out quickly. "Thank you, Mr. Mascro, thank you."

"Now, leave. I'll be in touch when I'm ready for you. Do nothing until then."

He scurried up off the floor and hurried out the door. It was then I noticed the pee stain on the front of his pants. This guy wasn't going to make it. I would need to include that into my approach, or I would be fucked before I even started, and that would not do. Besides, the only fucking I enjoyed was when I was in charge.

"Mas?" Sax hollered into the room, a question on his face.

"Hey, how was Immy's appointment?"

He drew further into the room, giving me a peculiar look. Sax didn't like it when I handled family business without him, but I'd wanted Immy to have him with her today since I couldn't be there. They were just as close, and I'd hoped it would bring her comfort at least.

"It went well, I think. She seemed different afterward. Some of her Immy spark was there. I spoke with the therapist after about what we talked about," he reported, his face tinting a little at the end. Hmm, interesting.

"Did she understand the importance of confidentiality? Does she know we're using fake names?" I asked, needing to hear it. However, my question caused him to chuckle.

"She was offended, actually. Her spitfire came out, and it was *hot*," he grinned, leaning back against the wall. Shaking my head, I looked at my friend.

"Oh, I'm guessing you said something highly inappropriate then?"

"Who, me?"

"Yes, horn dog. *You*."

"Well, if you consider me telling her that I hoped her pussy would be as pretty of a red as her face and I wanted to feast on her as she rode me, then yeah, I guess." The shit-eating grin he wore caused me to laugh out loud.

Fucking hell, only Sax could say something like that and get away with it too. His whole mountain man ruggedness had the ladies dropping their panties at his feet. Course, I had my fair share of women throwing themselves at me, so I couldn't say anything against him. Women gravitated toward the danger we possessed and wanted the one-night stand—never anything more. After a while, you learned to accept it. It was part of this life and easier in the end. Too many liabilities made you weak.

"So, any info on the twerp I saw pissing himself as he ran out of here?" Sax asked once our laughter died out.

Sobering, I focused back on the problem at hand. Dragging my hand up my face, I felt the weight of the last hour. Exhaling, I looked over at Sax.

"It's how we thought. He's been shaving off the top and siphoning money to Delgado. He 'claimed' it was an attempt to gain favor with us by double-crossing them. He's full of shit, but I decided to use this situation as an advantage. It's time to see if we can get some leverage on Delgado and how much they had a part in 'the Reapers' actions. There's a piece of this puzzle I'm missing. I just know it," I mumbled the last part, deep in thought.

My ascension to the boss wasn't the grand plan I'd heard my whole life from my father. I still couldn't decide if it had been a long con on my father's part or if he'd gone crazy in the end. I *hated* him for what he'd done, but there was still a tiny sliver of the boy in me who'd idolized his father. Against all logic, that part wanted there to be a reason for his dad killing his wife and having his daughter kidnapped. But nothing justified those actions or excused them. *Nothing*.

Instead, I became the boss and head of the Mascro family and was left hating a man who'd once been my idol.

"What time is your next meeting?"

Sax's question pulled me from my inner ramblings, causing me to glance at my watch, forgetting I'd already been running behind. I was now thirty minutes off schedule. Dammit. Squaring my shoulders, I smoothed my shirt and rolled my sleeves back down, redoing the cuff links as I did. Grabbing my suit jacket, I started to head toward the door.

"Thirty minutes ago," I sighed, "Come on, let's go meet with the next asshole of the day."

Sax followed and fell back into his guard role once we stepped through those doors. We both had a role to play, and we were great at playing them.

"Send in the next one," I instructed, rubbing my temples.

It had been a long day of meetings, most not being pleasant. No one tells you that being the boss of a crime family is 90% administrative. I was beginning to loathe meetings. Jotting down some notes, I looked up a few minutes later when no one entered. Picking up the phone, I hit the button to ring the desk out front. After a few rings and no answer, I started to get anxious that something had happened. Before I made it out into the hall, Sax walked in.

"All done, boss."

I looked at him quizzically, "I thought there was one more?"

"Ah, yes, there *was*, but not anymore."

"Care to elaborate?"

"Do you really want to know?" he challenged.

I thought about it for a minute. If Sax said there wasn't one, I believed him. Part of his job was managing the things I didn't need to, so I had to assume this was one of those. Besides, it was now 8 pm, and I'd been at this for twelve hours. If I didn't need to meet with someone, I didn't particularly care about the reason why. Sax had it handled, and I trusted him in his role. Shaking my head no, he smiled at my acceptance.

"We do, however, need to head out to the club. I have Nicco popping in at Climax tonight, so we can head over to Evolve."

"Hmm, is that so?" I challenged, raising my eyebrow at him. Sax did a dramatic bow before responding.

"At your will, of course, my liege."

"Fucker," I uttered, shoving his shoulder as I walked toward the garage.

His mention of Climax pulled the memory of our last venture there and the stunning woman we'd interacted with. There was something about her that had drawn both of us to her. That night had been exceptional. The way she'd owned her sexuality with each sway of her hips and the feel of her on my fingers was almost enough to make me say 'fuck it' to the whole mask rule just so I could see her face as she came undone.

However, it was a necessary precaution. No one knew who I really was at the club, and because of that, I had a relative sense of freedom I couldn't get anywhere else in my life. Climax had been a chance to do something as my own venture and hadn't been connected to my father. I'd opened it a year ago, and now, it felt even more important to keep it that way. Not having strings attached to the family seemed like a clever play when I didn't know who I could trust.

The other club, Evolve, or Club Bullet as it was previously known, was my father's establishment—*was* being the keyword. I'd taken it over six months ago when I inherited ownership of everything from my father. We'd been remodeling and rebranding ever since. The new name felt fitting and, hopefully, a positive change for the place. I wanted to leave the past where it belonged and hoped our family, and the criminal underground, could evolve into a new era.

While Evolve remained a 'family' company, at least this way, none of *his* stain would be left on it, and hopefully, we could start anew. My background was in business and management, both valuable assets for a life of crime. It was something Sax and I wanted to integrate more as we changed things. In a family built on history and legends, though, change took time.

It was why, while Sax was technically my personal guard, he actually had a more significant role he played in which we kept hidden—Consigliere. Sax was more than my guard; he was also my advisor and right-hand man. It made sense for us because we'd grown up together and worked through the ranks simultaneously. But to the family, it was untraditional. The mafia was all about a hierarchy, and it was meant to be adhered to.

The role of Consigliere was typically an outsider, a neutral party, and the Molinelli family had passed on heirs from one generation to the next for the Mascro line. Except now, they hadn't had any new descendants, and it was the perfect time to shake things up. However, they were rooted in tradition and wanted to push a third cousin onto me. While they were tracking him down and training, I'd bought myself some time to find a different candidate.

It was all a delicate balance, so to the family, he was my guard and in charge of training all the soldiers. In reality, he had access to all the family's little minions and his ear to the ground on what was actually taking place in the lower levels. It was the best decision I'd ever made. If you didn't even take into consideration that he was one of the few people I trusted implicitly, his access alone would help keep me more in the know than any boss before. Being different meant doing things differently.

My underboss was technically Imogen, but as she was a woman and still a teenager, her spot was temporarily being filled by our Uncle Seth. I hoped to get her out of the life if she didn't want it. I had no intention of forcing my baby sister into this darkness unless she wished to, but God, did I hope she would walk away. Immy was too good for this life.

The next level were my Caporegimes, or Capos. The

three currently there were on a trial basis during this transition period, and I was grooming guys I trusted to take over. However, one, in particular, was being resistant. I had six more months to get them ready to succeed. My father's men were still operating and "mentoring" my candidates, but I didn't trust them. I wasn't sure who was loyal to my father and who was faithful to the family, which is why I had Sax in the thick of it so I could be aware of any duplicity if it were coming.

The Mascro's biggest venture was money laundering and gave us an edge of power within the criminal underground. The other families needed us more than we tended to need them. Through gambling, antiquities, and front businesses, we could distribute dirty cash, and even counterfeit, back into clean money. We had a foolproof system that had served our family for years.

Despite that, my favorite form of currency was one we didn't advertise. *Secrets.* I'd been building a network since I was a teen coming up the ranks, and it was even stronger now. The best part was no one, not even my father, knew I was the secret keeper. It was a power I held solely on my own and also why I beat myself up for the events that occurred. There wasn't much I didn't know in regards to the major players in Chicago. I should've known what Dayton was up to. There was no excuse.

I'd discovered after the fact that the Reaper had been preparing to take our family down a path we'd sworn never to touch. Drugs, guns, and murder. Now, that didn't mean we didn't kill our fair share of people. It just wasn't our source of income. The Mascros gained power, or leverage even, by being the best and above it all. Our power came from control of the underground's money flow.

My dream for our family was to get us out of the shady business and own clean ones, to have legal profits. The illegal gambling, point shaving, and fixed games weren't as dangerous or criminal as other avenues, and I wanted to make our family as close to the right side of the law as possible.

A lot of the older 'made men' weren't going to be okay with my decision. They liked living outside of the rules. Still, as I kept buying businesses and diversifying our portfolio, I was headed in that direction. I wanted to exist in a world where the mafia didn't mean constant danger but was the great family it claimed to be.

I wanted a better life for Immy and, someday, for my own family. I didn't want to constantly fear for the life of the ones I loved, if it was even worth it to go down that path. From where I stood right now, it wasn't.

So, I'd take care of things in the meantime and be the hard-ass boss I needed to be in order to keep my family safe. Even if that only ended up being a few people, I'd never stop protecting them. The underground crime world might never sleep, but it didn't mean I wasn't biding my time, collecting the secrets I needed, and waiting for the right moment.

The world might think I was the mouse, but I was the motherfucking cheese just waiting for them to feel safe enough to spring the trap. I would reel those bastards in and lay waste to anyone who got in my way.

Just try and stop me.

TWELVE

LOREN

Tuesday had arrived, meaning it was time for my first kickboxing session with the surly trainer. I was apprehensive about following through. My earlier bravado had faded, and I almost walked back home three times. With only five minutes until my session started, I forced myself to walk through Windy City Gym's doors. In the end, the thought of his smug look for not showing pushed me to enter. Something about his cocksure smile made me want to smack it off his face.

"Well, kitten, color me impressed. Here."

He tossed me some fingerless gloves, and I barely caught them before they hit the floor. Hiding my reddened cheeks, I hastily shoved my hands in and fastened the velcro. He had moved over to the punching bag, so I followed.

"It's Loren, not *kitten*," I bit out.

Surly looked at me oddly before grunting and turning back to his own gloves. He nodded at my hands when he was done, and I assumed he meant to start hitting. I looked from him to the bag, but he just kept standing behind it and holding it still. I framed myself up like I'd seen on TV. One foot slightly in front of the other, hands braced in the same stance, and I rocked back and forth on the balls of my feet. Okay, I could do this, I mentally chanted.

Taking a step, I moved my arm in the same direction to hit the bag. It had felt like a significant amount of energy, but when I made contact, it sounded more like a love tap. The sound was my only judge because as I moved to hit the bag, I'd closed my eyes before it landed.

When I opened them, Surly's smirk confirmed my fears. He expected me to be terrible and was testing me. *Asshole.*

"I thought you were supposed to teach me!"

"I need to see what level your skills are at first."

Why did that sound reasonable and entirely plausible but likely a bald-faced lie from his mouth? I ground my teeth together as I stared, daring him to smirk again with my eyes.

"Okay, fine, let me see how long you can run for. Laps around the gym."

Dropping my hands, I decided to trust the pushing he was doing. He was the teacher, and I didn't need to question him. This was his domain, and I needed to follow his lead. I took off running in a jog around the space. This, at least, I could do. I've been running my whole life in one way or another.

Thirty minutes in, and I was still running strong, much to the douche's surprise and eventual annoyance if the sighs and shuffling he was doing were anything to go by.

"Enough," he barked, "*Clearly*, you can run. Sit-ups, now."

He pointed his finger to where he was standing. I slowly walked toward him, but instead of stopping like I assumed he wanted, I walked over to the wall and grabbed my water bottle. Taking a long swallow, I drank it down before using my towel to wipe off the sweat on my face. Once I was done with those things, I walked over to the surly bear, whose face was definitely redder than a bear's, it was more like a crab. Guess he fit a crabby crab too. From the look on his face, I think he wanted to strangle me. This obstinate self of mine was kind of fun. Who knew pushing his buttons would feel so... freeing?

Dropping down, I got into a sit-up position and waited until he finally decided to spot me. Huffing as he dropped down, he grabbed my feet and leveled a deadly glare at me. Starting my sit-ups, I seemed to have surprised my surly crab bear with my ability to perform sit-ups. I was beginning to think he wanted me to suck at everything.

I might not be able to throw a punch, but I'd been athletic my whole life, and thanks to my recent barre obsession, I was fit. His assumption I was weak or lesser than pissed me off, and I sped up. Once I hit fifty, he let go of my legs, causing me to fall back unexpectedly. Glaring at him, I righted myself as I waited for his next command.

"Push-ups," he growled out now. His tone had gotten more and more pissed with each demand.

Oh, was Mr. Surly not happy? Was I making him look bad?

I mean, it was only to himself since no one else was in this gym, but still, it made me feel self assured he wasn't getting his way. He'd assumed one thing, and it had been wrong. And now, I was rubbing it in his face.

Making sure to do the full push-ups, I began my count out loud since he didn't, and when I hit twenty-five, panting and my arms shaking, he finally seemed happy at my distress.

"Enough," he commanded, turning and fucking *walked* out of the gym.

I collapsed onto the floor in a heap, feeling completely spent, but a broad grin spread across my face. I think this kickboxing class was going to be just what I needed.

"Have a good night, Loren. See you tomorrow," Daphne shouted as I left New Horizons Wednesday night.

The day had been relatively slow for a Wednesday. After class last night, I'd finally been able to sleep solidly for a full six hours! The extra sleep to my system had boosted me earlier in the day, but now, I was feeling the humdrum of everything as I headed home. That antsy feeling of panic was crawling under my skin, and I needed an outlet.

Making an impulsive decision, I pulled out my phone

and ordered an Uber to take me to Climax. Something was calling me back there, and I hoped it would be the mysterious stranger. The Uber arrived a moment later, and the driver smiled at me as I got into the backseat. Music played softly as she headed toward the club.

Not wanting to go home first for fear I'd chicken out, I hoped my work outfit would suffice. Looking down, I took in my skinny black slacks and black Louboutin heels. They were both designer brands, even if on the professional end, and would give me some leeway. It was tamer than what I'd worn on my last incursion, but they should suffice, I hoped. Glancing at my grey collared shirt and burgundy blazer, I wasn't as confident I could get away with them. I'd stick out like a sore thumb if I walked in there like this. Hell, I doubt I'd even be let in this time looking like a librarian.

Panic started to set in and I was about to ask the driver to turn around when she spoke. "You have something under that top?"

Looking up, I saw her eyes in the rearview mirror regarding me. I slowly nodded, unsure I could use my words with the amount of anxiety coursing through my veins. This was weird, right? I should just go back home. This was why I didn't do impulsive things. I didn't have the stomach for it.

"Take off the button-down and stash it in your bag. They have lockers if you ask, and you can store them. Take your hair down and pump up the roots with your fingers, and if you have any lipstick, add it."

Blinking, I wondered just who this woman was because right now, she was my fucking hero. "Um, thanks," I quietly replied. I started to undo the buttons of my shirt, my fingers fumbling a little with the action.

"I recognized the address, and then when you started to look at your outfit, I figured you were trying to gauge if you could get away with it. Once you get inside, no one will even notice, though," she smiled.

Relaxing a bit at her words, I smiled gratefully back and started to make the changes she suggested. I had on a black bustier top underneath. She was right. It would give off just enough sex appeal. Folding my shirt, I placed it in my bag as I scrounged around for my lipstick I hadn't worn in forever.

I pulled out a nude shade and the red from the other night. Deciding on the red, I applied it to my lips and hoped it helped as much as it seemed to have last time. Though, what I was hoping I'd get out of this visit, I wasn't entirely sure. I just needed to do something to stop the crushing feeling that had been rising.

Lastly, I pulled my hair down from the french twist and shook it out as I pumped up the roots. The driver's nod of approval helped settle my nerves even more. By the time we pulled up to the club, I almost didn't recognize myself and the accompanying confidence.

"Thanks for your help. It was kind of a spur of the moment thing,"

"No problem and those are my favorite kind of things. Go and rock someone's socks off now," she grinned. Opening the door, I was surprised when she stopped me again.

"Wait, here, take this. It's my card. You can text me

directly if you get yourself into a jam or, you know, just need a lift. Okay?"

Looking down, I read the business card, *Rides by Natalie*, and a number was printed on the front. Her kindness melted something inside me, and I hoped to be able to repay her kindness someday.

"Thanks, Natalie. I'm Loren, by the way. And I will," I gestured to the card, "send a message if I need to."

She nodded, a kind and understanding look on her face. I shut the door and turned toward the club entrance. It was Wednesday, so there wasn't as long a line out front, but there was still a line. Just as I was about to walk away, the window rolled down behind me.

"Oh, tell the bouncer working that Natalie sent you, and they'll let you in straight away."

Before I could utter another thanks, the window rolled up, and she took off. That had been the strangest Uber ride I'd ever had, but also the friendliest. *Sister solidarity!*

Once I could no longer see her brake lights, my trance with her vehicle broke, and I made my way to the door. The bouncer, a different one from the other night, looked me up and down but didn't move to lift the rope. I wasn't showing enough skin tonight, I guess. Leaning forward, I found my voice as I whispered to him, "Um, Natalie sent me."

Almost as if I'd said the magic word, he immediately reached for the velvet rope, and I was ushered in. I'll be damned, that had worked. Natalie was a freaking miracle worker and officially, my hero. I was going to give that woman the best Uber review ever. This time when I headed down the darkened corridor, it wasn't as daunting since I knew what to expect. When I came to the end, a different girl waited between the two doors. I didn't understand why I was surprised. I didn't expect everyone to work every night.

"Welcome to Climax, where you skirt the edge of darkness. Which side are you venturing in tonight?"

"Illusion," I stated firmly. I didn't think I was ready for the other door, and I was hopeful that Tall, Dark and Handsome would be here again.

"Excellent choice. Do you need a mask?"

Nodding, she walked around me and tied it on before returning to her station. I shuffled on my feet, not sure what to do now. I mean… I knew, but like I didn't at the same time.

"Do you need to check your bag?" she questioned, noticing me still standing there awkwardly.

Realizing I did indeed need to check it, I started to rummage through for the crucial things: phone, card, license. Pocketing those things, I followed her to an area I hadn't noticed before. It was a little cubby spot with locked doors. She opened an empty one, and I placed my bag within. Taking my hand, she programmed it to match my thumb and then stamped something onto my palm.

"This is your locker number; it's black light so that it won't be seen unless with this light. It's also now programmed only to your thumb. Just come back at the end of the night and retrieve it. Items left in there for 48 hrs will be removed and donated. Enjoy your evening."

At that, she directed me back to the main area and

almost pushed me through the door. Geez, she wasn't as lovely as the last lady!

Squaring my shoulders, I reminded myself I had on a mask, and unlike the one I wore daily, this one made me feel powerful and sexy. Affirming myself with my new mantra, I made my way into the club area. I took a glance around the dance floor, but no one stood out or called to me, not like before.

Making my way toward the stairs, I decided to try my luck up there again. It was emptier than the other night, but I kept reminding myself it was Wednesday. I suppose most people in my age group didn't go out during the week. Those people also had families and—

Stopping myself from heading down that direction of thoughts, I headed toward the bar to grab a drink. The bartender was a woman this time, but seemed just as friendly as she smiled at me. Her red hair cascaded down her back and I was envious of her eye make-up. She had mastered the cat wing eyeliner that I could never get right.

"What can I get you, gorgeous?" she purred. Damn, all the bartenders in this place were mega flirts. I kind of liked it, though. It definitely gave a girl confidence. Taking off my blazer, I laid it across my lap as I situated myself.

"What would you recommend?" I leaned forward over the bartop just as suggestively, trying to get myself into character.

"Oh, gorgeous, I have just the thing for you. Sit tight."

She walked off to fix me something, so I turned on the stool, glancing around the bar. I didn't see my mysterious strangers. I didn't know why I expected them to be here at the same time I was either. I guess in my mind, everyone here remained in stasis, so to come back and not see the same people was poking cracks in my illusion. Disappointment filled me as I turned back around. Fortunately, the bartender was back with a drink. It was a different color from last time but looked scrumptious nonetheless.

"Here you go, try this. It's called an Apex."

She sat the drink down on top of a napkin and waited for me to try it. It was purple and looked pretty with the garnishes lying across it. Carefully, I picked it up and lifted it to my lips. What I thought was salt on the rim turned out to be sugar as it hit my tastebuds with sweetness before the cool liquid traveled down my throat.

"Mmm," I moaned. Her eyes dilated, flattering me even more. I wasn't attracted to females, but it was nice to be hit on by a beautiful woman , even if she did nothing for me below.

"You like?" she asked, all eager puppy-like.

"Yeah, I do, actually. It's perfect. Thanks…"

"It's Cami," she purred at my pause, leaning toward me over the bartop.

"Loren," I smiled.

"So, Loren. I know you don't swing my way, but what are you doing here all alone on a weeknight?"

"Oh, is it that obvious?" I chuckled.

"Only to me because I'm here most nights, and I'm going to school to be a psychologist. I read people's body language fairly well."

"Oh, that's interesting. I don't know what's allowed, but I'm a therapist myself."

"No shit! That's badass. So, what's your field of study?"

And that was how I spent the next hour at Climax. Cami was very energetic and friendly, and I instantly liked her. We talked about psychology and laughed at how she was an amateur therapist being a bartender, which was how she got into the field in the first place. There were some answers she dodged, and I wasn't sure why, but since I wasn't one to judge another person's need for secrets, I let it slide.

"Incoming," she proclaimed, a look of pain crossing her face.

"What? Who is it?"

"My brother, but please, don't hold *that* against me," she begged, making me laugh.

Why she thought I would hold it against her, I didn't know. She was one of the friendliest people I've ever met, and I liked that she didn't know anything about my past or who I'd been. She just knew *this* version of Loren, the slightly damaged, broken around the edges but perhaps fun, me. The fact she'd talked to me all night led me to believe she happened to like that version.

"Camster! What's up, sis?" an obnoxious voice shouted, and I immediately understood her previous statement. Well, you couldn't pick your family. My mom was a prime example. I wouldn't judge her based on him.

"Mason."

"Who's your friend?"

He had made it to the bar now and leaned close to me, his hot breath fanning across my cheek. Ew, gross, dude. Personal space was not a suggestion. Subtly, I leaned in the other direction, trying to get out of his, which, unfortunately, he didn't appear to notice or take the hint and just kept moving closer.

"You know she's into vags, right?" he slurred to me, "You need a real man to stuff you full," he panted. His eyes were dilated, but I could tell it wasn't from lust, but drugs. Mason's face had a ruddy hue to it, and he was sweating profusely. His hair wasn't anywhere near as gorgeous as his sister's, and he dressed like a wannabe gangster.

Mason was probably in his late twenties and had a decent body, but his breath reeked, and his conversation topics were awful. His dismissal and invalidation of his sister's sexuality were what really pissed me off though. My new friend's face fell at each of his comments, angering me even more.

Just as I was about to open my mouth and tell this bastard off for the things he was spewing, an arm dropped over me from the opposite direction. The scent of leather and ink with a touch of ginger filled me. My head was gently turned, and I was met by dynamic grey-blue eyes peeking out from the mask. His hair was short on top, a little curl on the ends, and shorn close to the sides.

"There you are, *beautiful*. Thank you for waiting for me. I'm sorry to have kept you, but it looks like Cami kept you company at least."

The sound of his voice wrapped around me and

melted my insides as he stared into my eyes. I was speechless. All my words had left me. Nodding, I stayed entranced in his eyes, feeling that spark roar to life. This man had me feeling alive with his touch, his voice, and his eyes. My body was tingling from head to toe, and all I could think was I wanted more. Whatever he had to offer, I wanted to bathe in it.

THIRTEEN

NICCO

This was the third night this week Mas had asked me to stop by and check in on Climax. It wasn't a complicated request, and I could do it on my way to and from the shop, so I'd readily agreed. The first two nights were dull and nothing out of the ordinary.

Tonight, I had class earlier and felt pumped up from it. Since I didn't have any appointments, I'd taken the night off. My plan had been to have a couple of drinks, make my rounds, and then head home early for once. I was working on an acrylic painting I'd gotten sucked into, and the muse was riding me hard to finish it. A night at home with my easel sounded perfect.

I was just about to close out my tab when she walked in. I was in a private booth, but I had direct sight of the bar area. This beautiful enchantress had sat down gracefully with an allure I'd never felt before. Her raven hair cascaded over her shoulders in a waterfall of silk. She had class and was refined. Her clothes alone screamed this, but how she carried herself and her mannerisms spoke of an upper-class upbringing. That would usually turn me away, but the more I watched her and Cami chat, the more I wanted to hear what they were saying.

Cami had hit on her initially, but once she had her drink, it shifted, and I saw they were genuinely having a conversation. This piqued my interest even more as most people blew Cami off when they became uncomfortable with her flirting or treated her with disrespect since she was only the bartender. People were stupid and didn't understand they shouldn't mess with the people who filled their drink orders.

I was debating walking over and asking her name when Mason strolled in. He was a walking, talking piece of shit, and I hated that I was related to him, even if very distant. He was the type of Mascro I wanted nothing to do with. Mason kept breaching her boundaries, and I could see how uncomfortable both she and Cami were with his presence. I felt like something terrible was about to happen, and I couldn't take it anymore. Tossing back the last of my drink, I made my way over to them.

"There you are, beautiful. Thank you for waiting for me. I'm sorry to have kept you, but it looks like Cami kept you company for me."

The instant my arm touched her skin, I felt as if I'd been zapped. However, that was nothing compared to the entrapment I felt staring at her. The deepest brown eyes bore into mine, and I wanted to give her everything she was asking for at that moment. Needing to gain some clarity, I forced myself to turn to Cami to break the hold she had me in.

"Hey, Cams, how are things tonight?" I asked casually, hoping to push her asshole brother off the scent.

"Oh, hey, Mason. I didn't see you there. How are things with you?"

Mason swallowed quickly, backing away, "Oh, hey, Nicolai. Sorry, I didn't realize she was your girl. I'll catch you guys later."

He scurried off so fast, I could almost see smoke tracks in his wake. Cami and I both broke into laughter at his display. Mason was a jackass and a coward.

"Sorry, beautiful. It looked like he was about to cross a line, and I didn't want that to be the case, so I intervened. Hope that was okay with you?" I asked hesitantly. I wouldn't change what I did, but I could still feel remorse for not thinking through all the options.

"Uh-huh," she nodded in some trance. I brushed a piece of her silky hair behind her ear, and her whole body shivered. Damn, she was responsive. It made me wonder what else she was that reflexive with. Biting my lip, I tracked her gaze as I let the strand fall from my fingers.

"Loren, this is my cousin, Nicolai. *I do* claim him," Cami teased. "He's a good guy. I'm going to leave you in his hands while I take care of a customer, okay?"

Her eyes were still fixed on me as she nodded. I noticed Cami smile out of the corner of my eye. I didn't really care if she was laughing at us. I was hooked.

"May I sit down?" She just nodded again. At least I wasn't the only one under a spell.

"So, Loren, is it? I'm Nicco."

Finally, that seemed to grab her from the trance she was in as she repeated my name. "Nicco," her voice rang out, making me feel like my name had never sounded as perfect as it did coming from her lips. "Not Nicolai?"

"Not unless you're family. First time at Climax, Loren?"

"Second, actually."

"What do you think?"

"It's seductive and freeing. I love it here."

"I'm glad." I grinned, thinking these babysitting hours of the club just might've gotten way more interesting. I ordered her another drink when Cami came back, and we started talking more.

"So, what do you do, Nicco? Wait, is that allowed? I'm not sure about the rules," she mumbled.

"The rules are whatever you want them to be. You just have to keep your mask on inside these walls, and the lights signify if you're open," I said pointing out to both of us. "And, I'm a tattoo artist. I have my own shop."

"Wow, that's cool." She smiled, taking a sip of her drink. I watched as she twirled her tongue around the rim of the glass, and I'd never been so jealous of an inanimate object before. "I can tell it fits you, if that's not too stereotypical. You just have this cool vibe about you. I'm just a therapist, nothing cool here. Hopefully, you don't quit talking to me now because that's happened before, too," she rambled in the most adorable way.

I liked that she appeared poised and had beauty to run the world with, but she wasn't arrogant. Loren had charm, and it was drawing me into her bubble.

"No, I'm enjoying talking to you, and I think that's a great job," I assured. I did too, and I wasn't afraid she would start to diagnose me. In a way, I got what she was implying because as soon as people heard I owned a tattoo shop, they immediately either started asking me what kind of tattoo I would give them or wanted to show me their tats. I didn't always want to see them.

Loren and I talked for around an hour as the drinks flowed between us. At some point, she had turned, her legs crossed over, and between my open sprawl. I had one hand on her leg, touching her as we chatted. Everything about our interaction felt natural, and I couldn't recall ever having this attraction and chemistry before with a woman. When I realized I hadn't been pretending to be the party Nicco either, I was even more captivated by her.

Each tiny movement she made had me yearning to touch her more. My hands longed to roam her body with no restrictions. Each brush of my thumb on the outside of her pants was already making her melt. Her voice was husky, and she had a hand on my thigh as well. Our faces were imperceptibly close as well, our lips only centimeters apart.

"Do you want to get out of here?" I asked, finally finding the nerve to do it.

"Oh, thank fuck. If you didn't ask me in the next minute, I was dangerously close to throwing myself at you in the hopes of seducing you, but since I haven't had to do that in over twenty years, it was probably going to be an utter failure."

"Well, that can still be arranged. Throw yourself at me all you want. There's no way you'd fail," I growled. The thought of her throwing me down on the bar had me straining even more against my pants. "Let me settle up our drinks, and then we can head out?"

"Yes, please," she begged, and I wanted to bow down to whoever would let me make her demands happen.

Cami was there instantly, handing me a credit card receipt. She had my card on file and had apparently planned ahead, the little matchmaker. In this instance, I was happy she had. Signing, I made sure to leave her with a generous tip before taking Loren's hand and pulling her from the barstool in quick succession.

"I'm hoping you didn't drive because I don't think it would be wise for either of us to try tonight. I don't want to take chances with your safety, so I was going to order an Uber, if that's okay with you."

"I Ubered here, so that works. I have someone we can call, but I need to grab it out of my bag from the locker."

We headed to the lockers, and she pressed her thumb down to retrieve her massive bag. I stared in wonder as I tried to fathom what one put in something that big.

"Shut it, not a word," she smiled as she dug through the contents.

"It's just, wow. That is some bag."

She rolled her eyes but smiled with me all the same. She pulled out a card, entered the info in her phone, and asked for my address before hitting send. I didn't even question it. Something about her didn't have me worried about bringing her home with me. Once she stuffed her things into her purse, I grabbed her hips, pulled her body flush to mine, and pressed her up against the wall.

"I can't wait to get you undressed so I can touch every inch of you, but first, may I?"

She looked at me quizzically, unsure what I was asking, so I slowly moved my hands to the strings of my own mask. Untying them, I revealed my whole face to her and waited for her reaction. Loren licked her lips once I was visible, making the small, vain part of me thrilled she didn't hate what I looked like. Loren nodded again when I looked back, so I slowly pulled her ribbon, letting the mask fall free of her face.

"Wow, you're even more gorgeous than my imagination," I whispered, causing her cheeks to tint pink.

"You're not so bad yourself," she purred.

Not wanting to wait any longer, I descended to her mouth and brushed mine against hers. Her lips were soft and pliable, her lipstick having left her with each sip of her drinks. Slowly, I began to trace my tongue over them, grinding myself into her core. Loren's soft moan opened her mouth, and I flicked her tongue, tangling ours together. I could taste the sugar on her lips and it had me craving more.

I pulled back after a minute, already breathing heavily, and not wanting to get started only to be interrupted when the car arrived. Her moan of protest was affirming as I grabbed her hand and pulled her to the side door to exit. Just as we got there, I felt her pocket against my thigh buzz, presumably announcing the Uber.

She followed me, biting her lip as she looked at me with liquid desire dripping from her. Just before I opened the door, I yanked her hand, drawing her into my body.

"Luscious Loren, I can't wait to have you all to myself, but before we step out this door, are you sure this is what you want?" I searched her eyes for the truth. I didn't want to take her home if she would regret it later or was too intoxicated to make a safe choice for herself. Her eyes were clear when she looked back.

"I'm sure, Nicco. I want nothing more than to spend the night with you. I'm a little tipsy. Those drinks Cami made are strong, but I'm good, I promise. I have full function of my decision making abilities."

Her voice was firm, and the fact she could state all that reassured me. Kissing her once more briefly, I drew back to head out to the car. I'd come back tomorrow and grab my bike. It would be amazing to take her on it, but she wasn't dressed for it tonight, and I didn't want to chance the few drinks I had to impair my driving with Loren in tow.

"There," she pointed to a silver SUV, and I chuckled. Of course, it was Natalie.

"Well, well, look what you caught." She grinned at Loren when she opened the door. I shook my head, laughing at Natalie's antics.

"I take it you two know one another?" asked Loren.

"Oh, yeah. Nat and I go way back. She had the unfortunate luck of dating my dumbass cousin. You know, the one you met tonight?"

Loren cringed at my comment, connecting the dots as Nat groaned out a laugh.

"Sorry?" Loren questioned, unsure.

"Ha! Good riddance. The only good thing Mason ever did was give me Lily. He's too stoned half the time now to worry about, and I have full custody. She's my world. This one, though, he's a good egg." She motioned to me.

"I knew I liked you, Nat," I grinned at her.

"He does seem pretty sweet," beamed Loren, looking at me.

"Oh, I can show you so much more than sweet, babe," I growled into her ear as I pulled her closer.

"Keep it in your pants 'til I drop you off, Nicco!"

We laughed at her comment and settled back into the car, buckling in.

"So, how do you know Nat?"

"She gave me a ride here and helped me figure out my wardrobe situation. When I got out, she gave me her card and told me I could call her if I needed a lift."

I smiled down at Loren as she snuggled into my side. She had sat in the middle instead of the other passenger seat, and our hands were roaming one another. I glanced up and caught sight of Nat in the rearview, and she nodded at me. I wasn't positive, but I expected that Mas had hired Nat to watch out for women who came to this address unofficially. Even when Mas wasn't around, he was still taking care of everyone, protecting them from the villain he saw himself as.

I hoped one day Mas saw himself for the anti-hero he was. He might not be your modern-day Prince Charming, but well, he was a Prince. It just came with bullet holes instead of glass slippers, bodyguards instead of fairy Godmothers, and enemies instead of dwarves.

As much as I wanted out of the family obligations at times, I didn't hate being part of his family. I just wanted something different, something just for me to leave my mark on. Some days that felt impossible, but when I was snuggled up with a beautiful woman, it felt as if perhaps dreams were possible.

Heh, maybe I had it all wrong. Maybe Natalie was the pumpkin carriage, Cami my fairy Godmother, and Climax the ball. Perhaps I was already living my fairy tale, and I just had to open my eyes to see it.

Pulling Loren closer, her body fit into me, and I wished for the first time in my life for magic to be real and that it wouldn't disappear at the stroke of midnight.

FOURTEEN

LOREN

The ride to Nicco's place felt exhilarating and a tad torturous. The light touches he placed on my leg were driving me wild, and I couldn't wait to feel his hands on my skin. Snuggling up in the backseat with someone was sexy in a classic charm kind of way. The nostalgia pulled at me as I tried to recall the last time I'd done something like this? High school?

Time felt like a blur, and panic weaved its way into me as I realized I'd only been with one man my entire life. My. Entire. Life. What was I doing? I wasn't this person. The other night had been the first time someone new had even touched me, and now? Now, I was planning on sleeping with a total stranger? Fuck! Shit, this was bad. How did I get into this? How do I get out of it? Thoughts pinged around my head faster than I could catch them.

"Hey," Nicco murmured as he lifted my chin to him, gazing into my eyes with assuredness. "We don't have to do anything. We can grab a drink and watch a movie. Whatever you're comfortable with, okay, beautiful?"

My eyes flicked back and forth as they searched his eyes, but all I found was pure honesty, creating an instant balm for my racing heart. Despite the bad-boy vibe Nicco had about him with the leather and tattoos, he was proving to be a sweet gentleman. I was discovering how deceptive looks could be.

I mean, the man still screamed sex and that he knew how to have fun, but I was learning he was a man of honor and wasn't going to pressure me into anything. As far as one-night stands go, I doubt I could've picked a better person for it. Deciding I would never get out of this panic if I constantly stayed in my comfort zone, I pushed myself to calm. Plus, I wanted to feel something good for once. Closing the space between our mouths, I placed a soft kiss against his plump lips in an answering kiss.

"I want this. I'm sure." I smiled.

Nicco's returning grin was blinding, and for a second, my heart skipped a beat, confusing me. Pushing it away to deal with another day, I snuggled back into his chest. His arm was draped around me in a warm embrace, and his hand rested on my hip. Nicco's thumb softly moved against the bare skin that was visible between my pants and top. He'd somehow snuck his hand under my blazer, but I wasn't complaining as each little brush of his thumb sent tingles to my core and promised all the things he would give me soon.

The car rolled to a stop in front of a building a few minutes later, and Nicco reached over to unbuckle my seatbelt. It was a sweet gesture, and I found myself wondering if he was even real. Gathering my stuff, I turned and waved bye to Natalie. She'd been my Uber guardian angel tonight.

"Thanks for looking out for me. I guess I'll see you around?" I asked awkwardly.

"Definitely! And no problem, girl. We've got to look out for one another, you know." She smiled. Natalie paused for a second before continuing, almost like she was debating with herself. "Nicco's one of the good ones. Just… just be careful, okay? Call me if you need anything. I'll answer."

"Sure," I nodded, not sure how to take her cryptic goodbye. "Uh, thanks again. Bye."

Stepping out of the car, I took Nicco's hand that was offered. He'd waited out of range, so my conversation had been private. When I stepped onto the curb, I realized instantly where we were. In fact, the dog park from my condo was on the north side of this building, meaning my condo was just around the corner. Well, that would be handy in the morning, I supposed.

"Ready?"

"Uh, yeah." I swallowed. "Nice area."

"Yeah, it's not bad. Close to my shop, and a lot of my family live around here too."

Nicco's voice sounded strained on the last part when he mentioned his family, and I didn't know how to decipher it. When I realized what I was doing, I told myself to turn off that part of my brain. I wanted to enjoy this, and if I started to analyze all the little nuances, I'd drive myself crazy. He pulled on my hand and led me toward the doors. The doorman smiled as we walked through, and I couldn't decide if it was an all-knowing look on what we were about to get up to or if he was just used to Nicco bringing random girls home.

Shut up, self. It didn't matter. He's not your boyfriend. It's a one night stand for crying out loud! Get your shit together.

Feeling properly chastised, I vowed to be present and quit overthinking. The elevator was waiting as we walked up to it, and Nicco pulled me in close to him as he hit the number for his floor. I laid my head against his shoulder and breathed in his leather and ink scent.

His shirt was soft against my cheek as it rubbed against it. I felt him start to nuzzle my neck as the elevator rose and goosebumps broke out over my skin. My heels gave me a nice height increase, putting my neck at a perfect angle for him. The higher we climbed, the more his hands began to roam my body, quickly building an inferno in my body.

"You smell amazing. I can't wait to smell you all over, Loren."

A slight moan escaped me as he palmed the globes of my ass in his hands and turned me fully into him. Nicco was fully traveling my body now, mapping it out with his hands. I moved mine lower and placed them under the hem of his shirt. Nicco's skin met my fingers as I explored his back muscles. His skin was warm, and I could feel his muscles flex as I caressed them. I couldn't wait to touch all of his tattoos and trace them with my fingers. I turned even more, so I was flushed with his front, pressing his hard length against my throbbing center.

Gazing up, I found his lustful eyes staring back at me

mere seconds before he descended in a tornado of tongue, hands, and heat. One moment, I was rubbing myself against him as he devoured my mouth, and the next, I was against the back of the elevator wall, consumed by passion. His tongue danced with mine in a seductive dance, and I wondered if I'd ever been this thoroughly kissed before.

The elevator's ding accompanied by the momentum shift was the cue Nicco needed to lift me, my legs wrapping around his waist naturally. A slight squeak left me at the change in position, and I draped my arms around his neck tightly. Fear that I was choking him tickled the back of my mind, along with the fact that I'd never been picked up by a man before. I worried I was too heavy and would cause us to fall. My bag began to slip down my arm at the movement, and another squeak left me as I tried to balance my equilibrium.

"I got you," Nicco affirmed confidently, and everything in me believed him.

The fact he wasn't panting helped as well, and I loosened my death-grip slightly, causing him to smile as he walked us to his apartment. I watched the doors as we passed and noticed we were on the fifteenth floor. Dropping my eyes back to his, I found him watching me as I took in my surroundings. It was a little disconcerting since he was the one carrying me and walking, but his smirk was panty-dropping hot, and I couldn't help but kiss him again. I didn't want our lips to miss out on any more time together.

Nicco came to rest us against a wall a short distance later and set my feet back on the ground. I wasn't sure if it was his place or if he just decided he had enough and needed to stop here. I didn't care either way as his tongue continued his assault on all my senses. Taking a breath, he traveled down my neck, licking and biting in little nips and causing me to gasp with each one. Tingles rushed through me and I couldn't wait a minute longer not to feel his skin against mine.

"Nicco," I managed between moans.

"Yes, beautiful?"

"Inside, now!"

"Good idea."

He moved back for a moment, and I whimpered at the loss of contact despite having asked for it. It didn't matter if I knew why he moved; I didn't want him to move. Thankfully, he was back an instant later and pushed me toward the now open door. Guess that answered my earlier question. We had stopped at his door.

As soon as it was shut, he locked it and leveled me with such a predatory stare. I understood then that this was his true panty-dropping smile—scratch that, panty decimating smile as liquid heat erupted from my pussy. Dropping my bag to the ground with a thud, I kicked off my heels and shed my jacket and blazer in record time. Noticing my actions, Nicco kicked off his shoes and shed his coat as well.

Standing in front of him in just my bustier and pants, my breaths were coming out fast and made my chest rise with each one. My nipples strained against the rough lace of my top, and I saw him zero in on them. Nicco's thumb was on his lips as he stared, and when he licked them, it sent me into overdrive. We both seemed to move at the same time, crashing into one another with combustible force.

"Oh, God, that feels so good," I moaned as his hands roamed over me, his thumbs seeking my pebbled nipples. Nicco traveled down and unbuttoned my pants and shoved them over my ass as he pushed them down. Pushing up his shirt, I was temporarily stunned by the beautiful ink on his body. I'd seen peeks of it earlier, but the whole view was a masterpiece. Before I could gawk too long, Nicco had me step out of my pants and moved us further into the apartment.

Nicco picked me up again, and this time, I didn't squeak. He moved quickly through the apartment, and I dropped kisses wherever I could reach. In what felt like unnatural speed, Nicco had us in what I assumed was his bedroom. My back was gently placed on a soft comforter as he leaned over me. Nicco stared down at me, capturing me in his gaze. Slowly, he began kissing me again, taking his time to slow down the level of passion as he enjoyed himself.

"Loren, you're so beautiful," he muttered as he broke the kiss.

His words melted me as he simultaneously set my body on fire. Moving down my body, he sucked my nipples through the lace, leaving wet trails behind. Running my fingers through his thick dark hair, I tugged on the strands as my back arched, a moan escaping. I was wriggling underneath him, searching for the hardness I'd felt earlier. When Nicco made it to my panties, he lifted off me and started to unbutton his pants.

Shucking them to the side, he was left in some very tight briefs that soon followed his pants. I heard them hit the floor in a plop, but my eyes were focused elsewhere.

They nearly bugged out of my head as I took in the sight of Nicco's cock. I'd always thought Brian was on the larger side, but the dick staring at me now begged to differ. Nicco stood watching me with hooded eyes as he fisted his thick erection in slow movements.

I swallowed as I took him in, unconsciously licking my lips in the process. His cock was much longer than I'd imagined one to be and thicker. I could make out some veins that pulsed on the side, and his tip was already leaking precum, and I wanted to lick it down. Suddenly, I felt like I'd been tricked my whole life and just discovered Santa wasn't real.

It was on that *level* of a revelation, and a curious urge encouraged me to discover all the other things I might've been lied to about. Just what had I missed out on? If Nicco's cock was anything to go by, a whole fucking lot.

"I uh, um, wow," I spat out. I wasn't positive, but I'd wager my eyes were a combination of bugged out in shock and rapid growing curiosity. Nicco's chuckle at my statement did nothing to quell the heat burning through my body.

"Don't be scared, beautiful."

"I'm not. At least, I don't think I am. It's just, well, um, I've only been with one person, and his thing," waving my hands at his appendage, unsure why I was suddenly feeling embarrassed and shy. "Well, let's just say you have *way more* in that department than I've ever seen, and I'm starting to wonder if I can handle it and if I'm even good at sex, like how would I know? He did cheat on me, so maybe *I am crap*. Do I even remember how to have sex? Oh, God. This was a bad idea. I can't do this. I'm not this person—"

I'd lowered my eyes to the bed in my panic, so I didn't see Nicco move closer until he was stopping my panic with his lips. His kiss was demanding and tantalizing as the anxiety left my body, and I melted into him. When he pulled back, I was slightly breathless and no longer freaking out. Nicco's thumb gently brushed my cheek in a soft caress, and I fell headfirst into the soothing abyss he offered.

"I'm not going to tell you what to do because that has to be your choice. But, beautiful, there's no way in hell you're crap at sex. Whatever shithead made you feel that way isn't worth the pleasure you bestowed upon him. Loren, you ignited me tonight with a look before I even spoke to you. Your mind enraptured me, and you made me excruciatingly hard with a simple touch. When I pressed my lips against your luscious ones, my whole body yearned to be pressed against yours. I don't need to know anything else because that level of heat and electricity can't be faked. Just listen to your body and do what feels natural. But again, we don't have to go any further. We can stop right here and cuddle."

Nicco kissed my lips delicately, and I felt his words sink into me, giving me the courage to trust myself and stop living in the past. For this moment, for this night, I could be a piece of Loren that wasn't grieving. A version that didn't have a truckload of baggage or insecurities. Recalling what it felt like to wear the mask earlier, I channeled the version of me that had been free from it all.

Wrapping my arms around his neck, I pulled him forcibly to me, needing his kiss more than I had ever experienced before. My hunger and desire were in control now, and I wanted to be devoured by this man. To allow him to take the pain and fear and only feel the absolute bliss of release. Pulling back from the intoxicating kiss, I looked at Nicco, and with a strength I'd forgotten I possessed, I surrendered to him.

"I don't want to stop, Nicco. *Please*," I pleaded.

No more words were needed as he entirely took control, tantalizing me with his touches and kisses. His fingers worked the back of my bustier in a delicate caress as he unsnapped the clasps. My top fell away, sliding down my body, baring my breasts to him. Nicco stopped for a moment to take them in, and I prayed they were still perky enough.

"Beautiful, your breasts are exquisite," careened out of him as he lavished me. Arching my back, I pressed them further into him. He started his now-familiar path down my body, and this time, he didn't stop when he reached my panties and met my dripping cunt. Nicco sucked on the material, pulling my clit into his mouth despite the barrier.

Damn, that felt amazing.

I'd never been a fan of oral before, but now, I wondered if it'd just been the giver. Because whatever Nicco was doing, I was a massive fan of. Whimpers poured out of me as I thrashed on the bed, lost in a sea of ecstasy. Damn, I've been missing out. Absorbed in my lust haze, I barely noticed him slipping the soaked panties off me.

When his tongue hit my pussy lips and licked up my full length, I knew I'd never experienced anything this amazing before. My eyes rolled to the back of my head the instant he speared me with his tongue and gave me long licks as he swirled around my clit, sucking it into his mouth. Nicco's finger started in slow, long pumps as he coated himself in my liquid heat. As my moans increased, he sped up as well, driving me quicker to reach the pinnacle.

"Oh fuck, Nicco. I'm going to cum," I moaned.

"Yes, beautiful. Cum around my fingers and make my cock jealous about what he's missing out on. I love how responsive you are to my touches, and your cream, as it coats my face and fingers, is intoxicating," he purred, pulling back for a second.

When Nicco finished turning me on with his dirty talk, he started fucking me with his fingers at a quicker pace as he sucked and lightly nipped at my clit. Before I knew what was happening, the most intense orgasm overtook me, and I cried out as my body spasmed around his fingers, searching for something thicker to clamp down around.

With one final lick up, Nicco pulled back with a smug expression on his face. He earned it. That was, by far, the most amazing thing I'd ever experienced. He slowly took his fingers into his mouth, sucking them clean of me. The raw desire in his eyes and the enjoyment written all over his face called to the animalistic urges in me. Rising on my knees, I trailed my hands over his incredible tattooed body. His muscles were well defined, and I eagerly felt them all up.

I started to drop kisses on them and traced some with my tongue, making my way across his body. Cautiously, I wrapped my hand around his thick cock and started to move it up and down, trying to find the rhythm he liked.

"Fuck, beautiful. That feels good."

Nicco threw his head back, and I was becoming a little more confident when he grabbed my hips in a firm grasp and pushed me flat on the bed. This time, his body settled on top of me.

"Beautiful, I need to be in you, so I can feel the exquisite torture your pussy is sure to be wrapped around me."

At his words, he reached to the side of me, and I realized he must've placed a condom there during my panic, that or he had a magic pillow that produced them at a specific time of the evening. Not wanting to think that way, I watched as he rolled the condom on his thick dick. Something about it was erotic as hell. He smirked again when he saw me practically drooling over it, but he had every reason to be smug. Hell, I was arrogant *for* him.

Looking at me again, Nicco watched my eyes before he slowly started to push into me. It had been over two years since I'd had sex to begin with, and by then, it had become perfunctory at best. As he slid his cock into me, it felt almost like the first time again. I decided to treat it as such in a way. It was the first time I was choosing this for myself. I was accepting my sexuality and all that came with it. I was embracing my womanhood, and I felt something in me finally break free.

Opening my legs wider, I accepted him as he started to move more and thrust deeper. Wrapping my legs around him, I used the heels of my feet to push his ass harder into me. Fuck, had sex always felt this amazing? No, I didn't think it had. Nicco kissed me as we found a rhythm together. Our bodies were fused, and I felt the flutters of another orgasm surprising me as it built within me.

Suddenly, I was pulled up, in a move I wasn't sure was possible, as he lifted us on his knees. Our bodies were still joined as he leaned back on his haunches, impaling me deeper as he now was able to thrust up in me. I tightened my legs as he used my ass as leverage to lift me up and down. The level of athleticism for this move briefly astounded me as he pistoned his hips up. His dick was hitting me deep, and I was sure the world had collided with the number of stars I saw.

"Oh my God," I extolled, my head falling back as my hair brushed against my ass.

Nicco took my moans as the sign of praise they were and ramped up his movements as his arms tightened around me. Laying me back on the bed, he pulled my hips up higher, anchoring me to his dick as our skin slapped against one another with each plunge of his cock into my welcoming pussy. Everything in me exploded, and the most exhilarating feeling coursed through my body, alighting every nerve ending I had.

"Ahhhhh," flowed out of me in a long string of obscene sounds.

"Fuck, beautiful. You're gripping me so tight. I can't—"

His words were cut off as he submerged his cock into me, holding me tight to himself. My whole body felt alive, and I had a feeling I would be craving this feeling of ecstasy again. It was a high I would willingly chase.

Gently, he lowered my legs from around his waist as he slowly pulled out from me. I laid on his cool sheets in a boneless heap as he discarded the condom. He exited his room, and my eyes began to close slowly in a haze of sweet bliss. A time later, I felt the bed shift as he scooped me up and pulled me into him in a comforting embrace. Nicco threw the covers over us, fully enclosing us in his bed. His warm body wrapped around me, and for the first time in my life, I fell asleep in the arms of a man.

FIFTEEN

LOREN

Something nudged me from behind right before I was pulled into the chest behind me. It took a moment to remember where I was, but as the orgasmic encounter flitted across my memory, all I could do was smile. *I had sex last night.* I had sex with a man who wasn't my husband, er, ex-husband. In fact, it was amazing, mind-melting, toe-curling *sex*.

Confidence I'd long forgotten surged to the surface, and for a brief period, I didn't feel the crushing weight of a new day. I wouldn't say I was magically happy now, but it felt a little less hopeless. Almost as if the sun was peeking through the clouds a diminutive amount, and I could see the flower of hope starting to peek through the hardened snow-covered ground. Everything in my life still felt heavy and bleak, but perhaps, for once, not so lonely.

Hands began to roam my body as I fully awoke and felt his cock rub against my ass. I was surprised when my arousal flooded me with desire. Nicco and I were still naked, and as I laid in his arms, a realization occurred to me. I experienced a lot of firsts last night.

It might seem strange to think I still had firsts to encounter at thirty-two. Then again, if last night was anything to go by, my life had been sheltered in ways I'd never known. Brian had been my first and only boyfriend, lover, and heartbreak, and I'd always considered that to be a good thing.

I'd made a lot of assumptions and compromises now that I thought about it. Having no one to compare him to, I'd accepted that some things were only in romance novels and movies and that real men didn't do them. Maybe the most glaring was assuming our sex life was great and adventurous. I'd been led so fucking astray. If the sex last night was any indicator, I had a lot to learn. Starting with how the small things were just as vital as the toe-curling orgasms.

Brian didn't cuddle, and after sex, would roll over and fall asleep. There was no tender care or softness, and there definitely weren't any naked sleeping or morning romp opportunities. As sad as it sounded, we'd become a Saturday and Wednesday sex schedule couple, and if we missed a night, I wasn't upset. It had become as dull as our life.

The kissing on my nape intensified, and the early morning philosophical thoughts evaporated as goosebumps covered my skin. Nicco's hands started to roam up my front, heading for my breasts, and cupped them when he made contact. Earlier than I expected, I was on the verge of an orgasm. This was another first.

It was a rare occasion I would cum during sex with Brian, and *never* two times in the same night. Now, I was about to cum again in just a ten-hour or so span, which fucking blew my mind. Brian always made me feel as if I was the problem. But according to Nicco's skills, that was not the case.

As he twisted my nipple in one hand and plunged his fingers in my wet cunt with the other, I fell apart within seconds.

"Holy shit," I breathed as I came down from the best type of wake-up call.

"Morning, beautiful," Nicco purred and kissed the space between my collarbone and neck.

It would forever be known as Heaven with how amazing it felt to be kissed there. All my insides liquified to goo from his kiss alone. I shivered in response, and I could feel him smile against me. *Fucking hell, this guy.* He was the type of guy you wanted for a one-night stand, but I was starting to wonder what he'd be like as... *more.*

Flipping around, I took in a sleepy Nicco. His hair was ruffled all over, the dark strands falling into his piercing grey-blue eyes. I traced the tattoos on his chest with my hand, going over the outline of a Celtic symbol on his pec.

"Did you sleep okay?" he whispered.

"Um, hmm."

"I grabbed your bag. I hope you don't mind, but I plugged your phone in with an extra charger I had. I didn't know what your schedule was like and didn't want you to miss anything or be without your phone."

The skip in my heart I felt last night briefly resurfaced as I contemplated his thoughtful gesture. Tears sprang to my eyes, and I hid my head in his chest, embarrassed about my reaction.

"Beautiful, look at me. It's okay. You don't have to hide from me."

Why was that the most profound and romantic thing anyone had ever said to me? The tears I'd held at bay a few seconds earlier were no longer contained and started to flow down my cheeks. Instead of Nicco becoming uncomfortable, annoyed, or even upset with me over them, he just brushed them off with his thumb in a gentle motion.

"Ssh, I got you."

He kissed my forehead, my cheeks, my nose, and then my mouth. I tasted my tears on his lips, and that comforted me for some reason. It was like he was taking my tears for himself and turning them into something else. I was about to open my mouth to take the kiss further when my alarm to wake up went off, jolting me in his embrace. Chuckling at the reaction, I rolled over to the nightstand where he'd set my phone and hit the stop button.

The sheet had moved with me, so when I turned back, it was to the beautiful landscape of ink along Nicco's body. My eyes drifted down as I took them all in, and I found his very erect dick standing at full attention. He'd laid back, arms propped behind his head with his muscles and tattoos on display—the very picture of sex mere inches from me. He must've felt my stare because he turned his eyes on me, and I audibly gasped at the amount of desire I saw reflected.

Had Brian ever looked at me this way? No, he absolutely had not. I was briefly speechless as I drank in everything Nicco had to offer. The surreal nature of waking up next to a beautiful naked man who wanted to ravage me struck me, and for a moment, I felt like I was living someone else's life.

"Do you have work today?"

It took a minute for the words to penetrate the arousal surrounding me, but when a fucking sex Adonis was lying next to me on display, all casual-like, it was really hard not to lose focus.

"Mmhm," I bit my lip, concentrating on what I had for today. Work, right that place I went to, and kickboxing because it was Thursday.

If the satisfaction of rubbing it in Mr. Surly's face each time I showed up wasn't so gratifying, I might've skipped tonight if it meant I got another Nicco workout. Clearing my head, I focused back on the present only to be met by a grinning Nicco, and I couldn't help but match him with my own.

"Yeah, I have clients to see today, and then I have kickboxing tonight."

Nicco rolled closer to me, pulling our bodies flush, his dick nesting against my stomach. I wanted to grab it and slip it into me, but I focused on his smile instead. If I got sexed up before work, I would never leave this bed. Let's face it, I wasn't that strong. What woman would be?

"Kickboxing? That's hot. I didn't get to ask last night,

being all consumed by your lips, but what kind of therapy do you do?"

And that's how I had the weirdest conversation about my job, naked in bed, with a cock pressed against my stomach. Nicco had to be the strongest man alive because at no point did he indicate I needed to pay him back with a blow job or a quickie. In fact, he listened to me intently and asked me wonderful questions about what I liked and wished was different about my job.

We finally rolled out of bed at 7:30 am, and I took a quick shower at his place. When I'd finished, Nicco had coffee for me and a toasted bagel. He loaned me a pair of his boxer briefs to wear home, so I didn't have to wear my destroyed underwear. There was nothing more uncomfortable than wearing dirty cum panties.

Nicco rode down in the elevator with me, holding my hand the whole way, and even kissed me passionately at the door. I walked the few blocks to my condo in a daze as I replayed the events of the night and morning in my head. It wasn't until I was riding up my elevator ten minutes later that I realized we never exchanged numbers.

He was only meant to be a one-night stand, so it was probably standard operating procedure. However, the thought of never seeing him again left me feeling morose, and all the sunshine I had following me moments ago was once again covered by darkness and storm clouds.

The few hours break I had was lovely, at least.

Entering my condo, I felt the sluggishness in my body take over as I dropped my bag on the ground. Leaning back against the door, I banged my head against it a few times. The jarring pain was grounding me back in the shadows I was accustomed to.

What was wrong with me? Why was I sad about this? This had been what I wanted—just a one-night stand. I needed to explore my sexuality more. I needed to figure out all the things I'd never done. I was in charge of my life now, and I didn't have to stay sheltered. Feeling somewhat emboldened with my new life motto, I headed into my closet to dress for the day.

"WHAT I HEAR you're saying is that you want things to be different but struggle to put those things into action? Is that correct?" I reflected back to my last client of the day.

"Yeah, that's exactly it! There just seems to be something that always stops me from taking that final step."

"In my experience, what's usually holding us back is fear. Whether that's fear of the unknown, fear of change in general, or fear of stepping out of our comfort zone… the barrier that hinders us the most to change is fear."

"Yeah, I think you might be right. I'm scared it won't be any different."

"It will never change if you never try," I affirmed, some of my own message hitting home as well. "Well, we're out of time for today, but I would like you to think about what it would mean to push that fear aside for our next session. "

"I can do that. Thanks, Loren. You always have a way of helping me put things into words and see them outside of myself," she stated as she got up. "I'll explore this and see you next week."

"See you next week, Claire." I waved and shut the door, glad to have this day over.

It hadn't been horrible, but with each walk back and forth as I grabbed clients, I could feel the stretch from Nicco in my cunt, and it only served to remind me I'd never feel that again. My confidence and the after-sex glow had helped in the morning sessions, but by the afternoon, I was dragging and headed on a fast train to despairville. Pushing Mr. Surly's buttons was the only thing keeping me from going home, curling up in bed, and ordering an entire cheesecake.

Somewhere inside, I was having a rational talk with myself, and I scolded my inner voice that I'd only known him one day, had known the score from the beginning, and only had myself to blame for getting attached. The hardest part to swallow, though, was when I realized I was more distraught over never seeing Nicco again, than I'd ever been about Brian leaving.

Granted, fifteen years of layers were built around us, with many in the last five being rough. Nicco had the advantage of having no baggage with me and only the fun, lust-fueled layers to our dynamic. Logic and rational thought were not my friends today, though, because I missed him, and I didn't care about all the reasons why I shouldn't.

Finishing up my note for Claire, I packed up all my stuff and headed out the door. I had an hour before class, and I wanted to grab something to eat. Bundling up my coat, I bid my farewells to the girls as I headed out. I wasn't expecting to find Mitzi waiting in the lobby for me when I exited.

"Mitzi?"

"Loren! Oh, I'm so glad I caught you. I was headed to the foundation and remembered your office was close by. I hope that it's okay to stop by like this? I wondered if I could interest you in a drink or some dinner?"

I shuffled on my feet. I literally hated being ambushed, but I'd also told her I would call at the beginning of the week, and I'd forgotten. I did have a small amount of time and needed to eat, so I guessed I could do those with Mitzi in tow. It wasn't inconveniencing me this way, at least.

"I'm headed to a kickboxing class, but I was going to stop over at the deli next door for a salad and sandwich. You could join me if you wanted?" Her smile was bright at my words.

"Sounds perfect. I've wanted to try that place out forever. Come on, my treat."

Following her out, I debated on how I wanted this dinner to go. I liked meeting Jude, but I didn't know if I had the time and energy to commit to something so important. It wasn't the type of thing I could bail or flake on. These kids would depend on me, and I would need to be dependable to them, or I'd only create more chaos in their lives. I couldn't bear to be that type of person.

"How did you find the fundraiser the other day? I saw you talking to Jude, but didn't get to catch up with you before you left." She was smooth, I'd give her that, hitting me with the kid from the start.

"I did like Jude. He's talented. It was a well-organized

function, and it seemed like the kids enjoyed themselves. I was impressed overall. But to be honest, Mitzi, I'm not sure I'm the best candidate. I would want to be reliable, and I don't know if I have the amount of time or energy needed to commit to something," I informed her. I felt proud of myself for articulating it well.

"Hmm," was all she said as we made it to the counter of the small deli.

I ordered a small garden salad and turkey club combo and then moved over to a small table area they had. I went ahead and paid for myself as I didn't feel right taking a meal from her if I wasn't going to volunteer. She grabbed a salad and drink and then sat down across from me. It was a few seconds before she finally spoke. I felt like I'd just disappointed my favorite teacher, and anxiety rose in my chest as I waited for her to respond.

"I hear what you're saying, Loren, and I would like to counter that with a suggestion. Instead of feeling like you have to commit to volunteering as a mentor or thera-pist, how about you just come by and hang out with the kids a couple of times a month? Come to some functions if we need people? That sort of thing. This way, it's not a huge commitment, but I'm hoping it will be enough to entice you back for more." She grinned.

I liked that she was honest with me. She wasn't calcu-lating or manipulative. In fact, she was using some of my own therapy techniques against me. What she was saying had merit too. I had felt good for the few minutes I spent there, and I could use some of that in my life. Not having to be required to meet any quota or beholden to a rigid schedule lifted my anxiety as well.

"You're good, you know," I teased as I speared salad onto my fork, dipping it in the balsamic vinegar dressing on the side.

Mitzi smiled wide, taking a bite of her salad as well. "Contrary to most of the 'ladies who lunch', I earned my degree in something I was passionate about, Business, and minored in Psychology. Both have served me well, running foundations and caring for kids. I truly believe you will be a great advocate for us, and I think even for yourself. I know the past year hasn't been kind to you, and, believe it or not, I get it. My life might seem like the picture-perfect portrayal that everyone sees. But I've seen heartache at the loss of a child. I've seen betrayal from friends and death of loved ones. No one is exempt or has it all together, Loren."

I was shocked by her words, not that she knew about my life because that had been front-page country club gossip fodder for months, I had no doubt. No, I was shocked that she had experienced some of the same things as me, and yet, I saw her as someone who had a wonderful and full life. I guess you really didn't know everything from the outside looking in. Perspective was paramount. Mitzi took another bite as we both quietly ate, digesting her words.

When she finished, she delicately wiped her mouth before putting her salad to the side. She was naturally the epitome of class and grace—everything my mother tried to be and failed miserably at.

"I know you will understand the next part I'm about to say, but sometimes, knowing and hearing it from someone else can be the thing that alters it for you. It's hard to see past the haze depression coats everything in. I know that. I've lived it. So, hear this, if you hear anything I've said tonight. *It's temporary.* The depression will lift at some point, and you'll be left with a life that's been on autopilot. The joy from being part of these kids' lives is not a fix for the pain; nothing takes that. But it can be a healing salve, a nightlight in the darkness, and a moment where you can look outside yourself. Think about what I said, dear. Enjoy your class, and I hope to hear from you soon."

She stood casually, patting me on the shoulder, and I watched her leave gracefully out the door into the Chicago cold. Mitzi was a freaking fairy or something with the mind trip she just gave me.

As I finished off my dinner, I let her words permeate and float around in my head. Nothing Mitzi said rang false, and she was correct in her assessment that it would be precisely what I would tell a client in my own care. Therapists really did make horrible clients.

I couldn't dwell much longer on her statements since I needed to walk to Windy City and change for class. But they were there, in the back of my head, planting themselves, just waiting for me to be ready to water and cultivate their growth in my life. Jude's face flashed briefly, and I knew I would be giving her an answer soon, one way or another.

Maybe her words were what pushed me through those gym doors, ready to take on Mr. Surly and his fucking punching bag.

Perhaps it was pent-up aggression for having

amazing sex for the first time and knowing I wouldn't be having it again any time soon.

Or maybe, I was just tired of feeling weak and sad and people telling me I could 'just get over it'.

Do you know what I was going to get over? Their faces when I punched it.

Yeah, maybe all of that was what caused me to go into kickboxing class with a purpose.

SIXTEEN

WELLS

The door banged hard against the wall as she walked into the room. I'd been standing with my back to the door, rolling the tape across my hands as I waited to see if she'd show. Every day I endured these rich assholes, and I barely managed to keep my temper under wraps around them. On Tuesday, I'd wanted to punish her, to make her pay for all my and their sins. I knew it was unreasonable, but it didn't stop me from feeling that way.

For some reason, her presence grated on my entire being, and while her sad eyes had pulled me in, it made me want to push her far away from me even more. Kitten was dangerous, and I doubted she even knew the power she wielded over me.

I'd been impressed she'd shown up on Tuesday, and despite her dismal punch, she'd done well with the fitness test part. It grated on me to admit, but she was in good shape. I never knew those ballet classes were good for more than just watching girls in tight pants bend over. I wasn't the only guy on the other side of the glass who'd gotten hypnotized a time or two by the view.

Today would be the real show of her abilities, but I had a feeling it would be harder for me not to snap at her than I wanted to admit. Everything in my being wanted her to be the recipient of all my hatred for the rich, the privileged. She embodied everything I hated and yet had the audacity to call to me. Her sadness was a drug I wanted to drown in, her body a pleasure I wanted to indulge, and her claws a welcome relief to my pain. *She was a weakness I couldn't afford to have anymore. I couldn't afford anything.*

I remained facing toward the wall even when I heard her steps behind me. Continuing to ignore her, I finished wrapping the tape around my hand even after it was good. She huffed out like the pissed-off kitten she represented. If it wasn't so damn funny, it might be considered cute.

"Yes, kitten?"

"For the last time, it's Loren, Mr.-Mr.-Mr. Surly!" she bellowed.

Okay, someone came to play today. I could use her anger to my advantage. I'd ignore how much hearing her call me a nickname turned me on. It would be so much easier sparring with her when she didn't make me want to fix whatever made her sad.

"Mr. Surly, huh?" I chuckled. She seemed momentarily taken aback by the sound, losing some of her sass.

"Well, yeah. I mean, you never told me your name, and since *you're* so fond of nicknames, it seemed only fair."

Laughing, I shook my head until I caught myself. I couldn't find her charming, it would only end in disaster. Shoving it down, I finally turned around and took her in. She was wearing a matching sports bra and leggings today that hugged her frame in all the places I wanted to explore. *Fuck.* Why did she have to torment me with more of her body on display? Growling now, I sneered at her for making me want her.

"What makes you think I want you to know my name, *kitten*? Enough of this. It's coming out of your training time. Now. Let's start. Laps. Go!"

Her face fell for a minute, and I felt like the biggest jackass, which was how I felt most days anyway. So, I welcomed it, morphing it into fuel to keep the sadness at bay. Kitten steeled her spine and took off running around the gym. Her form was lean and long as she ran, doing nothing to stop my body from reacting.

I might know not to get involved with her, but biologically, my body wanted to fuck her six ways to Sunday and didn't care about my feelings on the matter. Despite my jackass nature, there was a part of me that stopped myself from giving in to the constant temptation. My job might be hell most days, but the buffet of hot women wasn't a hardship to see every day.

I could plow my way through a whole spin class in a month and drop them like the asshole I was the next day, and no one would blink. But I didn't. Maybe it was wanting to stick it to these rich bastards and not be the person they assumed I was. Perhaps it was because, despite my bitterness, I wasn't that much of an asshole. Or maybe, I just didn't feel I deserved any pleasure in my life, even if only fleeting. Whatever the reason, I wasn't going to discover it today. There wouldn't be any giving into the sad eyed temptress.

After about twenty laps, I had her transition into some other warm-ups to get her muscles ready. I didn't know why I was constantly shocked she was in shape. She did attend those classes regularly. And unlike a lot of those spoiled princesses, kitten did seem to participate rather than being here only for show. And she definitely wasn't here just to snag a sugar daddy. No, kitten was actually a member of this overpriced establishment for actual fitness.

It felt like the rest of my clients were the opposite, if the amount of times I got hit on were any indication. It was almost comical at this point. What was even funnier, though, was the instant they got a whiff of who I really was, how quickly their lust shifted. Only the really desperate girl who worked at the counter still tried to ride my dick every day. A sick part of me received a lot of satisfaction from the look on their faces.

I was damaged goods, baby, better run far, far away before my taint rubbed off on you.

"Wrap up. Stances today, kitten."

Her slight scowl every time I called her that was becoming addictive and made me only want to say it more. I needed to watch myself, though, and push her further away. Getting caught up in someone like her would only end in disaster, and there was no guarantee I'd survive. Kitten was the type of woman men wrote sonnets about and went to war for. As much as I wanted to believe I was immune, having already paid my recompense, I wasn't a fool not to see the trap for what it was.

At the end of the day, I would always be trash, and she'd glisten like gold. I'd learned the hard way you could dress any monkey in a suit, but it was still a monkey in a suit. I might look like the real deal on the outside, but at my core, you couldn't turn my fake alloy into pure gold, leaving nothing but a green finger to remind you how wrong you were. I could only offer disappointment. It was the one thing I was good at.

Demonstrating how to wrap her hands with the tape, I showed her the different stances to take as I ignored my thoughts. She followed along, listening to my instruction intently, which only pissed me off more. Why couldn't she be more like those other prima donnas?

"Okay, *kitten*," I sneered, needing to take back some power. "Let's see if your punch has improved any from the pathetic slap you gave the other day."

Her eyes narrowed at my declaration, and I felt vindicated at her anger. I could deal with this. With her rage. It was the only emotion I was comfortable with, after all. Anger and I were good friends.

Moving her arm, I showed her the follow-through motion with the proper stance, none of that TV bullshit she tried the other day. Once I felt she had the movement correct, I stepped back and held the sparring mitts out front.

"Let's see if you paid attention, kitten," I smirked.

Her eyes thinned, and she braced herself, breathing in and out deeply before pulling her arm back and making contact. It was a solid hit on the glove I was holding, much to her surprise.

"Again, don't stop."

Loren started trading her punches off one by one, and a small part of me was proud of the progress she'd made in such a short time frame. When she'd barged in here wanting to take kickboxing last week, I figured it would be fleeting, a whim, and she would quit after the first session. Having her standing here, keeping up with my drills, and making her hits, seriously made me want to reassess her. But that would only lead to trouble, and trouble had no place in my life.

After thirty minutes, she was panting, and her arms were lagging, which was probably why I didn't expect her fist to slip and nail me right in the stomach. Doubling over, my breath knocked out of me. I wheezed a little and was stuck between feeling angry and impressed. Not even an opponent had gotten the slip on me, and this sad-eyed woman had. The irony, really.

"Oh my God! I'm so sorry. I didn't mean to do that. My arms are just jelly, and I followed the momentum. I promise, it was an accident."

"It's fine, kitten. I'm kinda," I panted around the loss of air, "impressed, actually," I finished. Finally, I was able to stand upright as my breath returned to me. "It's nice to see your claws, kitten. I knew you had it in you." I smirked. She folded her arms, her shock and anxiety over hitting me melting back to her anger.

"Why, I outta—"

"You, outta what?" I breathed out, cutting her off as I stalked forward into her personal space. I didn't know why I was doing it. This had bad idea written all over it, a horrible idea actually, but my body had decided to take matters into its own hands and was no longer listening to me. Her breathing increased at my proximity, only making it harder to resist as her perky breasts raised higher with each inhale. Her cleavage became a beacon to my lust, and I zeroed in on my target.

"Well, *kitten*," I purred, "just what are you going to do to me?" Licking my lips, I didn't give her time to respond as I held her trapped in my gaze. "Hmm. I want to hear all the filthy things your little brain is telling you," I demanded, wrapping a strand of her raven hair that had fallen around my finger.

I was banking that I would either piss her off and she'd quit, push her to give in to the things I could see in her eyes, or scare her and she'd leave. All options sounded reasonable at the moment, but my hard cock screamed for option two.

"You make me…"

"What do I make you?"

"Stop interrupting me and let me finish speaking, asshole!"

"Why, what's so important you have to—"

Her lips crashed into mine, and I growled out with relief she'd given in. She tasted of salvation, and I wanted to drown in her grace.

The kiss was aggressive, and we both fought for dominance, if the smashing of lips and teeth were anything to go by. Growling again, I bit the bottom of her lip, yanking her body into mine. A soft gasp left her, spurring me on even more. I was no longer consciously thinking about how bad this would be and only powered by sexual desire to make her mine and satisfy my urges to dirty her pristine image. It was part lust and part revenge against all she stood for and represented.

I ground my hardness against her, feeling some relief, but not enough. My hands roamed over her, grasping her hips. I lifted her, needing more contact. I could feel her slightly damp skin as I smoothed my hands down to her plump ass. The fact she had this ass was criminal. Bracketing my arms under her cheeks, I moved until I slammed her back against the wall, our anger for one another fueling our passion.

Dropping her legs back to the ground, I turned her, pressing her breasts against the wall. Her gasps combined with her moans, and I wanted to consume them all. Rubbing my leaking cock against her ass sent wicked visions I'd been denying myself and wanted to do to her. Loren was sin wrapped in an angel's body I wanted to worship.

"Kitten, your mewls are adorable, but show me your claws. I want to feel the burn."

She whimpered in response as I wrapped my arm around her body, skimming her waistband with my fingertips. Driving them under the band of her yoga pants and panties, I found the treasure I sought when my fingers grazed her hot pussy. Loren's gasp at the pressure spurred me on as she rubbed her ass into my hard dick. Kissing down her neck, I plunged two fingers in as I released her breast from its contraption with the other.

I wasn't gentle as I consumed her. I twisted her nipple, and when she moaned loudly, I wrapped my hand around her throat, bringing her face closer to my lips. Dominating the kiss this time, she was forced to submit to me in this position. Her dripping wet cunt was soaking my fingers as I thrust them in and out, twisting up as I went. I felt her legs begin to quiver as I plunged my tongue into her mouth, owning her.

Pulling back, I kept my hand on her throat as I watched her come undone. When I felt her start to cum around my fingers, I fell headfirst into the pits her eyes held. They were dilated and wide as she watched me, and for a moment, I felt vindicated and powerful. All these rich men were walking around swinging their big dick energy all fucking day, but I was taking what I wanted for once. I was getting my fucking cake and eating it too.

It would be a good story she could tell her friends as she gossiped around the barre class. She would quit kickboxing now, and I wouldn't have to deal with her anymore. I'd be able to focus on getting out from under the pile of shit I was currently in, and she'd be gone finally from my head.

Leaning down, I kissed her briefly again, nipping her lip some more. Her body was pliant after her orgasm, and I was about to suggest moving to the locker room for more privacy to finish when I saw it—a tear. Something about that single tear, trapped in the brim of her eyelid, disturbed me, and almost as if a bucket of ice had been poured over me, I jerked back away from her.

She watched me, confusion in her stare, as I released her throat and pulled my hand out from her pants. Her pussy had hugged my fingers so tight, I was almost coming in my pants from the thought of what she'd feel like around my dick.

But that Goddamn tear… Rage filled me, and instead of comforting her, I lashed out. What did she have in her perfect life to cry about? Too much money? Not enough attention from daddy? The one time I'd chosen to get mine, and she had to ruin it with her emotions.

"Happy now, kitten? Hmm. Did you make your little trainer fantasy come to life? Well, that's all you're going to get from me. You can leave now. The lesson's over."

Turning, I walked away from her before I said anything else. I wasn't sure if it would've been more hate or if I would've broken and held her in my arms. With each hateful word I spewed at her, that single tear had been joined by a silent stream of them down her cheeks, breaking everything I had left inside of me. I was a fucking asshole, there was no pretending anymore, but at least now, she knew it too.

I pushed through the locker room doors, tugging off my shirt as I went heading straight toward the showers. My whole body felt as if it was on fire and itching from the inside out. I didn't like it or know what to do other than try to wash off the encounter. Turning the knob, I cranked it up all the way on the hot setting. Discarding the remainder of my clothes, I stepped into the scalding heat as I let the water burn me, accepting my punish-ment. Taking my hard as steel cock between my hands, I tugged aggressively at a punishing pace, needing relief but not deserving to enjoy it.

Her kitten mewls and the feel of her body would forever be imprinted in my memory, and as much as I hated to admit it, *I fucking wanted her.* And not for the bullshit reasons I thought before. I didn't want her just so I could punish her or get her out of my system.

No… I wanted her because, despite all the things she represented, she wasn't any of them. I think I knew it from the start, I just hadn't wanted to believe it. But from the moment I'd locked eyes with her sad ones, I'd been captured. And if things weren't black or white, and I couldn't separate the likes of her and me, then I had to acknowledge she had pain too, forcing me to take responsibility for my own.

I would be the villain of my own story.

I had it right from the beginning. She was the salvation I didn't deserve. It would be better to stay far away from kitten before I destroyed us both. It was obvious now. I was the type of man to cause her tears, not take them away.

Resolving to let her go, I envisioned her body one last time as I came with a strangled grunt. My cum washed down the drain taking with it any hope I had of redemption.

SEVENTEEN

LOREN

T he oatmeal glooped back into the bowl as it fell off my spoon. I was trying to force myself to eat it, but my mind wasn't having it. The ticking of the clock sounded in the background as the silence enveloped me. Usually, I enjoyed it. Today, my mind was racing with thoughts, and I was beginning to feel out of control.

When I stopped the spinning and laid it out, it was no wonder. All the things that had changed in the past week were paralyzing compared to what I was used to. To be fair, changing my shampoo used to be a big event, so the three acts of indiscretion on my part momentarily felt insurmountable. I wanted to hate myself and berate my recklessness. I let a stranger finger fuck me in public, I went home with a guy I'd just met, and I kissed my kick-boxing instructor!

Mr. Surly aside, the first two had been a mind-blowing experience of self-discovery and freedom. Owning my sexuality was awakening something in me that I'd kept hidden for so long. In a way, I was finally discovering who I was. Things with Mr. Surly, however, were a bit more *complicated*.

Convincing myself to be strong and kick some ass had fueled me through that session to listen to his orders and learn. I wanted to feel physically strong, hoping it would help me believe it internally too. Something must've translated since I'd been the one to kiss Mr. Surly. The tension between us snapped, and *I wanted him.* I didn't think, I just acted, and it'd been scorching… until it wasn't. I was still trying to figure out what happened and when it had shifted.

The beeping of my phone broke my Ferris wheel thoughts, and quite frankly, I was ready for the reprieve. I was starting to get motion sickness from my mind. It was a mystery I wouldn't solve today. The sound perplexed me; I wasn't used to getting many notifications. No one called me but my mother.

Mitzi: Loren, I thought you might be interested in this. *link*

Clicking on the link took me to the Ignite website and an article about Jude and others competing in a local competition today. It started around lunchtime at one of the high schools. I was headed to my closet to change out of my loungewear before I even realized it. Maybe doing something good would help rebalance my chi or whatever it was. Either way, being there for Jude would be a good thing.

It was Friday and I was off, and since my social calendar was mainly filled with Netflix and barre classes,

I could easily attend this event. Working longer days at the beginning of the week to accommodate people's work schedules, my Fridays were free for me. Not that I ever used it for more than another day to do nothing and hide from the world—but today I was making plans!

Dressing simply in jeans, a soft navy sweater, and grey booties, I was ready to tackle high school. Bundling up in my coat and scarf, I walked out my door and was surprised to find 18D. He was walking down the hallway with a young boy in tow. The child had an overnight bag, and they were animatedly talking to one another about something. It was such an unusual sight that I ended up standing stock still in the hallway with my scarf wrapped halfway around my neck.

"Hey, Loren," 18D greeted me with a smile. I felt even more like an asshole now.

"Hey…" nope, nothing came to me. Fortunately, his smile only widened and let me off the hook.

"Monroe."

"Right, Monroe." I nodded. "Sorry, names take me a minute," stumbled out of me, my face flaming at my lie.

"Headed out?"

"Ah, yeah. I'm going to the Senior Fall Event at—"

"Pine Hill Day, perchance?"

"Yeah, actually." My brows scrunched up at his answer. "How did you know that?" Then I remembered seeing him at Ignite that day. Duh, he probably mentored someone.

"I'm guessing the same reason you are. I meant to talk to you after seeing you there that day, at Ignite. I didn't know you were volunteering or—"

Monroe was cut off by the little blonde haired, blue-eyed boy as he tugged on his coat. He looked down at the motion, a look of love covering his face, shifting something in me.

"Yeah, buddy?"

"Dad, we're going to be late," the little boy whined. "I don't want to miss out on the good cookies you promised."

"You're right, kiddo, I did. How about you drop your bag in your room, and I'll wait out here? Maybe I can convince Loren to ride with us?"

I was taken aback at the suggestion. I mean, it made sense, but I hadn't expected it. To be honest, I wasn't entirely sure how I felt being trapped in a car with a stranger, but I'd be lying if I didn't say there was part of me that was also a tiny bit intrigued. *Monroe had a son.*

Why that stood out to me, I didn't know. The boy smiled shyly as he walked by, heading into his dad's apartment, leaving us standing awkwardly in the hall-way. He was practically a miniature replica of Monroe.

"So how about it? Want to share an Uber since we're headed to the same place?"

That sounded reasonable and environmentally responsible, and I couldn't think of a valid reason to say no. So that was how I found myself nodding mechanically as I stared at my neighbor.

"Uh, yeah, sure," I replied when a brilliant idea came to me. "Actually, let me see if my friend is free. She's a driver."

Natalie would be perfect, and maybe I could get Nicco's number from her. Sending off a quick text, I anxiously waited to see if she was available. Just as Monroe's son exited the apartment, my phone chimed with a message.

Natalie: Hey, girl! You're in luck. I'm on your side of town. I'll be there in a jiffy!

"Awesome, she's headed here," I relayed, and we made our way to the elevator.

"Is this the new version of having your friend call during a date to fake an emergency?" Monroe joked.

"Ha! No, I mean, I don't think so." I shrugged, feeling rather called out. We stood staring at the elevator awkwardly, neither of us sure what to talk about now, I suppose.

"Oh, this is Levi, my son." He beamed, his love for his son evident.

"Nice to meet you, Levi. I'm Loren." I smiled as he looked at me oddly. "So, what's this I hear about cookies? I happen to be a big fan of them."

Apparently, that was the right question as Levi explained the difference between the crappy and good ones. The kid loved his cookies. Not that I could fault him, they were pretty awesome. My stomach growled at the thought, and I remembered I hadn't finished my droopy oatmeal earlier. I hope they had more than baked goods at this thing.

When we walked out into the cold, Natalie was pulling up to the designated rideshare spot. They were so common now that most places had an area out front to reduce traffic hazards. I wasn't complaining. It made finding your ride so much easier. Impulsively, I thought about riding in the front seat of her SUV and therefore leaving the back for them, but when I opened the door, it was full of books and things. Oops.

"Sorry, I didn't realize you had more than one person, but the back is clear," she cringed.

"No, it's fine." I smiled, my people-pleasing nature making an appearance despite screaming on the inside. I wasn't sure why I was mad at her. She was right that I hadn't told her it was more than me, and she was doing me a favor, so I just needed to relax. Monroe left me the driver's side spot and buckled Levi into the center. Flashes of myself sitting in that spot filtered through my head, and I immediately had to stop that line of thinking as I looked to the little boy next to me.

"So, Levi, besides knowing your cookies, what else do you enjoy?"

Thankfully, the boy was a chatter bug, and he filled us in on his favorite YouTubers and ranking on Roblox. I was well versed on the fact that kids didn't watch actual TV anymore from my clients. They just streamed shows or watched videos of other people playing games. None of it made sense to me, and I often wondered if their generation spoke a foreign language. I enjoyed learning that Levi was eight, in the third grade, and wanted to be a hockey player like his dad. I lifted my eyes to Monroe at that statement. He played hockey? Just who was my neighbor?

"I thought you were a lawyer?"

"I am," he stated, clearing his throat. "I played in high school and college, but I didn't go any further with it. I play in a pick-up league now, which is basically a bunch of old dudes trying to live out their glory days again," he joked, laughing.

Monroe might've been boisterous about the whole thing, but I could hear the self-deprecating tone underneath it. Wow, I never would've guessed he felt that way. Monroe appeared so polished and nice. To know he was even divorced was blowing my mind. Who would divorce him? The version of my neighbor I'd always had in my mind was changing, and I wasn't sure what to do with it.

I'd been unfair to him and assumed a lot of things about his life. I'd cast him into a role that didn't fit. He wasn't like the men I'd known or grown up around. Despite his wealth, Monroe wasn't elitist. I'd unfairly put on him all the things I hated about that world. It probably had been an attempt to not be reminded of what I'd lost. *It was hard to look at yourself when your reflection in the mirror had become someone you no longer recognized.*

The rest of the drive was quiet, just Natalie's radio playing softly in the background. When we pulled up to the school, I blinked, not realizing we'd already arrived. Monroe and Levi exited the vehicle on their side, but I held back, wanting to talk to Nat briefly.

"Thanks for the ride. My neighbor mentioned riding together, but he's basically still a stranger, so having you here helped me not freak out as much. Though, now that I say that, I see how stupid that sounds, considering I did go home with a stranger two nights ago. Man, I'm a fucking disaster." Dropping my head, I felt the tears brimming my eyelids, ready to overflow.

"Hey, none of that. I'm glad you called, girl." She turned in her seat to look at me. "It's what I'd intended when I gave you my card, remember? Now, wipe your eyes and go and be the awesome person you are. Besides, if you don't get out of my car, I'm going to have to charge you to drive around with me while I do boring errands. And then I might forget to give you a message, so, it's your choice," she teased.

Snapping my head up, I caught her blinding smile at my reaction.

"I take it you want that message?" Nodding, I waited with bated breath.

"Here."

She handed me a note, and I looked at it curiously for a moment. It was a hot pink post-it note with a company name at the bottom, *Ignite Ink*. Scribbled in a messy scrawl, it said, *In case you want to find me.*

Smiling, I looked up to find Nat was doing the same. "Guessing it went well the other night, huh?"

Blushing, I didn't even have to answer as she laughed at my reaction. Grabbing my stuff, I put the note in my pocket and opened the door to get out.

"Thanks, Nat. You've been kind to me when I've needed it the most."

"No problem, girlie. Give me a call sometime, even when you don't need a ride, okay?"

"Yeah, okay. I'd like that."

Waving, I shut the door and found Monroe and Levi waiting just inside the school entrance. As soon as I entered, Levi grabbed my hand and led me toward a table stacked full of, you guessed it, cookies.

"Whoa, you weren't kidding, Levi! These look amazing. Okay, how about this? Let's pick out a dozen, and we can share them when we get back to the apartment? Of course, we need a few right now too, so pick one for us to try." I beamed at him. His enthusiasm was contagious, and I found myself excited to try these with him.

"Oh yes! You can come over, and we can have a taste test and rate them all!" he started to suggest excitedly.

Well, it looked like I had Friday night plans after all. What did it say about me that I was excited about them? Huh.

Once we had our cookies sorted and boxed up, we walked around eating our treats as we took in the art exhibit. Monroe had hung back, talking to a man who looked to be the principal while Levi and I'd gone crazy over the options. He'd kept one eye on us the whole time and had a genuine smile when Levi handed him the one he'd chosen for him.

Now, the three of us walked around taking in the exhibits almost like an actual familial unit. It was scary how natural it felt. I noticed that most of the students were surrounded by peers or parents, so my heart broke for Jude when we got to him, and he was alone. However, when he caught sight of us, his face lit up, and I knew I'd made the right call coming today. This kid needed support and to feel like people believed in him. I think I could be that person for him. I wanted to try, at least.

"Hey, Jude. How are you doing today? How's your art?" I asked when we approached.

"Loren, um, hi," he stuttered, shyness washing over

him. "I wasn't expecting to see you, but I mean, it's nice to see you. And it's, um, yeah. Well, I think I'm doing okay," he finally finished, rubbing the back of his neck in embarrassment. His countenance was endearing, and again I just wanted to hug the kid.

"That's fantastic. I found the perfect spot in my office for the prints I bought the other day. Everyone keeps asking me where I got them. So, you just might have some more customers soon."

"Wow, really? That's, wow. Thank you."

Jude genuinely seemed so floored that I had done something for him and looked like he might cry. Shit, Mitzi's diabolical plan was working, and I knew I would do whatever I had to in order to help this kid. Wanting to distract attention from his almost tears, I introduced my two companions.

"I don't know if you know Monroe or not, and this is his son, Levi, aka the cookie expert."

"Oh, hi. It's nice to meet a cookie expert. What does that all entail?" Jude asked Levi, and they started a conversation.

"You know, Jude is new to the program at the center and hasn't connected with anyone," Monroe stated. "I think that's the first time I've ever seen him smile," he whispered.

Monroe was standing just behind me, leaning down slightly to whisper in my ear. His breath tickled my neck, and his deep smoky voice had my body shivering before I could stop it. Tilting my face up, his mouth was incredibly close to mine as we stared at one another. Swallowing, my lips moved a millimeter, almost touching him.

"Did Mitzi put you up to this?" I managed to get out. "Are you part of her plan to get me to commit?"

"No," Monroe replied, his eyes boring into mine. "I'm here to see the kids I'm mentoring. It was just happenstance, I guess."

Neither of us moved as we continued to chat this close to one another, almost as if we were daring the other to move just that small distance more. I wasn't sure where this magnetism had come from. I hadn't felt it last week or ever before on the elevator. His good-guy vibe was throwing me for a loop with how devilishly seductive he was at this minute.

Apparently, awakening my desires meant opening my eyes to more. I saw the possibilities in front of me and was no longer blind to them. Or perhaps, no longer scared to act on what I wanted. Levi interrupted our stare off a second later, and I didn't know if it had been a fortunate event before anything further occurred or disappointment that it hadn't.

When I cleared my head, I realized gratitude was owed because I was still trying to figure out so many things. I didn't know what I wanted or felt, and I'd end back on my thought Ferris wheel, which was becoming more like a tilt-a-whirl by the minute. I wouldn't deny that there was some chemistry brewing between us now, but whether or not I acted on it, that was a whole separate thing.

I might be discovering new things, but I was still fundamentally me. I didn't want to throw myself into new experiences to chase away the grief, and lose what made me Loren to begin with. It was a boundary I needed to keep.

"Dad! I see Myles and Miley. Come on. I want to see their robot!" Levi exclaimed, pulling him away.

Monroe looked back at me, with almost a sense of longing on his face, before heading off with Levi to a different section. I watched the pair walk off chatting and I found myself glancing around taking in the space. The area was set up into four sections, dividing the exhibits into categories. Turning back to Jude, I found him with his head down, shuffling his feet.

"Do you mind if I hang out here, Jude?" He looked up, surprised at my question.

"Of course not," he smiled. "Um, thanks."

Smiling, I walked closer and took up the spot next to him on the wall as we watched people walk by. He had a few pieces on a table, and the rest were on partitions, filling the front and back. There were more prints out than he had the other night, and I knew I'd have to look at them again before we left.

Jude and I stood and watched the crowd in silence, not worried about making small talk. He was a kindred spirit. I liked that about him. After a few minutes, I decided to take a leap and get to know him better.

"How did you get into photography?"

"Oh, well, my mother was into it and used to take me out with her on shoots. She was a small-time photographer, but she did work for a few papers and did a few print ads. She loved nature shots, though, and we'd go on adventures together. I miss doing those."

His voice sounded sad at the end, and based on him

being at the center, I could deduce this story wouldn't have a happy ending. Wanting to divert that topic for another time, I shared how I fell in love with photography.

"My first camera was a Polaroid, and you wouldn't find me without it," I laughed. "When I got my first film camera, I wanted to know everything about the process. It's hard to imagine everything digital now."

Jude smiled at my comment, and I resolved myself to be bold. "You know, I haven't been out shooting in a while. Perhaps, you could show me some good spots and help me get back into it? If that's cool with the rules and whatever."

"Yeah, I think it is. I mean, I'm in a foster home right now, and I just go to the center after school and on the weekends. It's better for me not to be home as much as possible," he admitted.

Well, shit. I couldn't walk away now. I had a feeling I was going to be reporting something too. Each second I spent with this kid, he tugged on my heartstrings. I wanted to say I could walk away and be fine, but I was only kidding myself. Jude had imprinted on my heart already with his shy smile and kindness.

"Well, in that case, how about you join us for lunch? After this, I mean, and then we can make a plan to go?"

He looked at me hesitantly, I think unsure if I was sincere. "Maybe," he started, "where would we go? I wouldn't feel right about you paying for me. You don't have to give me any handouts," he stated firmly.

"Oh, of course, absolutely. I would never assume otherwise. But just in case you would allow it, we could celebrate. No handouts, but a reward for doing something brave today. Everyone deserves a reward when they put themselves out there. I'm pretty sure that's in the rulebook," I teased, lightening the tension. I understood his need to provide for himself. He knew all about strings.

"Well, if it's in the rule book and a reward," he said with some relief in his voice, "then I guess I have to, huh?" he finished with a grin. I was glad to find a loophole he could accept.

"Perfect. Let me check out your new prints, and then I'll go see where the others went."

As I was browsing, a few people walked up, so I made sure to ask him questions about his work, helping to garner interest from others. Selecting a few new photos, I paid him and motioned I'd be right back while he talked with his new customers.

Heading in the direction Monroe went, I wasn't prepared to turn the corner and run headfirst into the last person I expected to see at a random high school. Now, I remembered why I didn't leave my condo. If you didn't go anywhere, you couldn't run into people you never wanted to see again.

"Loren!" He grabbed my arm as I barrelled into him, steadying me. "What are you doing here?"

Looking up, I found myself frozen as I stared into the eyes of Brian, my ex-husband. *Fucking hell.*

Eighteen

Monroe

Myles and Miley showed Levi their robot as they knelt on the ground, looking over the parts. I'd been mentoring the twins for about a year now through the foundation. Their mom was working hard to stand on her own feet after leaving an abusive situation and had sought the help of the foundation for her kids when they were homeless for a time last year. They were in a much better place now, and I loved seeing them flourish.

Levi had immediately latched on to the ten-year-olds when he met them and saw Myles as a big brother figure. They were both great with him, though, and being close in age, they got on reasonably well. I was excited to learn Loren was heading here when we'd seen her in the hallway. I'd wanted to speak with her after spotting her last weekend, but the week had gotten away from me, as usual.

The mess with Levi's mom hadn't helped either, and well, it had been a stressful week. Today was a professional day for school, so the kids were out while the teachers attended some conferences. I'd taken the day off to spend time with Levi and attend this event with the twins. Their mom couldn't get off from her day job since it was during the week, and I wanted to be here to support them. That was the most challenging part about being a single parent, being there for all the small things.

"Dad, look!" shouted Levi, as he pulled my arm for attention.

Glancing down, I saw they were doing a test run. The kids were really into the robot wars where they had to fight another robot in their age group. It was pretty entertaining to watch, and I loved helping them tinker with things. I'd gone to law school because I thought it would be a successful career path for me, and it had, but my love had always been building things.

Helping out at the foundation, I assisted the board with legal aid, but I also got to volunteer by mentoring kids, which was a passion of mine. It had been something I started after the divorce to occupy my time. However, it had quickly turned into something I'd loved and begun to pour more and more into it. I hoped to instill in Levi the importance of helping others as well.

"Whoa, guys! That's awesome. You're going to do great today. What time is your match?"

"We're up next!" chirped Miley, her curly brown hair bouncing as she practically danced in her spot.

"Well, let's head over to the match area then and get ready. I'm going to check on Loren real quick. Levi, do you want to stay with the twins?"

"We'll watch him," Myles replied, looking up from a piece he was adjusting.

"Okay, stay together. I'll be right there," I pointed.

"Of course, Dad."

I headed back to Jude's area, but I found her standing rigid as she faced off with a tall man. He looked to be berating her as she stood frozen in place. The protective string in me snapped, and I was moving across the room before I had put any conscious thought into it.

"Lo, there you are!" The nickname flowed out before I realized it. "I was starting to get worried," I proclaimed. Putting my arm around her waist, I hoped I wasn't taking too many liberties in my rescue attempt. Her body tensed at the first contact, but then, she relaxed into my hold, and I felt validated in my assessment of the situation.

"Um, hey. Sorry, I ran into, um, Brian, and um…" she trailed off, barely speaking above a whisper. Loren's face was ghostly white and stricken. None of her earlier exuberance was present, and I felt her slightly shaking in my embrace.

Twisting to the man, I took in the scowl he wore, disdain dripping from every inch of his expression as he stared daggers at her. If I had to take a guess, I'd place money on this being her ex. Just a wild hunch.

"Who the fuck are you?" he sneered.

"Monroe Miller, nice to meet you," I greeted, cheerfulness thick in my voice. Being polite, I stuck my hand out for a shake, but he stared down at it like it was covered in shit. I kind of wished it was so I could smear it all over his pristine white shirt. When he didn't take my hand, I dropped it back to my side, my grin in place.

"Well then, I would say it's been a pleasure, but that

would be a lie, so I'll just leave it at that. Excuse us, we're needed—"

Before we could escape, a slim arm slid around the asshat's waist, a very noticeable engagement ring on her finger. As I traveled up the arm to the woman it belonged to, I was momentarily appalled to find it was Christine. My upper lip wanted to curl at the sight, but I held it back. Barely.

"Monroe," contempt heavy in her voice. "Surprised to run into you here and with a woman. I thought you only fucked dudes now?" the high-pitched nails on a chalkboard grating voice proclaimed. *Fucking bitch.*

"Oh, Christine," I sighed, "I'm sorry to report that you've been misinformed. It was just your dried-up cunt I wanted nothing to do with each time you threw yourself at me while I was married to your sister. Well, this has been fun, but we're needed elsewhere."

Quickly, I pulled Loren with me as I made my exit. Nevertheless, Christine hurled one last jab at me, "I'll be sure to let my sister know then. Tell my nephew hi for me."

I tensed but didn't stop moving until I had Loren outside the double doors. Stopping against the wall, I placed my hands on her face as I checked her over. She was cold and had been silent since the moment I'd found her.

"Hey, it's okay. They're gone," I soothed.

Loren's body was shaking even more violently now, and her face was blank like she'd just shut down. She wasn't responding to me, and I began to get worried. What had that asshole said or done before I got there?

Fire filled my veins, shocking me at the level of protectiveness I felt for her. The thought of someone hurting her infuriated me.

"Lo, hey, talk to me. What can I do? Water? Cookies? I'm here, Lo."

I kept smoothing my thumbs over her cheeks until I felt her shaking start to subside, and she could track me with her eyes. Exhaling in relief as she blinked, my body relaxed a fraction as I waited for her to return to me fully.

"Monroe?" her wobbly voice asked, and my heart hurt for her.

"Lo, I'm here. Do you need anything?"

Her big brown eyes peered back at me, full of emotions as she began to calm. I watched closely as she swallowed and licked her lips before speaking again.

"Thank you," she started, "for rescuing me. That was, um, my ex-husband, and well, I haven't seen him in over a year. Figures the one time I leave my house for a new location, I would run into him. I don't even know what he's doing here…" She trailed off, her eyes going vacant as she tried to solve the problem of how she'd missed this danger.

"I'm guessing," I admitted, "it has to do with Christine. She has a daughter that goes here, my niece, Paisley."

"Oh."

"Yeah."

"Well, that's just fucking fantastic." Loren laughed a little manically.

I couldn't blame her. It was a bit ridiculous. The odds

that my ex-sister-in-law happened to be engaged to my neighbor's ex-husband had to be very slim, and yet, when I thought about it, it made perfect sense.

While Chicago might have a large population, there were definite divisions, and most didn't date outside of those arbitrary lines making the dating pool tiny and incestuous over time. Especially after a certain age. It was like trying to throw a rock and not make a ripple. You'd inevitably end up with a dating partner that was connected to someone you knew or had dated. This only affirmed it.

"I need to get back to the kids. I was coming to get you to watch their match. If it's not over now, do you want to check it out?"

"Oh shit, Levi! I'm so sorry, Monroe. Let's go."

She pulled away from my hands, and I missed touching her. Deciding to 'shoot my shot', as the kids were always saying, I grabbed her hand and led us back into the auditorium. Loren didn't let go, and I was doing a victory lap inside my head. She'd intrigued me from the moment she moved in, and I'd always wanted to get to know her more. Loren's heartbreak and despair called to my own, recognizing the pain.

I took her around the outside to hopefully make it to the match before it was over. I could hear the cheers as we neared and picked up my pace. Slipping through the crowd, she tightened her grip, sending shivers down my spine. Spying an open spot, I pulled her with me to the outside of the ring and spotted the twins and Levi. Thankfully, Christine was a shit aunt and hadn't realized

Levi was here, thus allowing us to avoid running into her again.

I would look to see if Paisley was around before we left and if she was alone, I would check in on her. I liked the kid and didn't fault her for who her mother was. She and Levi were close in age, so they enjoyed one another's company too. Hopefully, she would stay sweet and not let her mother's influence infect her.

"Dad! You almost missed it. Look, look!" Levi directed as he pointed to the dueling robots in the middle.

"Whoa, that's cool," I heard Loren exclaim as she took in the battle. Pride filled me at her statement, and then I laughed at myself since it wasn't about me. However, part of me liked that she got this side of me, or appreciated it at least.

Myles controlled the panel that operated the movements, and Miley gave him strategy plays as they watched their robot ramp up at the other one. It always amazed me the skill these youngsters had, and I loved that programs emphasized them earlier. It was evident to me that if we gave kids opportunities, they could do amazing things. I never wanted to limit Levi, even if that meant supporting his dream of playing hockey.

Loren moved closer, my hand staying firm in hers as we watched the battle at hand. The time was almost out, and it looked like it would be a close battle. The other team's robot was a little faster, and it might edge them out in the end.

Myles made one final push to topple over their robot but

misjudged the angle and hit the corner as theirs whipped out of the way. Unfortunately, the momentum sent their robot careening over as it lifted onto one wheel. The crowd held their breath as we waited to see if it would land or fall.

Just as the buzzer sounded, it landed back on the wheel, and a collective sigh of relief on our side could be heard. It would cost them, though, but at least it wouldn't be an automatic win for the other team. If you didn't win, you hoped to at least come out with your robot mostly intact with the least amount of repairs.

"That was great, guys. I can tell the areas you've improved your strategy. Great work, Miley." Both kids beamed back, affirming my commitment to be here for them since their mother had to miss it.

"That was awesome. Dad, can we go to lunch at the place with crazy straws to celebrate? Please," Levi begged. Turning to Loren, I hoped she would join us.

"What do you think, Lo? Want to go to lunch with us at the crazy straw place?"

Her eyes raised to mine, and she smiled as she nodded. "Yeah, that's what I was coming to ask you, actually. I invited Jude, so as long as he's cool with it, then I am too."

"Well, that can be arranged. But I think we're going to need a bigger vehicle or take the L train."

At my statement, all the kids started chanting "train, train," making Loren and I laugh at their enthusiasm. Guess we were taking the L.

"Okay, I'll go grab Jude and meet you upfront once you have your score?"

"Yeah, see you there."

She released my hand, and it felt like the world slowed as our fingers separated, wanting to cling to one another as they were pulled apart. Perhaps, it was a bit dramatic, but I felt her absence immediately and the calm she had unknowingly provided me. Looking back to the kids, they all had little smiles on their faces, and I laughed at their ability to understand things. Children were more intuitive than people gave them credit for.

A few minutes later, the judge walked into the middle of the pit and declared the other team the winner by one point. The twins were disappointed, but as we walked to the front, they began talking about how they could improve. Their enthusiasm and ability to shake off the loss was refreshing.

We made it through the exhibits and thankfully, found Paisley without her mom. She and Levi hugged, and he gifted her a cookie before we said our goodbyes. Paisley hugged me after looking twice for her mom, and my heart broke a little at that. She understood on some level what was going on and I was persona non grata.

"Loren!" Levi happily sang, skipping over to her as they came into view.

His enthusiasm for everything he did was endearing. I'd worried his mom would fill him with lies and deceit about me when I wasn't around, but Levi hadn't acted differently around me if she twas. I tried to keep our divorce out of conversations with him but wasn't confident the same courtesy was given.

"Hey, cookie monster," Loren greeted him, a smile on her face as she did. "You ready to tell me all about these straws you're a fan of?"

I watched them chat as they made their way out the door. Jude appeared a little lost but walked along with us all the same. Dropping back, I kept the twins between us as Loren and Levi led the way.

"Hey, Jude. How did you do today?"

"Um, pretty good, I think. After Loren bought a picture, some other people came over and did the same. More than I expected." He shrugged.

"That's awesome, man. How's your new foster home going?"

He shrugged again, and I knew what he was feeling. Foster homes could be hit or miss. The good ones didn't tend to have openings or want teens, leaving the bad ones and people only in it for the money. The terrible ones made you wish to be anywhere else. He'd come to the center a couple of times the past few months after running away. I wish there was more I could do for him, but with my current custody legal proceedings, I wasn't in the position to do anything.

Our group walked up the stairs for the train platform and headed to an empty spot where we could all stand. It was weird how natural this felt, strangers made of four kids and two adults, and yet, we felt like a unit. The kids enjoyed the train ride to the restaurant, and I smiled at the simple pleasure they got from things. I needed to channel more of that freedom and enjoyment.

Lunch was filled with shakes, burgers, and fries as we all stuffed ourselves full. When we were all so full to the point it felt like we may need to be rolled out the door, I discreetly left the table in the guise of using the restroom. Instead, I paid the bill out of sight, hoping to make it less of an issue for Jude. I knew it would be a touchy subject, and this way, it helped take that fight away. The kids would be oblivious to things, but Jude would be very focused on it, expecting strings—I always had been.

"Okay, who's ready to go?" I chirped, clapping my hands together, grabbing their attention.

The group began to gather their belongings and bundled themselves up to head back out into the cold. Loren gave me a secret smile, knowing what I'd done. As I hoped, Jude looked suspicious but didn't bring it up in front of the little ones.

"Loren, I don't expect you to keep following along since I kind of hoodwinked you into riding with me all day," I joked. "I've got to drop the kids off at their mom's work and then head back to the condo. Jude, where do you need to be? Are you going to the center?"

He glanced forlornly between the two, torn on how to answer. It hit me that he might be unsure about us or Loren going to his foster home. Loren, recognizing the situation as well, jumped in. "I need to talk to Mitzi. Jude, how about you accompany me to the center and Monroe can handle the twins?"

Jude nodded in relief, and while I understood Loren's reasoning, part of me was sad it was all ending, our crazy little impromptu date. The kids gave her hugs as she and Jude walked off toward the center. Levi looked sad to see them go, almost as much as I did. Looking back one last time, I forced myself in the other direction, directing the kids as I formulated a plan to see her sooner this time.

NINETEEN

SAX

"Do you want to try that again?" I seethed to the asshole on the ground. I cracked my knuckles and flexed my wrists as I waited. It was part intimidation and part warming up for the ass-kicking I felt coming.

"I'm s-s-s-s sorry, Sax. I'll do better. It's just been a hard month, I had—"

"Do I look like I give a shit, asshole? *No.* Don't mistake me asking, for caring about what's going on in your miserable life. You're to give me 10% of the monthly earnings. Period. Yet, here I stand with only 5%. Where's the rest of the money, Corey? Hmm?"

"I-uh-I-uh…"

"Spit it out before I break your teeth for annoying me."

"Delgado, he… he…"

At the mention of Delgado, my blood boiled. This fucker was causing more and more trouble every day. It was going to come to a head soon, and I hoped it wasn't on us. He was increasingly becoming a thorn in my side. I still haven't forgiven myself for the events six months ago. The fear started to crawl up my spine as I recalled that night, and I shoved it way down, locking it behind the vault in my mind. Too much shit had happened in my life to keep it on the surface.

Though, some days I feared I was one memory lock away from snapping and killing everyone. Some days… that didn't seem like such a bad idea. The world was full of despicable men and women, and I just wanted to keep my family safe. Whatever the cost. Sometimes, that meant I had to be the bad guy to do it. I regretted nothing in my pursuit of that goal—only when I failed at it.

"Here is what you're going to do, *Corey,*" I sneered, grabbing him by the collar. I yanked him to me as I knelt by his head. This guy pissed me off so much, I took offense even with his name.

"You're going to pay back the money you owe, *and* you're going to pay me early for next month. I don't trust you anymore, so you're either going to find a way to make it work, or I'll break your face. Got it?"

The sniveling snot was shaking, and the smell of his piss wafted up to me. I was done with him. Punching him in the face, I dropped him back on the ground before wiping my hands down my dark jeans, grateful they'd cover any bloodstains. I'd dressed more casually than usual since it worked better to blend with the masses when I was collecting. Not that I blended all too well due to my height, beard, and tattoos, but it made me feel like I at least tried.

Walking out of the storefront, I zipped up my leather jacket and pulled out my riding gloves as I mounted my bike. I had one more stop before checking on the guards to see if there was any new info on the mole. I was certain now that there was one. Too much shit was getting to Delgado right under our noses for there not to be. We weren't this incompetent.

An ass in a pair of jeans caught my attention across the street, and I realized it was the pretty therapist. Something about her drew me in like a bee to honey. She had this vulnerability that intrigued me, and yet, I could see the sex Goddess just there waiting to emerge. The night at the club, she hadn't recognized us, but I'd most definitely noticed her. I still wasn't sure if Atticus knew it was her. He liked to be in denial about those types of things until it smacked him in the face.

When she'd talked to me while the couple danced, I saw that spark, that adventure hiding deep within. It'd been one of the few times I was jealous of Mas as he'd been the one to feel her and bring her to ecstasy. It was apparent she had no clue, though. I'd tested her in the office the other day and saw no recognition in her pretty eyes.

I imagined I was just as good as she was at reading body language and expressions. It was part of my posi-tion as a guard, and even more so now as his advisor, his Consigliere. It was a skill I'd honed over the years. At thirty-seven, there wasn't much that got past me. And the one that did… haunted me to this day.

Spitfire was walking with a teen that looked vaguely familiar, but I couldn't recall from where. Part of me wanted to follow them, but I needed to get to my last stop more. I had a feeling she was quickly becoming an obsession I wouldn't be able to let go of, though.

Women had always been a dime a dozen for me. I wasn't being callous, just honest. Having a different bed partner each night wasn't uncommon, and it allowed me the level of freedom and invisibility I needed. Mas, well, he was pickier. Often he would limit himself, and I'd come to expect it was some sort of penance, but it wasn't unusual for us to share women. And the way we'd both responded to her, I hoped we found her between us soon. Mas just had to get out of his own way first.

When they went around the corner, I strapped on my helmet before revving my engine and heading toward my next stop. There was a part of me that enjoyed this job because I got to smash heads when they didn't follow the rules, and *people never followed the rules*. Everyone always thought they were above the law and wouldn't get caught.

Jokes on them. I was *the law*, and I always caught *my prey*.

The winter chill rushed around me as I drove through the Chicago streets. Until there was snow or ice, I rode my baby everywhere. It was much easier to navigate the busy streets, and parking was simpler. The cool breeze whipped around me, and I felt invigorated. Nothing could replace the feel of the engine as it rumbled and hummed between my legs. My bike, punching Corey, and seeing the sexy spitfire had my blood pumping for this next tenant.

Parking, I climbed off my baby and strode into the barbershop. It was cliche, but Daddy Mascro wasn't the cleverest, not like Mas. Many of these businesses helped run the gambling rings we had, the fights Nicco ran, to bookies for every type of sports, horses, and racecars. If it could be bet on, there was someone, somewhere, willing to take the odds. Most of these shops had been in the family forever and wouldn't dare think of double-crossing, thus making my job easy.

At the end of each month, I visited and collected the 10% they owed us for 'rent' and exchanged dirty money from other families into the businesses and gambling pools. Our system was practically flawless, and no one could match our reach or versatility. The Delgado's were the lowest of the three families operating out of chop shops, drugs, and violence. They were the scum of our world, and their honor was decreasing with every secret I uncovered. They were reckless, which got people killed. I just hoped it wouldn't be us this time.

The Rawle's were in the business of import/export and could get almost anything you needed to be brought here or shipped. They specialized in weapons, with some counterfeits mixed in, and the lesser of their business—people. They only advertised that they could extract people and transport them across borders, but Mas and I had a feeling they were dipping their toes in human trafficking, and if that were the case, we would need to put a stop to it. There were lines you didn't cross, even in the underground.

There were several other smaller families in Chicago, of course, but they all tended to align themselves with one of the big three, just waiting for us to take the other out so they could take up the mantle for power. The dynamics hadn't shifted in ten years, with Mascro being groomed under Dayton "the Grim Reaper's" control. The shift in leadership left us in a precarious position, and we found ourselves waiting for one of the other families to make a play.

Fortunately for our family, Mas was a fucking genius, With an MBA and savvy business sense, he was moving us in a new direction. One I eagerly awaited to see come to fruition. I owed everything to the Mascro family, but especially Mas. He was my best friend and brother, and we'd been through a lot in our thirty-year friendship.

"Pops! How's it going?" I warmly greeted the older man as the sound of clippers buzzed amidst the chatter.

"Saxon Wessex, as I live and breathe. It's been ages since I last saw you. How's it going, boy?"

Pops was an old-timer, and a great uncle something or other to Mas, plus a genuinely great human being. We spent a lot of time here growing up, learning the ropes from him.

"A little trouble with some of the new tenants, but I think we came to an agreement." I grinned mischievously.

"Meaning your fist met his face?" he joked.

Smirking, "You know me so well. So, what do you have for me today?"

Rubbing my hands together, I was excited to see the beauty he'd been hunting for me. Pops was the connoisseur of rare items and could find almost anything. He'd been hunting for a specific thing for me over the past couple of months now, and he'd sent word that he might've found what I was looking for. Excitement raced through me at the prospect of finally having my hands on this treasure.

"Ah, yes. I think I've finally located it. Come, come, I have it on that fancy contraption Atticus bought me."

His aversion to computers made me laugh and yet take comfort that some things never changed. Walking into the cramped space at the back of the barbershop, I scooted around boxes of shampoo and shaving cream. Pops sat down at the rickety desk made from old plywood, and he turned on the shiny new computer. Squinting, Pops pulled his glasses up from around the chain on his neck before clicking on a few things.

Despite his complaining, Pops appeared to be able to navigate the thing, and I wondered if it was all a show at times, a way to present the image to the world that he wanted. He might be inching toward seventy, but there was no doubt he was sharp as ever. What better way to fool your enemies into thinking you were inept than to pretend to hate something? I guess the mafia facade never faded. The thought left me feeling exhausted, but perhaps after doing something for so long, it felt comfortable?

"Ah, here it is. Fender Telecaster. I found a shop in California that has one for sale, $18,900. Is this the one you've been looking for?"

My breath hitched as I took in the magnificent guitar. It was just as I imagined it, a true classic, the 1968 Fender Telecaster. I'd become obsessed with the Telecaster after stumbling across an alt-rock band when I was a teen and subsequently idolizing Jonny Greenwood from Radiohead ever since. Something about the song "Creep" was beautifully harrowing and spoke to my inner demons.

"That's the one alright," I whispered, awe thick in my voice.

"Do you want them to ship it to you or here?"

"I'll take care of it. Just send me the link. Thanks, old man. My childhood dreams are coming true!" I joked.

"Ha, the only dream you had as a little boy was being the biggest badass to protect those close to you, and I think you've succeeded there, Saxon."

His voice had a warm quality to it that I wasn't used to hearing from him. Pops was right, in a sense. I had wanted to be the biggest badass only because I knew I wanted to be valuable for Mas. We'd bonded in our brotherhood, and I couldn't picture my life without him even at the age of nine. He was two years younger than me, but he'd always felt like my big brother in a way, and I wanted to make him proud.

"So, how is the rest of the business? Having any trouble with Delgado?"

"I see them peeking around. But they know better than to mess with me. They're getting braver, though. I fear they'll attempt something soon. You're preparing for it, right?"

His question made me bristle a little, and I had to remind myself he wasn't criticizing me but only offering advice.

"You know Mas, he's always three moves ahead."

Pops looked at me wearily, and I knew he recalled the night six months ago too. The night everything changed, and I saw the real face of evil. The lock on my mind vault blasted open before I was able to shut it down this time.

Screams ricocheted off the walls as the guards and I rushed through the dilapidated building trying to locate our missing princess. She'd been taken a few days prior, and we'd been looking for her ever since. I'd never forget the fear I felt when Atticus rushed into my room, stating Immy and her mother were gone. His face was ashen, and it was one of the only times I'd ever seen him scared. The guards were exhausted, but none of us wanted to stop until they were back with us, me the most. Immy was a little sister to me.

Dayton hadn't been seen either, and Atticus was suspiciously quiet on the topic. I chalked it up to shock and fear for his sister and moved on, too focused on the task at hand. The guards and I couldn't determine if this was a big play to take out the family by killing the don and kidnapping his wife and daughter, or something else. But with no ransom, the extent of the damage was undetermined, and we were all on edge until we knew the score. Screams rang out again, sounding all around me, and I took off in the direction I'd heard them.

It was Immy. This time, I was sure.

Busting down the door, it smacked against the wall with a bang and started to ricochet back to me. Stopping it with my fist, I glared down the fucktard over Immy who hadn't even noticed as he—

Blinking, I took in the cup of water Pops was pressing into my hand, grounding me back in reality with the coolness of the cup. He smiled at me with his all-knowing eyes, and I just nodded. He knew. Pops hadn't been at the warehouse that night, retired from that part of the family, but he hadn't made it through this life and not seen horrors.

"Thanks."

"It wasn't your fault, Saxon. You can't take on the sins of the father, or you'll never be cleaned."

Pops' words hung in the air, and I wanted to believe him… I just couldn't yet because *it had been my fault, just like it had been with Jaz.*

"Hmph. Yeah, well, I better get going. I'll go and collect the dues from Robbie upfront."

"Saxon, be…" he paused, gathering his words, finally settling on, "safe."

I had a feeling he wanted to say something else but had known I wouldn't hear it at the moment. I couldn't hear anything other than the anger pumping through my veins that Delgado would pay and regret the day he decided to mess with *my family.*

Walking out, I stopped by and grabbed the envelope from Robbie and exchanged a different one. Constantly moving money to make it clean was a never-ending job, and only a few were actually in the know of the full-scale operation. Things had to be shifted when Dayton had betrayed the family, and only three of us knew the full scale now. Mas, me, and Seth Mascro, the only uncle Mas trusted at the moment.

Heading back out into the cold, the excitement I'd felt at finding the guitar had dissipated with the flashback. Immy's screams would forever be permanently etched in my mind, along with the cries she tried to hide at night.

Each one decimated my heart until soon, there would be nothing left.

I accepted my punishment for failing her and would only be forgiven when I'd avenged it. She was owed that much, and with every breath I had, I would see to it that she was free of this nightmare, no matter the cost.

I'd failed once before in my life with Jaz. I couldn't leave it as it was with Immy. I wouldn't survive another failure.

I was the night now, and the quiet was my weapon. I weaved my way through the streets, casting shadows as I went, hiding the sins of my past. When you had nothing left to lose, there was no risk. I'd gone all in, and I was ready to collect. That asshole would never see me coming.

TWENTY

LOREN

Saturday morning brought a slew of emotions I wasn't prepared for. Yesterday was so unexpected. Spending the day with Monroe, Levi, and Jude was everything I'd wanted for years but felt so foreign now. Even today, I wondered if I'd merely dreamt it all. Luckily, the box of cookies on my counter told me differently.

When I'd gotten back from dropping off Jude, they were sitting in front of my door with a handwritten note in a kid's scribble.

Loren,

You forgot your cookies. I wanted to eat them all, but my dad said that wouldn't be nice. I hope we can hang out again.

Levi

It was unexpected and sent a smile to my face. Even now, I couldn't bring myself to eat a cookie because I enjoyed looking at them and remembering the little boy who had talked to me for twenty minutes about why these cookies were the absolute best. Levi's dad also kept replaying through my head. When I'd been facing off with Brian, his tenderness, the understanding way he accepted my answers and hesitation, and his kindness toward the kids made me feel things I wasn't used to experiencing.

I had to face facts, Monroe was a great guy.

Part of me wondered if my subconscious knew from the beginning, and that was why I tried to ignore him as much as I did. Because if I had allowed myself to want, to dream, to believe… then I would inevitably be hurt again. Hope was dangerous, and I wasn't sure I was ready for it yet. The warm and comforting feelings that lingered, though, begged to differ.

Deciding to ride this momentum, I grabbed my gym bag and coat and headed out my door. As I walked by 18D, I unintentionally slowed, but no sound or movement escaped the door as I continued to the elevator. Disappointment filled me, and I chastised myself for expecting them to be waiting for me. This was why it was better not to care. I was swinging 0-2 though, maybe even 0-3. Hell, now that I thought about it, none of my recent encounters had panned out past the initial tryst.

Slumping against the wall, I debated heading back upstairs. Was it even worth it to go to Windy City? What would it prove? Nothing.

When I hit the ground floor, I pushed the button for the 18th floor and rode the elevator back up, acknowledging that I was just as much of a loser as I thought. Entering my condo, I tossed my bag on the floor, no longer having the strength to carry it. I trudged to my bedroom as the weight of despair pressed down on me. Each step was heavier than the last, and I felt the tiny shards of the quicksand piercing my skin as I pressed on. Pulling the covers over my head, I hid from the world for the rest of the weekend.

I wasn't strong.

I was a fool for thinking otherwise.

IT WAS TUESDAY, and I forced myself to get up and go to work today. I'd been able to cancel my sessions yesterday, but I couldn't do that two days in a row. One of my colleagues would be knocking down my door if I did, and it wasn't fair to my clients to brush them off just because I was feeling weepy.

I'd barely left my bed in the past three days, only leaving to get up for the bathroom or food. I was a bit of a disgusting mess, and even I knew it. Washing my hair for the second time, I tried to get my mind to jump tracks. I'd been stuck in this roundabout thinking for the past three days, and I was only going in circles. Quite frankly, I was dizzy and over feeling this way. The buzz of the recklessness called to me and I wanted to take another sip, but I couldn't. I wouldn't.

Thinking about my recent failures was only bringing me misery, so I tried to focus on what I had done well instead, but nothing was coming to my mind. I was about to fall apart in the shower and cancel work again when the music changed, and the Beatles floated through my speaker. "Hey, Jude" crooned through the room as I stared at the white tile of my shower wall.

Jude.

Jude was something I was doing right, at least I hoped I was. He was quiet, but it seemed he was happy to see me when I showed up at his exhibit. He'd blended in with the other kids, and so he hadn't needed to speak up a lot. But there had been a few smiles I'd seen, and that was something I could count. Focusing on him and my clients, I was able to rally and dismiss the negativity running rampant like the poison it was.

Dressing, I picked out a deep purple sheath dress with a belt, black heels, and a long sweater cardigan. Pulling on my tights, I wondered why women put up with these. They were a nightmare to get on, and Heaven forbid you needed to pee at any point during the day. Sheesh, they were the worst, I thought as I jiggled myself into them, making a weird dance jump move to pull them up. Somewhere in the world, there had to be someone else making that move too, I decided.

Panting, I waited a few minutes to catch my breath before slipping on my black lace bra and slip. Drying my hair, I curled it under and finished putting together my outfit. Women had an unfair disadvantage when it came to the amount of time it took to get ready. The number of steps we had versus men was obnoxious.

My gym bag was still sitting by the door from the other day when I'd dropped it. It was Tuesday, which meant a kickboxing night. Did I want to see Mr. Surly after the last one? What had started as a hot kiss and prelude to sexy times had shifted partway through. I wasn't sure by who, but the emotions had changed from a scorching sizzling to a heavy loathing. Even in the sexy moment, my empathy had registered what was happening and I couldn't help the tear that fell.

It had been playing over and over in my mind this weekend, and I'd finally concluded it had to be that. The emotions had shifted, and I went from feeling sexy and powerful to cheap, dirty, and weak. I didn't like those feelings. It wasn't who I was or wanted to be. I wanted to explore my sexuality, but I didn't want to feel self-loathing. The hardest part was, I didn't know if it was from him or me.

At the time, I'd been angry at him for leaving me and walking away, but now, I was glad. I would've hated myself if we had fucked right there. I didn't even like him most of the time, and if he didn't want me either, exploration or not, I wasn't sure if I could go through with it. I needed at least mutual respect to get naked with someone.

It had been a valuable discovery for myself at least, and I realized I could face him. He'd done the right thing, and I was glad he had. Grabbing it off the floor, I proceeded out the door, determined to face this. Leaving my apartment was giving me the courage that I'd lacked all weekend. I guess I just needed to restart myself.

Monroe was already at the elevator, and I picked up my pace when I heard the ding. Thankfully, he held the door like the gentleman he was, and I slid in a few seconds later.

"Thanks," I greeted, a little breathless from my sprint.

I positioned myself facing forward as usual, but I felt awkward and unsure how to act now.

"No problem. How was the rest of the weekend?" He sounded genuinely interested and not like he was making polite small talk.

"Uh, it was okay."

"I didn't see much of you. Levi wanted to ask you to join us for a movie, but I figured you were busy or out."

"Oh, really?" Shocked, I turned this time to him, trying to gauge the emotion on his face.

"Yes. Why is that shocking? Did you not have a good time on Friday?"

"No, I did," I started, "a blast, actually. It's just, I guess I'm surprised you wanted to spend time with me after, is all." I shrugged, my face flaming.

"Of course I would. Levi had a blast and thought you were cool. He even shared his cookies with only minimal grumbling. He never shares with me."

"Oh. Well, that makes me feel special, actually."

"You should. He's a hard critic." He beamed.

When the ding of the elevator sounded for its arrival on the ground floor, I realized it was the first time I'd found myself not wanting to get off. Monroe held out his arm for me to go first, and I buttoned my coat as I made my way out of the building. Surprisingly, Monroe followed me, or perhaps, just headed in the same direction as me.

"You go this way?"

"Yeah. I usually walked slower so you could get ahead. You always seemed ready to get away from everyone and in your own world, and I didn't want to disturb that." He cringed in embarrassment, but it was me who felt it.

"Wow, I never realized how I must've seemed to others. I was just trying to… deal."

He searched my eyes before nodding. "Yeah, I can understand that. I mean, you weren't mean, just kind of not there, I guess. I always wondered what you were thinking," he admitted shyly.

"Nothing mostly, a break from all the things I have to pretend to be," I responded honestly, shocking even myself.

"How long have you been divorced? If that's okay to ask."

"Oh yeah, it's fine. I mean, you did save me from my ex, so I believe that earns you the right to ask," I joked. "We've been separated for two years and officially divorced for just a little over a year now. The day I moved in here was the same day I signed the papers. It honestly feels like it all happened to someone else."

"It's been about a year and a half for me, but separated for about the same amount. It's been messy, though, with Levi, and his mom, Brittni, keeps trying to get full custody. We split time, but it's like she wants to punish me by taking him completely away."

"Wow, that does suck. I guess in some ways, I'm lucky not to be dealing with that, and wow, that sounds so insensitive. I'm sorry."

"No, it's fine. I know what you mean, and I agree. I love my son, and I'm happy to have him the time I do get. I just wish it was more and that his mom wasn't such a conniving bitch."

"Ah, well, yeah, that makes it difficult."

"Sorry, I don't mean to dump my ex-baggage on you. She just called right as I was leaving, and it's been on my mind, I guess."

"I get it. Wait, I don't think I really processed it until now with everything that happened. But do I remember correctly that your ex's sister is the one dating my ex? Is that right?"

"Uh, yeah. That would be Christine."

"Oddly coincidental."

"I guess, but also, not so much. The elite circles…"

"Say no more. I get it now. You're right. I forget that I choose not to be involved in those, but I'm part of the few who do that."

"Same. I didn't grow up in this life, so it's all foreign to me. My ex was into the title and zip code, and it was maddening at times."

"My mom is the same way, and it's pure torture trying to get out of her events every month, it seems. Though she did send me to Ignite, so I guess I can't hate her for that one," I joked.

"Do you think you'll volunteer more? Jude asked about you yesterday when I stopped by."

Smiling at that, I nodded, "I think I will. I like him too, and I think we could be good for one another. I'm going to talk to Mitzi today about it and see what I need to do in regards to paperwork and such."

"That's great. I enjoy working with the twins, and it feels nice giving back to the community. I wish I'd had programs like these when I was in the system."

"You were a foster kid?" I asked with surprise, then

realizing how rude that sounded backtracked instantly. "I mean, that's cool. I didn't mean that to sound weird or anything. I'm just surprised, is all. Fuck, I'm making it worse. I'm going to shut up now."

His laughter warmed me, and I was glad I hadn't seemed to offend him.

"Wow, that was the quickest I've ever seen someone go tomato red and then curse. That was super cute, by the way. It's like when a toddler uses a cuss word. You know you shouldn't laugh, but it's just so dang adorable, you can't help it. That's you. I don't expect it, but when I hear it, it definitely makes me wonder what other things can come from your mouth."

For a moment, I was stunned, and then the laugh flew from my lips, leaving me feeling lighter. His sweet little smirk warmed my heart, and I found myself liking his company.

"Thanks for not taking offense. I'm usually much better with words," I admitted.

"It's okay. You can confess I fluster you," he joked. "But, nah, I'm used to people responding weirdly, unfortunately, not that yours was weird. Ugh, it seems your word vomit is contagious, or I'm not much better at this talking thing, at least with women. I've always been the awkward nerd with the crush on the cheerleader."

"I don't think you're awkward at all. Not unless I'm awkward too? I mean, I haven't dated anyone since I was sixteen, so maybe I'm not the best judge."

Sadness wanted to creep in at that thought, but I shoved it way back and instead focused on the friendly chatter of a new friend. Redirecting the conversation back to him, I tried again. "So, you were in foster care? What was that like, if you don't mind me asking?"

"I don't mind. My mom died when I was young, and my grandmother tried her best to care for me, but she didn't have much to give between her diabetes and living off government assistance. When I was about ten, I was removed from her home after coming to school for a week in the same clothes and no food. The foster homes weren't bad at first, but as I got older," he winced, "the ones willing to take in teens, well, they aren't the people always in it for the right reasons. I ended up at a group home when I was fourteen and stayed there until I graduated. It wasn't all bad, though," he finished, but something in his voice didn't ring true, and I began to worry even more about Jude.

I know other kids struggled too, but at the moment, he was the only one on my radar. The coffee shop was looming closer, and I wondered if he would follow me in or not.

"I usually stop and get coffee. What about you? Are you a coffee drinker?"

"Oh yes, and I love this place. Come on, let's get some life-sustaining juice."

"Oh, no. You're one of *them*."

"One of them?" he asked, looking at me oddly.

"Coffee fanatics," I joked. "I mean, I'm addicted to the stuff, don't get me wrong. I just don't see it as some life-altering substance. So to me, those people who do are the true crazy coffee junkies," I reasoned.

"Huh, well, I'm a proud member then." He grinned. I was finding I liked his smile more and more. Monroe was easy to be around. He didn't make me nervous, and I liked that we had the divorce thing in common. For some reason, it seemed to put us on equal ground, and I quite liked it. After we ordered, we moved off to the side to wait for our drinks.

"I was wondering," Monroe started, "if maybe you would want to come over for dinner sometime this week? Friends, if you're not ready for anything more," he added quickly.

The feelings that rushed through me confused me, and it took me a minute to wade through them all. Monroe patiently waited, maybe understanding what I was feeling. Once I stopped the emotional flood, I evaluated them individually and pinpointed the two strongest.

Fear—expected.

Excitement—interesting.

Meeting his eyes, he smiled down at me, recognition passing through me. Monroe would be okay with whatever answer I gave him right then. It was freeing in the sense that I didn't have to manage his emotions for him. I could answer how I felt and not be held accountable for his reaction. He was a rare man who exhibited kindness and understanding, and I realized I did want to get to know him more. Whether that was just as friends or more, I wasn't sure yet.

"First time being asked since the divorce?" Monroe finally asked as our drinks were handed to us.

"Yeah, actually," I chuckled. "Surprisingly, it wasn't as scary as I expected, but I also don't know where I stand on things. I know the thought of having a meal with you makes me excited, so that's what I'll concentrate on. I just can't give you an answer if it's more yet. I hope that's okay."

"More than okay. I think we can be great friends and potentially more, Loren. But if we have to start as only friends, I'm good with that. I'm not a rusher in these matters. I can't be with Levi, but since you've already met him and do live across the hall, it's freeing. I don't have to hide either of you from one another. I feel like you get this more than anyone else I've met since."

I nodded, understanding hitting me. Sharing all the parts of you could be risky. I did get that. "I do, Monroe, and I look forward to continuing our friendship and seeing where that leads us. I do hope you can cook, though, because it's one thing I'm absolute crap at," I joked.

"You'll be pleased to know that I do make a mean chicken carbonara. So, we will have something edible to enjoy. I get Levi in a few days, so we can plan for then, if you don't mind him being around or we can wait until some time next week. Does either of those work better?"

"This weekend works for me. I might run to the center at some point, but otherwise, it's not like I do much," I rambled.

"Perfect, I know he'll be excited to see you again. He bugged me *all* weekend."

We both smiled, and I realized we were at that awkward pause where it got quiet. "Well, I guess I'll see you tomorrow at the elevator," I started to walk off before remembering. "Oh, anything I can bring?"

"Nope, I got it covered. See you tomorrow, Lo."

"Bye, Monroe." I waved and headed into my building.

A smile pulled at my lips, and I felt happy as I entered my office. Crazy how just an hour ago, I was contemplating calling in sick. I guess good things could happen outside my door. I just had to take a step out.

TWENTY-ONE

ATTICUS

"Immy, we need to leave, now." Sighing, I leaned against the banister as I waited for my sister to leave her room. Finally, she emerged wearing an oversized sweater and leggings. Her style had changed drastically since the incident, and it only served as a gut-punch reminder to me how much she was struggling. It pierced my damn heart every time I thought of it, and the desperate need to punish someone would rise in me.

It was difficult to know who to punish, though, when you felt responsible.

"Sorry, Attie," she mumbled, head hanging low.

"It's okay, Ims. Let's just get moving. I don't want you to be late."

At her nod, we headed down the stairs and into the garage where Sax and the driver were waiting. Sax gave me an imperceptible look as we exited. He was struggling as much as I was, even if he didn't think I noticed. We were both just too stubborn to admit it. The drive to New Horizons was quiet, all of us lost in our thoughts.

"Do you want me to go in, or are you okay on your own?" I softly asked.

"I'm good. Thanks." Immy gently smiled and kissed my cheek before she got out of the car.

"I think this is good for her," Sax quietly asserted before following her out the door.

"Yeah," I answered to myself. I watched them walk into the building and hoped Sax was correct. Resigning myself to waiting, I pulled out my tablet to review the contracts and deposits the team had sent over. Something wasn't adding up there, and I needed to look at it more closely.

Scanning through everything, I signed the contracts for Sushi Roll and emailed them back to the lawyers. Switching to the other files, I thoroughly researched them, but nothing stood out on the invoices and deposits. I'd have to wait until 1 could investigate it more on my computer. The bank slips all seemed accurate, but something went missing from there to the bank each time. I just knew it.

My phone vibrated in my pocket, and I pulled it out to see who it was. *Nicco.*

"Hello, cousin. How are you fairing?" I greeted him.

"Hey, Mas. I'm good, man. Just confirming the line-up for this week's fight. I have Crash against Manic, Boom against Stonefist, and Bolt against Trst Knuckles. There are a few smaller fights for status, but those are the three showliners. Will you be stopping by?"

"I plan to, if I can get away. How's Crash doing?"

"Dodgy, but he hasn't caused problems."

"Just keep an eye on him. His background is… interesting."

"Now you have me curious," he laughed, "but I will see if I can actually get him up to the box this time and get a read on him."

"How's the shop?"

"It's great, man," he answered quickly before changing the subject. "Have you finished the documents for the sushi place?" I allowed his redirection knowing he was anxious I would ask him to do something underhanded. Nicco didn't believe me yet when I said I wouldn't, so I would show him with time.

"Yeah, just now. So, I'll send that over before long so you can see how it's doing."

"Sounds good, Mas. How's the princess?"

Pausing, I closed my eyes as I thought about Immy. "She's strong. I just hope she opens up to this therapist, and it helps her. I just want her to be okay."

"Oh, you got her into a therapist? That's great. You're doing right by her, Mas."

"I hope so because I feel like I'm failing around every corner with Immy lately."

"What happened… " he trailed off, unable to say the words as much as I was, "it wasn't your fault. I know that doesn't change anything, but you can't carry that guilt—"

"Yeah, I know. Hey, listen, another call's coming in. I'll catch you at the fight."

Hanging up, I tossed my head back against the seat. Exhaling, I tried to calm my heart. Why did everyone think telling me it wasn't my fault helped? It didn't. It only highlighted where I failed and that someone innocent had been hurt in unimaginable ways.

"Son, I want to bring our family to the next level. I've secured a deal that will allow us to branch out and acquire more advantageous ventures." The Reaper grinned.

"I don't understand. What ventures are you talking about, Dad?"

"You will address me properly, or I will remind you," he raged.

"Reaper," I gritted through my teeth, "what ventures are you referring to? Grandfather always harped on the need to stay out of some areas. How keeping our noses clean and controlling the money gave us a layer of protection."

"My father couldn't see the potential lying before his eyes. No, Atticus, we're finally going to be taken seriously for the power that we have. We're going to join forces with a family and branch out into more lucrative sources. Unfortunately, Cynthia disagreed on the cost, and so I had to get rid of her. It was a small price to pay to align our families. Well, that and your sister."

Fear ran through me at his words. My father had gone mad. This wasn't how we operated as a family, and until this moment, I'd never even heard my father talk about changing it.

"What does Imogen have to do with this?"

Dayton, the Grim Reaper, had gone back to looking at some papers on his desk, broadcasting loudly how little he thought of our meeting. "Oh, nothing. I just had to give her to Delgado in exchange for aligning our families. To think after all this time, she finally had value," he stated dismissively.

Ice filled my veins at what his statement indicated. Fuck. Fuck. FUCK.

My heart started to race, but I couldn't show it. Locking down my features, I forced myself to push away my worry. I needed to enact my plan now. He'd gone too far, and I had to assume when he said "get rid" of my step-mother, it wasn't a sending away type of gesture. He'd killed her or had her killed. And now, my baby sister was at the hands of that sadistic asshole, Delgado.

This infraction was the last straw, and I could no longer ignore his increasingly erratic behavior. I'd been in denial, but the Reaper wasn't the man I'd always thought, and my subconscious had been screaming at me for a while, but the boy who loved his father struggled to accept it. Now, with the truth slapping me in the face, I could no longer ignore it. It was time to take the boss down.

The door opening pulled me from my thoughts, and I was surprised to find an hour had already passed as Sax and Immy got into the car. Sax faced me, a look of concern on his face for me as he took me in. Locking down my features, I sat up straighter, smoothed down my suit. Assessing my sister, I noticed she looked okay, even better, maybe. A foreign emotion of hope sat heavily on my chest at the prospect of therapy helping. I needed some reclamation for that night, and I prayed she would find it by talking with Mrs. Carter.

THE MUSIC lightly lofted through the crack in my door as I scoured the excel spreadsheets, giving me pause. *Immy.* She hadn't played in almost six months now, and I'd missed hearing her melodies as I walked through our home. Imogen was a talented piano player, and it only firmed my belief that she was too good for this life. She could have a whole future outside of this place, and I wished she would.

Sax's knock had me raising my head from my reflection. When I made eye contact, he stepped in, shutting the door and effectively cutting off Immy's melody.

"Have you found anything?" he questioned, straight to the point as he sat down in the chair across from me. I stared, surprised he could fit in it comfortably with his muscular frame.

"I'm able to tell when the discrepancy starts. It's just where it's going that's still a mystery."

"So, you've pinpointed where it's leaking from?"

"Yep."

"Care to share, asshole?" he chuckled at my nonanswer. I was being difficult on purpose. Sax was the only person I could be a shit to and get away with it without any blowback.

"As we expected," I smirked. "Most appears to come from Joel's operations, but I did find something fishy in Marcel's as well. I'm wondering if they were both involved, or if one is a cover-up to throw suspicion. I highly doubt my father would've allowed two people to steal from him. It's more likely that he was using one of them to siphon money for himself."

"Seems Dayton had been preparing for this for a while then," Sax mused.

"It does appear that way." I brushed away the anxiety that coursed through me at his revelation.

"What's the play here?"

"We need to plant someone we trust in both operations and see what they can find. It feels more complex than just the money."

"Agreed. Jasper is under Marcel. He's trustworthy and loyal to you. And… maybe Hugo for Joel."

"Can you set something up with them? Have them meet us at the fight."

"Will do. Any other plays at the moment?"

"No. It's more a wait-and-see thing, which I hate. But we need intel before we can make a move. Any news on our Delgado spy?"

"No. He's been suspiciously quiet. I'll have one of the guys run by his place."

"Good."

Saving the sheet, I placed it in my secure server folder before exiting. It was way too easy nowadays to get access to things, so I was as thorough as possible. I was sifting through my emails when Sax spoke again. I'd forgotten he was still here, zoned in to what I had to do next.

"Saw the pretty therapist today," he smirked.

"Oh."

Ignoring him, I went back to my screen. The amount of time I spent unsubscribing junk mail I received was ridiculous. It was one of my biggest pet peeves, and I couldn't stand to have any notifications on my phone showing red. It gave me hives if I couldn't delete some-thing as soon as I saw it. On the other hand, Sax was one of those people who had over 5,000 emails unread. It was pure insanity.

"She looked nice today."

"Uh-hmm."

"Especially when I fucked her against her desk."

Snapping my head up, I stared at my friend, my jaw open and anger leaching into my face and voice. "You. Did. What?"

"Oh, nothing. I just wanted to get your attention. *Not that it won't happen.* You can't be the only one to know what she feels like."

"Excuse me! I haven't touched her," I scoffed, outraged at his claim.

"I thought this whole time you were just being smug. But you don't know, do you?"

When I gave him the 'boss cold' stare, he only laughed more wholeheartedly, and I was ready to shoot him. This was the thing about having your life-long best friend as your second. I didn't intimidate him.

"Oh fuck, Mas. Can I record this? This is going to be epic. You remember the woman from the club?"

"Yes."

"Well," he gestured. I stared, not quite getting what he was meaning.

"If you're trying to say the woman that night and our Mrs. Carter are one in the same, you're fired."

"Come off it, Mas. You're only lying to yourself. It's her, and ever since that night at the club, my cock gets rock hard when I see her. Those moans she made, *fuck*."

He bites his knuckles, his eyes rolling back as he recalls the sensational way she'd looked and sounded that night. Memories flood me as I start to put the pieces together and my cock begins to grow hard as well, remembering how she'd grinded herself against me.

When I recalled how wet she'd been from watching the other couple on the floor, I groaned. Fucking hell, I'd been seconds away from slamming my cock into her right there. *Into Immy's fucking therapist.* My brain had finally put the pieces together and I hated that Sax was right and how much more I craved her now.

"She's Immy's therapist," I tried to deflect.

"Yeah, and that means jack shit to me."

His smirk was annoying me, and for the first time, I felt possessive over a woman. The realization shocked me, and I sat back staring at him. Did that mean something?

"What? You got a weird look on your face."

"I… I don't know. I just got annoyed with you a bit… and *possessive*, I think over Mrs. Carter. I don't know what to do with that, though, honestly."

Sax and I didn't keep things from one another. He was the one person I could be candid and authentic with. I didn't have to pretend to be this big bad mafia boss, someone who was tough and strong all the time. With Sax, I could just be, and that was the most freeing thing in the world. So, we didn't have secrets. It would ruin our bond and everything we had.

I'd convinced myself I wasn't keeping one about my father.

At my statement, he sat up, a serious look crossing

his face. "Do you… do you have feelings for her? Do you want me to step away?"

This was new to us both. I'd never attached myself to anyone, and we had often shared women if we found them attractive. Sometimes, together and other times, just sharing her company. So to feel possessive was an area we hadn't encountered before in our history.

"No. Don't be ridiculous," I brushed off. "It just surprised me. I mean, I barely know her, and it's not like I can bring her into this life," I stammered.

Sax looked at me oddly, like he was trying to decipher a complex code, and I had to admit, I was as well.

"Hmph," he muttered finally.

"What?"

"It's interesting, that's all."

"It's interesting, that's all," I mocked, resorting to juvenile banter. Fucking hell. His answering smirk confirmed something he'd already figured out. Changing the subject, I quickly asked a safer topic, "Did you hear Immy playing?"

"I did. It was nice to hear those sounds again. This place has been way too quiet."

"It has… maybe we should see about getting her involved in some teenager things. Do you think she's lonely? She only has the guards and us. Why haven't I ever thought of this before?"

"Don't beat yourself up, Mas. You're doing what you can to be better for her, and you are. Immy was withdrawn the past six months, and I doubt she'd have gone if you'd offered before now. So drop the guilt. I carry enough for both of us. It's something to consider, and we should ask Mrs. Carter. Which brings us back to the subject you were avoiding." He smirked.

Shaking my head, I ignored him as I went back to my computer, but I couldn't deny a certain brunette wasn't on my mind. The hard cock in my pants wouldn't let me either. *Shit.* I needed to get laid if the thought of fingering someone was enough to make me rock hard. Especially someone who had just become off-limits. I wouldn't risk Immy's treatment for getting my dick wet.

Adjusting myself, I focused back on the money and made some notes to look more into. One thing was always accurate in business. Follow the money.

TWENTY-TWO

NICCO

The buzzing of the tattoo gun did nothing to settle my irritation. Usually, it was a calming sound that settled around me as we worked. Today, it felt like a million bees were attacking my ears each time I tried to read anything for school. I was incredibly unfocused and distracted, and I knew why. I just hadn't expected it.

Loren.

Ever since the saucy brunette walked out of my apartment almost a week ago, I couldn't stop thinking about her. I'd cleverly put my name in her phone so that she would have my number. I didn't want to be too forward and text me from her phone, so I just added me instead, hoping she would see it. When I hadn't heard from her for a few days, I'd sent a note with Nat, but still nothing.

Had she not enjoyed that night? *Was* it just a one night stand for her? Neither of those options felt right to me. Maybe I was too subtle?

Determined, I decided if I wanted something, I would need to make it known. Loren was older than me by a couple of years, so she was probably used to men treating her a certain way. I would need to prove that I was just as sophisticated. Feeling confident in my resolution, I found I could finally focus on my lesson.

This class was my favorite because I could work at my own pace. Because of that, I was already on the final. After this one, I would only have three more to go before obtaining my teaching degree. It felt surreal that I could be doing something I loved in a year, and I wished my mom was alive to see this, to see the boy who'd been a burden achieve something outside the life she couldn't escape.

When my mom had overdosed, I was grateful that Uncle Dayton had taken me in, but he'd never been a father figure to me. He was just a reminder of the life I didn't want to live. Over the years, I saw the violence and abuse he inflicted on all those around him. Living with Atticus and Immy was the only bright spot and helped me retain myself.

When Atticus went off to school, Immy and I had one another, and she became my little sister. The bond we had was special to me, and she was one of the few who knew I wanted to be a teacher. She might only be seventeen, but living the life we did, she was beyond mature for her age. And after the past six months, I'd seen the weight of the trauma on her. I wanted to get her out too, but knew it needed to be her choice.

Finishing off the last lesson plan for the unit I was working on, my phone beeped with a message, and I felt nervous butterflies build as I hoped it would be from my illustrious bed partner.

Lil Sis: I played today… It was weird. Good, but weird.

ME: MoMo, that's great! Anything after a time away is going to feel weird. Don't sweat it.

Lil Sis: Yeah, you're right. My therapist told me the same.

ME: I love hearing how right I am. Tell me again, please, lol. Your therapist sounds smart too.

Lil Sis: Yeah, she's cool. She doesn't treat me like I'm fragile or a little kid, so that's a plus. It sucks monkey balls talking about this shit though.

ME: Hey, I get it. It's never easy talking about the crap we've lived through, but from my own experience, if you don't, it eats you up. Then you end up as a 29 yo with over thirty tattoos and alone.

Lil Sis: Well, I think you're cool, so it can't be too bad. But you're wrong… you're not alone, dork.

ME: Okay, you're right. I'm being melodramatic.

Lil Sis: Yeah you are. Lol. Still nothing from your mystery woman?

ME: No. I've decided to make a play, though. No more subtle messages.

Lil Sis: Yasss. Shoot your shot, Nic! I think you're pretty great, so that counts for something.

ME: Ah, look at you with the feelings.

Lil Sis: I'll deny it if you ever say anything, lol.

ME: Love you too, MoMo

Lil Sis: Yeah yeah, I love you too. Let me know how it goes, loser. Later

ME: Oh, you slay me with your confidence

Lil Sis: I'm the balance to your giant ego

ME: Ah, at least you admit it's giant
Lil Sis: Ew, gross. I feel like you just crossed some weird boundary. Take it back! *Gagging emoji*
ME: Wow. The hurt I feel right now. *Wide eye emoji*
Lil Sis: LMAO. Ugh, gotta go. Tutor asshole is here.
ME: Be nice. He just wants to help.
Lil Sis: Now you sound like Attie.
ME: Well, in this case, I agree. Be good
Lil Sis: Uh huh, laters

A smile graced my lips as I packed up my stuff. Imogen always made me happy even when she was a resistant teenager—probably because she *was* a resistant teenager. Grabbing my leather jacket, I shuffled my bag over to my shoulder and headed upfront. Cassie and Davis were off today, meaning Jack and Brad were the only ones in the shop. They were both with customers, so I nodded as I headed out the door.

Mulling over what information I knew about Loren and wanting to be as un-stalker-like as possible, I remembered she told me about her practice. Quickly, I googled her name and found her practice, New Horizons, located in an area I was very familiar with. Straddling my bike, I headed in her direction and hoped I wasn't about to make a fool out of myself by showing up.

Ten minutes later, I pulled up to the office building and parked a few blocks over. I spotted a coffee shop and impulsively popped in to see what they served. It couldn't hurt to bring baked goodies with me. Who could say no to a pastry? I needed to make a big impression since I'd apparently failed the other times. Laden with my box of goodies, I trudged my way into her building next door.

My palms began to sweat, and I realized how nervous I was. I hadn't felt this way about talking to a girl since I was a blushing pre-pubescent boy. *Whoa.*

Shaking away those thoughts, I pulled up my bravado and headed into New Horizons, hoping my fate was about to change. The waiting room was nice and homey, and I felt at ease just from entering. It had warm tones, comfortable furnishings, and soft music playing overhead. At a window, a woman sat as she scrolled on a computer.

She didn't see me as I walked up. Knocking, I tried to grab her attention. Unfortunately, I hadn't noticed the earbuds, and my motion had surprised her. She jumped, clutching her chest as she turned to peer wide-eyed up at me. Shit, this wasn't off to a great start.

Waving, I hoped I hadn't just ruined it. This lady seemed like the gatekeeper and just might be what stood between Loren and me. She looked me over thoroughly, assessing my threat level, before pulling back the glass partition.

"Can I help you?" she asked politely.

"I really hope so… Doris," I said after I'd found the nameplate on her desk. The name drop helped soften her, along with my 'ah shucks, aren't I so cute' smile. "You see, I have a problem, and I'm hoping you can help me with the cure. I can't stop thinking about Loren, and I need to make a good impression. Could you help me out?"

"Hm, how do I know you're not some creepy stalker? Loren's special. She doesn't need to be hurt again."

Ah, her momma bear had come out, and it warmed me that she was protective of Loren. I could tell she needed that in her life. Taking a different approach, I shook the box I held in my hands.

"Well, that's why I wanted to drop these off. I didn't think about the fact she might be in session when I raced over here after deciding to take a chance. It's my running through an airport moment, Doris. Can you tell me what time she has lunch?" Her stern scowl softened a smidge but wasn't promising in getting the answers I needed. I had to keep trying, though.

"Alright, Doris," I started, leaning against the counter. "I can tell you play hardball, and I like that about you, so how about this? I'm going to write my name and number on top of this box. I want to meet Loren for lunch. If she's interested, have her meet me there."

I plucked a pen out of the cup holder and wrote my number and a quick note of where to meet me. Clicking it closed, I winked at Doris before turning to leave. She kept the partition open and slowly slid the box across as I walked backward. The further I was, the more she pulled the baked goods to her.

Before I walked out the door, I smiled. "And Doris, I'm glad she has someone like you in her life."

Her shoulders relaxed at my statement, and I could see the genuine approval in her eyes. She still remained as the stern gatekeeper on the outside, but I took the small win for what it was. As she read my message, the smile on her face had me feeling hopeful that this one might finally work. I wouldn't give up if it didn't. It just meant I'd have to be more creative.

Loren was someone I wanted in my life, and I was beginning to think even needed. There would be a way to get there, somehow. As scary as hope was, I chose to believe in the connection we had and the rarity of finding someone you connected with like that. I headed in the direction of the restaurant, and I hoped her lunch was soon. Otherwise, I might go crazy from waiting. I needed to know one way or another. Walking there, I couldn't help the pep in my step with each stride I took.

Settling in at City Bistro, I ordered a water and pulled out my sketch pad. I'd been working on a drawing for a few days of her face. It didn't have the same punch as she did in person, though, and I didn't know what I was missing.

Flipping a page, I started messing around with some tattoo ideas I was working on. I had a custom order for a woman with fire wings and a sword. I played up different angles, trying to find the one that worked the best for the area she wanted. Focusing on the drawing, I lost myself in the motions as I waited, hoping the start to the next chapter of my life was going to walk through those doors soon.

TWENTY-THREE

LOREN

"This week will be hard. You're at that stage where you have to push through the yucky stuff and choose to put your skills into place. It will be challenging, but it doesn't mean you can't get through this. Remind yourself of all the things you're capable of and how you've managed before. You got this."

"Thank you. I think I just needed to hear I wasn't losing my mind and that someone believed in me."

"Absolutely. I think that's what we all want to hear." I smiled. "I have you scheduled for next week on Tuesday. I'll see you then and I look forward to hearing how you conquered this," I affirmed.

Walking my client out, I was ready for my lunch break. Today was going well, I was just in a weird mood, and I didn't know why. I'd woken up feeling all out of sorts and was dreading the training class tonight. Mr. Surly had canceled on Tuesday, so I hadn't faced him since a week ago when I'd kissed him. I wasn't sure how to deal with it.

Sighing, I turned to go back to my office when I caught sight of a grinning Doris beckoning me over. She was talking to Daphne and Jewel as they both refilled their coffee mugs. Hmm, maybe coffee was what I needed. Deciding I'd grab some next door, I walked over to see what had them grinning so big first.

"Hey. What's going on over here?"

"Doris had an interesting visitor," Jewel teased.

"Oh, did you now? *Spill.*"

"Well, *he* was actually here to see *you,*" she interjected.

"Oh? A 'he' you say?" I asked, pondering who she could mean. I was confused when she handed me the box from the bakery downstairs. Glancing down, I saw it had something written on the top.

"Beautiful, you're a hard woman to track down. I want to take you to lunch. Your gatekeeper wouldn't let me pass go, so if you're up for this idea, meet me at City Bistro. Nicco."

A warm blush spread across my cheeks. He'd found me. Peeking up, the three women were watching me closely and smiled back at me.

"He's a hottie, Loren, seems nice too. And all those tattoos?" Her whole body shivered. "Whew wee! Gave this old woman a hot flash," chuckled Doris, waving her hand in front of her face.

"You didn't say anything about tattoos, Doris! You've been holding out on me," joked Jewel, smacking her on the arm.

Looking at my watch, I realized I would need to leave now to enjoy my time with him. When I looked back up, Doris reached for the box, pulling it from me.

"Go. You're 2 pm rescheduled, so you've got time."

Beaming, I nodded and headed back to my office to grab my coat and purse. Giddiness filled me as I rushed through New Horizons and out into the cold. The wind didn't feel as hard today, but maybe that was due to the redness in my cheeks. *Nicco*. I'd thought he didn't want to see me again, but this… Smiling, I rushed up the street to the little hole in the wall restaurant.

Stopping for a second, I checked my hair in the window before heading in. A hostess was leaning against the counter on her phone as I entered. At the sound of the bell, she didn't even glance up but pointed to the left. Assuming she meant for me to go in that direction, I cautiously walked there. I wanted to be offended by her behavior, but nerves filled me more. I was anxious as I thought about what seeing him again would be like.

Should I kiss him? Hug him? What would we talk about now? Maybe this was a bad idea. It had been a great night and a good memory. Perhaps it should stay that way. Before I could bolt in the other direction, I spotted him in the empty room. He'd been staring at the opening to the room and stood as I walked in.

Stopping in my tracks, we stared at one another assessing the situation. He looked as amazing as I'd remembered. Maybe even more so now that I knew what was under his clothes, his dark hair was rumpled in that deliberate look, brushed over his eyes. Nicco's grey-blue eyes zeroed in on me as I cataloged the rest of him. He was dressed simply this time, in a black t-shirt and jeans, motorcycle boots, and there was a leather jacket that was tossed over the back of a chair.

When I looked back up, he instantly moved forward, but I stayed stopped in my tracks as I waited. Our magnetism was just as strong as I remembered, and there was only one course of action—collision.

"Hey," he purred, his sexiness slamming into me with force, and my body reacted instantly. Nicco's smirk told me he'd noticed as well.

"Hey."

It was all I could get out as I stared at him inches from me. My hands were itching to reach out and touch him. When he broke the space by grabbing my waist, it was like a tidal wave of feelings crashing into me.

"I'm so glad you came," he stated, his hands flexing as he did. "I kept hoping you would call me. I've been going out of my mind, actually, and I decided to take another shot. I'm-I'm." He cleared his throat, a nervous chuckle leaving him. "I'm glad I did."

Nicco smiled, and my heart took off. Confused, though, I quirked my brow at him. "I don't understand. Call you? But how?"

His laugh wasn't the answer I expected, and I felt it all the way through my toes.

"I deserve that." He grinned, lighting up his whole face. Shaking his head, he continued, "and here I thought I was clever and mysterious, but instead," that nervous chuckle returned, "I'd left us both miserable thinking the other wasn't interested. At least, I hope you're interested. Here, let's sit down."

He grabbed my hand and pulled me over to the table. Nicco pulled out my chair and helped me out of my coat, placing it with his. Instead of sitting back where he had been, he scooted close to me, our chairs practically touching. Turning, he put his arm on the back of my chair, effectively enclosing me in his presence as his smell, and everything Nicco, surrounded me.

"I'm glad you're here. I've missed you." His thumb brushed my shoulder as he talked, his eyes intent on me. "I don't care if that's not cool to say. I just want you to know how much I've been thinking about you."

"I've been thinking about you too," I admitted, a blush returning to my cheeks.

"I'm glad to hear that, beautiful."

Nicco's gaze bore into me, firmly on mine, and I found myself falling into his eyes. He started to toy with a lock of hair as he talked, and I was transfixed. Everything else faded away, and it was just the two of us.

"I put my number in your phone that night when I plugged it in. I didn't want to assume or be weird and send it to myself without your approval. It felt like a romantic gesture at the time, but then when I hadn't heard from you, I got nervous. It crossed my mind that you just might not want to hear from me, but I didn't want to believe that until I knew for sure."

"That was kind of romantic, but I'm horrible with my phone," I cringed. "I, uh, I barely even check it as no one calls me, so that's on me."

"Well, that makes me feel marginally better." He grinned. "What about the note from Nat?"

"Note from Nat…" I trailed off. I tried to recall what he was talking about when it hit me. Leaning across him, I reached into my coat and pulled out the slip of paper she handed me last week. As I was moving back, his hand slipped down to my hip, holding me in place. His nose nuzzled my ear as he breathed me in.

"I could've gotten that for you, beautiful," he breathed, a hint of strain in his voice. At his words, I noticed the hard length growing where I'd put my hand on his leg, my breasts grazing his other arm. Sucking in a breath, my face heated again at the realization we were in public, yet how incredibly turned on I was. Slowly, purposefully dragging my hand across his erection, I sat back into my chair. His groan at my touch had me shifting my legs.

"Um, sorry. I wasn't thinking," I mumbled, embarrassment at my brazenness filling me. I dropped my head and let my hair cascade around, effectively hiding me.

"Loren." Nicco gently lifted my head, tucking a strand of hair behind my ear as he did. "You have nothing to apologize for. I don't want to see you withdrawing into yourself for something that isn't your fault. I'm not upset. It makes me happy that you felt comfortable enough to reach over. The attraction part is a bonus."

Listening to his words, I realized he was right. I hadn't even questioned reaching across him. That was something I never would've done with my ex from fear of his ridicule alone, but also not wanting my body to touch his in any capacity. Wow, how had I never pieced that together before? Nodding softly, I accepted what he was saying. Looking at the piece of paper, I unfolded it and reread it.

In case you want to find me. I rubbed my thumb over the writing.

Looking up, I cringed. "I, uh, I remember her giving

me this and being excited it was from you. I was heading into this art thing, so I put it in my pocket. Then everything kind of went awry and I forgot."

"Hey, beautiful, remember what I said about not apologizing?" He smiled, caressing my cheek. "If anything, it's me. I was trying to play it all cool and act like I wasn't thinking about you every minute of the day." Nicco somehow managed to move closer, his mouth inches from mine. "I was thinking about you, and I hoped you were thinking about me. But then I realized you weren't some young floozy into games, and I needed to be direct, so that's how I ended up here."

His words made me blush at the indication that he was thinking about me enough to keep trying to find me. I didn't know anyone who'd tried that much; well, Brian had never tried that hard. It was more a, 'Hey, you're cute, want to date,' and then we were just always Loren and Brian. The realization I've never been adequately wooed hit me like a punch to the gut.

"As embarrassing as this may sound. It wasn't that I wasn't thinking about you, because believe me, I was… I just didn't expect it, so I wasn't looking for it. It just occurred to me that I've never been courted or whatever you call it. I mean…" Stopping myself, I dropped my head again. Nicco made me too comfortable, and I was continually disclosing my secrets to him.

"You mean what?" he encouraged, lifting my head again.

Just as I was about to answer, a waiter came over to drop off glasses of water and take our order. I hadn't even looked at the menu, with panic in my eyes, I was grateful when Nicco took over for me.

"Any food allergies or things you don't like?" he asked quickly. Shaking my head in response, I watched him as he responded to the waiter.

"We'll have two Asian fusion chicken rice bowls."

Once he was done ordering, he focused back on me. Nicco's attention was the thing of romance novels.

"Beautiful, what were you going to say?" he gently prodded.

His eyes were so kind, and again, my feelings of safety emerged, making it feel okay to tell him. The night I'd spent with him had opened up this part of me, and I wanted to explore that more. I liked who I was with him and the ease I felt in his company. Deciding to trust, I gave Nicco my truth, as dangerous as it was.

"You were the first man I've slept with since my divorce."

"Okay, but I feel like there's something more to this. You've been divorced, what, a year?"

"Yeah, that's correct," I swallowed.

"That's not anything to be nervous about, beautiful. How long were you married?"

"Ten years."

"Wow, okay, that's a long time."

"Yeah, it was."

"You must've married young. I know you're older than me, but not by much."

"Yeah, we married after college. I was 22."

"So none of your boyfriends before your ex, they never wooed you or what did you call it, courting?"

Chuckling, I nodded. "Yeah, courting. But boyfriend, not boyfriends. Brian was my only boyfriend."

He paused for a minute, assessing my statement. "Was he the only person you dated and, er, slept with?"

Nodding again, I gauged his expression.

"When did you two start dating?"

"Sixteen."

"*Sixteen*?"

"Yup." I popped my 'p' like my teen clients and watched his face waiting for some reaction. Whatever I was expecting, I didn't get.

"Well then, beautiful," he grinned wide, "I guess that means we'll have to correct that, now won't we." His seduction was a tangible thing, thickening the air with it.

Butterflies erupted in me again, and I wasn't sure if it was nerves or anticipation, but either way, I had a feeling this lunch had just shifted something drastically in my life.

Our food came, and we chatted as we ate, our conversation natural and companionable. Nicco shared more about his shop and admitted he wanted to be an art teacher. I told him about Jude and how I was thinking of mentoring him. He choked when I told him where, and an odd look crossed his face.

"So, this might be a weird request, so feel free to say no if it makes you uncomfortable," he paused. "I want to see you. So, I'm hoping my request won't be too out there. I have this *family* thing I have to do tomorrow. We sort of host these fighting matches, and I wondered if you might want to go with me. I don't think it's really your scene, but I promise you'll be safe with me."

He seemed nervous as he asked me, and while I wasn't sure if I would enjoy watching people beat one another up, the thought of doing something on his turf excited me at how much I wanted to say yes.

"I would love to, Nicco. It sounds like exactly what I need. When is it?"

"It's tomorrow night. Does that work okay?"

"Yeah, it works." I grinned, not wanting to admit I didn't have a life and therefore had no plans.

He smiled at my answer, and my body temperature began to rise again. Moving closer, he whispered into my ear, "What time do you have to be back at work?"

Looking at my phone, I realized that unfortunately, I didn't have enough time to do anything his eyes were promising. Sighing, I looked back up at his handsome face. Man, he was attractive.

"Regrettably, I have a session in about 20 mins."

"Well then, I'll just have to live in anticipation of tomorrow night. Here, give me your phone."

Handing it over, I watched him scroll through my contacts, landing on a name I hadn't noticed. *Stud Muffin.* Chuckling under my breath, I watched as he typed a message and sent it to himself, I assumed.

"There. Now I can text you every time I think of you and properly woo you."

"Okay, *Stud Muffin*," I teased.

"Why, thank you!" He touched his chest in jest, a smile blooming on his face. "I'm humbled by your words, beautiful." Nicco winked, and I found myself laughing at his fun personality.

Slowly, he leaned in and pressed his lips to mine. It

was gentle and soft and filled me with enough heat to set the room on fire. When he pulled back, a sound I would deny escaped, heating my cheeks even more. Thankfully, Nicco ignored it, only smirking. His damn smirk was too cute to be annoyed by it.

Gathering our belongings, we headed out after he paid for lunch. When I tried to pay for part of it, he gave me this look that made me put my wallet away without saying anything. I guess he was taking this wooing thing seriously. Nicco walked with me to my building and left me with another mind-numbing kiss.

My face must've broadcasted how well lunch had gone based on Doris' smile as I entered New Horizons. I didn't even care. It felt amazing not to be thinking about all the crappy things in my life and to feel wanted by a man. I had about ten minutes now before my session, so I put my coat and purse away as I tried to focus on my job.

My phone buzzed, and I remembered I hadn't looked after he sent a message. There were now two messages from Stud Muffin.

Stud Muffin: Prepare to be wooed
Stud Muffin: Just so we're clear. I want to hear
your screams of pleasure as you moan out my
name. I can't wait till tomorrow night. Plan to stay
over, beautiful. I have so many things I want
to do.

Heat filled my face again, and I felt myself grow wet at his words. *Shit.* Fanning myself, I pulled up a relaxation track I used with clients and hit play, needing to center myself. Five minutes later, I wasn't completely relaxed, but I wasn't feeling aroused, which was good before heading into a session. Locking away my thoughts, I pulled on my therapist mask and tackled the rest of my day, feeling invigorated.

TWENTY-FOUR

WELLS

I couldn't blow off another session with sad eyes, so I needed to pull my head out of my ass and face her. I was frustrated that I'd let her get to me, causing me to miss Tuesday. A day's worth of pay down the drain just because I couldn't keep my dick to myself. It had nothing to do with being rejected or embarrassed—nope, none. I didn't have room for that emotion in my life. Not anymore.

"Hey, Wells. Want to grab a drink after tonight?" Missy or Kristy asked. I never learned her name, and yet, she continued to talk to me and ask me out.

"No."

That never worked, though, and as I felt her hands trail up my arm, I stiffened, trying not to grab it like I wanted and throw her off me. I needed this job to stay afloat in my debts, but I didn't want to be assaulted. Yet, another prime example of me being blamed for something if I were to do anything. Fucking unfair, sexist shit. Besides, she wasn't the one I wanted touching me. Not that kitten was a real option.

Moving off the bench, I put space between us and ignored her comments as I made my way out of the locker room. I could finish getting ready out there and away from her. Her cries of frustration did nothing to my already annoyed state. Sorry, not sorry, but not happening.

Leaning against the gym wall, I methodically wrapped my hands, falling into an easy rhythm I'd learned as a teen. Fighting had been a way of life then, a way to survive. My thoughts were interrupted as I heard the door to the gym open and close. I hoped it wasn't Barbie trying again. I just didn't have it in me to be nice today. That was a lie. I didn't have it in me to be nice ever.

Looking up, I was momentarily stunned when I caught sight of my kitten. She looked different today, and I couldn't place my finger on the why. Blanking my features, I grunted and walked over to the bag. Thankfully, she trailed behind me, so I didn't have to talk. I counted in my head to slow my heart at her nearness. She smelt fucking delicious, and I had to school myself not to throw her down right here and devour her. The pain of rejection rolled through me after our last encounter, helping to defuse my arousal.

"Warm up," I barked, ignoring her as I started my own stretches. I swear I felt her eyes roll at the back of my head, but a few seconds later, the sound of her stretching could be heard. Keeping my gaze trained on the bag in front of me, I went through my warm ups, zoning out.

"Now what?" she huffed, pulling me from my trance.

Looking at her face closely, I saw she had a rosy complexion and had taken off the long shirt she was wearing a few minutes ago. *Shit*. Averting my eyes, I turned back in the other direction, ignoring her until I was done.

"Here." I motioned, pointing her to the bag. Holding it, I waited until she was in position.

"Give me as many jabs as you can until your arms get tired, and then we'll switch to kicks."

A fierce look of determination took over her face as she centered herself and started attacking the bag with exuberance. Sighing, I dropped the bag, causing it to swing with her next punch. Walking around the bag toward her, I gently placed my hands on her hips, correcting her form. Moving her arms from behind, I tried to keep my distance from her, not wanting my body to touch hers.

"Like this."

She nodded, I guess adopting the no-talking rule we'd decided on. Once she had her rhythm of punches, I moved back and held the bag. I was surprised how long she punched, not stopping until she was tired like I'd told her.

"Take a break, get some water. Then we can resume."

She nodded again, communicating in head shakes and grunts becoming our norm. I didn't hate it. It was easier to control my urges when she didn't open her mouth, making me want to shut it with either my dick or tongue.

Kitten moved toward her stuff against the wall, downing a bottle of water in the process. Some spilled over, rolling down her neck and cleavage, and I swear I'd never in my life been as jealous as I was then of that glistening drop of water. Turning back, I breathed again, rearranging my dick and warmed up my legs by practicing some kicks. I was trying to distract myself from her intoxicating presence. When I heard her steps, I pulled the bag back to me, using it to hide any lingering evidence.

"Okay, get into the position you stand in," I directed, waiting for her to move into place. "This is the height you want to shoot for," I motioned to an X tape on the bag, "Don't get fancy and try to go higher. You're not ready. Trust me and do it here for now."

A fire lit in her at my words, and I knew she would do it higher. They always did. Letting go, I walked around to my position and held it as I waited for her to make the same mistake all rookies did.

Surprisingly, she kept it at the level I had indicated, slowly thrusting her foot forward with barely enough force to kick a leaf over.

"Harder," I demanded, my voice going rough with the command.

Sad eyes narrowed on me, and I watched as she steeled herself and started to put more force into it, finally getting somewhere. After about ten minutes, she showed signs of fatigue, which had been a good length of time for her first.

"Switch legs."

We continued in this pattern over the next hour, only a few words passed between us as she kicked the bag and I held it. When the time was up, I didn't think she'd said more than ten words to me the entire session. Usually, I'd prefer that, but I found myself missing her voice and combative remarks for some reason. I guess that was why I pushed her buttons at the end, wanting some of her fire, feeling I deserved it.

"Decent job, *kitten*. It seems you can listen when you want to. I bet you'd be pretty on your knees, submitting to me as I shove my cock down your throat."

I hadn't expected the smack of her hand across my cheek, but I *deserved* it. I'd crossed a line.

Part of me enjoyed her aggression, for the simple fact I got to see the fire back in her. The other side of me reveled in it because of all the shitty mistakes I'd made in my life. My kitten was everything I hated and desired wrapped up in a hot little sad package. Her sad eyes pulled to the darkness in me, and I wanted to wrap her in it, simultaneously fighting against the shadows and being hers.

"What's your problem?" she screamed before stalking off, her ass entrancing me as she did. Grabbing the punching bag, I held it to me, hiding the second erection she'd given me in an hour. I expected her to storm out, but when she got to the door, I watched her take in deep breaths, her back arching with each one. She turned, a look of fierce determination on her face.

"No. It's not ending this way… not again. You're going to teach me. *Now*," she motioned toward me with her fingers, "*teach*."

Despite what she'd intended, her claws coming out only sent fire through my veins even more. Needing to douse my arousal, I released the bag and picked up the mitts on the bench. Glaring at her, I positioned myself with my hands up, sending a death stare toward her. It seemed my kitten had taken her anger juice today. She wailed into my hands, not stopping until I called it. Sweat dripped from her brow, her breaths were heavy as she bent over, trying to catch her breath.

"You can try to outrun your demons. You can fill it with this," I motioned all around, "but they eventually catch up to you. They always do. *Trust me*, I should know."

Our time was up, and if I stayed in that gym any longer, I wasn't sure I wouldn't continue to open up my wounds for her to pour salt in. There was a level of torture I enjoyed, felt was justified even, and then there was just plain torture. At this point, being in her presence any longer than necessary was Hell. I wanted to deny my interest in her, but I was only fooling myself.

Giving in to that temptation would be catastrophic in ways I wasn't prepared to deal with. I'd given in to them in the past, and I was still trying to find my way out from the rubble. No, it was better that my sad eyed kitten stayed far, far, away from me.

Grabbing my stuff, I hastily made my way out. I needed to be far from the gym and her. My bike was parked in an alley behind Windy City, which ended up being my biggest regret of the day. Two burly goons stepped out from the shadows before I reached it, effectively blocking my exit and bike.

Halting my footsteps, I sighed, knowing this would inevitably catch up with me, but always hoping I would be lucky enough to miss it. Chuckling at myself, because who was I kidding… not being lucky was what got me into this mess in the first place.

"Fellas, I'm all booked tonight, but I can see if I can squeeze you in tomorrow. Let me just go back to the gym, and we can..."

"Not so fast, *Crash*," a voice sneered behind me, freezing me in my spot. A hand clamped down onto my shoulder and the small window I had at escaping fled. Hanging my head, I accepted the pain about to be bestowed upon me. He walked around to the front of me, a sinister look on his face. *Darren*.

"I thought we had an agreement, and yet, here you are, winning fights. You owe me money, Crash, lots of money."

"And I told you that I'd get you the money, but I don't cheat."

"Interesting, considering why you're in this *predicament*, isn't it, boys?"

The two goons laughed down the alley, my blood running cold at the sound. I was outnumbered and outgunned. Would I even be able to walk away from this?

A push from behind had me falling to my knees, catching me off guard as the gravel dug into my skin. I was still in my workout clothes, so the pavement cut my knee with the force. The punches that followed came in a whirlwind from all directions, impossible to track as the blows rained down on me.

I blacked out after a while, going to the place in my mind I'd learned many years ago in foster care, the place where I could be safe. When the punches stopped, it was hard to breathe as I dragged in the air. Every part of my body ached as I tried to catalog my injuries and stay present. One last kick to my ribs had me groaning as it felt like the boot left an indent in my side.

"This is your last warning, Crash. Delgados don't play. You might want to miss the fight tomorrow."

Spit landed on my face, followed by the sound of boots retreating. When silence descended around me, I relaxed as much as possible. Blackness crept in and out, and I had no idea how long I laid on that hard ground. Stretching, I groaned as I tried to reach the bag I'd dropped. It took a few tries, but finally, I reached the strap and pulled it toward me slowly.

Panting, I laid on the ground for a few more minutes as I regained my strength and courage to go through the pain again. The cold that seeped into my skin spurred me to move, and I was finally able to pull out my phone. Dialing the one number I knew by heart, I waited to see if the last nail in my coffin would fall.

"Hello? Wells, is that you?" His familiar voice rang out, and I wanted to ignore the comfort it brought.

"Yeah, it's… me. I… need… help."

"Where are you?" he questioned, the panic evident in his voice.

"Gym."

"I'm on my way."

"Thank… you… Mon… roe."

"You don't need to thank me, Wells. You know our creed. Anytime, anywhere—"

"—I'll… be there."

"Yeah."

"I just… wasn't sure. After… last time," I panted, each word harder as I laid there.

"You're my best friend, Wells. That supersedes anything. If you'd taken my call in the past six months, you'd know that." I could hear noise in the background as I assumed he was gathering his things to leave. "I'm just glad you did call. I have Levi, so let me see if my neighbor can come and watch him while I leave. It's after ten, and he's asleep."

"I'm sorry," emotion thick in my words, "I didn't… know who… else to call."

"No apologies. Enough, okay? I'll be there soon. Just hang in there."

"Thanks, Roe."

"I'm on my way."

The phone clicked as I heard him knocking on a door. Relief that someone still cared coursed through me, allowing me to push myself up into a sitting position. Struggling inch by inch, I was exhausted by the time I made it against the wall to wait.

In some ways, I felt lighter. I'd been dreading the moment when the goons found me, and my reunion with Monroe had been plaguing me for months. Now, they'd both occurred, settling my anxiety and allowing me to breathe, even if that was difficult right now.

Fuck! I needed to find a way out of this debt. The crushing weight of it over me each day was slowly suffocating me. I didn't know how much longer I could live with that pressure, that fear. Always wondering if next time would be when they killed me.

I must've passed out again because what felt like mere seconds later, Monroe was slapping my face awake.

"Wells, buddy. Wake up."

"Stop it. I'm fine," I mumbled, slapping off the hand touching me. "I just need help up."

"You're far from fine, Wells. *Shit,* who did this to you?"

"Ow, man," I hissed, "careful. I just had the shit beat out of me."

"You don't say. Fuck. Okay, on the count of three, ready?"

"No," I groaned, "but let's do this."

"One, two, and three."

Monroe heaved me up, pain ricocheting through my body with the movement, as a groan left me.

"Come on, just a little further. We'll have to come back for your bike later."

I heaved one foot in front of the other, shards of pain slicing into my sides with each step. Shit, I'd definitely broken a rib or two. Fucking hell, those took forever to heal, meaning I'd be out of fighting for a while. At least I had a good reason not to see my kitten for a bit. Each time I was around her only served to remind me of what I would never have. *Happiness.*

A car sat at the end of the alley with its lights flashing. How Monroe found me here, I wasn't sure, but I was grateful. A girl came around and opened the door when she saw us, looking me over with a critical eye. She looked familiar, but in this light and with my eye partially closed, it was hard to say honestly.

Groaning, I landed in the car with a sigh of relief at

finally making it. Monroe got in on the other side and started tending to my wounds as I passed out again from the effort. The ride to his apartment felt quick as I blinked open my eyes and found the car stopped in front of his building.

"Thanks, Nat, I owe you for coming out so late," I heard Monroe say as he got out of the car.

"Don't mention it. Be good to my girl," she responded, eyeing me like I was getting blood all over her upholstery. To be fair, I probably was. Oops.

The door opened, and I almost fell out of it from how I was leaning against it, Monroe barely catching me in time.

"Shit, man. Sorry."

Grunting, I focused on the steps I needed to take instead of the pain I was feeling. So close, and then I could sleep, I kept reminding myself. Monroe helped me into the building, past his doorman, and into the elevator. I sighed in relief at the break from the pain. The ride was quiet as we both waited for his floor, my head leaning back against the wall, eyes closed. Preparing myself, I sucked it up and pushed off from the surface to make it the last few steps.

I was leaning heavily against him now, slowing our trek, but I was scraping the bottom of the barrel on energy.

"Almost there, Wells. Come on."

We stopped in front of his door, and he knocked. I found it strange but then remembered he had someone watching Levi, so the bolts must be in place. It was a weird thing to focus on, but it helped me not think about the pain for a few brief minutes.

The door opened, and I heard a gasp, causing me to raise my head, expecting to find a high school kid or perhaps an older lady shocked with my wounds. Instead, I locked eyes with my kitten.

"Sad eyes," I whispered before everything went black.

TWENTY-FIVE

LOREN

I'd been surprised when Monroe knocked on my door late tonight asking if I could watch Levi for an hour. I was even more shocked when I opened the door to find him with Mr. Surly.

"Oh my God. What happened?"

I jumped into action and helped Monroe carry my now passed-out gym instructor to the couch. Once he was down, I ran to the kitchen to grab ice, water, and paper towels. Monroe had the T-shirt off Mr. Surly by the time I returned and was inspecting the dark bruising. It was extensive, and I cringed as I began cleaning up his face.

It was covered in dried blood and was starting to mottle with bruises along his jaw as well. It was not going to be a pretty sight when he woke up. One eye was swollen shut, and I winced as I gently dabbed it. What the hell had happened after I left? It had been only a few hours since I saw him walk out of that gym in a huff.

After a few minutes of working diligently in silence,

we had him mended to the best of our ability. I placed an ice pack on his face to help with the swelling before throwing away the bloodied towels. Washing my hands, I realized I was shaking with adrenaline, either from shock or even fear.

Monroe came up behind me, his body blanketing mine in heat as he took my hands into his, stopping the tremble. I relaxed back into his embrace for a moment, soaking in his comfort. He was a giant snuggly blanket, and his presence reminded me how much I missed this part of a relationship. Though, to be frank, it hadn't been present in years and never felt this solid. What did that say about my marriage? I was starting to realize I'd been wearing a mask longer than I thought.

Perhaps my marriage wasn't as flawless as I'd always believed, and I'd been blind to the deficiencies long before they were obvious. There were pitfalls to only having one relationship in my life. The things I thought were normal might not be, and now, as an adult, I had no clue how to navigate all these feelings, expectations, and rules I found myself in.

"You okay?"

"Yeah, it's just, I don't know," I mumbled as I dried my hands. Turning, I looked up into his kind green eyes, finding nothing but assurance. "I sort of know him." I shrugged.

"You know Wells?"

"Uh, yeah. I mean, I didn't know that was his name. He never really told me, so I call him Mr. Surly."

Monroe chuckled, his arms wrapped around me now.

Despite our friendship being new, I felt safe with him, and I didn't question the motives behind everything he did. He was a solid and upfront man, and I knew he would never play games with me. It was refreshing. His attention was centered on me as he waited until I had my thoughts under control.

"It was jarring seeing him like that. I just left him a few hours ago, and he was fine. My brain is having a hard time piecing it all together."

"Yeah, I can see how that would be confusing. Plus, I bet you weren't expecting to see him in this place. Two different parts of your life colliding in a way."

"Yeah, that's true." I nodded, biting my lip. "How do you know, what did you say his name was?"

"Wells Young." He smiled before continuing. "Uh, remember how I said I grew up in foster care and at a group home? We'd been placed in a few homes together and then at the group home became friends. I haven't heard from him in a few months, though. We disagreed about something, and he tends to pull away when he feels threatened."

"That makes a lot of sense…" I mumbled.

"Oh, does it?" he teased.

"Just how he is with me, I guess in lessons. Anyway, that's not important. Do you, um, need anything else? Do you want me to go?"

"I think he's probably good at this point. He might need to see a doctor tomorrow for his ribs, but I can't do anything with that tonight. You can stay though… you don't have to leave."

His words had been muffled on the last part, hesitant to throw out his offer. The heat between us grew as I stared into the pale green depths, conflicted on what to do.

"I..."

Before I could finish, a loud moan came from the living room, followed by a crash. We broke apart and raced into the room to see what had caused the noise. Mr. Surly was face down on the floor, apparently having rolled off the couch. He groaned as he laid there, unable to move, curses flowing from his mouth.

"I think I like it better when you're asleep," I muttered, helping Monroe lift him back up. Some of his cuts had reopened and were dripping blood down his face.

"Easy buddy, lay down," Monroe admonished the brute who was thrashing around in our hold.

"Either I'm dead or dreaming."

The moan sounded out of Mr. Surly from the couch. I decided I was refusing to call him by his name until he told me himself. Though, maybe Surly was more apropos. He hadn't really earned the Mr. title either.

"Why is that?" Monroe questioned, already re-bandaging his injuries. I could see his level of care for the sour man despite his horrific personality. However, I didn't have much room to talk since I'd wanted to jump him last week. Taking in their history, I could understand their bond. And despite his asshole brashness, there was something about him that pulled me in even when I tried to deny it.

"Because my sad eyed kitten is here."

I stopped what I was doing, my hands freezing on his arms, as I peered up at him. Did he mean *me*? Monroe glanced over as well, confusion on his face. Shrugging, because I didn't know how to answer that.

"Do you mean Loren?" Monroe asked, a furrowed look on his face.

"Lo-ren. I like it," he slurred, his eyes closed. "I think she told me that, but I'm an asshole. Besides, she's *kitten* to me. She's got those claws, but you still want to snuggle her close," he stammered out, his breathing evening out as he fell back into a deep sleep.

My face flamed at the description, causing Monroe to grin softly. We were able to bandage all the reopened cuts as Surly started to snore. We both collapsed onto the opposing smaller couch, panting a little at having to lift him from the ground. Surly was a heavy man with all those muscles. I couldn't help the lingering way my eyes trailed over his abs that were on display.

"Do you want to watch some TV?" Monroe asked a while later, both having been lost in our thoughts or perhaps, in my situation, transfixed by the sexy man candy. Surly was much easier to salivate over when he was unconscious.

"Uh, sure."

Monroe turned on the television, but it didn't take too long before I passed out, finding myself wrapped in his arms.

Low voices woke me the following day as I tried to recall where I was. A vague recollection of the night before floated through my mind, and I remembered falling asleep at Monroe's. I was now lying on the couch alone, a blanket over me. Voices on the other couch became more apparent as I woke up and heard what they were saying. When I heard my name, it piqued my attention, and I eavesdropped, despite knowing I shouldn't.

"I'm surprised she's here. I didn't think she liked me," a rough voice that had to be Surly's rasped out.

"I wonder what gave you that impression. Surely, it wasn't your winning personality," Monroe teased him. "She's my neighbor, Wells. I asked her to come over to watch Levi when you called. She didn't even know it was about you," he admitted. "We've kind of... I don't know what you call it, but I like her."

Monroe's words warmed my heart, and I found myself smiling. Now, I really felt guilty for listening in, but I still didn't stop.

"Did she tell you we kissed the other day?"

Anger rolled up in me, and I was about to jump off this couch and slap the douchecanoe when Monroe's words stopped me.

"How... was it?'

Okay, I hadn't expected *that* answer. The rage left me when I took in the conversational tones and familiarity between them. There hadn't been any jealousy in Monroe's words, and while I thought Surly had been trying to throw my reputation under the bus, it seemed he was only sharing with his friend.

"Hot," he admitted. "Until I fucked it up like I typically do. I spouted off something assholery once, and she kicked me in the balls." They both laughed, and the sound was pleasant.

"You say something dickish?" Monroe asked sarcastically. "Though, I'd like to see you getting a swift kick to the groin."

"Haha, jackass," he deadpanned before his voice softened. "Thanks for coming and getting me. I know I said it last night, but I feel I need to readdress it this morning as well when I'm not out of my mind in pain."

"You don't have to thank me, Wells. You know I'm always here for you, no matter what."

"I know you say that, Roe," he sighed, "but after how I left things last time, I didn't know if I could trust it."

Surly's voice was soft, and I could hear the emotion. It was a foreign sound coming from him. Feeling guilty like I was an emotional voyeur, I started to make noise and move around, mimicking how I assumed waking up looked. Stretching my arms over my head, I slowly blinked my eyes open.

"Oh, hey. Good morning," I dramatically yawned.

The smirk on Monroe's face told me I might not be as sly as I believed. Surly was avoiding looking at me, though.

"Good morning, Lo."

"I'm sorry I fell asleep on you so soon. That couldn't have been comfortable." I cringed.

"It was fine. I was able to move to the bedroom after the show and get some sleep. I need to go wake Levi now, so," he looked between us both, unsure what to do. Eventually, he made a decision and got up, "I'll, uh, be back."

After Monroe left, the silence intensified, becoming awkward as I looked around the room at everything but the man on the couch. I was surprised when Surly broke the silence, pulling my attention back to him. His chest was still on display, the bruising easier to distinguish in the daylight. His eye was still swollen shut, the swelling decreasing some.

"Thank you... for last night. I didn't deserve your kindness."

"You're welcome," I answered, surprised by his honesty. "You're right, you didn't deserve it, but I'm not one to hold grudges. If you'd have taken the time to get to know anything about me, you'd know that."

I watched as his jaw ticked, and I realized how confrontational I'd ended it on. Surly pulled all the frustration out of me, though. Trying to be better, I blurted out the first thing that came to my mind, "Um, your face has seen better days."

"Ha! Kitten has jokes. Well, it hurts enough to match it. My whole body feels like I've been run over by a Mack truck."

"You ever wonder how that saying got started? Like, did someone actually get run over by a truck and knew it was the most painful? Did they do a study of different brands to determine the rating?"

Surly barked a laugh, followed by a grimace, grabbing his ribs. "Ow, kitten. Don't make me laugh."

"Sorry. Not my intention. I'm not usually funny."

When it became quiet again, my societal niceties flared up and I asked another question. "Why do you call me that? Kitten, I mean. I do have a name." Despite hearing last night, something in me wanted him to say it out loud, to admit it to my face.

"Ah, yes, Loren, right?"

I nodded, even if it was rhetorical. Being out of Windy City was throwing me off our usual banter.

"Kitten fits you." He shrugged with one arm, his one eye intense on me.

"I disagree," I scoffed, feeling offended. I protectively crossed my arms and rolled my eyes at him. "I'm not a baby cat."

"No, *that* you are not," he purred, causing a blush to rise to my cheeks. He kept staring at me, offering no other explanation.

"Fine, if you're going to call me that, you will stay as Surly," I huffed, annoyed at myself for feeling flustered and a little turned on. Why did I always end up acting like a petulant child around him? His responding smile did not help the situation between my legs, my whole need to be obstinate with him in the first place.

"Surly, huh?"

"Not like you ever introduced yourself properly," I defended, not liking that he was getting enjoyment out of this. "But yeah, between all the brooding commands you give me, I felt it fit."

He watched me closely, taking me in. I felt very uncomfortable with his inspection, almost as if he saw me for the first time. *The real me.*

"Your turn to tell me why you really call me kitten?"

"What's the fun in that, *kitten*?" he teased, a panty-dropping look coming over him even with one eye swollen shut. "It's a lot more fun to tease."

"Well, you can keep your teasing remarks to yourself. I need to go. I have things to do that don't revolve around bandaging up arrogant men."

Standing, I stalked off toward the doorway feeling bad I wasn't telling Monroe bye but figured I could just text him. As I reached the door, Surly called out one more time, apparently needing to have the last word.

"It's Wells, by the way. In case you need to know what name to moan out when you think of me. Though, I quite like how Surly sounds coming from your mouth."

"Ugh!" I screamed, quickly exiting. Every time I started to like him, he opened his damn mouth and reminded me why he was such an asshole in the first place.

Unlocking my door, I stalked into my kitchen, needing my coffee. The timer had already gone off, meaning I didn't even have to wait for it to drip down into the carafe for once. Pouring some into my mug, I sat on the barstool with my phone to text Monroe before I forgot.

When my phone lit up, I saw I had a couple of messages too. Quickly, I sent one to Monroe.

ME: Hey, sorry. I had to leave. I'm still looking forward to dinner tomorrow.

Hitting send, I felt weird with my message. There

was so much unsaid dialogue in texting. It might be convenient, but the subtext was filled with minefields that were difficult to navigate. Add in emojis, and I was lost. What did they all mean anyway? How did a peach refer to something sexual? I was utterly clueless about it all. Another disadvantage of not dating in your twenties, I suppose. Looking over the other messages, I smiled as I read them.

StudMuffin: I've decided I'm going to be your tour guide.
ME: Tour guide? Are we going on a trip?

I was surprised when he responded immediately. Direct Nicco I could deal with. There weren't any minefields that way. Part of me was feeling guilty for my upcoming dinner date with Monroe. But neither man had said anything about exclusivity, and wasn't *this* part of dating? Dating more than one person at a time?

Monroe and I were friends, but it felt like more was there. I could do this, I decided. I could. Well, I at least wanted to try since I found myself liking them both.

StudMuffin: Good morning, beautiful. And yes, we are going on a trip to debauchery land.
ME: Oh, this sounds serious. Debauchery, huh?
StudMuffin: Yep, and I will be your sexy tour guide.
ME: I'm both excited and nervous about what this means. LOL

StudMuffin: Have no fear. I will take care of you. Wear something sexy tonight. Preferably a dress.
ME: Okay, I can do that.
StudMuffin: What's your address? I'll pick you up.
ME: Okay… just don't be mad. *Dropped pin of location*
StudMuffin: Why would I be mad?
StudMuffin: Well, well, well… that's convenient. Guess, I'll be seeing you soon, beautiful.

Smiling, I couldn't help the arousal that coursed through me at the thoughts Nicco surged through me. Scanning the following message took it straight away.

Mom: We require your attendance this Sunday at brunch. Don't be late.

Rolling my eyes, I went to the next.

Mitzi: Do you have time to talk today?
ME: Yes, I can come by in a few hours. I was planning on it anyway. I wanted to see how Jude was doing.
Mitzi: Wonderful. I will be available whenever you're here.

Finishing my coffee, I headed to get dressed for the day, for once not dreading my shower as much. Despite the weird night of sleep and occurrences, I felt more rested than I had in a while. My visit with Mitzi, my date with Monroe, and my night with Nicco were all filling me with happiness.

I was choosing to ignore the brunch on Sunday. That was a problem for another time. Those two days could feel like a lifetime, no use worrying about them now. That ship would sail regardless when I was in my mother's presence, so I might as well enjoy the time I had.

TWENTY-SIX

LOREN

Walking into the center, I realized how much I was looking forward to meeting with Mitzi today, unlike my last visit here, where I was dreading it out of social obligation. The teen girl at the counter still appeared as happy to be there as last time, but it didn't bother me as much today.

"Can I help you?" she droned, twirling her hair as she doodled.

"I'm here to meet with Mitzi."

At my words, she looked up, taking me in. Slowly, she grabbed the phone, punched in some numbers, and then sat it back on its cradle. I wasn't sure how she communicated anything that way, but a few minutes later, Mitzi came walking out with a smile on her face.

"Loren. So happy you could come in. Come, come." She gestured in the direction of her office.

Walking to her, I smiled in return, noticing how different things felt this time. Sometimes, I had these moments as a therapist where I realized the stuff I preached to my clients did, in fact, work. Not that I hadn't believed it wouldn't before, but more that I hadn't needed to use it in the same way. Now, my life felt like a constant example of what not to do. Taking the same seats we had last time, I waited to see what she had to say.

"How are things going, Loren?"

"Well, that's a hard question to answer, but in general, I guess well."

"I'm happy to hear that. I was hoping to see if you had decided on anything we talked about last week?"

"I have, actually. I think," I started, swallowing, "I would like to take on a more hands-on role with Jude and be his mentor."

"Oh, that's wonderful!" She clapped, a massive smile on her face. "He'll be so thrilled. I really think he connected with you. He talked about the art show last week in detail to anyone that would listen." She beamed.

Happiness filled my chest briefly, so foreign, I'd almost forgotten what it felt like, but at the sunny flutters, a small amount of hope planted itself in my chest. The darkness in me wanted to root it out and shun it away, having gotten used to reigning, but a small part of the person I used to be clung tightly to it like a life raft drifting at sea.

"What are the rules and limits of this type of relationship? I just know with counseling, I can't do a lot of things."

"Oh, well, it's very different here. Once your background check clears, which we know it will, then you're allowed to spend time with your mentee however you choose. Under certain circumstances, there can be overnight visits, but that has to be pre-approved, of course."

"Wow, okay. I didn't realize I could do so much with him."

"Most of these kids don't have adult relationships at home, so finding someone they connect with can be the difference between staying off the streets and ending up in desperate situations. You're doing a good thing here, Loren." She patted my hand on the table, offering me reassurance.

"Thanks, I think I'm ready for this."

"What about the other things we discussed?"

"I want to see how this goes first, and then we can see about more if that works?"

"Of course, absolutely. Well, let's get you signed up, and then you can tell Jude the news."

I spent the next twenty minutes filling out forms, and I half wondered if I'd just signed over my firstborn. Despite the intensive details they needed, I did understand the reasoning. It just sucked when I was on the other side of it. It was early afternoon, so I was hoping he'd be here, but Mitzi had also given me his foster parents' address in case I needed it. They lived in an area I wasn't familiar with, and I had a weird feeling I'd need someone to go with me. Oddly, it felt nice to know I had people in my life at the moment to do that.

Scanning the common room, I didn't see Jude among the other kids there. Deciding not to waste time, I was hoping they would know where he was so I wouldn't have to play hide and seek.

"Excuse me, have you guys seen Jude around?"

One of them looked up from the game they were playing, assessing me before answering.

"Down the hall in the darkroom," he nodded.

Waving my thanks, I headed in the direction he'd indicated and hoped the doors were labeled. Thankfully, I found the red light outside one, so I knocked, knowing how imperative it was not to ruin the film development. A minute later, the light turned off, and the door opened, a disheveled Jude in tow. He blinked at me as he adjusted to the light, confusion covering his face.

"Loren?"

"Hey. Wow, I feel awkward all of a sudden." I laughed. Rolling my shoulders back, I braced myself to state my purpose. He was a teenager, and I, the adult, could handle this. "So listen, I really enjoyed meeting you and—"

"But you can't do anything else, yeah, I get it. It was nice meeting you," he answered, cutting me off. He started to shut the door back, and I put my foot in it to stop it.

"Actually, no. I get it. You're used to people letting you down, or telling you that they would love to do something but can't, so you jumped to conclusions to protect yourself. But I think you should give me the chance to speak for myself. It's the polite thing, at least."

He motioned with his hand for me to continue, and for the first time, I saw the teenager attitude coming out of him. Fortunately, this was what I was used to and could manage. Smiling, a thrill of excitement coursed through me at the thought of cracking that wall of anger he held around him.

"I met with Mitzi today," I started, some doubt leaking through on how he might feel about this, "to, uh, inquire about being your mentor. I just wanted to make sure you were okay with that decision," I acknowledged wanting him to know he had a choice. At my words, his arms dropped, his anger dripping away, and he straightened his posture, and I saw the hopeful boy he kept hidden peeking through.

"Oh, I'm sorry about before. I…" he shrugged, dropping his head.

"It's okay. I get it. Thank you for apologizing, though. It's always good to own up to our mistakes. So, is that okay?"

His head snapped up, and he regarded me. I could see hope and fear flashing across his face. Slowly, Jude nodded as he warred with himself. Finally, he swallowed, clearing his throat.

"Yeah, I would be okay with that."

"I'm happy to hear that." I smiled. "I was really hoping you'd say yes. Are you busy right now? I wanted to maybe take you out for some lunch?"

"I'm just playing around. It's nothing important. I can go," he rushed out almost as if he thought the offer would disappear. My heart broke for this boy, and I vowed then to be the adult in his life who was steady and reliable. I could push through my own feelings to be better for him. It was a heavy task, and I knew I would need to prioritize it to make sure I didn't do any damage either.

"Great. Grab your things, and we can walk out together."

Jude nodded and hurried back into the room to grab whatever he needed. Remembering the texts I sent earlier, I decided to check to see if I had any responses back. This concept of having people want to talk to me throughout the day was still so new to me. Even in my marriage, our communication consisted of when we were leaving work and if we needed anything from the store.

It was peculiar to me to text people, but I found myself liking it. The rush of emotions at seeing a new text, often accompanied by the heat of reading them, and the anticipation of what was to come next had me reaching for my phone more.

> **Monroe**: Sorry if Wells was rude this morning. He's not entirely housebroken. Thanks again for your help, especially in watching Levi. I enjoyed our conversation, and I can't wait to have more at dinner.
>
> **ME:** That's funny. I will have to remember that about Surly. No problem with Levi and the help. I was happy to be able to, and I'm looking forward to dinner as well. I'm taking Jude to lunch now.

Before I could read the next one, Jude exited the room, shutting the door behind him. I put my phone in my purse, not wanting to be rude in his company. He smiled shyly, and I realized he was waiting on me to lead the way.

"So, I'm new to this whole mentor thing."

"Oh, well, me too." He shrugged one shoulder in response.

"Really? You've not had one before?"

"No, people usually pick younger kids."

"Ah, I see. Well, then I'm glad we can figure this out together. Team no-clue?"

"Team no-clue." Jude smiled, and I felt like I'd done something good today by getting him to do it. The seed planted earlier to be better began to lengthen its roots, spreading more into the darkness and pushing it out.

"What kind of food do you like?"

"Oh, you don't have to. I'm good."

"Well, first rule. When we're together, I get to pay for things, but no hidden strings or return favors are expected."

Jude watched me, trying to figure out if I was sincere. I could understand his fear and knew it would be a battle to get him to accept this, but I hoped he would.

"How about I promise not to go too crazy, but once a month we do something fun and decide that together? If you don't like the terms, we can renegotiate at the end of the month, but I would like the opportunity to show you first that I'm different."

"I think I can accept it," he finally said, a smile in his voice.

"Perfect. Well, it's cold out, but I'm craving some street food. How about we head over to this area I know with several street vendors, and we try it?"

"Yeah, that sounds good to me. I don't mind the cold."

We set out in the direction of the plaza, taking in the

area as we went. "So, Jude. You like photography. What else do you enjoy?"

"Oh, well, that's my main thing. I guess I enjoy reading and music. School's okay." He shrugged.

"That's cool. I like those things too. You'll have to show me some of your books sometime. I could let you borrow some too, if you wanted."

"Really? That would be awesome. I'd take good care of them, I promise."

"Absolutely. Books should be shared and enjoyed," I enthused, excited about this common interest. Turning the corner, we came upon the food vendors. "Ah, here we are! What would you like to try? I'm thinking a hot dog and a giant pretzel!"

"Oh, sure, same. I've never had any of this," Jude stated sheepishly.

"Well, have no fear. I will be your guide today, and we shall try it all! Come on, I'll need your hands," I laughed.

We scampered around the vendors, getting a little of everything, and made our way to a table. We deposited our food items as we took it all in. We had BBQ chicken, hot dogs, pretzels, nachos, and some pepper jack breaded cheese cubes. It all looked delicious, and I didn't know which I wanted to dig into first.

"What do you want to try?" I offered as I saw him eyeing it all. He looked as excited as a kid on Christmas morning, and my heart solidified in my decision to be a person he could count on. Having someone who needed me was a push I needed. I didn't want to let him down, and to do that, I couldn't let myself down either.

Jude tentatively picked up a hot dog, cautiously watching me to make sure it was okay. Nodding in encouragement, I picked up some of the nachos, making a big show of it as I took a bite. Thankfully, it had the desired effect, and Jude eagerly bit into his food. We were making our way through our smorgasbord, talking about what we liked best when I heard my name.

"Loren?"

Looking up, I spotted Imogen. When she realized it was me, she walked over with a slight smile on her face. Curious, I looked around to see if she was with the sexy mountain neanderthal or the seduction in a suit brother of hers. I spotted her brother, Atticus, a few booths down paying as he talked with the beefcake, Sax.

Looking back to Imogen, I waited to see what she would do once she realized I wasn't alone. Her steps faltered halfway when she spotted my companion but continued toward us. Jude was oblivious to the looks passing between us as he continued to eat pretzels and cheese cubes.

"Hey, how are you?" I vaguely asked.

It was always tricky running into clients outside of New Horizons. I'd always defer to them, and since she'd called out to me, I took that as her consent to greet her. Now, I'd see how much she would reveal about our connection.

"I'm okay. Attie had some business to do, and I wanted to grab some new sheet music. We missed lunch, so we decided to grab something here. Attie won't admit it, but he's a sucker for a good Chicago Dog, but it's not really in his *brand*," she chuckled, rolling her eyes.

"Well, he's not wrong there. The hot dogs here are the best in the city," I affirmed as I took a bite, mustard coating my lips as I did. Crossing my eyes with exuberance, for some reason, I felt the need to be the comic relief with these two. Grateful for their laughs, I fixed my face back to normal, preparing to make another comment when I was faced with the alluring gaze of Atticus.

"Oh, hello, Mr. Masters," I stuttered, grabbing a napkin quickly to wipe off the mustard. Jude laughed at me, making me happy he felt comfortable poking fun at me in front of others, but simultaneously shot daggers with my eyes for it. Unfortunately, it had the opposite effect as Jude only laughed harder, Imogen joining in.

"Mrs. Carter," the stiff man nodded.

"Um, would you like to join us?" I cringed. Why did I ask that? My polite social niceties were always getting me in trouble.

"Well, we—"

"That'd be great!" chirped Imogen as she shyly sat next to Jude, cutting off her brother. He narrowed his eyes at her, but allowed her to sit down.

Atticus eyed the picnic table, probably assessing its cleanliness. I'd been so busy observing Atticus that I forgot about the other one. The bench dipped a little as sexy Sax clambered down next to me, not even hesitant to join. Turning to look at the man, he took up the rest of the bench, his frame touching mine.

His heat seeped into my body, and I felt every movement he made as he shifted himself and his food. Slyly, he winked at me when he caught me gawking at him. Atticus finally sat down on the other side of me while I'd been observing Sax, effectively making me the middle in a hot guy sandwich.

Imogen and Jude were both shyly looking at their food, only taking small bites. It was the most awkward table in the history of awkward tables. Clearing my throat, I decided to be the grown-up and try to salvage Jude's and my lunch.

"Imogen, this is Jude. Jude, this is Imogen, Sax, and, uh, Atticus."

"Hello," Jude returned, doing a little wave, warming my heart. Everyone returned his greeting before another awkward silence descended.

"So, what's your favorite? This is Jude's first time, and we had to try all of these things first," I gestured to our spread.

"Oh, have you tried..." Imogen started, turning to Jude to share her favorites. They delved further into a conversation from there, effectively tuning the adults out as they began to talk about bands and shows they had in common. It was endearing seeing two kids who I knew struggled with their peers find a connection in one another.

Quietly, I ate some food, as I watched the two teens and soon became lost in my thoughts. Sax's leg brushed up against mine, halting my hand to my mouth. Heat began to lick up my leg, and I swallowed to try to dispel it. Carefully, I placed the chip I was holding in my mouth, my focus entirely on his leg.

"So, Mrs. Carter, how do you know Jude?" Atticus questioned, pulling my focus to him.

"Oh, um, we're out of the office. You can call me

Loren. And, well, we're just connected," I stammered. I didn't know what Jude wanted to say about our relationship, and since we hadn't had time yet to discuss it, I just left it open. Fucking hell, I was acting like a nervous schoolgirl around these two men.

"If I'm to call you Loren, then you should call me Atticus."

"Fair," I nodded, "but I kind of already did."

For some reason, my mouth had decided to be flirtatious, causing him to smirk at my answer, sending tingles from my belly to my core.

"Ah, so it seems you have."

"So…" I trailed off, unsure where to go from there. The two teens watched a video on Imogen's phones, effectively ignoring us.

"I'm curious, spitfire," drawled the hard rock man next to me, "have you thought any more of the proposition I gave you last time I was in your office?"

His question was asked innocently, but the undeniable heat in his eyes belied otherwise. Sax pressed his leg more firmly into me, causing me to shift closer to the other man. They were both wearing suits, and for some reason, the sight of them dressed so well sitting on a picnic bench got to me, and I broke out into hysterical laughter.

Everyone stopped and turned to me, unsure what I was laughing at. By the time I was able to get my giggles under control, I had tears in my eyes. Wiping them, my uncharacteristic laughter had lightened the mood, and we all delved into a conversation on food and what Jude needed to try next.

Despite some intense and awkward moments, our little impromptu picnic downtown became an epic affair. Jude and Imogen exchanged numbers, much to Atticus' disapproving glare and Sax's scrutiny, but I thought it was a perfect idea and that maybe these two could find a new connection in one another.

I didn't miss the smile on Imogen's lips, or the heated look Sax left me with, but most confusing was the look on Atticus' face. It was a mix of desire and contempt, almost as if he was angry he found me attractive? But why would he be interested in me? I was probably reading him wrong. Shaking my head to dislodge the thoughts, I reminded myself it wasn't a thought I could entertain either way. Focusing back on the teen next to me, we enjoyed our walk as we made our way back to the center.

"Hope that was okay, the meal. I didn't know what to say when they asked about our relationship either. What would you be comfortable with me saying?" I finally asked.

"Oh, it was the best afternoon I've had. Thank you, Loren," Jude offered, a warm smile lighting up his whole face. He looked like a different kid at that moment. "And I don't know, I guess it depends on what you're comfortable with, I mean?" he awkwardly chuckled.

"How about we just keep it simple? We're Jude and Loren, Loren and Jude. It doesn't need a label."

"That sounds perfect to me." He grinned, making me feel like I was finally getting something right this year. Granted, it was still the beginning of the year, but the concept still counted when the past year had felt like a million.

Jude and I exchanged numbers and made tentative plans to go out again soon. He left me with his wave, and I felt freer as I walked back to the train. Catching my reflection in the window as I walked by, I realized I had a real smile on my face. Filing that away, I relished in the knowledge that I'd done something good for myself and how great that made me feel for once.

I didn't hate the person I was today. In fact, I think I was starting to like this new version of myself just a little. It was a start, and that was something I could accept.

TWENTY-SEVEN

LOREN

Tossing the third outfit on the floor, I admitted defeat. Huffing in exasperation, I fell onto the bed in a sea of shirts and pants. I had no clue what people wore on dates now or what was even considered sexy. The dress I'd worn to the club the first time was the only thing I had like that in my closet. The second time had been Nat's suggestion on what I was already wearing. Ugh, this was *pointless*.

Sitting up on the edge of my bed in my bra and matching underwear, I pulled out my phone and debated canceling on Nicco. It was like he had a sixth sense to my emotions because right as I opened my texts up to send one, he messaged me.

StudMuffin: Hey, beautiful. I can't wait to see you later.
ME: Full disclosure, I'm freaking out.
StudMuffin: What's got you scared? Is it me?
ME: No, you're the one thing I'm not scared about. It's just all the other stuff.

StudMuffin: Well, I'm glad to hear you're not fearful of me. What is the other stuff? Let's find a solution together.

ME: That's some good therapist shit there you just did.

StudMuffin: Well, maybe you've rubbed off on me. Speaking of…

ME: Yeah?

StudMuffin: I was going to go all dirty sex-crazed but thought I better not.

ME: I don't mind. I kind… of like it. It helps me know how you feel, actually.

StudMuffin: Oh, beautiful, I can't wait to feel you again.

ME: Why is that making me feel all hot and bothered?

StudMuffin: Because it's hot. So tell me, beautiful, what is all this other stuff?

ME: Ugh, your persistence is both annoying and charming.

StudMuffin: It is one of my finer qualities. So…?

ME: I have no idea what to wear or how even to date. I was 16 last time. I'm so out of my comfort zone.

StudMuffin: Solution 1, text Nat. She can help. Solution 2, there isn't a hard or fast rule to dating. Do what you're comfortable with, and if you don't know what that is, then we'll explore that together. In my opinion, open communication is the key, and I think we're finding our sweet spot with that.

ME: Thank you. Those are helpful. I will text Nat.
I'm glad my first date after my divorce is
with you.
StudMuffin: Me too, beautiful. Me too. I'll see you
in a few hours.

Leaning back, I did feel better after my conversation with Nicco. He had an uncanny ability to make me feel at ease and courageous. I'd probably do just about anything he suggested.

Taking a deep breath, I took a chance and texted Nat. I didn't have girlfriends outside my coworkers. All of my friends prior had been married couples, and after the divorce, they all took sides. Despite Brian cheating, I didn't have it in me to disclose his transgressions. So all they saw was my downward spiral into depression.

No one wanted to be around depressed people, so it was easier for them all to side with him and leave me to wallow. I never really got along with those women anyway. They were all focused on status, their figure, and gossip. If I thought about it, I'd been bored with their friendships for years.

ME: Hey girl, weird question, but are you busy at
the moment? I could use a favor.
Nat: I'm not doing anything. What's up? Need me
to pick you up somewhere?
ME: No, actually, this is more of a personal
request.
Nat: Well, I'm even more available now! Spill
girl.

ME: Nicco asked me on a date, and I have no clue what to wear. I'm freaking out.

Nat: Say no more. I'll be there in 10 mins. I'm already on your side of town.

ME: Wow, thank you. I owe you.

Nat: Nah, say no more. It's what friends do. I'm getting in my car now. I'll be there soon. Do I need to do anything when I get there? You live in that nice building, after all.

ME: I'll let them know to send you up. 18B.

Nat: Sweet. See you soon.

Deciding I should probably put something on over my undergarments, I slipped on a silk robe and decided to make some coffee. It had been a long night with Wells. Despite knowing his name now, part of me still wanted to call him Surly. It suited him so well after all. Then the day had been emotionally exhausting with Jude and my surprise lunch companions.

My age was going to kick my butt tonight if I didn't do something. Hopefully, the coffee would help wake me up and give me a caffeine boost. Calling down to the front, I let them know I'd be expecting a visitor as I waited for my energy boost. Just as the coffee finished, there was a knock at my door. Assuming it was Nat, I opened the door without checking the peephole.

"Uh, hey?"

A confused but slightly heated look met me as I opened the door to Wells and *not* Nat.

"Oh, hey. Do you need something?"

Pulling my robe tighter, I tried to conceal my bra that

was peeking through the slit. Wells stood silent for a moment, his jaw slightly open, as he looked me over from head to toe with his unwavering gaze. When he looked back into my eyes, the want was no longer present, locked behind his guardedness as he stared at me as if I'd just insulted him.

"You knocked on my door, *Surly*. So what do you want?" Even though he'd knocked on my door, I shifted on my feet as I waited for him to explain.

"Yeah, well, you answered it looking like *that*, and I can only guess what it means," he huffed, annoyed.

"*What*?" Shock radiated through me, not liking what he was implying. Pulling some of the fire I often felt at the gym, I gave it back just as good. "You know what? We're not in Windy City, and this isn't your territory. It's *mine*. So, I'm not going to play these mind games with you today. Either tell me why you knocked on my door, or I'm shutting it in your face."

Surly didn't like that answer, and I could practically hear him clenching his jaw as he ground his teeth. Ha! Good. Surly needed to understand that not everything was about him. He always acted as if I went out of my way to offend him. Get a clue, dude. I was barely keeping my head above water most days.

He took a few deep breaths, and the therapist part of me wanted to congratulate him on regulating his emotions for once, but I was afraid it would come across as more snark than encouragement at this point, so I decided to reign it in.

"I just wanted," he cleared his throat, "to thank you," he gritted out, "for helping last night."

"Wow, that was really hard for you, wasn't it?" I teased, taking too much pleasure in his discomfort. "You're welcome."

I watched as he took a deep breath, letting it out slowly. "That's all."

"Okay."

We stood awkwardly staring at one another, a million thoughts hanging in the air between us. It was almost a dare to see if either of us would move. As much as he pissed me off most days, I couldn't deny the sexual chemistry between us. The ding of the elevator broke our trance, and I glanced at it to see Nat walking toward me, a few garment bags draped over her arms.

When she saw me, a smile crossed her face and when she spotted the angry hot guy, her eyes raised in a question I wasn't sure how to answer. Wells finally seemed to find his feet, turned abruptly and stalked off, leaving me standing there waiting for Nat.

"Hi," she chirped as they passed, his only response to her was a grunt of acknowledgement. She smiled wide, and moved her eyebrows up and down at me as she continued down the hallway. I stepped back as she made it to my door so she could enter.

"So… that looked intense."

"Oh yeah, you could say that. It's *complicated*."

"Uh-huh. I find most things that are *complicated* really aren't all that complicated. You want to fuck each other. Sounds pretty simple to me," she teased.

My cheeks heated at her words, not denying her statement but felt the need to protect my image.

"Yeah, well, there's no denying that it's there," I

disclosed, shutting the door and following her into the apartment as I continued, "but he's such an ass most of the time that I mostly want to punch him. He's just so hot," I groaned, sitting on the back of the couch. "And then, he opens his mouth and ruins it!"

"Damn girl, you don't hold your punches. I like it," she laughed. "Though, you answered the door looking like sex on a stick." She gestured at me. "I'm surprised he was able to walk away with the third leg he was rocking." Nat moved her hands to emphasize what she meant.

My face was entirely red now as I tried to dismiss her statement. I'd felt it rubbing up against my ass a week ago, and it definitely could pass as a third leg. Stuttering out, I tried to defend my state of undress for the second time.

"I thought it was you when I answered. I didn't intentionally try to tease him. You sound as bad as Mr. Surly."

"Oh, you even have a hot nickname for him? Yeah, you want to bang him if you haven't already," she laughed.

"Why did I invite you again?" I groaned, dropping my head back in effect.

"Oh, so you have." She grinned. "So, how was it?"

"Oh my God," I laughed. "You're impossible. Fine, I will give you all the details, and *then* you drop it. I don't want to focus on him anymore than I have to," I started. Sliding down onto the cushion, getting comfortable to have 'girl' talk.

"He's my kickboxing instructor, and last week, there was a heated moment between us if you will, and I, um, kissed him." My face flushed as I recalled it. "It started to go further, but then something shifted," I swallowed, "I think in me, and well, he stopped. Surly left me panting up against a wall as he stalked off and then avoided me at the beginning of the week, so yeah, complicated is the best word for us!" I finished with emphasis, throwing up my hands.

"Okay, okay." Nat put her hands up in front of her in a pleading gesture. "You win. It's definitely complicated. But damn, how hot would that be? You just know he fucks good with all that *angst*." Now, she was fanning herself, and I couldn't help but laugh at her shenanigans.

I couldn't disagree with her. It had been some of the hottest foreplay of my life. While I didn't have a lot to compare it to, it still seemed hotter than any story I'd even heard from girls, and blew anything I'd experienced with Brian out of the water.

"Do you want coffee or anything? I was making some before Wells knocked on the door."

I made my way into the kitchen and grabbed a mug to pour the hot liquid into. Nat jumped up on the counter, and I realized it was the first time I'd seen her out of a car. She leaned back on her arms, kicking her legs under the open space of the bar. She was shorter than I expected, probably a few inches shorter than me. Her brown hair was long and ran down her back in waves. Nat's style was both comfortable and fashionable in a very hipster sort of way. It was then I realized how much younger she was than me.

"Are you done checking me out?" she teased, pulling my attention back to her.

"Ah, sorry. It's just that I've never seen you outside your car before now, and I was just taking you in and filing away the info, I suppose." I shrugged as I tried to throw off some of my embarrassment.

"Girl, you can check me out any time. I know you don't swing that way, but it's a huge compliment and makes a girl feel good."

"Well, okay, I'll make sure to check you out longer from now on."

Nat had a way of making me feel not embarrassed about things. She didn't judge, and I realized how different she was from the ladies I used to be friends with, and how loose of a term that really had been. A knock sounded at the door, and Nat hopped down as she headed over to it.

"Hope you don't mind, but I invited a reinforcement," she said over her shoulder, a smile on her face that told me she was up to no good. "I'm not great at style, as you might've noticed by my own outfit. I'm better at hair and makeup."

"Uh, sure. Who did you invite, though?"

My social anxiety started to flare as I took in the state of myself. I was practically naked and about to meet a stranger. I was hitting it out of the park today with first impressions, I supposed. I stayed in the kitchen, hoping it would provide me some level of security. I could hear them talking as they neared, and I was about to run into my room, lock the door, and cancel everything when they turned the corner. Instantly, I deflated as I took in the familiar redhead.

"Cami," I greeted the newcomer. At my voice, she

bounced over to me and wrapped me in an exuberant hug taking me by surprise as we rocked back and forth.

"Loren! Oh, it's so good to see you, and without a mask on. Girl, you're stunning! This is going to be so fun. It's like having a human Barbie doll." She beamed back at Nat, talking a mile a minute.

Nat was leaning back against the counter now with a smug look on her face. I shook my head at her knowing she'd probably sensed my fear at her words. Nodding to her, I acknowledged her brilliance at inviting Cami over as well.

"Sorry, I'm not used to having guests here. Do you want any coffee?"

"Girl, we need something stronger than coffee," Cami chirped as she made herself at home and started opening my cabinets as she looked for glasses and God knows what else.

"Oh man, Loren. We need to stock your liquor supply better. Please, tell me you at least have some wine," she pouted.

"Um, maybe in the fridge?" I hedged.

Rolling her eyes, she opened the fridge to find an old bottle of Pinot Grigio I'd probably had for a few years hidden in the back. I was almost positive that it had been a gift from my colleagues after my divorce. At the time, I hadn't seen the need to celebrate the demise of my picture-perfect life. Now, I was starting to understand how fake that picture had been. Tonight was the perfect night to open that wine and toast to a new chapter.

Finding the corkscrew, I handed it to the experienced bartender and allowed her to do her thing. I would muck it up and leave bits of the cork in it. Brian had constantly ridiculed me for it. I probably had PTSD over all the things he criticized me on and why I hadn't opened the bottle in over a year. Though a dark part of me admitted that if I'd started drinking at home, I might not have stopped. There were some dark days I had there, *still had*, if I was honest.

"To new friends and makeovers!" cheered Nat as she passed out glasses and raised hers.

"To new friends and makeovers!" Cami and I joined.

"Wait, makeovers? I don't know about all that, you guys."

Unfortunately, they only laughed at me as we drank our wine. Nat pulled me by my hand and out of the kitchen but stopped when she realized she didn't know where she was going.

"Where in this massively exquisite place should I go?" she asked, turning to me with a grin as she waited for me to direct her.

"Oh, thanks. Um, I guess my bedroom. Down the hallway on the right."

She pulled me along as she skipped to my room, Cami giggling behind us. I went along with them, starting to catch some of their energy. Cami had the garment bags Nat had brought and tossed them on the bed before going through my clothes piled there.

Nat set down another bag and started pulling hair products and makeup out of it. Cami started some music on her phone and began to dance around as I sat and watched them, mesmerized. They were effortlessly cool and fun.

Nat and Cami were the epitome of cool girls from movies you wanted to befriend. Thankfully, they were the type of cool girls you wanted to be and not the mean ones you feared. I envied their light-heartedness and ability to be easygoing in moments like these.

"So, where's this date? Wait, it's the third Friday, so," Nat mused, turning and lifting an eyebrow, "fight night?"

Her question piqued my interest as Nicco had been very mum on the topic other than 'an untypical place'.

"Uh, yeah. I think so. I mean, he didn't really say." I shrugged. It was becoming my go-to expression, it seemed. Which was uncharacteristic of me to be so unsure, or well, allow my body language to communicate it. Being the 'perfect persona' for every walk of life meant I often presented as confident when I was anything but that.

"In that case, you need to look fierce," she decided, nodding in confirmation.

"So, I'm guessing your evening went well the other night if you're having a second date?" Cami asked, raising her eyebrows suggestively.

"Uh, yeah. It went well," I blushed.

"Oh, girl, give us the deets!"

"Ha, well okay, it was the first time I was with someone after my divorce. Well actually, ever," I admitted.

"Wait. Are you saying that you've only been with your ex-husband? Were you religious or something? Waiting for marriage?"

"Don't look so shocked, but no, it wasn't a 'waiting 'til marriage' thing. Just a high school sweetheart thing.

We met when I was sixteen, and I never dated anyone else."

"Oh, I see. Harsh."

"Yeah, you could say that," I uttered, sadness leaching from my voice.

Nat heard the sadness and took my hand to lead me over to the bench seat in the corner. She started to mess with my hair, and I realized I'd never had this experience before, not even as a teen. It was kind of nice to get to enjoy it now, even if I was thirty-two.

"Cams, listen to this though, not only does she have Nicco clambering for dates, she had some angsty-looking hottie at her door smoldering with sexiness when I arrived as well."

Cami was sorting through my closet and rummaging through the drawers in there that held all my under-things. Blushing a little at the thought of her seeing them all, I decided to let it go. I had several matching sets, and they always made me feel sexier than I did in general. At Nat's statement, she poked her head out, an eager look on her face.

"Oh, this I have to hear. Spill the tea, sis!"

"Um, I'm not sure I get that reference," I cringed.

"What! You've never seen RuPaul's Drag Show?"

Shaking my head, I hoped it wouldn't be a deal-breaker as I liked the friendship we were starting.

"Well, next time, we must watch it. It's *fabulous*. But besides that, it just means tell me about it already!" she laughed. "Who's this hottie that smolders? Hmm, tell me!" She had a very eager puppy dog look going on.

"Oh, well," I started, feeling nervous again, "he's my

kickboxing instructor, but there isn't anything between us other than mutual hate."

"You know they say there is a fine line between love and hate, and I find it's best to work it out in the bedroom," she purred.

"I'm just surprised you're not calling me a slut or angry at me since you both are friends with Nicco," I admitted.

"First, no slut-shaming here. Second, you're not in a committed relationship, so do your thing, girl! And third, whom am I to judge? I have two girlfriends and a boyfriend myself!" she laughed.

Her words took me by surprise. The non-judgment was refreshing after living in a world where people like my mother thrived. I was starting to see just how lacking the upper class were despite their bravado at being the best.

"You have three lovers?"

"Yep," she stated smugly, lounging back on my bed, a look of bliss on her face. "They all know about each other too."

"Wow, that sounds complicated."

"Not at all. We're open and communicate with one another, and the sex is," she groaned, making an exaggerated moaning sound, "*fucking amazing*!"

We all broke out in laughter at her comment, but it did have me thinking about my own situation if things progressed with Nicco and Monroe. Maybe I could have them both? It was too out there of a concept to think about now.

"Nat, any men in your life?"

"Ha, you're funny! No, my ex was enough of a reason to stay away from a relationship. Sorry, Cams."

"Not hurting my feelings. My brother is a jackass. Loren met him the other night as well. She can contest too."

"Oh, shit, I forgot he's your ex."

"Unfortunately. Now, I have my fuck buddies I use when I have the need, and I'm good with that. Lily is my main focus."

"That's your daughter, right?"

"Yeah, she's seven and already thinks she knows everything."

"She's the best, despite having my dumbass brother as a father."

"Yeah, *there* is that."

"So, I think I have an outfit!" Cami clapped from the closet. She'd gotten back up and resumed her rummaging when Nat told us about her asshole ex. After having the unfortunate pleasure of meeting him, I was glad she wasn't with him any longer.

By the time the girls were done with my hair and makeup, I barely recognized myself. I was dressed in a short black silk dress with lace along the bottom hem and the top. Cami had paired it with a short leather jacket she'd brought and some black booties I had.

Nat had paired it with large silver teardrop hoops, a silver bangle, and a long silver uneven chain that ran right between my breasts. Cami had picked out a very sexy black lingerie set as well that had me feeling all kinds of hot and needy. Nat had twisted up my hair in a messy bun I would never be able to pull off on my own.

Tendrils fell strategically around my face giving me an edgy but airy look. The makeup had my eyes standing out in a smokey cat eye and deep red lipstick. I was digging the look and felt nothing like myself. Not only did I feel sexy, but fearless. The woman in this outfit looked badass and like she could take on the world. Bottling that courage, I hugged the girls as I profusely thanked them both.

"I can't thank you ladies enough."

"Uh, yeah, you can. Well, first you don't need to thank us, but if you wanted to, that is, then just invite us over for a girl's night sometime. It would be fun."

"You know, that sounds like a blast. Yes, definitely," I found myself readily agreeing, not an ounce of apprehension in sight.

They both smiled wide, and I felt I'd made some actual girlfriends for once. We all walked down together after Nicco had texted he was here. They both made obscene comments as they walked past him, but he only shook his head, all his focus on me.

Nicco's eyes blazed with the heat of a thousand fires, and I reveled in it. The fear and anxiety I'd felt earlier today vanished, and I embraced the woman I was tonight. If a guy could look at me with so much heat it could melt the ice caps, then maybe I could believe in my sex appeal for a night. Feeling emboldened, I walked up to him, wrapped my hands around his neck, and pulled his lips to mine.

His hands cupped my ass as he pulled me into him, and I briefly forgot where I was. Nat and Cami's hoots and hollers brought me out of the sex haze I'd been pulled into.

"Damn, beautiful. You're reminding me of Luscious Loren from the first night. I can't wait to see what else this night brings if that's how it's starting."

Famous last words.

TWENTY-EIGHT

LOREN

We made it two steps before Nicco realized the outfit I wore wouldn't work on his motorcycle causing him to chase after Nat, promising to pay her double to give us a lift. She pretended to be put out by the request, the slight smile giving away her act.

"Ugh, I guess. You're so demanding, Nicco," Nat teased, rolling her eyes as she shoved him off.

"You're the best, Nat. Our chariot awaits, beautiful!"

Nicco swept out his arm in a dramatic fashion making everyone chuckle at his overzealousness. Even the doorman appeared amused by his gestures, and I felt relieved he didn't think I was a floozy from my earlier kiss fest in the foyer. The doorman nodded at me as Nicco wrapped his arm around me, and I returned it with a smile.

Nicco walked with me out the door, declaring to everyone I was his. An uncommon feeling filled me with his gesture. It was a combination of desired and cherished, and I realized once again, Brian never made me feel this way. Everything he did had a purpose, a precise deliberate intention to it. If he wasn't getting something in return, he wouldn't do it.

Cami waved bye as she continued in the other direction, pulling her jacket closed as she braced against the wind. As it swirled around us, too, my dress clung to my skin, and I held it down with my free hand. Instant gratitude filled me for Nat in giving us a ride. Nicco's motorcycle sounded exciting, but I needed to be wearing warmer, and well, more clothes in order to enjoy it.

Buckling up in the backseat, Nicco wrapped me in his arms as soon as we were both settled. The move was becoming so familiar, I started to worry I'd miss it when this was inevitably over. I wasn't deluded into thinking this had the potential to be something more... real. I was older, broken, and had nothing to offer in the future department for Nicco.

In the past, that would've terrified me and caused me not even to try to engage in this relationship. The freedom in understanding everything was temporary allowed me to jump in with both feet. I knew it would end. Everything did.

When the one thing meant to be forever dissolved into nothing, what value did anything else have? *None.* Understanding the future this way liberated me. If nothing mattered, nothing had consequences.

"You okay?"

"Hmm? Oh, yeah. Sorry, I'm just lost in my thoughts."

Nicco tipped my chin up, his grey eyes glimmered softly, and the blue seemed to sparkle more as he peered at me, drowning me in his essence. *I could get lost in these eyes.* They held warmth and hope with a tad bit of danger, pulling me into his domain with unspeakable promises. Slowly, he lowered his lips to mine and caressed them in a sensual kiss, effectively pulling me out of my thoughts.

"Beautiful," he breathed, pulling back, rubbing his thumb on my cheek. "Tonight, I want you to get out of your head. Just do what feels good. Let me be your guide, remember?"

Nodding, I stared into the comforting blue depths his eyes had become and hoped to discover the answers to the questions that plagued me. While I didn't find the magic solution making everything clear, I found a sense of absolution, allowing me to let go.

Tonight, I would drop the reins of pressures and societal rules that had held me back my entire life.

Tonight, I would embrace the woman I felt in these clothes and give in to the danger lurking in my soul.

Tonight, the mask would fall away, and I could emerge unrestrained to flirt with the darkness that marred my skin.

"So, what is this place exactly?" I was standing in a warehouse where people rushed around setting up. Nat had dropped us off thirty minutes earlier, but I wasn't quite sure what was going on, yet. Nicco had been busy directing people, and I'd been quietly following along. It wasn't boring, but I did feel out of my element. Everyone stared, and I started to feel self-conscious. Nicco turned to me, his eyes alight with mischief as his grin spread wide.

"This is an abandoned warehouse."

"Yeah, I gathered that much, smart ass," I quipped, rolling my eyes. Huh, I guess these were my sassy underpants.

"Ooh, I quite like the sass, beautiful. Say something else."

"Uh, it doesn't work that way. I can't just on-demand something. I'm not Netflix."

Nicco belted out a laugh, causing everyone in the vicinity to turn and stare more. Shrinking inward, I tried to be as inconspicuous as possible as I curled into his side.

"It seems you can, babe." He smirked. "But to answer your question, there will be a fight later, and I guess you can say I'm in charge of hosting it."

"Why do I feel you're being purposefully vague, Nicco?" I pulled back, crossing my arms, not liking this feeling of caginess between us.

"It's not... Okay, that's a lie. There are just some things about my family I haven't shared, and it's complicated, and I don't want you to run away before I can explain it properly. Can we table this discussion for another time and just enjoy the night?"

I thought over his words. This was our second date together, maybe third if you counted the first night as a date. We were still working up to all the get-to-know-you bits that I'd taken for granted as a teen dating someone she'd known her whole life. My job was also making this difficult. I could feel he was hiding something, and my natural tendency was to pull and find what was underneath the covers.

But this wasn't either of those situations. He didn't owe me anything. We had to work up to it. A feeling of excitement at the process of discovering things about him organically ran through me, and I nodded in understanding. Nicco relaxed, and I realized now how much he'd feared my response. I didn't want him to feel obligated. I wanted him to tell me because it was where our relationship was headed.

"So for tonight, just know that people might treat me differently, and I might have to check in from time to time on things. But, from this point forward, I am all yours."

He pulled me back into his arms, his hands possessive on my hips as they gripped me. His voice filled with desire, and I had to squeeze my legs together to stop from rubbing them. My pulse was racing, and it was like I could almost feel my blood zinging, ready to coat me in recklessness.

Stepping even closer, he pulled me completely into him, and I could feel his hard cock rub up against me. An involuntary moan escaped my lips as Nicco bent down, licking up my neck, nipping my earlobe.

"Seeing you come undone is the sexiest thing I've ever seen," he purred, effectively destroying my panties. My breath hitched as I waited for his following words. "Do you trust me?"

Shivers ran down my body, and words wouldn't come to me, nor did I think I'd be able to utter them. Nicco had encapsulated me with his lust, immobilizing me to the spot as I greedily basked in his smell, his touch, his carnal desire... him. Slowly, I nodded my head into his neck as a slight gasp left me.

"*Good.*"

He stepped back, and I instantly felt the loss of his presence. Nicco had the whole world around him, and I always felt brighter by association. He shone so brightly, it cast out my own shadows, allowing me to dance in the warmth of his safety. I hadn't understood that until this moment when he asked me, but I did. I trusted him, and that was monumental to me.

Draping his arm around my hip, his fingers flexed as he possessed me. Guiding me to an upper level, I noticed a guard type person standing at the stairs. In a move that had to be rehearsed, the large guy moved aside and allowed us entry. I observed him nod at Nicco in reverence, piquing my curiosity. Nicco carried on, not thinking anything of the behavior. However, the gesture had stuck out to me, causing me to falter.

When I didn't naturally drift with him, Nicco stopped and observed me trying to see if something was wrong. My facial expression must've seemed disconcerting because he was instantly in front of me, his swagger leaving as his concern for me shone through.

"If you're not comfortable with this, I can call Nat and have her take you home. I thought it would be fine, and I just wanted to see you so bad. I never want to push you, though, so if you're nervous or anything, you can tell me. This is about you, beautiful. Just say the word."

His hands cupped my cheeks, and his thumbs

stroked gently across them. It was soothing and loving. Shaking my head, I found the words I'd lacked before.

"No, that's not it. I just noticed how respected you were. I don't know if I've ever had people treat me the way everyone here does you. It was just one of those moments where I had an epiphany, and I didn't know how to think about it, I guess."

"Beautiful, I think people show you more respect than you know. Doris adores you and threatened to maim me if I hurt you. Nat and Cami would pick you over me in a heartbeat too. I think you're so used to helping everyone else, you don't see how many people are tripping over themselves just to talk to you."

Shaking my head, I couldn't process the words he said. It was ridiculous. That was nowhere near being true. Nicco stopped my movement before I could retort.

"How about we make a bet? If I can prove three people tonight look at you in awe, then you have to let me design a tattoo for you," he smoldered.

"And when they don't?" I bantered back, licking my lips.

"If they don't, then you can make me do something boring, and I won't be able to complain about it one bit," he teased.

Giggling, I couldn't help but nod as I started to plot what ridiculous thing I could take him to. His tattoo bad boy exterior would give the ladies who lunch a frightful start and would almost be worth it to see their reaction. The sad reality was Nicco outmatched any of those "desirable" bachelors they tried to set me up with. He was a good man and the real deal.

"Scared I'm going to make a run for it?" I joked when he showed me the booth, motioning for me to scoot in. His devilish smile made my pulse spike for the things it promised and how much I wanted them.

"Just you wait, beautiful. I think you're going to be glad to be on the inside real soon."

Leaving that cryptic statement alone for now, I took in more of the room. From above, we could see over the railing to a makeshift ring below. Fight night made sense now, and if I had to guess, this was an illegal event. Something about the illicit part of this situation excited me. I wasn't fearful of being arrested because I did trust Nicco, and he wouldn't bring me to something that would put me in a position to lose my job.

He leaned close, seeing what I was looking at. The railing was on my side of the booth, making it easier to see down. At first, it was what I thought he was referring to. It was a better vantage point to view the fights, at least. As he kissed my neck, I was happy my hair was up, allowing him to leave trails of kisses in his wake. I could get used to this adoration he bestowed on me. It felt nice to be desired.

The light touches he kept dropping to my skin were driving me wild. I almost wanted him to stop, but I couldn't bring myself to utter the words. They were just enough to build the heat of desire, yet not enough to satisfy. The thought of him stopping altogether was more tragic, though, so I let him tease me with his soft kisses and touches as I offered my neck to him.

A waitress stopped by the table, and my hackles went up when she put her fake nails on Nicco's shoulder. To his benefit, he leaned away from her and wrapped me in his embrace. The glare she tossed me would kill if her eyes were laser beams. When she asked me in her sickly sweet voice what I wanted, I shook my head no. I knew a mean girl when I saw one. Odds were she'd spit in my drink, or worse, spike it. Neither option sounded fun or part of the reckless debauchery I wanted to partake in.

"You didn't want anything?"

"More like I didn't want the loogie or date rape drug she was sure to put into it," I shrugged.

Nicco looked astonished for a second before laughter rang out of him so hard, he couldn't breathe. I didn't understand what was particularly funny, but at least he didn't tell me she wouldn't. I hated when guys acted clueless about other girls' intentions and then defended the behavior of the mean girl. It only perpetuated it and made the one who spoke up feel unheard. I wasn't a fan of the whole thing, so as long as he didn't come back with "she would never", I wouldn't have to punch him in the junk.

"Loren, I live for the things that come out of your mouth. I'm constantly surprised and amazed at your brilliance."

Okay, so that wasn't what I expected him to say at all. Quizzically, I tilted my head, trying to understand the point he was getting at and, more importantly, why he laughed. When I couldn't come up with a rationale that fit, I gave in and asked him.

"Why did you laugh then?"

"Because she *so* would do that, and I've never heard a woman call another one out like that before. It struck me as funny." He shrugged, pure mischief on his face. "She's actually the absolute worst person and never takes no for an answer. I've often worried about my own drinks. I'll get her switched because I want us to have fun and not worry about jealous bitches."

Smiling wide, I threw my arms around his neck and squeezed tight. It had been purely instinctual, and I was discovering with Nicco how natural it felt to be myself. I didn't doubt or second guess. It was odd and different, but it felt right.

"What was that for?"

"Just wanted to say thanks for believing me, and, I don't know, it felt right."

"Well, you can hug me anytime, beautiful," he purred into my hair, and the heat started to sizzle again. Pulling back a smidge, I stared into his eyes as we held the embrace. A million promises swam in his depths, and I felt seen by him.

A glass slammed down on the table and sloshed over onto me. The noise and liquid caused us to jump as we took in the pissed-off waitress staring daggers into me. Old me would've started to apologize immediately, feeling I must've done something to offend her. Emboldened me had a different idea altogether.

My cheeks blazed red with outrage at her entitlement, her belief she deserved Nicco despite his non-interest in her. It was the Barbie wannabe from Windy City version 2.0, and I was sick of being treated inferior. Narrowing my eyes at her, I zeroed in on her face and imagined I could shoot fire from them, burning her to a crisp.

Unfortunately, or perhaps, fortunately, before I could say or do anything, Nicco motioned, and in a flash, the bitchy waitress was pulled away as she screamed profanities. I had to give it to her, she fought against a guy twice her size and didn't let up. I wanted to feel bad for her, but she didn't have to be rude. I'd done nothing personally to her, and yet she had zeroed in on me from minute one because I was with Nicco.

Sorry, but if he wanted to be with you, sweets, he would be. Get over yourself and your fake boobs.

There was a small part of me that didn't like how I was feeling. Her behavior was rude, but I didn't have to belittle her. Was I any better by demeaning her or her body parts? Shame sat heavy in me, and while I knew it was an ingrained belief to feel bad for wanting to stand up for myself, the quicksand was strong, and I sank. For a moment, though, I had felt pretty bitchtastic.

Trying to focus on that and not the shame, I calmed my racing thoughts and felt better after my self-chastise. The patriarchy wanted us all to hate one another, but screw that. We got nowhere as women by knocking each other down. Even the bitchy waitress deserved some kindness. If I didn't show her, who would?

Feeling self-empowered, I held my head high as I watched the bottom of the warehouse begin to fill up. Nicco had apparently gotten up during my inner turmoil and returned with some paper towels and two drinks, non-spit-filled ones.

"Thanks, Nicco."

"You're welcome, beautiful."

Comfortably leaning back into his arms, we sat and

watched the people milling about and the energy the crowd infused into the space. Only a select few joined up top, and I began to understand the importance of this section. Nicco kept a light graze over my body in different places, causally leaving me breathless as we sipped our drinks.

I was a panting mess when I recognized a person below who'd just walked in. Shock hit me first, not expecting to see him in this setting, except when Nicco leaned over and pointed him out, anger built within me at what he was implying.

"There's Crash. He's a badass fighter and often brings in a lot of money for his matches."

Twisting my head, our faces only centimeters apart, I zeroed in on Nicco's eyes. "There's no fucking way he's fighting tonight!"

Nicco blinked, taking in my pissed-off expression, unsure how to respond to my declaration. Crossing my arms, I glared at him to make sure he understood.

"I mean it, Nicco. He *can't*. If I mean anything to you, stop it. *Please*."

My voice broke a little on the plea, but I think it was what swayed him to take me seriously. He slowly nodded his head and waved for someone to come over. He whispered into the man's ear before sending him off to hopefully stop Wells from getting killed.

"Okay, Loren. I asked Beau to gather Crash. What don't I know?"

Ascertaining he trusted me and didn't doubt my demand, I exhaled, some of the anger leaving me. "He was attacked last night and had at least a couple of broken ribs, a concussion, and several bruises and cuts. If he fought again, he'd probably puncture a lung and die. He *can't* fight, Nicco. *He just can't.*"

As I'd been detailing this out to Nicco, Wells had been delivered to the table, hearing my plea.

"Well, well, *kitten*. It seems someone has been keeping *secrets*."

Glaring at the asshole whose life I was attempting to save, I almost wanted to take it back and let him suffer for being such an insufferable ass. Nicco stepped in, stopping Wells and me before we could throw any barbs.

"Crash, just the man I've been trying to gain an audience with for months now. Please, have a seat. It seems we have something to discuss."

Wells sent me a death glare as he gingerly sat across from us, only proving my point.

"Now, where would you like to start?" Nicco questioned. His voice had this whole new level of authority, and while it wasn't the right time to feel aroused, I couldn't help the slow buildup he'd been doing the past hour to my body. Warring emotions filled me as I attempted to focus. Logically, I knew I needed to take this seriously and maintain my guard around the surly asshole. Yet, Nicco's hand kept up an insistent movement as he rubbed up and down my leg while he spoke. Unabashedly, I found myself spreading wider, tempting him to touch me where I wanted him to.

"There's nothing to discuss. Whatever kitten here told you, is a lie," spat Wells.

"Hmm, is that so? Well, okay then, there's an easy way to prove this. Let's get Beau back here and let him hit you in the stomach, and if you stay standing, then I guess beautiful was mistaken. Fair?"

Wells swallowed but knew he couldn't deny it, so he nodded. I saw him flick his eyes to me before he stood up, derision heavy in them. Sorry, asshole, I tried to save you, but you threw a temper tantrum. It was time you made your voice heard. Admitting your weakness was the strongest thing you could do. I just didn't know if Wells was strong enough.

TWENTY-NINE

WELLS

What the hell was my kitten doing here? In *this* place of all places? And with *him*? Fury pumped through me as I watched him paw at her. I wasn't sure which made me angrier. The fighting ring boss with his hands all over her or the fact she ratted me out? Either way, I couldn't let her know I had an opinion. Keeping my distance from her was the best course of action, even if I wanted to take her away from here as fast as I could hobble out of here.

I glared at her from across the table, attempting to burn her to the spot with my rage. However, her little gasps of air had me curious about what his hand was doing below, which infuriated me even more. I didn't want to be interested. I didn't want to care. And I didn't want to be jealous right now.

But I fucking was.

She hid it well, but after our tête-a-tête last week, I had intimate knowledge. I knew what she looked like when aroused, how her moans sounded in the throes of passion. And right now, her pupils were blown, and she was biting her lip to stop her exhales. Kitten's shifts reinforced her need to come. She was on the brink, and something about it sparked my own arousal, and I hated everything about it.

Pulling my focus from the sex kitten, I felt my anger burning in me, using it to push me through this next part. I *had* to convince the boss I could fight. It was a lie, and my kitten knew it, but I needed the money. More than needed to be exact, not knowing which reason was more dire at this point. The threat from the goons who did this to me in the first place, or the debt I had to contend with.

Either way, I was screwed, and not in a good way. I didn't know which option was better or worse, honestly. But I needed to fight. It was the only solution on the table currently.

Fueling my hatred, I tossed words back at them, "There's *nothing* to discuss. Whatever *kitten* here told you is a *lie*."

Using her name in front of him grated me, but I needed distance. I'd already fallen in too deep with her, and if I could do one thing right, it was to shield her from my shit.

"Hmm, is that so?" His hand tapped on the table in a rhythm as he regarded me. "Well, okay then, there's an easy way to prove this. Let's get Beau back here and let him hit you in the stomach, and if you stay standing, then I guess beautiful was mistaken. Fair?"

Fuck, he was more astute than I gave him credit for, especially if he trusted the Goddess next to him enough to listen to her concerns. I caught kitten's eyes and saw fear for me there, but I couldn't allow myself to ponder how it made me feel. Besides, nothing could be done now. I had to see this through. It was the only way. Nodding to Nicco, I stood as the burly bodyguard approached the table. Bracing myself for the punch, I prayed I didn't pass out or throw up from the pain.

Clenching my fists, I watched as Beau pulled back, ready to strike. When I didn't feel pain a few minutes later, I realized my eyes had closed. When I opened them, I found *her* standing in front of me. My body relaxed at the sight of her, but it had been a mistake. I wasn't free or safe. It was an illusion.

"You don't deserve my kindness, but I can't let you fight, no matter how much of an asshole," she paused, and I knew the last part would hurt the worst, "or *coward* you are."

They stung and struck me down to my core because they were true. I'd become caught in the landfill of her eyes. So many emotions warred with one another there, and I couldn't escape them. My focus on anything else in the room vanished, which caused me not to notice her move a hand and poke me in the ribs, the broken ones. Wincing, I doubled over in pain at her jab, and I knew I'd shown my hand.

Fucking hell—kitten just revealed her claws. If it hadn't been at my expense, I might've been proud.

"Have a seat, *Crash*. It seems we have something to discuss."

She was seated back in the booth, so when I straightened, I wobbled over to the spot I'd been in earlier. Carefully, I lowered myself down, continuing to only confirm her claim. I didn't care anymore. I'd already been found out, might as well be careful. My stubborn asshole tendencies did have limits.

"Care to explain why you were going to fight when you're clearly injured?" Nicco's tone had a hardness to it, and I feared I might've stepped in a big pile of shit with my duplicity. I couldn't afford to lose fighting here. It was the one thing keeping my head above water, giving me the outlet I needed to let my rage out.

"I guess I thought I could handle it." I shrugged one shoulder. "I was feeling better earlier, but obviously, I'm not. *I apologize,*" gritting the last part.

"While that all sounds lovely, I don't believe it for a minute. You were either going to pump yourself full with enough cortisone not to feel anything for the next hour or injure yourself to the point of death."

Exhaling, I nodded, acquiescing to my loss. It was the first one here, yet it felt more significant despite not being one of strength. A drink was delivered a few seconds later, and I downed it, my throat parched from all the bullshit I'd been spewing apparently.

"Before I blacklist you from ever fighting here again, perhaps you could enlighten me more about how you accrued these injuries and why it was so important to fight tonight," he regarded me, a calculating look crossing his face. "Because I don't take you as stupid. I've watched you fight numerous times, so there has to be a reason you were willing to risk your life tonight."

Nicco sat back, his arm going around *my* kitten, and I held back the urge to slap it off. She melted into him, but I could make out the worry on her face. Kitten bit her lip again, but this time from anxiety as she glanced back and forth between us, her concern climbing as the silence dragged out. I could almost feel her pleading with me to be honest with him. I debated it in my head. There was no way I would've shared anything with him prior to tonight.

But something about kitten trusting this guy made me reconsider. My sad eyed girl was a lot of things, but she wasn't a fool. Staring her down, I weighed my options as I held her gaze, finding some stability there. Trust was a fickle bitch in my life, and I'd only ever been able to trust Monroe. For some reason, it seemed like Loren kept falling into the trust column too, despite our tumultuous interactions.

It scared the hell out of me, but sad eyes kept showing up. She kept being there around every corner I turned, and sooner or later, I knew we would detonate. *Again*. The pull of that collision was like a promise on my lips, making me miss the way hers had fit mine in decadent perfection. It would most likely end terribly, and I needed to keep my distance for her sake, but each day got a little more complicated, and I wondered how long until I fell under her spell completely. Relinquishing the pull, I started talking.

"Last night, I was approached by Delgado and his enforcers," I said quietly, "and they *sent* me a message."

The mention of Delgado had Nicco's jaw tightening, and I knew he understood what I was saying.

"Understood. I will set up a meeting with Mas. I think it might be something he'd been interested in, and perhaps, we could help one another with the *problem*."

Unexpected relief washed through me, and my trust in the beautiful woman next to him appeared to have been a solid decision for once. Accepting his answer, I started to stand, assuming I was dismissed. His voice halted my movements causing me to stay bent half in the bench and half out of it.

"Stay. Any friend of beautiful's is welcome."

"I wouldn't say we're friends, more like frenemies," she grumbled, but not with her usual ire toward me.

Nicco smirked at her, fawning at every little thing she did as if he couldn't wait to see what she did next. I hated him a little but couldn't deny his response to her. She was a drug you never wanted to quit.

"How are you," he started, kissing her knuckles as he spoke, "frenemies with a record breaking, undefeated, amateur fighter, beautiful?"

Way to go ahead and spill all my secrets, jackass!

His comment had her tilting her head toward me, her mouth agape in surprise. She sat up, closing her mouth and pulling her shoulders back. It was her readying stance for our verbal sparring. *Guess I would still get to spar tonight after all*, I mused. Sadly, I had to admit the jabs with sad eyes, *my kitten*, were more fulfilling. She smirked, and I knew she was about to toss me a doozy.

"Well, he can't be too record breaking if I was able to knee him in the nuts," she proudly proclaimed.

Nicco roared with laughter, and I had to admit her statement was cute. Lifting a corner of my lips, I smirked back at her bravado.

"Oh, kitten, you wouldn't stand a chance if I was fighting you."

I hadn't meant to purr it, especially with the boss sitting there, but it indeed had come out full of lust and need. The heat developing between us had to be palpable by now, her breath caught, making her chest rise with each inhale. Nicco nuzzled her neck at the sound of her gasps and started to kiss down her shoulder. Shifting my cock, I tried to look anywhere else, but her eyes were locked on mine, and I couldn't look away.

This was pure torture. Pure. Fucking. Torture.

Deciding if I wasn't fighting, I didn't have to sit here in pain as my cock grew tight against my boxers. I might as well head home and get some sleep. Rest was the only thing that would heal my physical wounds now. The internal ones, well, that was a different story.

"Thank you for the offer to stay," I gritted, "but I think it will be harder to sit here and watch… the fights and," I stumbled, "not fight in them. I'll leave you two and wait to hear from you."

Nicco barely acknowledged me, only nodding at me, though it could've just been him licking her neck. It was hard to say. He did raise a finger, and Beau was next to us in a flash. He pulled away from the now blushing kitten and addressed me.

"Beau will walk you out to make sure you don't have any more *encounters*."

Exhaling in relief, I was thankful despite my scowl. Showing it would be suicide, but I was relieved beyond measure I didn't have to fight in this condition. There would be consequences, and they were going to be hell to pay. Hopefully, I would figure something out before they put me in a grave.

Beau quietly nodded at the command, and I headed for the stairs, ready to get the hell out of this place. I stopped before I descended, feeling the pull of her eyes on me. Kitten was watching, and I couldn't place the emotion shown on her face as she did. Eventually, Nicco said something to her, and she turned to him, breaking our connection.

It felt as if part of my soul stayed in the VIP area as I continued down the stairs. With each clang of my boots on the metal, it was a reminder of how unfair life had been for me. I couldn't let myself be deluded by things like hope and love. It would only be a recipe for heartbreak and disappointment. I'd lived a lifetime of those already.

The cold air hit me as we walked out the back door. Fortunately, we'd managed to avoid any Delgados in attendance, and I'd made it safely outside. Heading to the nearest train station, I shuffled my way there, each step harder than the last. The ride home was quiet since most people didn't venture out this late on this side of town.

I'd once lived in a condo like Monroe's in the center of the city. Now, I lived way out of town on a lot that was private and my own. The train only went so far and then the beat up junker was my chariot. It was undependable at best, unless stalling and breaking down were the key aspects you wanted. I didn't trust it to take me further than a few miles.

The house came into view, and the relief I felt was tangible. The house was the last thing I had left, but it was mine. It wasn't much, but I'd been slowly repairing it, one room at a time. The outside resembled an aban-doned house on good days, but I found it kept people away, adding to the appeal for me. It would be the last thing I'd remodel for that reason.

The dogs were excited to see me as I entered, their whines and pants greeting me in a cacophony of noises. Training and breeding dogs had become a passion of mine. One of my better foster families had an Alaskan Husky, and I fell in love with the breed. They were big and mighty, as well as good companions. As a small boy, it was something I was missing. When I'd become successful in my career, I fulfilled that boyish dream of getting my first dog.

Koda was loveable and high energy, needing proper training. I dove headfirst into everything I could find on the subject. It was one of those weird things I found I'd been surprisingly good at, just like I had with stock markets. After a month of working with Koda, the breeder had been impressed with the progress and asked me to join their training program for their dogs.

Underdogs Farm wasn't a puppy mill but bred and trained various breeds for professions such as police dogs, therapy dogs, search and rescue dogs, and even seeing-eye dogs. Huskies weren't the typical breed due to their jovial nature and high energy, but they could be brilliant assets with formal training in certain fields. It had started out as only a few hours on the weekend, and I would take Koda so he could visit his family and run out his energy on their farm.

Soon, I found myself with Nova, and that was when I started looking for a place I could live with two dogs.

The condo wasn't ideal with its limited space and neighbors complaining of the barking. I found this property and had just moved in when the shit hit the fan with my job. All my assets were seized outside my house and bike, and that was only because they'd been put in a different name—Monroe Miller.

Now, I trained dogs at my home, taking them for a few months before sending them on to be ready for their position. There were currently four dogs in the house, two of which would leave soon. It got a little crazy at times, but they kept the loneliness away and ebbed the depression. Dogs didn't care how successful you were, they just loved you. They were the purest form of the emotion, and I could easily give them my best because they deserved it.

"Here, Koda, Nova. Let's go outside. Ghost, Loki, you too. Come on."

They all skidded around me as they rushed for the door. Letting them do their business, I stared out at the landscape around me. The stars shone brighter here, and I settled into the safety of being home. The night sky was peaceful, the air quiet with only the sounds of the wildlife around us. Once the dogs were done, I followed them inside and filled their bowls with food. It was one of the mindless tasks I was in the habit of doing. I left them to eat and heated something in the microwave.

It was shit, but when I'd barely eaten anything all day, it was practically gourmet. The drone of the microwave became white noise as I leaned against the sink. I could get lost staring at walls in this place, my thoughts safe to wander. When it beeped, I jumped, pulling the hot plate from the device. Flipping on my TV, I found myself unable to focus on anything that played. Leaving it on a movie I'd seen a million times, I shoveled the cardboard food into my mouth as my thoughts circulated to Loren, my sad eyed girl, *my kitten.*

I was only half a man these days. I wasn't good for her at all. She deserved a good guy like Monroe. Yet, even with all of these solid arguments in my head on why it was a horrible idea and how someone like me didn't deserve her, I couldn't stop obsessing over her. It was clearly an obsession now. Her essence consumed me —her smell, the sounds she made, the way her eyes lit up, the corner of her mouth, the taste of her on my fingers.

A car pulled up, the sound of the crunch of gravel pricking mine and the dog's ears. Their eyes lasered on the door as we waited to see who it would be. The door shutting had me moving to the window to peek out at my guest. Only two people knew I lived here, so I wondered if I'd been followed after all.

Only one set of feet on the gravel had me exhaling, and when he came into view, I fully relaxed. Heading to the door, I opened it before he got there, leaning in the door frame as I waited.

"Hey," his kind voice rolled over me, easing away some of my hard edges the way he always had.

"Two nights in a row? This is a record. Especially when I hadn't seen you for six months."

My words came out more growly than I intended, and I saw the blush heat his cheeks. Fuck, I hadn't meant to embarrass him, but like usual, I was constantly fucking up relationships, especially the important ones.

"I just wanted to check on you, Wells. Is that a crime? And you know why we didn't talk for six months. That hasn't changed, but I'm not going to let you suffer just because you can't pull your head out of your ass."

Monroe's huff of outrage had my balls tightening, and I had to grit my jaw to not pull him toward me and kiss him into submission.

We'd fooled around with one another when we were teens living in a group home together. Limited access to girls, hormones, and sexual curiosity led to our relationship becoming more than just friends. Before he was married, we would hook up when we were both single. It had been casual and purely physical, or at least I had assumed it was. When he met Brittni, jealousy coursed through me like a roaring train, and I'd unconsciously pulled away over the years. One night, I couldn't take it anymore, and I reached out. It had been two years since I'd seen him at that point.

It was nice at first. I got to properly meet Levi and be part of Monroe's life again. We easily fell back into our friendship, and it felt like no time had passed. When things became more complicated for me at work, I snapped, unable to take the tension, and I kissed him. Which unfortunately had been the worst timing because Brittni walked in right as I did. I felt guilty when I found out she wanted a divorce, even though Monroe told me it'd been coming for a while. Yet, she used it as her reason for filing to avoid owning up to her own infidelity, which he'd already discovered. That kiss had set so many things on a collision course with no survivors.

Stepping back, I let him in. Needing some space between us, I walked over to the fridge and grabbed two beers. They were the cheap kind because I couldn't afford anything else, but they were still beer. Offering him one, he sighed at my silence but accepted it, clinking the heads together.

Retreating to the couch and TV, I silently sat as I stared at it, hoping he would drop whatever he'd come here to say. I couldn't confront my feelings, not tonight, not anytime soon. The one time I had, it had led to his divorce and my subsequent firing.

Bad things happened when I tried to be happy, and I wouldn't ruin his life anymore. I know the bitch was waiting for a chance to use his bisexuality as a weapon against him to either gain more child support or full custody of Levi. I wouldn't do that to him. I wouldn't be the grenade that blew up his life. If I had to suffer in silence, I would because it at least kept him in my life.

Embracing the silence, I'd become acquainted with, I prayed to whatever God would listen that we wouldn't have this conversation. Not tonight when I already felt as if my skin was inside out with how raw I felt. We sat there sipping our beers, neither of us watching the TV as a million words hung in the air between us. Once he finished, he set his bottle down on the end table, a look of purpose on his face when he turned to me, causing my stomach to drop.

"If you don't want to talk, fine. I just wanted to let you know I'm going on a date tomorrow. With Loren, the woman from this morning. I thought you should know. I thought… never mind. It doesn't matter. I just felt I should be honest. Hiding our feelings only ever leads to disaster."

Monroe stared at me for five minutes waiting for me to say something, do something. I know because I watched the clock above the TV the whole time, refusing to respond. How could I? The one girl I'd liked in forever and the one person who'd always accepted me were going on a date. It was perfect, they were perfect, and I wanted them to be happy. I could give them that. I could.

After those five minutes, he sighed heavily before getting up and walking to the door. Quietly, almost like a whisper on the wind, he uttered the words that would break me. "I love you, too," and walked out the door, closing it just as silently. The house felt emptier, the air stale as I continued to glare at the clock, cursing it for all the wrongs in my life. The dogs had even remained subdued, sensing the intensity.

The closing of his car door felt like a gunshot as it pierced my heart with the words that had landed there. A single tear rolled down my cheek as I let him walk away from me.

It was better this way. They would be happier without me. *They would.*

I wasn't sure who I was trying to convince anymore.

THIRTY

SAX

The clinking sound of the keys as I tossed them into the air acted as a meditative trance. I was propped up against the wall near the garage and had fallen into my thoughts. The motion of the toss, catch, toss soothed away some of my edges as I waited for Atticus. I'd been contemplating his retreat into the office after lunch. It wasn't an unaccustomed event, but this felt different, and I attributed it to our impromptu lunch guests.

I knew Atticus as well as I knew myself, maybe even better. It'd been my job, after all, as his personal guard for years. I'd learned to anticipate his needs before he even knew what he needed. It was a reflex at this point, even if technically, it was no longer my job now, since I was number two. Some habits were harder to quit than others.

My thoughts drifted to our magnetic lunch companion and how different she appeared outside the office setting. I supposed it made sense. You had a persona to uphold in the mafia, but it faded away when you were with people you trusted. Sadly, only a few people fell into that category nowadays.

Initially, I'd been enamored with her for her looks. She had a delicateness about her that craved my rough hands on her. The things I could do to her drove me wild at night as I thought about it. Imagining her fair skin and dark hair spread out on my black sheets had me hard in minutes. Add in the red lipstick she wore the night at the club, and I couldn't wait to see it wrapped around my cock as I fisted her long locks. The images haunted me, and no matter how much I'd tried to get them out of my head, I couldn't.

Even when I had some busty blonde on her knees, pounding into her the other night, the only person I could see was her—Loren. I ended up having to close my eyes and picture the scenarios I'd been beating myself off to in order to cum. The blonde tried to kiss me after, and a rage unlike any other filled me, and I had to stop myself from slapping her for daring it. I didn't hit women, but at that moment, I almost had.

That sobering fact left me dazed and unsure of what the hell was happening. Since the day I figured out what my cock was and how to use it, I'd been getting it wet by a new chick as often as I wanted. Pussy was easy to get when you were in the family, and I'd never had to try before. Spitfire had turned everything on its head and made me question everything.

I had no clue what any of it meant, and it was something I wasn't accustomed to. My role was to know every threat, enemy, and risk for any situation. This one had me faltering, and I had a feeling I wasn't the only one under her spell. The trouble was, Mas wasn't one to admit it. He would run from this, and it was my job to stop him from fucking it up. Yet, this situation had me questioning whether or not I wanted him to.

The selfish part of me wanted him to run, to avoid it, and leave her just for me. The part that was his friend knew it was a shitty thing to do. Besides, it wasn't the first time we'd shared a girl between us. Spitfire was just the first to make me want to keep her to myself. It was such a novel concept I didn't know what it even meant for myself. Atticus finally emerged from the elevator, breaking me from my thoughts.

"Everything good?"

"Affirmative. Just an issue to sort."

"Does this issue have a name perchance?" I teased. Evasive Atticus was putting me on edge, making me anxious. This wasn't how we were with one another, and I didn't like this new development.

Mas looked over and sighed, hopefully admitting to himself he couldn't hide this from me. He nodded and slipped into the car. Joining him in the back, I waited him out until he was ready to speak. I'd learned years ago that information was easier to gather if it was his choice. He expected me to pester him like his father always had, but waiting always had him spilling with little effort.

"I can't get involved with her. It's too dangerous, and Immy likes her. I can't risk that. *I won't.*"

Nodding because everything he said was true, I just didn't know if it mattered in the end. We were on a crash course set straight for her, even if he didn't acknowledge it. I wasn't sure how it would happen, only that I saw the eventual crossing of paths and was already weighing the risks and casualties likely to occur.

We were at war whether we acknowledged it or not. This turf war with Delgado wasn't over, and escalation was a guarantee. The likelihood of everyone surviving was slim. That was a fact and necessary reality of this life. When you accepted your inevitable death, it no longer carried power over you, or worse, fear. Hard to fear something you'd looked in the eyes and said, 'do your worst' to.

Loren and Immy were the kinds of people you dreamed of better things for. Until the incident, it had seemed like a probable future for our princess. But Immy had seen horrors now that most grown men never witnessed. That left a mark, a scar. She would be irrevocably changed. Time would tell just how much.

Hopefully, with the help of Mrs. Carter, it wasn't such a long shot anymore. Since we'd left the plaza, Immy had been on her phone texting, a grin from ear to ear. I didn't even care at the moment it was from a boy because it'd been so long since I'd seen her smile. I wanted to bask in its presence as long as possible. Mas evidently felt the same as he'd kept his comments to himself in her vicinity, but as soon as she'd gone, he gave me the *look*. The "I want everything there is to know about that kid, ASAP" one.

While he'd been hiding, more like sulking, in his office, I'd gotten to work. It had been easy to hack into the center's records. Being a not-for-profit, they had minimal security in place, the assumption being no one would want their info. *Wrong*. Information in any form was valuable and should be protected as such. I almost had the heart to install it for them. Almost.

"Run me through what you found."

Not even hesitating, I rolled off the info I'd uncovered.

"Jude Franklin, 17, currently resides in foster care with Sarah and John Edgar. Biological mother was Hannah Franklin. She died at age 32, killed in a drug-related shooting around five years ago. It was believed to be gang-related. Biological father, Clinton Franklin, also 32 at his *supposed* death. Whereabouts are unknown, but he was believed to have been with her. Several bodies were unidentifiable, and it is assumed he's one."

I took a moment for him to digest that info and then continued with what I knew about the boy. Atticus sat stoically, an unreadable expression on his face.

"Only other family member is an older brother, Cameron Franklin, age 20. Since he left the system at 18, there hasn't been much info on him. They were reported as close growing up and lived on the streets for almost a year before CPS found them. A teacher noticed them wearing the same clothing multiple days in a row, not having warm outfits during winter, and caught them stealing food. Jude is a smart kid. Mostly A's in all of his studies, and he is interested in photography and art design. No after-school clubs, but that seems more due to his living situation. He's now at the center and has been entering some art competitions to earn scholarships. He stays out of trouble and follows the rules," I paused, debating if I should offer my two cents. "I kind of like the kid."

Atticus watched me, assessing my features, but only nodded in response. For once, I had no clue what he was thinking. His emotions were on lockdown, and nothing was emitting from him, not even around me. This was so unlike him or our relationship. Hurt bubbled up in me, with a feeling of being left behind and tossed aside along with it. We'd been this duo for so long, to feel on the outside of it pierced me deeply.

I considered confronting him, but as soon as I began to open my mouth and challenge him, we pulled to a stop. Blinking because we were nowhere near the warehouse yet, I was surprised to find us at a high-rise apartment building in an up-and-coming part of town. Again, before I could ask what this was about, the door opened. My skin prickled, and my veins felt as hot as lava as I swallowed the pain of betrayal coursing through me.

This was not okay. He was leaving me out, and feelings aside, it broke family protocol. While we'd never separated our friendship and mafia relationship before, I could push my feelings aside as his friend. Cutting me out as his number two was a completely different story. This act of defiance could get people killed.

A skinny, plastic and basic bitch scooted into the car, and I wanted to explode. She greeted Mas with two kisses on his cheeks, and I already hated her. Just another pretentious basic bitch. Fortunately, outside Mas, I was known for my quiet, stoic nature, so I withdrew and ignored them both.

So this was his plan to ignore his attraction to Loren? It was ignorant, and if he'd asked me, I would've told him that.

The oddity of him shutting me out grated on me, and I realized how much I didn't like it. We worked because we had no secrets between us. Right now, it felt as if the most grievous sin had been committed. It wouldn't make sense to anyone else, but in our world it did, and that was what mattered.

Fury pumped hard through my veins by the time we pulled up to the warehouse. Each time the pretentious woman giggled, it was a knife slicing through my heart. She was taking the liberty to maw at him, and worse, he allowed her. I didn't know this version of Mas, and I didn't like it. Hardening my features, I locked everything away and went into guard mode.

Before the car came to a complete stop, I opened my door and headed for the back entrance of the warehouse. Sweeping the area, I spotted our guys. They checked in with me and confirmed the all-clear through nods. Greeting the doorman, I entered the warehouse all on my own for the first time in our thirty-year friendship. People turned to look at my entrance expecting to see Mas as well, but as I moved past, they had to glance further back to find him with the blonde wrapped around his arm. I wanted to regurgitate our lunch all over her dress. It would be an improvement.

Bypassing the bullshit down here, I moved to the top floor. I wanted to check in with Nicco while Mas paraded his floozy around for the night. My boots pounded up the stairs with each step, my anger exploding through my feet. Beau took one look at my face and rapidly moved to the side to let me pass. I typically had an asshole exterior, I wouldn't deny that. But as much as I'd wanted to lock it away, I knew my emotions were displayed for all to see tonight. The ruminating thoughts and betrayal I felt fueling them.

I spotted Nicco in a booth and headed there. He was talking with someone, and I found his behavior odd. It was the most gregarious I'd seen him at these fights. Nicco typically looked miserable, counting down the time until he could leave. Despite his 'fun guy' exterior, I could always read his discomfort. We'd grown up together as well, and while I wasn't as close to him as Mas, he was a close second.

Before I could find out who he was entertaining, I was intercepted by Mandy. She'd been my most recent fuck out of desperation, and I'd immediately regretted it.

"Sax, baby, I'm so glad you're here. Nicco's with some *slut*, and he made me go downstairs. I snuck back up, though. Please, you've got to talk some sense into him. She's no good for him. Please, baby, can you?"

She continued talking, and all I wanted was for her to shut the fuck up. Her voice grated on me, and I wanted away from the annoying blonde slut looking for someone to save her. Get a clue, ladies. No one was saving you *here*. If anything, you should run fast in the other direction. We were mafia men to our core and few respected women.

Staring down at her, I glared, not responding to her asinine request. Eventually, she stomped off in a huff, and Beau directed her where she belonged. Apparently, that part of her complaint had been factual, and I, for one, was grateful she wouldn't be buzzing around me all night. Deciding a drink was in order, I switched directions and placed my arms on the bar top.

"Usual?" one of the bartenders asked at my appearance, knowing not to make me wait. Nodding my answer, I waited as they poured my Jack and Coke. As I stood there, I succumbed to the job demands and completed a perimeter check with my eyes, locating all my guys. They conveyed back when they spotted me, and I felt confident things were secure at least. From my vantage point at the bar, I could partially make out the companion Nicco had with him.

Her head was turned, allowing me only a side profile. The woman appeared classy and sophisticated, distractedly at odds with an underground fighting ring. The pair held heated looks as they talked, and I could even feel the simmer from here. Damn, Nicco had found himself a real treasure. I watched them unapologetically as he began to trail kisses down her neck, leaving licks as he went. I wasn't the only one watching the two, either, as every eye up on the top level zeroed in on their booth.

When a gasp left her ruby lips, I found myself growing hard from the show they were giving me. Her head fell back, and I'd assumed his hand was making magic happen below. Nicco had lifted his head and turned to talk to someone who'd walked up to the table, and yet, she still appeared in bliss. Her eyes were closed, her head tossed back on the seat as he continued his ministrations. Something about her felt familiar, and I wanted a closer look. Like a magnet pulling me, my feet started for their booth before I even realized it.

As I approached, the person talking to Nicco must've

asked her a question, or perhaps she felt my energy nearing hers. One moment she was in the throes of passion, not giving a damn who saw as she chased an orgasm, and the next, her eyes opened and locked on *me*. My breath caught in my throat as her chocolate eyes seared into me, her mouth parted in a silent shout of pleasure.

My cock was rock hard now, and I would be remiss to admit that in that exact moment, thoughts of protecting the family, Mas, or even Immy were far from my mind. Everything in me centered on her and the energy coursing between us, intertwining our souls in a dance. Spitfire held my gaze as she came down from her high, her body flushing red from the climax, goosebumps erupting over her skin.

Almost as if I floated there, I found myself at the booth, transfixed in the heated moment with her. It felt tangible, and if I looked away, she would cease to exist and dissolve into nothing. Moving whoever stood in my way aside, I slid onto the other bench seat, never once losing contact.

At my arrival, Nicco tracked back and forth between us as we held eternity in our moment. I hadn't been the one bringing her to ecstasy, but I was the one who'd ridden it out with her. Locking eyes had fused us together, and I knew I'd been inescapably changed. I'd been rewritten and soldered to her.

"Sax? Loren?" Nicco's voice broke our hold, and a crooked smirk tilted up my lips.

"Well, well, what a surprise to find you here, *spitfire*."

Focusing on Nicco, I assessed him in a new light,

searching out his relationship with her. Was *he* going to be a problem? I'd only shared with Mas, but currently, he was burning his own bridges, so maybe it was time I found a new one to stand on. Nicco delivered me a smug look, and it said all I needed it to.

He recognized my reaction to her and understood it. Facing Loren, I sipped my drink as I took her in. She was dressed differently than I'd ever seen her before. Loren made dress pants look sexy as much as she did this ensemble. I had a feeling spitfire would look fabulous in anything because it was her that accentuated the clothes, not the other way around.

"Loren, how nice to see you here. Tell me, how do *you* know, Nicco?"

I thought my presence would throw her off or make her uncomfortable, but spitfire only lived up to her name, making my blood sing for her. She didn't know how much she pushed my libido, only my control holding me back. Her sass was making me want to take her right here and right now. I wanted to feel her tighten around me as I heard the moan I saw her feel a moment ago.

"Oh, *Mr.* Sax. You know trust and *confidentiality* are of the utmost importance to me. I would *never* tell my secrets," she purred.

I didn't know how it was possible, but my cock grew even harder at her words, straining against the zipper. Leaning forward on the table, I licked my lips, enjoying how she responded.

"If I remember correctly, spitfire, I told you the next

time you called me *Mr. Sax* would be when you're screaming my name as I licked up your wet cunt."

Her breath hitched, biting her bottom lip, the lipstick continuing to entice me. When she licked her lips, I knew things were looking up for me. Preparing to suggest we head somewhere private because despite my bravado of wanting to fuck her immediately, I didn't want all these asshats getting peeks at her.

I'd been locked onto her since I'd zeroed in, failing on my job for the first time in my life. My plan was thwarted by Mas and his plastic date when they arrived at our booth. Loren hadn't noticed him either, her focus on me. His voice had us both stiffening, and in my case, not in the way I wanted.

Nonchalantly, I twisted my head, all emotion gone as I stared down at the man meant to be my best friend. He'd become a stranger in the matter of a few hours this afternoon, especially when he dropped his latest news.

"Nicco, good to see you. I wanted to introduce you to my fiancée, Michelle Savor."

THIRTY-ONE

LOREN

Something had come over me at seeing Wells in this place, our usual tension pooling in my belly at being in his proximity. Nicco's lingering touches drove me wild, and with each heated look, I was on the verge of erupting. When he slipped his fingers in me while in a crowded room, the allure of the salaciousness had me careening over the edge.

Opening my eyes, I hadn't expected to see Sax, Mr. Sin personified himself, watching me. His magnifying eyes acted like a homing beacon, drawing him to me. I should be worried that all my worlds appeared to be colliding at an underground fighting ring, but I didn't care. Not now, at least. Pushing myself to feel everything, I embraced the recklessness, enjoying not thinking of the consequences for once.

My lust-riddled brain hadn't connected the dots. If Sax was here, Atticus was likely to follow.

When I heard his voice, the rough timber sent shivers down my spine. The memory of our lunch and the way they'd enclosed me on the bench together sent naughty images through my head in my current state. Tilting my head toward his voice, I hadn't expected to find Atticus with a blonde woman on his arm. When his words penetrated my brain, I couldn't stop the gasp from leaving my lips.

I wanted to ignore the crushing sense of disappointment and shock I suddenly felt weighing on me and the feeling of betrayal coursing under it. Opening myself up for one emotion had left me vulnerable to experience all of them. I couldn't focus on those right now, so denial became my best friend. We had one lunch. He was the guardian of my client. There was absolutely nothing between us. So whatever I was feeling would need to bury itself as it had no place in my life.

Atticus's eyes shifted over to me, shock and perhaps desire flared briefly as we were held suspended in time. He hadn't expected to find me here, and I guess, hadn't noticed me either when he'd walked over. Between my hair being up, the riskier clothing choices, and being in an abandoned warehouse altogether, I was probably the last person he expected to see here. I know he was for me.

A tiny tendril of fear coursed through me. Hopefully, since we were at the same place, he wouldn't judge me as being incompetent to help his sister. My private life had no bearing on my skill set, but not everyone could separate the two. I once had a colleague who'd been on a dating site, and when a parent of a client found out, they refused to allow their child to be seen by them. Forgetting the fact they only knew because they were on the same site. People were strange creatures.

A single blink of his lashes transported us back to the present, and the sound returned with a racket of noise. The words he'd spoken echoed around in my head. *Fiancée. Fiancée. Fiancée.*

Wrapping my hands around my glass, I wished it'd been colder so it could cool the heat my cheeks were feeling. I focused on the ice as it clinked against the glass, willing myself to quit showing my emotions so easily. Too many things had happened in the span of a few minutes, and it felt like I was on a tilt-a-whirl.

Peeking up through my lashes, I found Sax holding my gaze. I could hear Nicco speaking with the *couple*, but the words didn't filter through. Atticus and I acted like strangers, worse than strangers actually. It was standard protocol and part of the confidentiality agreement, but it didn't make me feel good about it. The fact it hurt was a red flag, but the alcohol coursing through me had muddled my boundaries.

The fact was, I could only acknowledge them if they acknowledged me. So why was I hung up over it? Sax's eyes swirled, and for the first time, I witnessed vulnerability from the sexy brute of a man. An arm wrapped around my shoulders, pulling my body closer to Nicco, but my eyes stayed firm with Sax's.

In his eyes, I found myself.

Recognizing the emotions churning within him, I offered him the one thing I could. Acceptance.

Sax's ice-blue eyes held fire and ice within, and at my silent offer, I saw relief. His pain was deep, his wounds considerable, and his soul dark. And I wanted it. The realization stunned me, but I couldn't deny it. I wouldn't.

"Mas, this is beautiful, but you can call her Loren," Nicco joked, obviously unaware of our history. I waited to see how he'd play it and if he would acknowledge me this time with the direct introduction.

"Ah, Mrs. Carter, what a pleasure to find you here. Though, I do admit it's not the first place I pictured you," Atticus's smooth timber proclaimed. The satisfaction he wasn't going to deny our relationship had me feeling bold.

"Oh, what kind of places do you picture me in?"

The question purred out in a seductive drawl I hadn't known existed. My earlier boldness coursed through me, filling me with more confidence than I've ever felt and made me daring. I placed my hand on Nicco's thigh, staking my own claim, and pushing the boundaries outside my office. A tiny voice told me to go further, but I didn't want to pervert anything between Nicco and me. I would never want to use him, so, fortunately, the sane part of me won out in the end. But the hand had been enough as I watched Atticus's nostrils flare a smidge, his jaw tense.

"I know where *I* picture you," Sax mumbled, but I heard it, and my skin heated at the undertone.

"I can assure you, *Mrs. Carter*, that was a figure of speech."

I didn't miss the biting tone or the way his eyes hadn't left where my hand laid. Nicco had been watching everything trying to put the puzzle pieces together and finally caved when he couldn't place anything.

"So, how do you know Loren, *cousin*?" Nicco inquired, jealousy and doubt in his tone.

Ah, shit. His words had the lust leaving quickly as I realized the implications and world of shit I'd placed myself in. Questions started to run through my head at the ethics of things that were admittedly harder to do with the alcohol in my system.

"Attie Bear, I'm bored. When does this fight start? Where are we going to sit?"

I could almost picture her stomping her foot as the whine left Michelle's mouth. I'd blocked her out of my vision, an unconscious desire to make her not exist, so her question had me jerking, the tension breaking between Atticus and me.

His arm tensed around Michelle, and for a second, it felt as if he wanted to push her away from him, but at the last second, he turned and addressed her.

"Michelle, darling, how about you find a table and order whatever you like? I'll be along shortly."

At his order, Michelle did one of those girly squeals before kissing his cheek. I'd zeroed in on him, and perhaps I was overanalyzing things, but I cataloged each little movement as they happened. He tensed at her gesture, and I'd even go as far to say he cringed as her lips brushed his cheek. Atticus' jaw ticked more, and he seemed to sag in relief once she stepped away. It didn't make sense to me, but he'd always been a beautiful enigma I'd wanted to figure out.

Atticus hesitated for a brief moment before unbuttoning his suit jacket and sitting down next to Sax. The sexy neanderthal barely budged over, leaving Atticus with a small space to fold his six-foot frame into. It was comical in a slightly cruel way. The therapist part of my brain wanted to dissect their relationship and uncover the root of the palpable tension between them. It was obvious something had occurred between them based on how differently they interacted from six hours earlier.

"I feel like I'm reading a book, but I'm missing a chapter or two. Anyone care to enlighten me?" Nicco quipped, but for the first time, I heard a hint of steel running through his words. He didn't like being out of the loop, but I couldn't be the one to inform him, so I had to wait it out as anxiety grew within me. I'd never been put in this situation before, and I wasn't sure how to handle it.

"To answer your question, Mrs. Carter and I know each other through Immy."

Relief rushed through my bones, and I sagged back into Nicco. His grip tightened around me as he pulled me closer. I nestled into his side, feeling the comfort he so readily offered.

"Through Immy? How?"

Well, I guess Nicco wasn't going to leave it. He was a bloodhound on the trail, and he smelt blood.

"Mrs. Carter here, well, she's mentoring a new friend of Immy's."

What the fuck? Okay, so I didn't think he would ignore the reason altogether and use Jude! I wanted to rant at him, but the damn confidentiality clause meant I couldn't do shit. That whole speech I gave Sax weeks ago suddenly reared its ugly head, and I wanted to shout. I hated keeping something from Nicco, especially if he was Imogen's cousin or second cousin, but I'd taken an oath and would never break it, even if, for once, I had a reason to.

"Oh, Jude, this is the teen from Ignite you were talking about mentoring?"

Nicco turned to me, a curious look on his face at the question. Selecting my words carefully, I made sure to be as honest as I could, "Uh, yeah. We made it official today and went out to lunch to celebrate, and it's where we ran into the three of them," I gestured.

"I'm going to have to get after Ims for not telling me about this," Nicco teased, causing the three of us to awkwardly join in. A waitress brought over more drinks right as an announcer came over the loudspeaker, startling me. The distractions were a nice break from the suffocating tension in our four-person booth.

"Well, I guess that's my cue to head to my booth. Nicco, I'll need to get numbers from you later, when you're not *otherwise* preoccupied."

Atticus rose from the bench and buttoned his suit jacket, straightening it before walking off, not even looking back as he did. His stride was sure, and I wondered what it was like to be that confident your whole life. It helped me not focus on the insult I assumed he'd just lobbed at me.

"It seems we have a lot of *similar* contacts, beautiful," Nicco touted, but for once, I wasn't sure of his intention and felt an underlying suspicion.

Fucking hell.

Figures when I met someone I liked, it would come with a whole list of complications. Nothing in my life was ever simple anymore. That fantasy cracked open five years ago when I first faced tragedy. The raw, gurgling, vitriol of life spilled out, spreading its tainted touch in every aspect it could.

Some days, I could visibly see the darkness coating me like a liquid, dripping with death and hate, sliding over my skin and trapping me in a world filled with corrupted gloom. It stuck to everything, leaving its murky mark. It would be easier if we could visibly see this darkness, the shadows of our souls where we hid our deepest fears and hurts. Yet, we huddled them together out of sight, simply fortifying them until we could no longer see the light.

Nicco had been a light in my life. I didn't need him to save me because I had to do that myself. But Nicco had reminded me what the light felt like. He provided me shelter from the storm and showed me all the things I'd forgotten, all the lies the darkness whispered to me that I'd started to believe. Nicco was my night light, and I needed him to stave off the monsters. If I lost him now…

I didn't want to think about it because I wasn't sure my answer would be comforting.

"It oddly does seem that way." I smiled, but it wobbled. The emotion was thick in my throat, and I tried to swallow it down. Turning my head, I watched the figures below and the crowd who were lost in a mass of adrenaline and aggression. Their voices diminished my fear, and I floated amid them as they shouted for their fighter to win.

A growl brought me back to the booth, and I realized it had come from Sax. Staring, I pondered what was going on. He had a fierce look on his face, his beard accentuating his scowl, making him look menacing. Sax's bulging biceps sat on the table, his tattoos peeking out of his tight black shirt. It was then I realized he wasn't in a suit like normal. Something about a relaxed-looking Sax had my mouth-watering, and I wondered if he was wearing jeans and how his ass looked in them.

Despite his growl, he didn't say anything. Sax glared daggers at Nicco as he leaned against the table. Observing the man next to me, I could tell something was passing between them, but I couldn't figure it out. Nicco had a stubborn glint in his eyes, and I wondered what he was refusing to do. That part was at least clear to me. Sax wanted Nicco to do something, and he was refusing. I had a feeling it involved me.

I didn't think their current animosity had anything to do with the eye fucking Sax and I had earlier. In fact, neither had seemed to care about it. No, this was something different. Focusing back on the brooding defender, I tried to break up some of the tension. "Did Nicco do your tattoos?"

They broke their battle and looked over to me, not realizing, I guess, I'd been aware of their staring contest.

"Yes, spitfire. The *kid* did my tats. He's quite good at them."

Nicco glared at Sax when he referred to him as "kid," and I couldn't help but laugh. "I'm not sure what's going on. I've felt out of place most of the night, and the fact all my worlds seem to be colliding has my mind a little boggled, to be honest. So, I hope whatever this current tension is about has nothing to do with me." Turning to my date, I took his hand in mine.

"Nicco, this has been one of the best dates of my life, and you've surpassed anything I've been on before. Thank you."

Leaning up, I cupped his cheek with my palm and kissed the other one. I felt his eyes flutter at the contact, and his body relaxed at the gesture. Pulling away, I tried to communicate how much I wanted him and the experience this night had been, even if it had been derailed. Nicco searched my eyes and finally nodded, finding an answer he could accept.

Turning to Sax next, I smiled at the burly neanderthal that was fastly becoming someone I couldn't ignore. "Sax, it was a surprise to find you here, but I can't say I'm disappointed. I know we don't know each other very well yet, but I can't deny the physical connection. I'm just not sure what I'm ready for. Nicco can explain more if he wants. He is, after all, my tour guide." I grinned back at the man in question.

Something about my statement had him looking guilty, but that hadn't been my intention. Nothing to be done about it now, though, so I let it be. Gathering my courage for the last part, I inhaled a big breath before beginning.

"This night has been amazing, but I think it's time I call it. I know I was supposed to stay over Nicco, but I was hoping I could get a rain check?"

He looked disappointed initially, but I didn't see how I could get back into the sexy Loren from earlier. Too much darkness had seeped into me and not the reckless kind. Thankfully, at the rain check part, he smiled softly.

"Yes, beautiful. I would like that very much. I'm not

sure where things went off course tonight, so I apologize for any part—"

Placing my fingers over his lips, I cut him off, "There's no need for apologies, Nicco. Save the words for when they matter," I affirmed. Dropping my fingers, I kissed him firmly on the mouth, now hoping to infuse my feelings for him and not whatever doubt had crept in during the past hour.

"Wait," Sax started, a look of panic on his face. Curious, I turned to him and arched my eyebrow. I'd always wanted to make the gesture but I'd never been presented with the perfect scenario.

"Yes?"

"How are you getting home?"

It came out more like a bark, and the deep rumble traveled through me and hit me right in the clit. Body shudders rushed through me for a second as I closed my eyes and exhaled, trying to control the tremors. When I regained my bearings, the smirk I found staring back told me he'd noticed and was feeling very smug about it. Well, I guess he could. His damn voice made me want to throw my panties at him. Add in his danger vibe, the caveman tendencies, and his sexy as hell beard, and I was officially a goner.

"I'll get home the same way I got here."

This time, it was my turn to be coy and I winked. Knowing what I was referring to, Nicco chuckled and exited the booth, so I could scoot out after him.

"Fucking hell, spitfire. You're wearing *that*."

Turning on my boots, my skirt flared out a little, and I smiled mischievously. It felt nice to bring the sexy beast to his knees, figuratively. Grabbing my phone, I sent a quick text to Nat asking for a rescue. I knew she'd be along soon. So, with one last kiss to Nicco, I batted my eyelashes and blew a kiss to Sexy Sax and sashayed my ass right out of there.

Or, you know, to the stairs at least, and then Beau walked with me out front until Nat pulled up. Nicco had to keep up appearances, and I didn't trust myself with Sax. He'd have me up against the wall with his cock buried deep before I even remembered my name. He had that look about him, I could just tell.

And while the image excited a part of me, and I wanted to give in to it, the other side knew I was about to hit my emotional limit, and any one thing could send me bolting over into the dark chasm. I had people in my life now that I'd started to care about. I didn't want to miss anything. I guess I was using some of my own advice after all. Suppose there *was* a first for everything.

Spoiler alert—therapists had feelings too, and weren't perfect.

At the end of the day, we were all just trying to get by and make it to the next one. If we could do it with others by our side, life was more enjoyable. So, I chose something different this time. I chose myself.

THIRTY-TWO

MONROE

Levi's voice broke my concentration as he walked into the room. "Dad, I can't find my other sock."

"Oh, um, did you check under your bed?"

"Yes," he huffed, almost like I was the one inconveniencing him.

"Well, Mr. Sassy Pants, if you know so much, where do you think it is then? Hmm?"

I turned and leveled him with a look of skepticism. Sometimes, you had to play into it, or you'd end up arguing with an eight-year-old, and no one won in that situation.

Rolling his eyes, he turned and walked back to his room, living up to the earlier nickname. Levi was already giving me teen angst, and I wasn't sure I was ready for more anytime soon. Chuckling, I shook my head and returned to thinking.

Sipping my coffee, I flipped the newspaper distractedly. I was probably one of the few people who still read the paper, but it was one of those odd things I enjoyed, plus it gave me a routine in the morning. Yet, this morning my thoughts were all over the place, and I couldn't focus on the words. Wells and Loren both swirled in my head, making it hard to concentrate.

"Found it!" Levi shouted, running back in the room with it held aloft like a victory prize.

"Nice! Where was it?"

"Under the bed," he mumbled. I held in my laugh, deciding to be a mature adult this morning.

"Wonderful. Does it mean you're ready to go?"

"Yeah, I guess," he muttered, hanging his head.

"What's wrong, kiddo?"

Setting down the paper, I focused on my son and tried to figure out what was bothering him. Levi's feet turned inward, rubbing the toe of his shoe as he stood awkwardly. This wasn't like him. He was usually full of laughter and joy.

"Is it true?"

Standing, I walked over to him, kneeling to his level. "Is what true, buddy?"

"I heard Mom saying I wouldn't get to see you soon."

"Well, that's a lie. Nothing could stop me from seeing you. I don't know why your mom said that. What else did she say?"

"I dunno." One shoulder shrugged as he peeked up from below his lashes at me. "She told her friend you were sick and needed help."

"Sick? Well, do I look sick, kiddo?"

Levi looked me up and down as he ran his eyes over me, calculating every detail his young mind could process.

"No, I guess not."

"It's not good to listen in on your mom, bud. I'll talk with her and see what's going on, okay?"

"Okay, Dad."

Levi hugged me tight around the neck, and I pulled him close. His slight frame always made me want to hug him closer to protect him from the world despite knowing it didn't quite work that way. There were far more dangers in the world than physical ones. Pulling back, I held onto his arms as I chose my words carefully.

"Your mom and I aren't together anymore, but that doesn't change how I feel about you. Nothing is more important to me than you. *Nothing*. I would move mountains to spend time with you, bud. Always."

"Always," he responded, a smile on his face. I pulled him in and hugged him again before standing up. Levi had started feeling too old to say "I love you, Dad" about a year ago, so we'd adopted 'always' from Harry Potter as our way of saying it since he'd become obsessed with the movie.

Grabbing his bag, we headed out the door, and his worries played over my mind. What was Brittni saying to her friends that would scare Levi? Frustration began to bubble up in my chest, and I prepared myself to face her.

Shuffling him out the door, we made our way down to the garage. Levi was meant to stay all weekend, but had asked to go to a friend's birthday party that was a sleepover. I couldn't deny him spending time with his friends, even if it was my night. Since his mom lived out in the North Shore suburbs where the party was, I'd agreed to drop him off early.

Unfortunately, it meant we had to drive an hour out there. Typically, I abhorred it, the traffic and pompousness were enough to give me hives. Today, though, I was excited about stopping by a specialty shop on her side of town, making the drive at least rewarding. I thought about checking on Wells again, but decided to let that sleeping dog lie for now. Things were complicated with us on the best of days, and, despite me wanting to know details, I'd learned long ago Wells wouldn't share until he was ready.

Levi put on an audiobook as we headed out to his mom's. His love of reading was something we had in common, and he'd been devouring books since he learned how to read. We were currently making our way through the Percy Jackson series. As the book played, we both fell into the story enjoying our ride out to Kenilworth—where Chicago's wealthiest lived. Brittni remarried last year, and even though we'd been in the upper tax bracket, she'd still managed to marry up. Now, she was Mrs. Brittni Kimpton, married to Larry Kimpton, hotel mogul.

Driving up to the two million dollar, red brick house, I felt a tension enter my chest at having to let Levi go. This was always the hardest part. I placed the car in park and waited until we came to a good place in the book to stop. When the chapter finished, I paused, saving our place. I think Levi and I both dreaded saying goodbye, drawing it out as much as possible.

"Alright, buddy. I'll see you on Wednesday after school."

Leaning over, I kissed his forehead as he gathered his

things. His phone beeped, and he checked it as he got out.

"Bye, Dad." He waved, taking off for the house before he stopped and turned around. "Mom wants to talk to you." And then took off again.

Sighing loudly, I turned off the engine and sat for a moment. I'd planned to talk with her, but now that it was her idea, dread filled me. I had to prepare myself for interacting with her. Brittni was a woman wrought with deceit and manipulation. She never did anything unless it benefited her. Finding the truth in what she spouted was a hard-won battle. It always felt like I needed battle armor when facing her. I'd been married to her for six years, yet it felt like a lifetime.

Levi had left the door open, so I strode in, knowing she would either be in the kitchen or study. Brittni liked to pick her room based on the conversation she was having. Not seeing her in the study, I headed to the kitchen, a feeling of doom and foreboding. This wasn't going to be good.

"Brit." I nodded, purposefully shortening her name. Now that she was married to a hotel mogul, she tried to put on airs of being high class. Rubbing in her middle-class upbringing as much as I could was, well, a bonus. It was petty, but the delight it brought me canceled out any guilt I felt.

"Monroe."

The ice in her words froze me to the spot, the chill tangible in the air. She placed her teacup on the saucer and turned around from the kitchen island. She'd dressed in tan slacks, a white silk button blouse, and a Hermes scarf around her neck for the day. Brittni looked the epitome of a bored housewife, and I wondered if she already had a fling on the side. Commitment had never been her strong suit.

"What do you need?" I crossed my arms, sighing as I waited for her to degrade me. "I have plans I need to get to."

"Fine. I'll cut to the chase." She rolled her eyes, acting as if I were the one inconveniencing her. "It's come to my attention that the company you're keeping isn't very *savory*. So, I'm going to request full custody."

The world stopped for a minute as I processed her words. Some of the things Levi said this morning started to connect. She'd been planning this despite her attempt to make it sound like it was new.

"I'm sorry, but you're going to have to be more clear on what you mean by *unsavory*."

"Humph." Brittni crossed her arms, not liking I'd questioned her. "Well, I have it on good authority you were floundering around with some floozy with Levi at a school function."

Brittni had stretched the truth and would have a difficult time getting any judge to believe her shenanigans. It amused me how often she seemed to forget I was a lawyer just because I didn't work in a courtroom every day.

"I don't know who you're getting your information from, but the only woman I've been out with is Loren Carter, and she isn't a 'floozy'. In fact, she's a trauma therapist. I think it will be hard to convince a judge of her *unsavoriness*," I challenged, a feeling of smugness coming over me. For once, I felt like I was ahead of her manipulative bullshit.

Panic flashed in her eyes for a brief second before replacing it with a condescending look of her own. I wanted to slap myself for walking right into her trap. It seemed I was the one needing to remember this time how good she was at this.

"That might be the case, but we both know that can't be said about all the *company* you keep."

Sighing, I planted my hands on my hips, dropping my head as I gathered myself. She was still using this shtick. Lifting my head back up, I hoped my eyes held the fire I felt within.

"Brittni, just *stop*. You already tried this once, and it didn't work. No one, except *you*, cares that I'm bisexual. And now that we're divorced, it isn't any of your business. You'll never prove to any judge I'm not a good father, and you know it. So just stop. I'm tired of playing this game."

Turning, I walked out, dismissing her as I did. I could hear her making sounds of frustration, but I didn't stop. It was the first time I'd ever had the last word, and it felt empowering. Larry was leaving his office as I passed, a glass tumbler in his hand and a cigar hanging from his mouth. Nodding, I kept heading to the front door, ready to escape this hell hole. I'd mistakenly assumed divorce meant I never had to deal with her manipulative bullshit again. They forget to tell you co-parenting was a new level of Hell of its own.

HUMMING ALONG TO THE MUSIC, I found myself swaying to the rhythm at the stove. Sprinkling seasoning into the sauce as I stirred, I jumped when there was a knock at the door. I'd been zoned into the music, and I'd lost focus. The hours I'd been home had flown by as I prepared for the date. Shopping had calmed my nerves as I meticulously picked out ingredients for the meal I wanted to make. I even had a bottle of wine and candles, pulling out all the stops for Loren.

Brushing my hands off on the apron, I headed to the door, a noticeable skip in my step. Loren had arrived early, bringing a smile to my face. Of course when she lived across the hall, she didn't have far to travel, but I was glad she was here. Spending time with her was enjoyable, and after the morning dealing with the villainous ex, I was ready to be around a woman who made me feel giddy. And Loren made me feel that and a whole slew of emotions.

Checking my appearance, I blushed when I realized what I'd done. Opening the door, I found a beaming Loren standing in front of me. She looked breathtaking, and I stood and stared at her for a minute, soaking her in. I realized I'd never seen her smile so big before. Loren had always been beautiful, but as she stood smiling at me in my doorway, the Earth stopped moving. Regaining my composure, I pulled my door open the rest of the way, allowing her to enter.

"Lo! Welcome! Come in, come in. I'm so glad you

could make it." I beamed, teasing her as I ushered her into the main room. "Would you like the official tour?"

"I'm good for now, thanks. I think I have a good idea what it looks like, after all."

"True, but you never know, my crown molding might be better than yours."

"Wait, you have crown molding?" she teased.

Things felt nice already, and I relaxed as we walked into the kitchen. She held a box out to me, and I set it on the counter without looking, my focus on her. Loren looked around, and I took the opportunity to check her out more. She'd worn jeans and a sweater, and I liked how relaxed she looked. When she turned, I looked away, pretending to check on dinner. The smile I caught let me know I hadn't been as sly as I hoped. Making a few adjustments, I returned my focus to Loren.

"Would you like any wine? I got both red and white since I didn't know which you prefer."

"Oh, that was nice of you. Either is good with me, whichever goes best with the meal," she adorably rambled, her face tinting. "I'll trust the chef."

"White it is then. I'll be right back with it."

Grabbing the glasses and the bottle I had chilling, I poured the wine into our glasses and lifted it up. Smiling, we clinked our glasses together, a bout of nerves flooding me at the implications of what this dinner could mean. Before, we'd just been neighbors hanging out together, but tonight, we were Loren and Monroe, two people on a date. It both excited and terrified me.

"I like your apron," she giggled before taking a sip of her wine.

Looking down, I realized I'd grabbed the apron Levi had gotten me last year. *Aprons are just capes on backwards.*

"Ah, thanks. Levi got it for me," I chuckled. "I started learning how to cook after we separated, and I try to make it fun so Levi can learn. I never really had that growing up and didn't realize how inept I was until I was responsible for making something other than ramen."

"Well, I could probably learn a few tips. I'm a disaster in the kitchen. Coffee is about the only thing I can do, and that's black."

Loren's cringe face was about as adorable as her smile, and I realized how much I looked forward to knowing all of her faces. Dating was scary in some aspects, but it was exciting in others. Learning about a new person and getting to know and understand what made them who they were invigorated me.

"I think that could be arranged."

"Where is Levi? I thought he was going to be here?"

"Oh, yeah. I forgot to tell you. He had a sleepover, so it's just us tonight. Let me go and grab the food. It should be done now. I ended up making fettuccine alfredo, so hopefully, you like that."

"It sounds wonderful, thanks, Monroe."

Heading back into the kitchen, I exhaled, the butterflies overwhelming me, the grin on my face beginning to feel like a permagrin. I plated the food and carried it back out to the table, glad to have something to focus on. Hitting the playlist on my phone, the soft tunes started to roll through the speakers helping to set the mood.

"I like this. It's soothing. What, or who, is it?"

"Oh, it's an Italian pianist, Ludovico Einaudi. It seemed appropriate. When eating Italian, listen to Italian musicians."

Loren giggled, the sound pure and erotic, hitting me simultaneously in the heart and dick. We started eating, both of us hiding our smiles between bites. The sound of our forks hitting our bowls and the music playing around us filled the apartment. It didn't feel awkward, though, both of us enjoying the food. When we finished, she placed her fork down, turning more toward me.

"Mmm. This was wonderful, Monroe. Thank you so much for cooking for me. I don't think I've ever had someone do it before," she admitted.

"It's my pleasure." I grinned. Wiping my mouth, I placed my napkin on the table, turning toward her more as well. "So, I know the basics about you. Your job, you're divorced, and you volunteer at Ignite. What else makes Loren, Loren?" I couldn't stop the smile that wanted to spread at my corny joke,

"Oh well, I'm pretty boring, actually." She blushed. Each time I got one, it made me only want more. She pushed her hair behind her ear before continuing. "I grew up in Glenview and was a high school cheerleader who married her high school boyfriend. I moved to the city after college and worked, and then at some point, my marriage didn't work. And now, I'm here."

Her voice had gone quiet at the end, and I realized the grenade I'd launched at her. Quickly, I tried to fill the silence. "Hmm, cheerleader. I don't see it," I joked. "I played on the hockey team, as I think Levi told you. I was kind of a weird loner kid, though, so it didn't help my social status."

"Oh, I find that hard to believe," she chuckled, taking a sip of wine. "Well, actually, I take that back. That first time we talked in the elevator was pretty awkward."

Feigning shock, I said, "I'm offended. That was some great chit-chat, some of my finest."

"Then I feel sorry for you."

"Ouch, that hurts, Loren, and here I cooked for you and everything."

"You're right, you're right. This meal was delicious, so I guess I can excuse any awkward small talk. I mean, does anyone sound cool in an elevator?"

"No, I guess they don't," I agreed.

"Okay, so now that we got the awkward part out of the way, maybe we could move on to the not awkward part."

"Yeah, sure. What part is that?"

"Would you like any more wine?" I offered.

"Not at the moment. It kind of all goes to my head, and I want to be present for this."

"That makes me feel incredibly happy to hear you say that. Although, I have to admit, this is the first date I've been on since my divorce."

"Really?"

"Yeah, and I was nervous," I confessed. "I had a confrontation this morning with Levi's mother, and this date was the good thing I needed tonight."

"I'm glad to hear you say that. I've been looking forward to it too. Though, I did have another date last night," she blushed. "A guy I met a week ago. I hope that's okay, I've never dated anyone outside my ex-husband, so I'm kind of learning the rules. But to be honest, it's been fun. I... I... don't know. I've never had these experiences," Loren explained shyly.

Admittedly, part of me was bummed she was possibly seeing someone else, but I couldn't deny I understood what she was saying. She needed to experience more in her life, and I wouldn't let it get in the way of what we could build. Loren was someone I could see myself with, and if it meant I had to deal with another guy in the meantime, then I would figure it out.

"I don't know if there are rules, honestly. Probably just honesty and communicating, which you nailed, so I think you're off to a good start."

"Yeah?"

"Yeah," I smiled. "So that box you brought, it wouldn't happen to be dessert, would it?"

"It is. In fact, it's a chocolate cake from Formento's," she beamed.

"Formento's! The 10-layer chocolate cake?"

"The very one."

Before she even finished her sentence, I ran into the kitchen to grab the box. Peeking inside, the smell of chocolatey goodness hit all my senses, and a groan left my lips at the Heaven awaiting me in the box. Grabbing two forks, I took the box back to the table, sitting it down with reverence as I did.

"I take it you like their cake."

Chuckling at her calling me out, I nodded. "Yes, you

would be correct. Though I've only had it once, it was the best cake of my life."

"You know, some say it's better than sex."

"I would almost agree."

Laughing together, we picked up the forks and dug into heaven in a box. Chocolate exploded on my tongue as the moist cake, icing, and pudding mixed to bring the perfect bite. Almost simultaneously, Loren and I moaned around our forks, chuckling when we both heard the other. Licking my fork clean, I cherished the flavor of each bite.

"You might be right, you know. That tasted pretty great, almost better than sex," I laughed.

"Well, maybe because you haven't had sex with *me*."

Before I could respond, she covered her mouth, her face flaming, unable to hold her laughter back anymore.

"Oh my God, I have no idea why I said that. I'm not some crazy sex Goddess. In fact, until last week, I'd only had sex with one person, and it wasn't all that great before. I mean last week's, wow. Shit, now I'm rambling, and I... I..."

Leaning over, I took a chance and kissed her lips. Loren hesitated for a moment before dropping her fork and returning it. I could taste the richness of the chocolate on her lips, and it officially became the best kiss I'd ever had. Pulling back, I tucked her hair behind her ear, trying to reassure her. "Regardless of how many people you've had sex with, Loren, I think you'd be great at it. I hope that doesn't sound pervy."

"No, not at all."

"Good. Now, shall we finish this cake? Or you can leave it all for me, if you prefer."

"Not in a million years."

We sat around the table, finishing the deliciousness, and I relaxed into our easy comfort. Our date hadn't been perfect, but it had been fun, and that made it the best in my book.

THIRTY-THREE

LOREN

Rinsing my coffee cup, I placed it in the sink when a door slammed down the hall, jarring me and causing me to jump. I'd been lost in my thoughts and hadn't been prepared for the sound. Memories assaulted me, flooding in emotions of panic and doubt, but I pushed them away, unable to deal with them right now. Blinking back the tears, the exhaustion I felt sat heavily on me like a coat.

The past two days had been great. I'd spent time with Jude, gone on two dates, and had the girls over to help me get ready. It was the most sociable I'd been in years. But I felt the drain today. The thought of having to deal with my mother on top of this made me want to throw my mug against the wall. I didn't know if I had it in me. Regrettably, I didn't get to decide whether or not I wanted to with regards to anything concerning my mother.

When the phone rang, I knew who it was without looking. Speak of the devil, and she shall call. Preparing myself, I cleared my head before answering. "Hello, Mother."

"Loren."

"How can I help you?"

"I was calling about brunch today."

"Yea, I was about to get dressed for it."

"No need."

"Okay…"

"Don't be rude, Loren. I'm hosting a dinner instead and require your attendance."

"Why do I feel like this will end badly for me?"

"Seriously, Loren. You act as if I'm out to embarrass you. I'm your mother. I only have your best interests in mind."

"It's just that I think our interests might not line up anymore."

"Well, who's fault is that? You're the one whose husband cheated on her!"

Taking a deep breath, I didn't want to get into it with my mother this morning. "What are the details I need for this evening?" I gritted out, trying my hardest to keep my cool. It was never easy when my mother was involved, though.

"It's a formal dinner. You do know what that means, yes?"

"Yes, Mother."

"Do you have anything in fashion to wear? You still need to act as if you care," she huffed.

"Yes, Mother."

"Very well. Arrive at the house at 7 pm. I expect you to be on time. It's imperative to your father and me."

"Yes, Mother. Do I need to bring anything?"

"Heavens, no, this isn't a potluck! How crass do you think we are?"

"I simply meant if you needed me to bring wine or a dessert, but I shall refrain if you do not wish for me to bring something. I wasn't implying anything, *Mother*."

"Some days, I wonder how I ended up with such an ungrateful child."

"I will see you at 7 pm, Mother."

"Be on time!"

"Bye, Mother."

"Bye, dear. Do make sure to look your best."

Hanging up the phone, I exhaled and inhaled several times until I felt my breath even out. As much as I dreaded this dinner, at least it meant I had my morning free. Deciding to double check I had something in my wardrobe 'in fashion' to pass her inspection, I headed to my closet. No point getting comfortable yet if I would need to head out to try on dresses.

Leave it to my Mother to give me the morning off only to end up spending it doing something for her, inevitably still making it about her. Except now, I'd been trapped for the evening as well. Never say that Jacqueline Hanover wasn't a diabolical manipulator. I often wondered if she took classes from psychopaths or if they took lessons from her. Crass thing to think about one's mother, but sometimes, you have to face reality. *Jacqueline was a royal bitch.*

Pushing things aside, I had a few dresses that would probably fit my mother's requirements, but as I tried one on, it hung off my frame, and the other had a rip in the hem. The last one was a summer dress and would never work. Heaving myself into a pair of jeans and a chunky sweater, I slipped on some boots and headed out the door, grabbing my bag and coat.

Slowing my steps as I passed Monroe's door, I hoped he'd hear me and try to catch me, but as I passed and listened, no movement could be heard from inside. Our date had gone well the evening before. He was a world apart from Nicco, but I liked how they were both different. Monroe was more of someone my mother would approve of, but I didn't know if I necessarily wanted that as a dating requirement. Though, his being divorced and a single father would be a slight in her book. Clearly, her book was shit.

Nicco had texted me a few times since Friday night. I think he felt guilty for how he'd reacted toward the end. I wasn't upset with him, but I needed some time to think and process. Though, it hadn't helped either. Not that I'd had an ample amount of time to myself anymore. Deciding to bite the bullet, I sent him a text.

ME: Hey, when are you free this week? Dinner at my place? Fair warning, I can't cook, but I can order like the best of them.

When I didn't see the bubbles, I locked the screen and put it away. I'd drive myself mad, staring at the screen, waiting for a reply. Sometimes, it was best to be absent with messages anyway. At least, that was what I was trying to convince myself. The cold wind whipped around me, reminding me why this was the 'Windy City' as I stepped outside. Tightening my scarf around me, I burrowed down into it, hoping to shield my face from the brutal wind.

The shop I liked was only two more blocks away. I hadn't been there in over a year, but it was my favorite place to splurge when I'd still been interested in clothes. Brian hadn't liked it when I spent a lot of money here. The freedom of only being responsible for myself bubbled up, and a sudden giddiness erupted in my belly. I could finally buy whatever the hell I wanted, and no one but me could complain about it. An unexpected excitement zinged through me, and I found something to look forward to.

Picking up my speed, I practically skipped there as I rounded the corner to the door. Pulling it hard, I almost fell over with the effort, my momentum throwing me off. Laughing at my exuberance, I gathered myself and headed in. Stepping into the rows of clothes, I swear I heard cartoon birds singing as I entered. This was my happy place. An associate walked up with a kind smile on her face.

"Hello, what can I help you find today?"

"I need something for a dinner party in Glenview and," I paused, feeling spontaneous, "something that makes me feel like a *woman*." I wanted a dress just for me.

"Well, I think we can handle that." She smiled. "Let's get you a room started. Would you like anything to drink while we find some items for you?"

"You know what, why not! A mimosa would be great."

"Absolutely, have a seat here. I'm Stacy, and I'll be your personal assistant today. Any colors or cuts you know you don't like?"

"Well, I'm not a big fan of yellow or anything too bright for that matter. I don't do 'in your face' pattern-wise. Other than that, I think I'm fair game. Besides, you're the expert, and I trust your judgment. Think of me as a blank slate, here to let you dress!"

"Oh, now, be careful with what you ask for! You just might regret that," she laughed.

"Nope. Today is a day to have fun. So, style me, please!"

"I wish more clients were like you," she chuckled. "Last questions, do you have a budget, and do you need accessories as well?"

"You know what, let's do it all for the sexy woman outfit. The dinner one is for my mother, and I can't be bothered to care where she's concerned."

"I hear you there. Okay, I'll get things started. Now, just sit back and let us dazzle you!"

The next hour was a fun montage of girls bringing me dresses and items to see if I approved. Stacy had an eye for detail and just about everything she brought me, I loved. Once we narrowed it down to a few for each category, I started to try them on. It was early enough on a Sunday that the shop wasn't busy. A few of the other sales associates were in the dressing rooms with us giving their opinion as I modeled the dresses we selected.

"Oh, no, that one isn't as sexy as the other one. It's gotta go!"

"Agree, the cut is all wrong on that one."

"I love the lingerie, though. You need to get it regardless."

"So, who is the sexy outfit for, Loren? Tell us, tell us!"

Blushing, I spun around in the skirt, watching it flare. It was fun, but it wasn't me. Giving them a wink, I stepped back into the changing room to try the next one. However, the blonde associate was right. This lingerie was delectable. I put it aside, deciding to go for it. Slipping on a deep red tulip dress, my breath momentarily stopped in my throat. *I loved it.* Walking out, I tentatively held my breath to see what their reaction would be.

"Oh, that's the one! Spin, spin!"

Spinning, I giggled as the skirt fanned around me. The top of the dress represented the top of a tulip with different layers that looked like petals overlapping. The skirt part flared out around my hips, creating a cute silhouette on me. It was very chic and sexy rolled into one.

"You know, if you wear a jacket with it, you could probably get away with wearing it for dinner, and then you could still get another dress. Then you'd have two dresses you love instead of just the one," Stacy suggested, slipping a short jacket over my shoulders.

"Stacy, I think you're a genius. This would be perfect, and it's just enough on the sexy side that it will annoy my mother, so bonus points there."

The women laughed and agreed with the choice. Feeling excited, I went back into the room to try on the rest.

"So, are you going to tell us his name?"

"Well," I called out from the dressing room, "that would be difficult since there are two of them."

"Oh, you sly thing. Walking in here like Miss Innocence and you're over here bagging two guys! Girl, I want to be you!" one of the girls exclaimed. Laughing at her exaggeration, I finished slipping on a black lace dress. I was momentarily speechless as I stared back into the mirror.

"So, tell us how you snagged two guys?"

"Well, one I met at a club, and the other is my neighbor."

"So who's better in bed?"

"I don't know that yet. I've only slept with one of them."

"Let me guess, the one you met at the club!"

"Not answering!" I laughed, a blush forming on my cheeks. "Okay, I'm coming out."

Stepping out, I took in all of their faces. Smiles, quickly followed by squeals, greeted me. Stacy ran over and started messing with the dress before deciding it was a perfect fit. Grabbing my hands, she started jumping up and down, squealing in glee. Her excitement was contagious, and I found myself joining her. I'd never had a friend do this before, so it was fun to join in, and I realized I was happy.

"Okay, okay. So yes?"

"Yes!" they all shouted out at me, causing me to laugh.

Stacy handed me some heels, and I knew they'd be perfect. Giving her all the items we'd agreed on, I dressed back into my clothes, which suddenly didn't feel as fun. Maybe I'd treat myself to a whole new wardrobe soon. It might be the thing I needed. It wasn't like I was reinventing myself, but more that I was discovering myself. It was hard to reinvent something you never invented in the first place. I'd been a copy of the person I was expected to be. In my case, my mother.

For once, I was discovering who I was outside of her wants and demands and not caring about the consequences. I was thirty-two years old, for fucks sake. If I didn't start living my life for me now, when would I? *Never*. It was now or never, and I, for one, chose now.

Leaving the store, I felt confident and excited that the social excursions hadn't drained me. I'd even made friends with strangers and plans to meet up with Stacy later this week for coffee. Headed back to my condo, I carried my purchases with a walk of stride. This dinner was going to be torture; there was no way around that, but when I bumped into a familiar face a second later, an idea to make it more exciting started to build in my mind.

"Sorry, I didn't see you there," he uttered distractedly before turning back, "Loren?"

"Hey!" I'd been just as shocked to see him on this side of town. Obliviousness to my surroundings had been worse than I'd known. Could it have been possible I was around these attractive men for over a year and never noticed?

"What are you doing over here?" Shaking my head, I restarted. "You know what, never mind. Better question, what are you doing *tonight*? Want to go to a dinner party with me?" I smiled wide, hoping my eyes conveyed my hope and mischievous intentions. His answering smirk had my panties melting and my heart racing, and now, I couldn't wait until dinner.

"THIS IS WHERE YOU GREW UP?"

"Yeah, it's not all rainbows and sunshine, though. Lots of shadows in this glitzy place."

My plan to spice up my mother's dinner party had sounded like a bit of fun hours ago. Now, as I stood on the doorstep waiting to ring the bell, I had doubts. She was going to kill me with her glare for this. I could already picture it. A spike of adrenaline for getting one over on my mother washed away the anxiety I felt and gave me the courage I needed.

"Are you going to press the button, or will we be served out here with the, what are these, rhododendrons?"

Turning, I smiled up at him. "Hydrangeas, actually. But I'm surprised you know your shrubs."

"There are a lot of things you don't know about me, spitfire, and I look forward to showing you," he growled, his voice pitched low in my ear. Sax's breath fanned out over my neck, causing goosebumps to erupt over my skin. Sucking in a breath at the sensation, a slickness developed between my legs as he ran a finger up my palm. The simple touch had me on fire, and I suddenly had thoughts of turning around.

Which, of course, meant my mother had to ruin the moment.

Before I could utter a word, the door opened, and my mother gasped as she took us in.

"Loren! What on earth are you doing out here? Standing around like a vagabond. I swear. Come inside, now!"

My cheeks flamed, but for an entirely different reason this time. I started to follow my mother in, my head hanging, when Sax grabbed my hand and pulled me into him.

"We *will* finish this later, spitfire."

Sax sealed his lips to mine briefly, taking me by surprise. Pulling me along with him, I found my mother's disapproving glare down the corridor. Of course, she'd seen everything. Nothing got past my mother's judgmental eye. Jacqueline took in my attire as we entered the foyer. Arms crossed and nose upturned, I wasn't sure if it was my dress or date she disapproved of. Actually, it was probably both.

"Mother, let me introduce you to my date, Sax…" Turning, I blushed as I looked to him for the answer.

"Saxon Bishop," he answered, offering a tattooed hand to Jacqueline.

Internally, I was dying from laughter as I watched the internal war flit across her face on what to do. Good manners meant shaking his hand in return, but Sax was not someone she usually surrounded herself with. Bearded, muscular, and tatted, he didn't fit into her country club dream. In the end, she presented her hand tentatively, throwing me a look of hatred as she did, knowing she had to or it would be considered rude.

"Honestly, Loren, bringing a man you don't even

know the last name of to my dinner party when I stressed the importance of not embarrassing me. It's like you live to torture me!" she bristled.

Sax turned her hand over and kissed the palm before giving it back to her. Jacqueline Hanover stood stunned for a moment before a slight blush crept up her cheeks. I kind of wished I had a camera to capture the look on her face. I didn't blame her for being disarmed by the man, he had a knack for it. Before I could grab my phone out of my clutch, she blanked her features back into the disdainful housewife she was.

"Hmph. Well, at least you're not *late*."

I was beginning to realize it might kill Jacqueline Hanover to say something complimentary toward me. Perhaps Mother believed for every nice thing she said to me, it subtracted the good she would receive. My mother was an emotional hoarder. I guess I should be more surprised by this than I was. Thinking about it now, she did kind of fit the profile.

Sax continued to hold my hand as we followed Mother. I'd asked him on a spontaneous whim, but his presence was already giving me confidence and strength to persevere through this meal. A maid stepped out and took our coats before we could step into the sitting room. It had always amazed me how they did that, be there precisely the moment Jacqueline needed something.

Earlier, I'd assumed this dinner was Jacqueline's way of forcing me to spend longer with them and a platform for her to remind me of all the ways I was a disappointment with my current life choices. Staring into the room now, I knew it was much worse. Standing stock-still in the entranceway of the room, I felt the bottom of my whole world drop away. If Sax hadn't been holding my hand, I might've turned and run from the house.

Almost as if he sensed my impending doom, Sax squeezed my hand, grounding me in the present. It seemed my earlier spontaneity to spice up this evening might be the thing that saved me. My mother's sweet smile as she took her seat communicated everything she felt about me. Maybe I'd never seen it before, or perhaps, I choose to ignore it, hoping for the best from my mother.

Nonetheless, as I stood motionless and stared across the room at the one person who'd broken me in two, I could only concur that my mother, Jacqueline Hanover, absolutely *despised me.*

THIRTY-FOUR

SAX

Loren froze in the entryway, her face going white as she took in the guests talking. Her focus was on some dickweasel chatting with a rail-thin blonde with balloons in the place of boobs. An older guy was next to the blonde and looked bored as his date flirted with the asshat. He was browsing his phone as the other two talked. As her bitch of a mother took a seat, the first man turned to us. Loren looked like she might retreat, so I squeezed her hand, reminding her I was here with her.

It was a complete happenstance I'd run into her earlier, but I was glad I did. I'd been lost in my head thinking about the events of Friday night and how lost I felt. Atticus and I had always told one another every-thing since the day I came to live with him. We were brothers. The past two days, he'd felt like a stranger, and I didn't know how to do this.

I'd been out, touching base with family members in the area, or at least that was the excuse I'd given to leave the house. In actuality, I'd been walking in a daze, hoping to clear my head of the chaotic turmoil I was experiencing. Bumping into Loren had been kismet.

When she'd asked me to attend a dinner party in Glenview, I'd been doubtful. It sounded like a bore, but her mischievous smile had won me over. I was curious about her and who she was outside her office. The fight the other night had been electric, and I wondered if that chemistry was natural or only a by-product of the environment. Based on our little tit for tat on the stoop earlier, I'd say it was palpable between us.

Being interrupted by her mother hadn't been the ending I wanted. For the second time in a week, I found myself wanting to punch a woman. The way Jacqueline Hanover spoke to her brilliant daughter told me everything I needed to know about her. She was the classic elitist bitch who thought her shit didn't stink, and everyone else was beneath her. Throwing her off with a kiss on her hand, as much as it pained me to do, was at least entertaining. The woman had probably never been properly touched by a man, resulting in some of her icy exterior.

When Loren remained frozen in the front of the room, I wrapped an arm around her waist, pulling her into me. Her body melded to mine, and I soaked in the sensation of having her this close to me. If her parents weren't in the room right now, along with whoever this asswipe was, I'd throw her down on the couch and finally give her the treat I'd been promising for weeks. My face buried in her sweet cunt.

Directing her toward a seat, I avoided the guy sending death glares my way. It was comical, and I rolled my eyes at his face. This corporate pansy wannabe thought he was intimidating. I'd laugh if it weren't so pathetic. I could kill him with my pinky in more ways than he could even think of. Using my asshole persona to my advantage, I ignored his death glare as I shifted my hand lower on her hip.

The room was quiet as we entered, and I wondered who the fuck these other guests were. The rudeness protruding from them amazed me, though. Taking Loren's willingness as consent, I pulled her along and sat on the sofa, dragging her into my lap and draping her across. Shock displayed across her face as she looked up at me.

"Time to shake things up, spitfire."

My words had her smiling, and some of the fire returned to her eyes. She stayed on my lap and turned her head to face her parents, crossing her legs as she did. The dress she had on was the perfect combination of her own style. It was classy but dared on the side of danger with little flares of sex. The deep red suited her, and it reminded me of the lipstick she'd worn Friday, the one I wanted wrapped around my cock.

At the thought, I felt myself begin to harden beneath her ass. My hand on her thigh rubbed small circles, slowly inching her skirt up. As I contemplated how far I could push up her dress, the room remained quiet. Everyone focused on us. I was about to give them a show they apparently felt they'd paid admission for when the dicknozzle spoke.

"Who the hell is *this*?"

Loren tensed at his words, yet her face remained

passive. She was draped over my legs, her back in the crook of my arm as she leaned against the armrest. Spitfire turned her icy stare to the asshole, and for once, I was glad not to be in her line of sight as she stared him down.

"That's none of your business, Brian. You lost that privilege a year ago. Well, more like two, but who's counting?" Loren's voice was steady, and if I couldn't feel her pulse racing from holding her, I'd believe she was calm as a cucumber. Dismissing, who I now assumed was her ex, she addressed her mother.

"Mother, I'm not certain why my attendance is required for this evening. Brian and I are over and will *never* get back together. The ring on *her* finger also solidifies that. I doubt you're so cruel as to invite me to dinner with my ex-husband to celebrate his new engagement. Perhaps, though, you are. Why else would you tell me to arrive after him, dressed to impress, if not to humiliate me on some front?"

"Now, Loren. I'm sure there's been a misunderstanding. Your mother meant no—"

"That's where you're wrong, Father. I'm done tolerating her abuse. I realized tonight, even before this hellish fiasco, how little of importance I am to her. So, no, I don't believe there was any other reason for her to invite me here with *him* unless it was to embarrass *me*."

"Why would I need to embarrass you, dear? You do that all on your own. Parading around with someone like *him*."

"Someone like him? Do you mean someone who respects me? Someone who sees all the fire within me?

Someone who thinks I'm worthwhile? That kind of person? Hmm?"

"Loren, you're being unreasonable and a bitch. I don't know what you're trying to pull, but if it was to make me jealous, it's not working," the douchenozzle scoffed.

"Give me a break, Brian. I wouldn't touch you with a 10 foot pole. There's no part of me whatsoever that wants to make you jealous. Besides, why do I need to make you jealous when I have him? Not to mention, I just stated I had no clue you were even going to be here until I walked in five minutes ago, so check your ego at the door, you arrogant bastard."

"Loren, now, there's no need to call names."

I assumed her father stated it as her mother shrieked at the language and fanned herself at the scene unfolding in her sitting room. The blonde and the older guy remained quiet, almost watching it like a tennis match in front of them.

Loren's breath came quickly now, and I could tell she was on the verge of erupting in rage. Standing in one move, I lifted her easily in my arms. A tiny squeak left her at the jostle, her arms going around my neck. I stood, facing toward the exit, wanting to get the hell out of this dungeon. Loren had been correct. It wasn't all it was cracked up to be. This house was worse than some of the crack houses I'd seen.

"Where do you think you're going?" Mrs. Hanover shrieked.

Not even stopping, I tossed over my shoulder, "No offense. Actually, all the offense, this place is a hellish nightmare, and if I spend one more second here, I'm liable to shoot someone. As I don't want to deal with cleaning up blood tonight since I plan to be balls deep in your daughter here, I figured I'd save us all the trouble and leave quietly, but if you prefer for me to stay… " I paused as I waited, their looks of shock laughable as their mouths dropped open. "Yeah, that's what I thought."

Loren's laugh at my statement encouraged my caveman tendencies, and I continued right on walking out of the house. No one else even tried to stop us as they sat mouths agape, watching us leave.

"That was the sexiest thing I think I've ever heard. I don't even mind you acting like a neanderthal and carrying me out of there. In fact, I think I want to travel this way from now on," she teased, not knowing I was on board with this plan. I'd carry her to the ends of the earth if it meant I got to hold her in my arms and fuck her brains out. I was romantic like that, after all.

"Did you see their faces when you joked about killing people? I thought my mother was going to faint!"

"Who said I was joking?"

"You're hilarious."

A sobering reality hit me as I realized she had no idea of the person she was with. I'd never cared before. They were just women to be used for a need, and then I moved on. I didn't care about them, and they didn't care about me. We were two bodies enjoying the pleasure we could create.

Spitfire was different. She wasn't from our world and didn't know the inherent risks. Setting her on her feet by the car, I realized we hadn't grabbed our coats on the way out.

"I'll be right back."

Almost dreamily, she looked up and nodded, a beautiful smile on her face. Returning to the house, I walked in, hoping to bypass any of the hosts and just grab our jackets and, most importantly, the keys to the car. Shouting came from the room we'd just left. Slowing, I dropped back to listen, some habits I was unable to break.

"You told me she knew he was going to be here!" a masculine voice I assumed to be her father yelled.

"You're overreacting, Kenneth. Loren's a spoiled bitch. You let her get away with everything and now look at her. With some lumberjack maniac in a suit! She purposefully did that to upset me and ruin *my* party. Don't you see? She's out to get me and ruin my life!"

Her mother started to cry, and it took all I had in me not to go in there and laugh in her face. Her manipulation was blatant, but it worked as I heard her father start to soothe his wife.

"I don't like the way he was holding her. You need to do something about this before she ruins her reputation and her value. If she's fucked him, the deal is off. I don't want sloppy seconds."

Rolling my eyes, I'd heard enough and turned to grab our coats. The other two guests, who I assumed must be a couple and acquaintances of her parents, had remained quiet throughout most of the ordeal, making me forget about them. So when the blonde spoke up, her disinterested counterpart remaining silent, I stood for a moment longer to hear what she had to add to the party.

"She's a slut! How is she with that man and my ex? Who was she with the other day?" her nasally voice asked.

"Brittni. I already told you it was Monroe, and your sister did the same. You'll get your custody. I just need to find out what my ex-wife is up to. Jacqueline, you said she was still a depressive waste, barely leaving her house. If that was the case, why did she look like that? Hmm? And why was she with that type of man? You've been lying, Jackie!"

"How dare you! I'm not the one who is lying here. It's obvious Loren has been lying to us all and sleeping her way through the city."

Disgusted by what I heard and tired of their bickering and putting Loren down, I gathered up our coats and stormed out, making sure to slam the door behind me. I hoped to send some fear into the cold hearts of those left in the house.

People believed the mafia was evil, vile, and corrupt. I'd say the upper echelon was where true evil resided. The hate and betrayal in that room from people who were supposed to be her family repulsed me.

The mafia might kill. The mafia might steal. But the mafia was a family you could count on.

Blood in, blood out. Mafia was family for life.

THIRTY-FIVE

ATTICUS

The pounding in my head hadn't stopped since Friday afternoon, and I didn't think it would go away any time soon. At this rate, I'd need to buy Tylenol in bulk. Massaging my temples, I couldn't make heads or tails of the note I received this morning.

It's time we meet. Corner of Union and Roosevelt. 7 pm.
Come alone.
   -D

Sighing, I buttoned my coat and headed out for the meeting. Sax had been avoiding me since Friday night, and honestly, it made it easier. I knew he was upset with me, and I didn't blame him. For the first time in my life, I had to keep something from him. Each second that passed felt like scorching hot lava burning me from the inside, and there wasn't an antacid on the planet capable of helping me.

With Sax making himself scarce, I slipped out of the building without being questioned and into my Bugatti before anyone knew I was gone. The engine purred to life, and despite my loathsome meeting companion, I could enjoy my drive. I needed to do this more, the simple feeling of switching gears calmed my mind. Nothing but the sound of the engine with me as I zoomed along the streets.

I didn't regret taking over the family. It was something I'd been bred to do my whole life, and after what my Father had orchestrated, the Grim Reaper couldn't be allowed to stay in command. It would've tainted the family we'd built and the respect we'd gained as Mascros for the past hundred years. I couldn't allow that. So, my father had to go, and I'd been the one to do it. I didn't regret it, but part of me had wished for more time.

Despite being in my mid-thirties, I still felt unprepared, and maybe, that was a joke life played on you. It always seemed simpler from the other perspective, when in reality, it was anything but. Coming into the role of boss like I had, it left a lot of loose ends, and I was still chasing them six months later. My father had made this part look easy, but maybe he'd lied about that too. When your role model turned out to be the devil, it threw everything you'd built your life around into chaotic disarray.

Shifting down, I slowed the car as I came closer to the intersection. It was already dark at this time of year, and not many people were out on a Sunday evening. Between the hour and the chill, most families were tucked in their warm homes, preparing for the start of their week. The location he'd picked was a park on the edge of a neutral zone. While the city wasn't precisely cut into sectors, we all did have our divisions we tended to stay in. It helped in the business sense to keep those lines clear.

Parking, I waited as the engine died, its clicking sound ominous. The night was eerily silent around me, and I couldn't even make out any insects. How scary must a place be if even the critters avoided it?

Accepting my fate, I stepped out of my car, straightening my suit and coat. My shoes squeaked with each step I made on the sidewalk as I made my way to the entrance at the corner. No one was present yet, but it was a power move to wait until I revealed myself before making himself known. Even if only to ensure I came alone.

Which was stupid on my part. I hadn't told anyone where I was going. If I didn't return, no one would know where to start looking. It had been a desperate move, and I hoped I wouldn't regret it.

I needed this to end. For me, for Immy. And for—

"I see you got my message."

His sinister voice coated me, my skin prickling as he strolled out of the shadows. Like I'd assumed, he'd been waiting for me to approach before he made himself known. It was the right move and what I'd have done in his position. It gave him an advantage, and in war, every little angle mattered. These might be neutral grounds, but I was under no pretense that we weren't currently on his turf.

"What is this about, *Darren*?"

"Straight to the point, Mascro. Can't say I don't like

your style. Your father was always so *chatty*. It got old after a while, though."

"My father was a *traitor*."

"Well, I suppose he was. But he owed me a job, and since he didn't deliver, you're going to pay instead. If not," he shrugged, "well, what happened to your sister will be child's play for what I have in store for your pretty little *girlfriend*."

"Girlfriend? You must mean Michelle, my fiancée."

Darren barked out a cruel laugh. "You must think I'm an idiot if you believed I'd fall for that line of bullshit. I know a fake arrangement when I see one. The others might have bought it, but I know you, Atticus. Don't *forget* who you're dealing with. I'm not *my* father."

"Forget? How could I forget? You're the reason why Jaz is dead! Why Immy was raped!"

A sardonic guffaw escaped him, and I realized too late I'd fallen into his trap.

"Tsk, tsk, little Mascro," he smiled, nothing but mirth in his glare. "I'd say we were all to blame for Jaz and well, *Immy*, collateral damage in our life, and you know it. I'd take it as a warning, though. Give me what I want, or I'll take it. *And you don't want me to take it.* I'll be in touch, Mascro."

Anger coursed through me, seething as I watched him walk away with no care in the world. His hands were casually in his pockets, whistling as he strolled away. Turning quickly on my heel, I headed back to my car. My hands were shaking as I approached, and I shoved them into my pockets. The Bugatti's automatic locking system engaged, unlocking the doors as I approached.

Opening the door, I slid behind the wheel and focused on my breathing. I couldn't lose everything this soon. I couldn't. I just couldn't. Slamming my fists on the wheel, all the calm I'd gained fled me, my hands shaking again. Starting the car, I buckled my seat belt before charging out of there. Spinning the wheel quickly, I did a quick turn and headed back in the other direction, speeding as I headed home.

Switching on heavy metal, I attempted to tune out the panic as I sped through the quiet streets of Chicago.

I'D BEEN HOME for about an hour and was thoroughly trashed as I sat on the floor of my office. I was hidden behind the couch, finally giving up the last time I'd come for a refill from my drink cart. I decided to sit right in front of it and save myself continuous trips back and forth. The way the room would occasionally spin had me wondering if it might've been a bad decision after all.

The empty tumbler spun around on the floor, and I watched the rainbow of colors as it reflected off the lights. It was quite beautiful and reminded me of a prism as the colors bent into one another. It reminded me of Jazzy, which wasn't surprising since she'd been firmly on my mind since my meeting. I tried to siphon through my memories to see if anything he'd said was true. Was *I* responsible for Jaz?

I'd always blamed Darren, but maybe? Memories

crashed into me, and suddenly I was eighteen again and on top of the world as her sweet voice filled my mind.

"Sax, you're coming over tonight, right? Convince Attie he needs to! It won't be the same without you two. Besides, I've taken some of my brother's stash. It'll be fun," pleaded Jazzy, a sweet smile on her face. She knelt next to him on the couch, pleading with him.

I watched as Sax rolled his eyes at her, but I could see his devotion for her clear as day, probably because it mirrored my own. Jazzy sashayed over to me next, straddling my waist when she neared. Her chestnut waves trailed down her back, and her hazel eyes sparkled as she smiled at me.

"Come on, Attie." Jaz combed her fingers through my hair, tingles coursing through me and my cock hardening. Her breath fanned my face as she leaned in, her lips close as she spoke. "My brother and father will both be out of town for meetings. This party is going to be epic. We can be together in public for once. No one will know who we are. Just three kids enjoying themselves."

Jaz began to kiss my neck, and my arousal kicked up with each kiss she left. I found my hands tightening on her waist as I held myself back from rocking up into her.

"How much does it mean to you, Jaz?"

"So much," she breathed, biting my earlobe. My body involuntarily shuddered at her ministrations, and I soon found myself kissing her, never able to resist.

"Say, yes, Attie," she pleaded one more time. Staring deep into her eyes, I gave in to what she wanted. I always did. Jazmine Delgado was my first love, and I'd do anything for her. Even defy my father to be with her. Romeo and Juliet

had nothing on us, and we were going to change the world together. Her fiery spirit had me saying yes. As I nodded, I heard Sax chuckle, knowing I'd give in. Her gleeful squeal filled the air, her hands wrapping around my neck, and I tackled her to the couch, finishing what she'd started as I rocked into her.

"Mas, wake up. Fucking hell, man."

A slap to my face woke me up as the sun streamed through the office blinds. I was sprawled out on the floor, my face stuck to a piece of paper, and my mouth dry. The noise and movement that had awakened me came into focus as I tried to wet my parched lips.

"Mas, get up. I'm too pissed at you to even try to carry your ass to the bathroom. You're going to have to do it yourself."

Sax's voice broke through the fog surrounding me, and I opened both eyes. Pushing up, I tried to gain my balance as the floor started to spin beneath me. A groan left me as I shut my eyes, willing the nausea to stop and the vomit to stay buried. I could not get sick right here. I could not.

"Jesus Christ."

Apparently, my lack of movement and pathetic state was irritating Sax. Though, it was more likely the ice out I'd done for the past, however many hours it was now, had left little sympathy for me. Peeking up at him, my plea appeared to work. He grunted and lifted me under my armpits, heaving me up. The movement was quick, and I had to slam my eyes shut hard to stop the room from the tilt it was currently set to.

"Sax, I'm sorry. I was trying to protect everyone," I slurred.

"Sorry to break it to you, pal, you're not protecting anyone in this state. Come on. I'm only helping because I don't want Immy seeing you like this."

He carried me to the bathroom attached to my office, my feet not cooperating with the direction. Sax leaned me up against the counter before he opened the glass door and turned on the shower. Before I could undress, I was hauled into the ice-cold shower, effectively waking me right the fuck up.

"Fuck! What the hell, man?"

Spluttering water out of my mouth, I tried to get out from under the spray, but the strong arm kept me pinned there. Cussing him every name, he didn't relent. Eventually, I was fully awake, shivering from the cold water, and Sax let me go. Pushing him aside, I stepped out of the shower, dripping water as I went.

Swiveling, I turned my anger toward him. "You have no right! I'm the fucking *boss*. I should have you beat for that," I seethed.

Sax glared at me, rolling his eyes as he made his way out, offering me no words. With shaky fingers, I unbuttoned my shirt and wadded it up into a ball. Flinging it at his back, I felt some satisfaction as the splat hit him squarely. Sax's tall frame had been a disadvantage to him in this situation.

He turned slowly, a glower on his face, but it had no effect on me. He didn't scare me. I was my own enemy here. My rage intensified, and I found myself having a standoff in my dripping wet, eight hundred dollar pants.

"You crossed a line."

"I crossed a line? Me? That's rich coming from you, Mas. You've done nothing but block me out since Friday evening. You got fucking *engaged,* and I was the last to know. Our brotherhood used to mean something, but these past three days, it's meant *shit.* You did that. *You.* So take your sorry ass excuses and man the fuck up. I might not be in your inner circle anymore, but I was still number two last I checked. So get yourself dressed and ready. We have a family meeting in an hour."

Sax's words struck me square in the chest and the hard exterior I'd been holding around me finally cracked and splintered all over the floor. He turned to leave, wanting nothing to do with me, and I didn't blame him. In my attempts to save everyone, I'd done the one thing we said we'd never do. Keep shit hidden from one another.

"You're right. I'm sorry. I'm so fucking sorry."

At my confession, he paused in the doorway. Sax didn't turn around, but he also didn't leave. Taking it as the olive branch I needed, I told him everything.

"When we got back from lunch, there was an envelope on my desk. It was a picture from our outing and had a bullseye around Loren's face. I panicked, okay? I thought if I pushed her way, made it known she wasn't anyone important, then she would be safe. I thought I was doing the right thing. I knew I couldn't tell you, though. You'd see through the lie, and I had to make everyone believe. I had to, Sax. I had to."

Tears I hadn't felt in years came to the surface, but I pushed them back down. I was the fucking boss. I didn't cry. Sax had tensed at my words, but with each spoken word, he'd softened and slowly began to turn.

"This isn't all about that, though, is it? What else are you keeping from me, Mas?'

Sax didn't sound angry anymore. His voice was filled with exhaustion and mostly pain. I'd done that. I'd self-ishly pushed him away in an attempt to be the hero. My own need to protect someone after my epic failures resulted in me hurting my best friend. That wasn't fair to him. Sax had always stood by my side. My failures and successes were also his.

Hanging my head, I nodded, exhaustion coating me as well. We'd become so occupied trying to protect others that we'd forgotten the most important rule. *Never take your eyes off the horizon because the mafia never sleeps.* The moment you looked away, your enemy moved closer. We'd grown so accustomed to the relative peace we'd held for years that we'd become soft. It was time to change that. If our family was going to survive the war brewing, then we needed to be stronger.

"I still hear her laugh at times, you know. She was my first failure, and Immy was my second. I didn't want to add another regret. Loren isn't involved in any of this They at least knew the score, the life. Not that they deserved it anymore, but…"

"You don't think I feel the same as well? Mas, you weren't the only one with Jaz. You weren't the only one who loved that girl. We both have to live with the regret until the day we die. But we *know* who is responsible for her death. While we might've been there, we didn't force her to take the pills, nor did we know they'd be laced. We *couldn't* have known, Mas. Beating yourself up for an accident does nothing."

"You're right. I know you are. But I can't make it go away!" I shouted, beating my chest. "It won't go away."

Clasping my wet undershirt in my fist, I ripped it until I was free of the sodden garment. Slapping the space above my heart where my raven tattoo lay, I tried to feel the pain I felt I deserved, even if only self-inflicted.

A hand grasped my fist before I could slap myself again, and I looked up to find Sax had moved closer to me. His blue eyes held sorrow, and it broke the last bit of strength I held. He wrapped his arms around me, and for the first time since I was a young boy, I broke down and cried in my best friend's arms.

Sobs wracked me as all the pain, guilt, and shame fled me as the tears fell down my cheeks. I grieved for the girl who was taken from us way too soon, I grieved for the man who'd never let anyone else in, and I grieved for the sister who'd been too pure to witness horrors. My only hope was that Immy could rebound from this. She'd slowly begun putting the pieces of her life back together, and I wanted it to be a full one.

After a time had passed and my tears had dried, I stepped back as I gathered myself. Sax's face showed every emotion he felt, and I realized the selfishness of my own behavior. We hadn't talked about it. We hadn't even mourned, nor did we relieve ourselves of the pain we felt at her loss. I'd been so young. Twenty years ago felt like a lifetime. Neither of us had been equipped to deal with her death, and Immy's close call had opened up old wounds. Now I had to take the penance my actions had caused.

"I met with Darren last night."

Silence met me as I knew it would. Meeting his eyes, I was surprised when I didn't find Sax's anger directed at me.

"That explains the whiskey binge," he answered, nodding in understanding.

Sighing, I leaned back against the sink, relieved as I prepared to disclose the last few secrets I'd kept.

"He says Dayton, the Grim Reaper, owed him a job, and if we don't pay, then he'll do unthinkable things to Loren. We were sloppy, and we've brought her into this mess now."

"Fuck."

"Yeah, *fuck*."

"Do we have any idea what this job is?"

"Nope. Just that he'll be in touch, based on what we've uncovered so far, Dayton helped them run things. He was trying to break into a different side of the business. I have a bad feeling it has to do with something we won't like."

"We need to find a way to get ahead of him."

"We've been so focused on picking up the pieces. We forgot to stay focused on the whole picture. He's had us jumping through hoops from the start, and I, for one, am done."

"Agreed. We need to source out the mole today. We can't keep chasing our own tails. I'm tired of playing his game. Darren Delgado wants a job. Well, I'm about to give him one. Cleaning up his own mess."

We stared at one another, plans unfolding in our minds, the tension gone between us. It felt so stupid now when I thought about it. I was better than my father because I didn't do things on my own. I trusted Sax, so I needed to trust him to be capable of handling things.

"I'll start making calls. Just one more thing," Sax stated, pausing in the doorway.

"Go ahead."

"The engagement. That's fake, right?"

"Of course. She's just some girl I found on Tinder and told her to act like my fiancée for a period of time, and I'd pay her ten grand."

He nodded, and I caught a slight smile on his face before he turned.

"Wait, why?"

Fully smirking now, Sax turned, leaning against the door jamb. "Just means I knew all along you had feelings for her."

"That's ridiculous. I barely know her. I just didn't want her to die because she's helping Immy."

"Sure, if that's what you need to tell yourself, Mas. But answer me this…" he paused, being dramatic.

Rolling my eyes, I started to undo my pants and shoved off the wet fabric. Gesturing for him to continue, I turned on the shower, hot this time, and discarded the rest of my clothes in a damp heap on the floor as I waited for him to spill. When I stepped into the shower, Sax finally answered.

"If you hadn't cared, why did you look jealous as fuck on Friday when you saw her with Nicco? Or why were you hard as you sat across the table from her? And how did you know I meant Loren when I asked?"

I clenched my jaw, not wanting to admit anything, and he nodded, smiling wide.

"Yeah, you're right. She's *just* Immy's therapist."

Laughing, he left, walking out of the now steam-filled bathroom as I cussed under my breath. I wasn't ready to admit yet the answers to his questions.

Thirty-Six

LOREN

S ax had dropped me off at home last night, and I'd been surprised when all he did was kiss my hand after walking me to my door. I watched him from my peephole as long as I could, but he never turned back. I should've been happy. I didn't need another man in my life to complicate things further, but I couldn't deny his sex appeal or the way I responded to him.

Now, in the light of day, self-doubt crept up, and I kept falling into the trap of believing I was crazy for even entertaining the idea. I was *meek* Loren, *mousy* Loren. Only ever been with one man *Loren*. I had nothing to offer these men, and once they found out I wasn't as exciting as I pretended, I'd be dropped to the curb faster than you could say "bye".

Sighing for the third time, I'd officially annoyed myself. Staring at my computer, I realized the one good thing about the day had been my mother not calling. The daughter, who always atoned and kowtowed to her mother, struggled not to pick up the phone and apologize profusely. The anxiety rode me hard all day, but then I would remember her smug smile and satisfaction at seeing me caught off guard by *his* presence, and I'd shut my anxiety down.

How could she invite my ex-husband, the man who'd cheated and abandoned me while I grieved in a pit of depression? And while wearing a smile? She acted like she had done me a fucking favor! The more I thought about it, the more self-righteous strength rose up in me. I was *angry*, and I liked it.

This time, *she* would need to apologize to *me*. I was done letting her control me with her manipulation and lies. It was sad it took me thirty-odd years to get to this point, but I was *here*. That had to count for something.

"Loren, I'm heading out. Do you need anything before I go?"

Glancing up, I found Doris in my doorway. Was it already after 6 pm? Blinking, I shook my head. "I'm good, Doris. Thank you, though."

"Okay, Daphne's already gone, so you're the last one. Don't stay too late. You look tired, dear."

"Yeah, I'm almost done. I'll see you tomorrow."

She waved and walked out, a look of concern on her face. A little too late to be concerned now, Doris. Though at that thought, a realization hit me. *My mask wasn't on.* I'd worn the metaphorical mask hiding my pain for the better part of two years. No one outside my condo had known the absolute despair I'd felt. If Doris thought I looked tired now, I must not be shielding my emotions anymore.

Was this a good thing or a bad thing? I couldn't decide.

Checking the screen, I realized I zoned out halfway through my last client's note. Finishing up the last bit, I locked my charts and signed out of everything before gathering my belongings. Quickly, I closed up and turned off all the lights as I headed to the door. Pulling out my keys, I felt something flutter to the ground as I locked the door. Reaching down, I picked up the card. It was a business card. Ignite Ink, Nicco's shop.

An idea struck me at the sight, and I hoped it would be a good one. Things had been weird since Friday, and while we'd texted off and on, it hadn't felt like it had before that night. While I couldn't do anything about the confidentiality thing and his trust on the concept, I could be vulnerable and reach out to him this time. He'd chased me down the first time, so now, it was my turn.

Fortunately, his shop was close to where I lived. He'd mentioned it that evening when we ended up at his place. Cutting over two blocks I didn't usually go down, I took in a part of the city that was new to me. I'd probably driven down this way before, but I hadn't stopped to see what was around me. Sometimes, life went by so fast you forgot you were meant to live it. Ferris Bueller and John Lennon both had it right. *"Life is what happens when you're busy making other plans."*

Before I made it to his shop, I spotted it from the other side of the street. A fire symbol in Neon with graffiti lettering of Ignite Ink was on the front of the window. Looking both ways, I crossed the road and headed to the door, pushing down my anxiety at entering a new place. The bell jangled, and the sounds of heavy rock music greeted me. An older woman with purple hair, several piercings, and dark lipstick looked up at my entrance.

"Welcome to Ignite Ink. How can we help you this evening?"

Despite her colorful exterior, she appeared sweet and engaging, helping to quell my nervous energy as I walked forward.

"Hi, um, yes," I stuttered, face flaming. "Sorry, I was wondering if Nicco was in?"

"Do you have an appointment, dear?"

"Oh, no. I don't have an appointment. I was just hoping to catch him. Maybe this was a bad idea. Excuse me. I'll just head out."

Turning, I was almost to the door when his voice stopped me.

"Loren?"

Letting go of the handle, I turned and took him in. Nicco wore a look of confusion, causing my anxiety to return. Shit, this was bad. I shouldn't have come here.

"Sorry, I was just leaving."

Turning quickly, I tried to get out of the door as fast as possible, berating myself in my head the whole while making me clueless to anything behind me

"Loren, please. Stop."

His words halted my movement, but I stayed facing the door, unable to meet him. My breathing came fast as I focused on my reflection in the door. I could see him behind me as he approached me cautiously like a wild animal.

"Beautiful, what's wrong? Is everything okay? *Please,* look at me."

Nicco cautiously touched my shoulder, and when I didn't pull away, he slowly turned me in his arms. I went willingly, my body seeking his touch. Nicco tilted my chin up and gently tucked my hair back as he did. My whole life, I'd read about that move, seen it in movies and TV shows, and yet, I'd never experienced it the way I had with him. Shivers erupted over my body, and I sucked in a breath at his touch. His eyes searched mine, and his question started to sink through the anxiety I'd been feeling.

"Everything's fine. I just," I shrugged, "wanted to see *you.*"

"You did, huh?"

My words had his eyes stop searching and land on me squarely. Being the center of Nicco's focus was better than any drug. He made me feel strong, beautiful, and capable with just a look. The heat coursing through his dark eyes had my breath spiking again, but this time for a completely different reason.

"Yeah."

"Well, what did you have planned once you got here?"

"I didn't think past that point, actually," I admitted, a smile gracing my lips. His chuckle did naughty things to my lady parts, and flashes of all the lustful things I wanted to do with him filled my head.

"Well, how about I introduce you to all the gawkers behind me, and then you can come to the back with me?"

He smiled and raised his voice on the last part, knowing we had a crowd of onlookers. I peeked over his shoulder and saw three people with guilty looks, but then shrugged, not caring at being caught. Laughing, I buried my head in his shoulder for a second, breathing in his leather and sandalwood scent with a hint of parchment.

Fuck, his shirt was soft, I thought as I rubbed my face against the soft cotton. Even in black jeans, a plain tee, and motorcycle boots, Nicco was sexy as fuck. I was beginning to think he was more than an addiction for me, more than a fun time. Nicco was fast becoming something I craved and didn't know how to do without. I hoped I wouldn't have to find out anytime soon. It wasn't a future I wanted to imagine.

Kissing my hair, he pulled me back and linked our fingers together. We had to make an interesting couple to his coworkers. Nicco in his casual attire and me dressed in dress clothes. We were two ends of the spectrum.

Walking over to the front area, he pulled me closer into his chest as he addressed the purple-haired woman.

"Loren, this is Cassandra. She keeps us running and does our piercings." Nicco beamed, proud of his staff as he provided me with the information. He dramatically turned to her, making a big sweeping gesture.

"Cassie, I'm afraid I have to end our torrid love affair. My heart has found someone new. Please, understand." I realized it was a joke between them when she laughed, and I smiled at being included in the jest.

"Well, I guess it was going to happen at some point, Nicco. No one can sustain a love like mine forever. You will be missed."

Joining in their laughter, I turned to the woman, "Nice to meet you, Cassandra."

"Pleasure is all mine, Loren. I'm happy to meet someone Nicco likes. I was starting to wonder if he'd be the eternal bachelor."

"Hey! I'm only twenty-nine. I'm not a spinster yet!" Nicco defended, making us both laugh more at him. In a surprising move, the purple-haired, pierced Amazon gave me a gripping hug before we walked away.

"I think she likes you," Nicco whispered as we moved further into the store.

"I'm glad. I like her."

Nicco smiled down at me, squeezing me tight to his side, a happy look on his face, and I liked the way it made me feel. As we walked to the back, he introduced me to two people working on tattoos, Dave and Julie, but they didn't talk for long since they were with others.

I was impressed with the layout of the shop and how clean it was. I'd never been in a tattoo parlor, of course, but it wasn't how I imagined it. I could see Nicco's love for the place and his pride in doing well. His designs were intermingled on the walls, and I found I could identify them by look alone. They were breathtaking.

Finally, he pulled me into an office space, shutting the door behind him. Nicco dropped my hand, walking around his desk to sit in his chair. A roguish look appeared on his face, setting all my nerves on fire. He leaned back, his legs spread out as he watched me. I didn't know what he was waiting for as I shifted from one foot to the next under his gaze.

"I like your place. It's nice, Nicco."

"Thank you."

"Are you going to say anything else?"

"What do you want me to say, beautiful?"

"I don't know!" I threw my hands up, my frustration at not having the answer getting to me. "But you staring at me like that isn't helping."

"How am I staring at you, *beautiful*?"

Nicco leaned forward on the desk, his hands clasped in front of him, all of his weight on his elbows. The glint of humor in his eyes stopped me from bolting when I realized what he was doing. Nicco was pushing me, trying to get me out of my comfort zone. Once I knew he wasn't playing a mind game, I relaxed, recognizing I was safe, and a feeling of boldness emerged.

"Like you want to consume me."

"Hmm, maybe I do." His voice wrapped around me, fueling my actions as I gave way to the urges coursing through me.

Slipping off my coat, I draped it across the back of a chair and set my purse with it. Walking around the desk, my hips swayed with each step, and I knew what I wanted to do. I slid onto the desk, pushing his arms off it as I did. At first, Nicco looked shocked at the move, but as I centered myself in front of him and used my legs to pull his chair forward, he started to catch on. Scooting forward, he bracketed my legs with his arms as he trapped me in his embrace.

"Hmm. I like this position. Now, what are you going to do, Luscious Loren?"

"Well, first I wanted to talk about the other night, and then I thought we could have a little fun."

He moved back, allowing him to see my face, a serious look crossing his.

"Of course, beautiful. What do you want to talk about?"

"I… I didn't like how things ended the other night. I know we've just started dating and have already discovered my ineptness at it." I smiled, hoping to lighten the tense atmosphere. "But, I forgot an important thing to tell you. With my job, it comes with a level of confidentiality, and there will be things I'm not able to tell you."

He nodded, watching me closely. Biting my lip, I prepared myself to say the hard part. "It seemed like you punished me for it, though, and I didn't like how you withdrew both physically and emotionally."

He sat quietly for a second, and I hoped he was considering my words and not figuring out the best way to tell me to leave.

"Wow, I guess I need to get used to mature conversations if I'm going to date a therapist, huh?"

Cocking my head, I didn't understand what he was saying. "I don't understand."

"Well, maybe it's your job, or maybe your maturity, or fuck, both, but I'm used to the words, 'we need to talk' to be accompanied by screaming, crying, name-calling, and me inherently feeling like an ass. So, to hear you address the situation calmly, lay out your feelings, and then allow me to respond, it's kind of blowing my mind, beautiful."

He stood leaning over me when he finished making us the same height on the desk. Leaning into me, he kissed me slowly, full of heat. His tongue licked at the seam of my lips, before swirling with my tongue. As things started to heat up, he pulled back, his eyes intense as he stared down at me, our breathing heavy. My lips felt swollen, and I wanted more, but I was glad he'd stopped before I lost my head. I needed to hear his answer first.

The physical aspect came easy between us, and in his hands, I felt safe to explore, and I wanted it in other areas. Vulnerability was scary, and I wanted to run and hide from it. The reward felt worth it, pushing me to share with Nicco and be *known*. Placing my hands on his chest, I waited for him to respond before I could give in to the pull.

"You're right, beautiful, and I'm sorry for withdrawing from you. It wasn't fair. I got in my head and was a little jealous. I'm sorry." He kissed me softly, sealing his words, and then pulled back, a question on his face. "I'm just confused about what you mean about your job."

"Oh, yes, sorry. My husband, I mean, *my ex-husband*, knew the drill. He'd been with me all through grad school and knew there might be times when I couldn't tell him how I knew something or how I knew someone." I paused, assessing him. "It's not me keeping things from you like in a normal capacity. It's different because of my job and what that entails. I meet a lot of different people and know a lot of personal details. I try to keep it all separate, but sometimes, life overlaps. Confidentiality is important to me, and I need you to understand that. My job and now the mentoring might create situations where I can't tell you things."

"Beautiful, you don't have to explain it to me. I get it. My family," he paused, "well, it's kind of the same way. We have secrets, and there are things I have to keep to myself. I don't want to lie to you either, but there might be times I have to. I messed up the other night, and I reacted poorly. I let my feelings get in the way of what I knew to be the truth. I promise to talk to you next time and not shut down."

Processing his words, I tried to understand what he was saying and if it was something I could deal with. "Will you ever lie about things that concern me?"

"No. Anything that concerns you and me is yours to know. I won't hide anything that will affect that. I promise."

Nodding, I sealed it with a kiss. "Okay."

"Okay?"

"Yeah."

"So that's what a mature adult conversation sounds like, huh? I like it," he teased.

"If you keep saying mature like it means old person, I'm going to show you how I kicked Wells in the balls."

"Ouch, okay, okay," he chuckled. "Healthy. How does that sound?"

"Much better. Okay, *young stud*," I winked. "Now that you have me on your desk. What are you going to do with me?"

"Oh, beautiful, I have… so… many… plans."

Between each word, he punctuated it with a kiss and started to trail them down my neck. The v-neck of my shirt offered him an excellent opening to pepper kisses on my chest. Running my fingers up his neck, I threaded my fingers into his thick dark hair as he began to lick and suck my sensitive skin. Wrapping my legs around his waist, I pulled him more into me and felt his hard erection hit me right where I needed it.

Moans escaped me as I rocked against him, my head thrown back as I reveled in the sensations coursing through me. Nicco's hands grabbed onto my hips and scooted me further, our bodies melding together.

"You smell so good, beautiful."

Nicco's hot breath fanned over my skin and my flesh pebbled at the sensation. His hands moved over me, exploring all I had to offer him. Inching up my shirt, his thumbs traced patterns along the bare skin he uncovered. I was a writhing mess as I held his head to me and rocked against him. With my other arm, I pulled his shirt up, feeling his hot skin beneath it. Our moans echoed around the room, and I didn't even care if all of his employees could hear.

In a frenzy, we both began to claw at one another, and I couldn't get his shirt over his head fast enough. Each time I glimpsed his inked chest, I marveled at the artwork there. Tracing his abs with my fingers, I journeyed down to unbutton his pants, looking up at him. Nicco had stopped, watching me as I ran my fingers across his skin. When our eyes met, he snapped and attacked my mouth with passion.

Clasping my face with both hands, he consumed me like I'd never been kissed before. Nicco possessed my lips in a way that made me feel like the most precious and sexiest thing in the world. I never had to be *only* one thing with him. He gave me the freedom to be all the parts of myself, both light and dark.

Dropping his hands, he pushed my shirt over my head. Our bare skin touched as he brought his body closer, and I needed the last layer removed. Thankfully, Nicco had the same thought, and a moment later, I felt his nimble fingers unhook my bra. As much as I wanted him to rip it off and make me his, the slow caress of his finger as it gently lowered my strap off my arm did things for me.

Nicco's hand trailed down, leaving light touches in its wake. As my breast became exposed, his mouth lowered, and he began to softly graze kisses on the top of my chest as his other hand performed the slow torturous trek with my other strap. I panted, the small touches and kisses arousing me in new ways. Nicco had mastered seductive and passionate gestures, effortlessly bringing me to the height of passion in the process.

"Beautiful, your skin is so soft and unmarked. My lips want to taste every inch of you and paint you with my art." Nicco continued to drop kisses but headed further down my body, stopping at my breasts.

"Nicco," I moaned, unable to form any other words. Almost as if his name had spurred him on, he took one nipple into his mouth, sucking it as he twirled his tongue over the hardened peak. His thumb brushed over my other breast, working in tandem with his mouth, dragging a long moan from me.

"Your moans are the most beautiful sounds in the world. I hear them in my sleep, and I wake up missing you."

A whimper left me, and I felt my body start to tense up in preparation for an orgasm. It surprised me, but I threw my head back, sensations assaulting my body as I came. No longer wanting to wait, I reached my hand down and rubbed the outside of his jeans, receiving a moan into my skin.

"*Fuck*, beautiful."

"Nicco, I need you. I need your cock inside me and stretching me."

"Fucking hell."

I finished undoing his pants from earlier and yanked down his zipper. Nicco was working on mine as well, and it was an unspoken competition to see who could get the other out of their pants quicker. Pushing his boxers down, his cock sprung free, and I wrapped my hand around the thick base.

At my touch, Nicco stilled, panting into my shoulder. I continued to pump him up and down, and a switch flipped in him. One second, I was stroking his cock in long pulls, rubbing my thumb over the tip, and the next, I was flipped around, my feet settling on the floor as he shoved my slacks the rest of the way down.

I barely had time to brace myself before he slammed inside of me with great force. Nicco's hands gripped my hips, and I was sure to have fingerprint marks afterward. Laying across the desk, I grabbed the other edge to brace myself from the impact as he pounded into me.

"Fuck, fuck, fuck," he moaned. "Jesus, Loren, you're so wet and tight. I couldn't wait a moment longer to feel your heat around me."

Damn, his words skirted the edge of poetic and dirty making me crave him even more.

"Yeeessss," I moaned, my sounds taking on a life of their own. There was no doubt everyone heard us at this point, and though I should be embarrassed, I couldn't find the energy to care, not when Nicco was bringing my body to incredible heights.

In quick succession, my body tightened, and I soared over into another orgasm as my body felt like it exploded into a million pleasure particles. Nicco slammed into me one last time, the force so great the desk moved as he pulled me tight to him when he emptied into me. Panting, he released my hips to fall next to me on the desk as we laid there trying to return to Earth.

"Shit," he cursed.

"Huh?" I mumbled. My brain wasn't functioning fully yet.

"I forgot to use a condom. I'm so sorry, Loren. I promise I'm clean, and if anything happens, I'm not going to abandon you."

Sobering reality slammed into me. My body tensed, and Nicco felt it. Slowly, he lifted off me and withdrew. I stayed face down, not ready to have this conversation. Nicco, thinking I was upset, softly turned and lifted me until he cradled me in his arms. Walking around the desk, he sat us down on the couch, both of us naked, but he didn't seem to care about that.

"I'm sorry, Loren. I wasn't thinking. I'll get the morning-after pill and get tested. Whatever you need, I'll do it. Just don't shut me out."

Lifting my head, I caressed his cheek, wanting to comfort him. This wasn't about any of that, and I didn't want him to freak out.

"It's not that, Nicco. I'm not upset about what

happened. It's just... I hadn't thought I would need to have this conversation so soon, you know."

"Whatever it is, you can tell me."

His voice was soft and comforting, and I knew I could tell him. Nodding, I took a big breath before sharing my deepest shame.

"You don't have to get the pill or worry about dealing with it later."

"Okay..."

"You don't have to worry because... I can't."

"You can't what, beautiful?" Concern was in his eyes as I stroked his cheek.

Sucking in a breath, I exhaled the part of me that could never be healed. "I can't get pregnant."

"So, you're on the pill?"

I shook my head, a tear rolling down my face.

"I don't understand, beautiful." Nicco wiped my cheek, worry showcased in his tender touch.

"No, fuck, I'm messing this up." My voice wobbled more, and I hated how much this still affected me.

"Hey, it's okay, Loren, if you're not ready to tell me, you don't have to."

His kindness gave me the courage I needed to say the words I hadn't been able to say aloud for two years.

"I'm not on the pill, Nicco," I paused, "because I can't get pregnant. I don't have any eggs."

"Oh, beautiful." He pulled me into his arms, holding me, and for once, I felt comforted in my pain.

THIRTY-SEVEN

WELLS

Any movement I made hurt, but I couldn't miss any more work. Not only did I owe the thugs and other debtors, but I still needed to eat and pay bills too. If I couldn't fight soon, I would need to take another job, or perhaps three at this rate. The amount Delgado wanted from me kept getting higher, and I couldn't see a light at the end of this deadly tunnel. I was in way over my head, with no clear direction of escape.

"Oof, man. You've seen better days!" One of the other trainers snickered when they caught sight of me in the locker room.

Pinning him with my eyes, I conveyed the pain I wanted to rain down on him for his asinine remark. Commenting on obvious facts always brought out my sarcasm. Add in my perpetual dark cloud, and my looks were deadly. Based on his swallow and quick exit, it seemed he got the picture.

Slowly, I placed my bag in my locker and sat down on the bench. I had two more sessions today, and then Loren. My feelings were a mixed bag with her, and the weekend hadn't made anything clearer. I hated her most of the time, but then her fire would ignite the pain inside, and I wanted to burn with her. It was dark and didn't make a whole lot of sense, but it was what I felt.

Taking a deep breath, I mustered the strength to get off the damn bench. The Advil I'd taken earlier wasn't cutting it, but I wouldn't take anything else. I couldn't go down that path. It was a future I didn't want for myself, even if my future was bleak. Pushing through the doors, I swallowed the pain down to deal with these last two clients.

Think of the dogs, think of the dogs, think of the dogs.

"Cynthia, are you ready to burn those calories today?"

"Oh, yes. Let's do this, *Wells*." She licked her lips, thrusting her chest out toward me as I approached. These MILF's all had fantasies of bagging a trainer, but I had no interest in them. This job was a means to an end and nothing more.

Ignoring the sexual undertones, I got to work. Lunge squats were in her future and perhaps would keep her away from me for a time. Running her through the warm up, I zoned into the process and tried to ignore everything else. The pain, the loneliness, *the guilt.*

"Great job today, Karen. I'll see you next week."

Smiling, I walked to the locker room, finally finished with my second client. Once I was through the door, I dropped the fake expression and collapsed onto the bench. My whole body hurt, and I wanted to do nothing but sleep for hours. How was I going to do this day in and day out? I might as well start digging my grave myself because I would be in it by the end of the week, either from Delgado when I didn't pay or the pain.

Both options felt about the same at the moment.

"Wells, you in here?"

"Hmm?"

"Wells?"

Footsteps followed the voice as they came around the lockers, but I couldn't find the energy to open my eyes to see who it was. Part of me hoped it was the Reaper finally coming to collect my soul. I'd welcome it at this point. A slap to the face had me blinking my eyes open a few seconds later, finding two Monroes in front of me. Lights shone around him in whites and golds.

"Mo?" I whispered, my head spinning. "Am I dead? I'm sorry I screwed everything up. It makes sense you're an angel. You always were the best thing in my life," I mumbled, my head falling back.

"Wells, can you hear me? You're not dead, buddy. Just in pain, I think. Can you keep your eyes open for me?"

Opening them again, I hadn't realized they'd been closed, and Monroe swam in and out of focus as I tried to find him again. Blinking helped some, and I found him kneeling down between my legs, his hands on my thighs as he watched me in concern. Thoughts I shouldn't be having about him started to form in my mind, and my cock took notice. Thankfully, Monroe was focused on my eyes and not my dick.

"There you are." He smiled, erupting butterflies I didn't want to admit to. Locking away my emotions, I shut down my wayward thoughts. I wasn't good for him. I wasn't good for anyone.

"What are you doing here?" I questioned. It came out harsher than I intended.

My words had him pulling back and standing. His hand slid down my thigh as he stood, and I prayed he didn't feel the erection I still had from his proximity. Monroe leaned back against the other lockers, blowing out a breath of his own before he answered.

"You haven't responded to my texts, and I was worried. Plus, Brittni's causing problems, so I thought I'd hit the bag for a few rounds and get out some aggression. I need to start back anyway. Hockey practice will be starting back up in a few weeks."

"What's the bitch doing now?"

There was no love lost between her and I. She'd never liked me, and after my fall from grace, it gave her even more reason to push me out of his life. Finding us together the way she had, only added gasoline to the fire where I'd been concerned. If she got hit by a bus, I'd buy the bus driver a cake. The bitch was trouble, and I didn't trust her.

Blowing out a breath, Monroe looked up at the ceiling, his tell he was about to hide something from me.

"Oh, just the usual. She's trying to fight me for full custody. It's like she forgets I'm a lawyer except for when it's about child support."

"She's a fucking bitch, and you never should've married her."

"Yeah, well, too late now. Besides, I have Levi. He's worth it."

"He is a pretty great kid," I admitted, a rare smile tilting my lips. Levi was the only good thing to come from their union. Changing the topic, I focused back on the other part of his statement. "You can hit some bags in the gym. I have my last session anyway."

"Thanks, man. You know you can ask for help if you need it."

"I know." I shook my head. I couldn't ask him for anything. I would never forgive myself if he became caught up in my mess. Monroe had made it out of the life we'd been brought up in. I wouldn't be the one to pull him back into it. "I'm good, man."

"Uh-huh."

Rolling his eyes, he walked over to the locker he used and started to undress. I caught myself watching as he slowly pulled his tie from his collar. Grumbling to myself, I focused on my breathing and slowly stood. The pain in my ribs was excruciating, but it was an effective boner killer, so at least there was that.

Heading out into the gym, I made it over to the water cooler when Loren walked in. Something about her was different today, but I couldn't place it. She regarded me closely, almost like she didn't know how to proceed either.

"Get started, kitten. Don't waste my time."

Rolling her eyes, she began her jog around the gym. At least I'd been consistent in earning eye rolls today. On her third lap, Monroe exited the other locker room. When he took in who was running, he gave me a funny look before moving over to the bags. I guess I hadn't made it evident she was my client. Oh well, not like he'd asked either. Rolling my own eyes this time, I ignored them both.

After ten minutes, I called out to Loren. "Enough."

She stopped and slowly walked over to her towel to dab at the light sheen to her forehead. Loren was in good shape and had barely broken a sweat, much less appeared winded after doing a two-mile run. As she headed to the bags, she finally noticed we weren't alone.

"Monroe?"

Her voice had him stopping and grabbing the bag he'd been pounding into. He smiled at her, a look of desire in his eyes, and I squelched the jealousy I felt.

"Hey, Lo. You don't mind if I crash your lesson, do you?"

"No, I don't mind at all."

Their smiles at one another made my insides burn. Shoving it down with all the things I couldn't have, I used my pain to mask my hidden desires. "This isn't chit-chat hour."

Sticking her tongue out at me, she skipped the rest of the way over. I tried not to take her happiness and change in mood personally, but yeah, it stung. It was what I'd wanted. What I needed even, but it still sucked. Loren began to wrap her hands like I'd taught her, and Monroe returned to his drills. The rhythm of his punches soothed me, a familiar sound to the backdrop of all the things I ignored.

Moving over to Loren, I held her bag, but when she didn't start her rounds, I looked up to find her scowling at me. My twisted soul took pleasure in it, and my dick wanted to wipe it off her face.

"What now, *kitten*?"

"You shouldn't be holding the bag for me."

"Yeah, well, it's my job, and you're not my boss."

"Maybe I should be," she sassed.

"What does that even mean, kitten?"

Flustered now, she blinked, "I don't know, okay!" Throwing her hands up, she started pacing before she finally turned, hands on her hips and a determined look on her face.

"I want to spar today instead."

"Fine."

"Good."

Picking up the mitts, I walked back out onto the mat, bracing my feet to steady myself. It was probably the more intelligent move as it would require less strength or movement on my part, but I didn't want her to know I was appreciative of her thoughtfulness. If I allowed myself an inch of space with her, I'd fall into her quicker than I could blink. I was a user, and I wouldn't use Loren or Monroe. I would shield them from me. Loren started her jabs, and I could see her improvements.

"Good. Now, faster."

Nodding, she started again as I counted off the rhythm. Increasing the tempo, she kept up with my counts until her arms began to fatigue.

"Okay, how do you feel about moving to leg kicks?"

At my question, a smile broke out on her face, and I couldn't help but return it. Her enthusiasm was beautiful, and I loved how excited she was about this. Most of the women only wanted to flirt and be seen, not here to learn anything. Loren wanted to be good at this for whatever reason. And seeing her learn something and enjoy it, gave me a sense of accomplishment I'd been missing.

"Okay, do you remember how I showed you?"

"I think so," she stated, biting her lip. Trying to ignore the way her lip looked between her teeth, I held the gloves up again for her to kick. She hesitated, then began to kick with her left leg. After she got a rhythm, she started to do better, and I gradually raised the glove higher. It became more difficult for her with each height, and I could see the frustration on her face because of it.

A sick part of me enjoyed frustrating her despite the fact she was doing well, and I pushed her to try heights most people couldn't do. When she kicked and almost fell over from the attempt, I dropped my hands, knowing I'd hit the limit for today.

"Nicely done. I'm impressed. Now, swap legs."

We went through the same routine, and Loren was able to get her leg up a little higher on this side until she made the same mistake and almost fell over. Dropping my hands, I removed the mitts and crossed my arms, studying her.

Loren was breathing heavily, sweat thick on her skin and her face red from the exertion. The smile, though, was genuine, and I realized it was the first real emotion I'd seen on her face outside her sad eyes. She hid behind a mask so often, you'd never know, but her eyes didn't lie. Not to me, at least. Most people avoided eye contact or didn't look deep enough to see what a person was feeling. I recognized her eyes, though. I saw the pain, the fear, and the grief bottled there.

This smile she shared with me felt intimate because I

was part of the reason she was smiling. My heartbeat sped up at the thought of seeing someone happy because of me for once. I hadn't felt that in a long while. Dropping my wall back into place, I realized how easily I let it go when she was around. Her ability to disarm was a risk I couldn't take.

"Good workout today. Do your cool down, and then you're dismissed."

I hated to do it, but I couldn't be around her anymore. Turning quickly, I caught the way her face fell at my words, at my dismissal. I walked away in a hurry despite the pain crying out to slow the hell down. Pushing open the doors to the locker room, I managed to make it over to the shower stall before I fell to my knees, the air panting out of me in spurts from the pain and panic.

I heard a door open and close behind me, and I prayed it wasn't her. I couldn't face her, not right now. She would see my pain clearly. My fear broadcasted for all to see. But mostly, she would see me, the real me. I couldn't let her do that. I wouldn't.

The footsteps approached, and by the weight of them, I knew it wasn't Loren. Relief flooded through me, and my panic started to dissipate at the knowledge. Gathering myself, I stood and faced the incomer, hoping it was a stranger. Of course, I wasn't that lucky.

"Why are you such an ass to her?"

Monroe sounded pissed, and as I took him in, I knew he was. He stood with his arms crossed, foot tapping, and red creeping up his neck. Monroe hated confrontation, a funny thing for a lawyer, but he did. His blonde hair and fair complexion did him no favors when he was upset, and his neck and ears would flame bright red.

"Because I *am* an ass, Roe."

Shoving past him, I headed back to my locker. Monroe had other ideas as he grabbed me by the arm and spun me around. My ribs cried out in pain at the motion. Monroe noticed my wince and let go but stayed close enough our chests touched, allowing me to feel each breath he took.

"Wells, you don't have to keep doing this. Stop punishing yourself. If you keep pushing everyone away, you're eventually going to be alone."

"Maybe that's what I want," I seethed, the vitriol heavy in my throat. Why couldn't he just leave me alone?

"*Bullshit.*"

Pushing his chest, I was tired of him constantly reminding me how much better of a person he was than me. "Just stop, okay? You're duty to make sure I don't die or whatever it is you're holding onto, it's completed. You're free. I release you of your servitude."

"You're such a fucking idiot, and if you weren't already hurt, I'd kick your ass myself."

"Like you could." I laughed, the coldness leaking from my voice making it hard as it echoed around the silent locker room.

Taking a step, he eliminated the space between us, making us practically nose to nose. Monroe got as close as possible to me and shoved a finger into my chest. "You don't get to be the only one hurting. You don't own it. So how about you quit telling me what I can and can't do and just fucking listen to what I'm saying for once?"

Monroe's breath fanned over my face, his finger still held on my chest, his cotton and waterfall scent engulfing me, and I couldn't handle it. Slapping his arm away, I stepped back out of his stratosphere where I couldn't feel or smell him enveloping me in his Monroeness. Everything felt safe and manageable in the bubble of him and me, but the moment I stepped out of it, the world crashed back in. It was a deception I couldn't afford.

"That day Brittni walked in, it was one of the best days of my life," he mumbled, some of his fight leaving him.

"How is ruining everything you built the best day?"

"Because it finally gave me a reason to leave the lying bitch who only wanted me for status. Because I finally heard the words I'd wanted to hear since I was sixteen. Because it was the first time in *years*, I heard someone say they loved me. Because for a moment," he paused, holding me to his every word, "everything in my life was perfect. *Because you and me, we've always made sense. Because whether you deserve it or not, I've loved you since I was a teenager, and that's not stopping just because you want to push me away.*"

Monroe looked downtrodden by the end, a tear struggling to escape his eyelashes. Everything in me begged to comfort him, and as I started to reach for him, he turned to leave. Dropping my hand, my head fell forward, shame coating me at his departure. What was I doing? Was it even the right thing anymore?

When Monroe reached the door, his footsteps halted, and I looked up, hoping he'd changed his mind and was heading back here. But instead, I found him paused at the door, his hand propped on the wall, almost as if he stopped himself from leaving. Staring straight ahead, no eye contact, just a voice in the room, Monroe left me with one more thing.

"I saw the way you both looked at each other earlier. I know you're doing the same thing to her as me. If you can only let one of us in, she's the real deal. Just don't push everyone away because you're scared. We're all adults here. Let us choose how we feel about things before you decide for us. You know where to find me when you stop punishing yourself."

Closing my eyes, I squeezed them shut tight, trying to hold in the emotions brimming there. I didn't deserve to feel pain or loss. I was a worthless human being, and it would be better for everyone if I left them alone. The memory of my fall from grace flitted in, reminding me how inept I was for anything good.

"Wells, my man! I've got the deal of the century for you. It's pure gold, man! We're going to make millions. Get all your clients on the phone today. They aren't going to want to sit on this one. It's a done deal."

Digging my nails into the skin on my arms, I squeezed until I could breathe again, pushing the memory away. Blood ran down in tiny streams on my arms, dripping onto the floor as I watched it. It wasn't healthy to suppress my emotions this way, but when you've been doing something for so long, it becomes a part of you regardless of whether you like it or not. I couldn't think about that time. If I allowed myself to recall one memory, they would all flood me, and I'd never make it off the floor.

Grabbing my bag, I left the gym, ignoring everyone as I went. I was still too sore for my bike, so I wobbled as fast as I could to the train. As I sat and watched the city fly by, I thought of what Monroe had said. Part of me wanted to hope things could be better, that they would work out this time.

Unfortunately, the only thing I could always count on was me, and I was way too good at goodbyes for me to ever hope for more.

THIRTY-EIGHT

LOREN

My mind whirled with uncertainty as I left Windy City. My feelings bounced all over the place, the last hour playing on a loop. I hadn't known if Wells would be in attendance when I arrived, but I had needed to do something with the energy rolling through me. I'd been prepared to do a barre class if necessary. I'd bumped into Katie the other day, and she'd made a comment about missing me, so I felt obligated to do a class now. Sadly, I hadn't missed barre. Kickboxing ticked all my boxes and fulfilled me in ways barre never had.

Whether that was to do with Surly or not, I wouldn't think about.

When Wells stormed out of the session, Monroe had told me he'd talk to him. When they both didn't return a few minutes later, I started to worry that something serious like his stitch had opened or he'd passed out.

Walking into their intimate conversation hadn't been my intention.

Thankfully, they were so engrossed in they hadn't

heard me enter. Grabbing my stuff, I took the other exit out and made my way home. I wasn't sure what I'd witnessed, but I could see the history between them. The pain and anguish on Wells's face was real, as was the longing.

Somehow I kept collecting these men with complicated pasts who made me feel more alive than I ever had. Yet, I still felt alone and on the outside looking in. Each time I seemed to get a tiny step closer to someone, distance would be inserted, whether by him or me. My mask had begun to slip, the darkness starting to leak out. Maintaining the facade of being the perfect 'everything' was wearing on me. Soon, I would crumble under it all, lost in the debris of all my failures.

I think it was what terrified me the most. That I would be forgotten to the mistakes of my past, haunted by the remnants of a person I no longer was but who no one would let go of. I would be trapped forever in a cycle of grief and despair.

The more I tasted the impulsive danger, the more I wanted it, craved it even. Wrapping it around me gave me a sense of freedom I hadn't expected. In my darkness, I could feel all the emotions I hadn't been allowed to. In the shadows, I could breathe.

Recklessness marred my skin like a tattoo now, and I wanted more.

Wanting to taste danger and walk along the edge of darkness, I made a spontaneous decision to head to Climax. Calling Nat, I found myself momentarily lost when she didn't answer. Chastising myself for treating her like my own personal taxi, I decided to take the train there. I could do this. I wanted to dance in the shadows a moment ago. Nothing said danger like the L train at night.

The train platform was empty as I waited, and I breathed deeply, reminding myself I'd wanted this. As I stepped onto the empty train car, I grabbed a seat and wistfully watched the city pass by, hoping to ignore the anxiety I felt. The lights created different images as we passed, and I soon became lost in their hypnotization. As the train stopped and started, people came and left the car, but I didn't notice.

Time passed as I sat there mesmerized by the lights watching the world spin outside the window. The buzzing of my phone had me jumping out of my skin. I'd forgotten it was in my hand after attempting to call Nat. I stared at the screen for a minute before I could compre-hend the name on the screen.

Jude.

Fumbling to answer, I dropped the phone, and it skidded across the aisle. Reaching for it, shock filled me when a boot-clad foot stepped on it. I'd been so zoned out that I hadn't paid attention to anyone else on the train. Stupid mistake as I now found myself seemingly alone with a stranger. When they didn't release my phone at my tug, I looked up to discover who the boot belonged to.

The man was handsome in a devil may care kind of way. He was muscular, his snug clothes showcasing his abs and biceps. Tattoos adorned his hands and arms, and as I traveled up further, I could make out a tattoo peeking out of his collar that wrapped around his neck.

He had light stubble on his chin, adorning a crooked smile. His eyes pierced me, mischief alight in them. His hair was dark as obsidian and brushed over on the top. The sides were kept short, offering a look of refined danger. The smirk had grown the longer I took him. It added to his appeal, even if it meant he knew I'd been observing him.

"That's my phone," I informed him, just in case me being hunched down with my hand on the device wasn't obvious enough. Kickboxing had made my inner voice sassy, that or the amazing sex from Nicco. I wasn't complaining.

"Is it *now*? Well, it seems we're in a quandary, gorgeous."

I didn't like the way he said gorgeous, and I had a feeling his words meant something different than what I heard.

"I'm not sure I understand what quandary we're in, mister. It's *my* phone. *Your* foot is on it. Move your foot, and I get my phone back. *Simple*."

"The mouth on you!" He slapped his knee, a wicked smile now playing on his lips. I didn't miss how his eyes lit with an emotion I didn't like. "Oh, the things I could do to that mouth." Seduction lay heavy in his voice. While I found his words crass and unwanted, I couldn't deny the way my body responded to him like a soft caress, his timber rolling over me.

"I think you're mistaken on what type of girl I am. Now, please. My phone."

I tugged at it under his boot again, but he stepped down harder on it, almost clipping my finger in the process. Narrowing my eyes, I felt my darkness skirt over my skin, pricking away the terror I'd been feeling moments ago. This wasn't a good situation to be in, but something inside me wanted the destruction it would cause. To unleash the wickedness in me with no discourse for my actions.

Slowly, I stood to my full height taking in the rest of the car as I did. There were two other people at the end of the train. The way they stood indicated they were with this asshole. Whether he was part of a gang or a wannabe rapist, I didn't know, but I would make him pay for the sins of all the men before him who'd underestimated me.

The train drew nearer to the next stop, and I would need to time this perfectly. Slinging my bag over my back, I approached the asshole who'd decided to tempt fate tonight. Walking seductively, I drew his gaze to me exactly how I wanted. His smirk and leer fueled the fire within, giving me the courage I needed to unleash the part of me I'd always hidden.

Faster than he could blink, I twisted his balls in my hand as I braced his throat with my forearm. The strangled cry coming out of him sent my pulse skyrocketing.

"Tell your *goons* to stay back, or I'll twist even harder."

The asshole glared at me, not believing I would or maybe could, so I applied a little pressure until I heard him whimper. "Stay… back…" he finally ordered.

Releasing his family jewels just a smidge, I bent down to whisper in his ear. "Just because I'm female doesn't mean I'm *weak*. Remember this the next time you decide to be an asshole to some woman just because you can."

He glared daggers at me, but the heat in his eyes was still there. He licked his lips, and I almost fell forward into them. Pushing my common sense up, I cast some light on the darkness to remind myself of my morals. I couldn't completely lose myself, no matter how seductive the pull was. The screech of the brakes had me remembering my time limit.

"Bit of advice, you're gonna want to ice these later. Bye, now."

In quick succession, I released his balls, grabbed my phone, and skidded out the doors onto the landing as the doors closed behind me. Panting from the effort, I turned at the banging and smiled at the goons who hadn't been fast enough. Waving my fingers, I turned and flipped them off over my shoulder. The adrenaline coursed through me hard as I jogged down the stairs needing to get far away from them. I had no clue where I was, but I felt invincible and like I could take on any of these asshats who tried to make me feel small.

My phone rang again, and I was quick to answer this time. "Hello? Jude?"

"Loren?"

"Jude, I'm here. Is everything okay?"

"Not exactly. Can you, um, can you come down to the police station?"

"The police station! What's going on? Jude?"

"I'll explain when you get here. It's the one on Lincoln. I'm sorry to bother you, Loren. It's just, I had no one else to call."

"It's okay, Jude. I'm glad you called. I'll be there soon. I promise."

"Thank you, Loren."

"Hey, I'm on my way, okay. It will be better soon. We'll figure this out together. Okay?"

"Okay."

Hailing down a taxi, I jumped in and gave the address to the police station. My heart raced, and my body shook as we merged into traffic. I was wired from the encounter and now with fear. Fumbling with my phone, I called the first name that came up, hoping he'd be available. I needed help.

"Hello?" the sleepy voice answered, making me feel like an asshole. Checking the time, I saw that it was almost eleven o'clock at night. How long had I sat on that train car unaware?

"Hello? Anyone there?"

"Hey, it's me. I'm sorry to bother you. It's just... I didn't know what else to do."

"Loren?"

"Yeah, sorry again. I'm rambling, I..." Catching my breath, my emotions started to crash from the high I felt moments earlier, and the tears threatened to spill. What had I been thinking?

"Hey, it's *okay*," he soothed, his voice deep and soft, instantly calming me. "What's wrong?"

"I don't know. It's Jude. He called me and said he needed help. He's at the police station. I'm headed there now. I don't know what's going on or if he's in trouble. I just, I..."

"Which one?"

"The one on Lincoln."

"Okay, I'm on my way. I'll be there in five minutes. I'm glad you called."

"Yeah?"

"Yeah."

"It *will* be okay. We'll figure this out together, spitfire. I promise."

"Thanks, Sax."

The breath I released felt huge as I hung up. Jude needed me, and I would do whatever I could to help him. A few minutes later, the cab pulled up to the police precinct. Paying the fare, I stepped out as I debated if I wanted to wait or head in. The image of Jude waiting alone pushed me to head in. Chaos surrounded me as I entered the doors, and I was over-whelmed by the activity in the station. It was down-town Chicago, so I suppose I shouldn't be too surprised.

But I'd never been to a police station before, so I wasn't sure of the protocol here. Spotting a desk with a woman answering phones, I decided to try my luck there. Plus, I figured she'd be kind to a fellow woman.

"Hello, I was wondering if you could help me find someone?"

"Fill out this form. If they haven't been gone for 24 hrs yet, you'll have to wait."

A clipboard and pen were shoved at me before I could register her words, and someone else stepped up to the desk.

"Um, no, actually, sorry, that wasn't what I meant. See, I got a call, and I'm looking for a teen."

Rolling her eyes, she grabbed the clipboard back from

me and replaced it with another one, and pointed to a bench for me to sit on.

"Next," she bellowed, clearly done with me.

My earlier assumption hadn't worked out for me, but at least I made a little progress. Inspecting the seat, I brushed it off before I sat down on the hard plastic chair. It was glued to another, so the homeless man who sat next to me was able to offer me his very fragrant aroma as a welcoming gift.

Smiling at him, he gave me a big toothy grin before he went back to picking at something in his hand. I wasn't curious enough to ask, afraid I'd be scarred for life if I did. Crossing my leg, I propped the clipboard on my thigh and began to fill in the form. However, I couldn't get very far because I didn't know much of the info.

Name: Jude Franklin
DOB: unknown- age 17
SSN: unknown
Address: unknown

As I kept going down the form, I could only fill in a few more blanks. Well, this wasn't helpful. Sighing, I signed the bottom before rerunning the clipboard back to the very accommodating desk lady. Her return glower mirrored the feelings I held for her as well. When I turned back around, the homeless man had taken over my spot and was now sleeping in both of the chairs.

Exhaustion filled me as I tried to find space against the wall hoping it would hold up my tired body. Using some hand sanitizer, I wanted to cleanse myself from the despair that lingered in the air here. The person next to me looked at me oddly as the antibacterial smell permeated the air. Tilting the bottle toward them, I offered them some. They looked at me curiously, trying to figure out my game, but eventually, the woman accepted slowly as she placed her hand out for me to squeeze some into.

Following her example, I moved slowly and dipped the bottle down to her, realizing how skittish these folks were. I guess if you had to spend time in a police station, you naturally became that way. Once I squeezed it out, I found she'd relaxed and even smiled a thanks to me at the gesture. Nodding, I deposited it back in my bag and braced myself against the wall for my long wait. I was under no pretense that the happy desk lady would get to me any time soon. I only hoped Jude was okay.

My eyes must've closed because what felt like only a second later, I jumped, opening them when my name was called out.

"Hey, spitfire. You okay?"

Blinking at the sexy man, I nodded, my mind starting to run away with ideas. The sounds of the police station filtered through, reminding me now was not the time to fall into his crystal blue eyes.

"Umm, yeah. They haven't told me anything yet. They haven't been helpful at all, actually."

Sax growled a little before kissing me on the cheek and striding up to the grumpy lady. I decided to call her how she was, no longer feeling like giving her a pass. Not unsurprisingly, the bitchy lady—okay, now I was just bitter—started fawning over herself to help Sax. Not that I could blame her, but still. The lady next to me elbowed me before leaning in.

"Where do you get one of *those*? Does he have a brother?"

Smiling, I looked over to her. "I'm afraid he's one of a kind."

"Damn." She returned my grin, becoming a co-conspirator with me.

"Yeah, damn." I giggled back. It helped lift some of the sadness I'd fallen into.

"You here for a kid?" Her question was kind, and it seemed she felt more trusting of me now.

"Yeah, he called, but he didn't give me much info."

"Ah, yeah. They only get a few minutes to call someone, and they don't want to say too much since the other side is listening in, you know."

"Oh, yeah. I guess that makes sense."

"First time?"

"Yeah, does it show?"

"Just a little," she grinned, "but hopefully, your only one. Especially if he has anything to do about it."

She nudged me, and I found Sax was no longer alone upfront. Atticus was there talking to a well-dressed man as Sax stood back, arms crossed. His demeanor reminded me of a bodyguard in a sense, and the puzzle of who they were became even more complex.

"Yeah." I agreed absentmindedly, but my focus had switched to the duo upfront. Atticus shook hands with a man and then nodded to Sax. The man, who I assumed was a detective or police chief based on his plain clothes, walked off in a different direction. When I looked back to

Atticus, Sax was gone. I furrowed my brow wondering where he went. I soon found him when he appeared directly in front of me. Jumping a little, he laughed at my fright, and I slapped him playfully in return.

"Don't do that. You scared me to death."

"You can scare me any time."

The woman next to me cooed, causing both Sax and me to laugh together this time. Sax didn't say anything but grabbed my hand and pulled me over to where he'd been. Waving over my shoulder to my wall companion, I smiled at the wink she gave me in return. I'd made a friend and an *enemy*, based on the scowl the desk lady threw me as we passed, during my first police visit. Blowing her a kiss, I curled under Sax's arm, happy to have him here to direct me. I'd been so lost and overwhelmed I would've ended up staying here all night before I'd been permitted to see Jude.

When Atticus saw us approaching, he nodded to me but didn't say anything before heading out of the station. It was strange. My brow furrowed in thought, wondering what I'd done to make Atticus so cold toward me. Perhaps he was upset about being woken up at this hour, though to be fair, I'd called Sax and not him. He'd probably been with his fiancée and was upset about leaving her. A weird feeling fluttered in my chest at the thought. Did I feel smug that he'd left her to help me? Yeah, I kind of did.

Once Sax and I made it through the front area and into a small room, he filled me in on what was going on.

"So it seems there was a drug bust, and Jude was in the wrong place at the wrong time type of deal. He doesn't have any priors and didn't have anything on him at the time. They brought him in as an attempt to pressure him to give up some people."

"What? They can do that?"

"Unfortunately, it happens with kids in the system far too often. They don't have anyone reliable to come to get them, and the police can question them without a guardian while they wait for the state to send someone. They abuse the system to try to get kids who are desperate to turn on someone, or badger them with scare tactics long enough they give in."

Anger rolled through me, and I was glad I'd answered the phone. The asshole who'd almost made me miss it flashed through my mind, and I wanted to punch him again. "That's bullshit." Huffing, I crossed my arms, my irritation evident in my stance. Sax smiled, cocking an eyebrow at me. He boxed me in against the wall and leaned down to whisper.

"As much as your spitfire turns me on, Loren, right now is not the time for me to get hard." He licked my earlobe, causing me to suck in a breath. "So, unless you want me to pull you into the closet right there and have my way with you while everyone out here hears you scream my name, you might want to save it for later."

He pushed his hardened length against me, rubbing against my center. My body flushed at the sensation and the way his words rolled over me, enlivening me with his promise. I was halfway to agreeing when the door opened. Spinning, I watched as they brought Jude into the room.

Not even thinking about it, I instantly went to him

and wrapped him in a hug. He tensed at first, and I started to realize what I'd done, thinking I fucked up. Before I could pull away, he wrapped his arms around me tight, relaxing into the embrace.

"Are you okay?"

I felt him nod into my shoulder, and I rubbed his back as I held him. Sax talked with the guy from earlier, and I glared at him, taking my anger out on him since he was the most available target. Chuckling, he lifted his hands up at my stare.

"Chill, little momma. It's cool. I'm one of the good ones, I promise. He needs to be signed out by a guardian, but we can't reach his foster parents. Are you willing to take him into your custody for tonight?"

"Absolutely," I answered without even questioning it. I wouldn't let him remain here for one more second, especially if I had the power to do something about it. Jude hugged me tighter at my declaration, and I held onto him, hoping to provide him with peace and comfort.

"Thank you, Scott. We'll be in touch."

Sax nodded at the agent as he left the room, and it went quiet as I stood with Jude in my arms. Stepping back, I took in his face. He looked okay and didn't seem to have any visible marks.

"Are you okay with staying with me tonight? We can take you to your foster's if you're not?" I hadn't meant to answer for him and wanted him to know he had a choice in the matter. My question had him dropping his head, shame coating his features.

"I can't go back," Jude mumbled.

"What's that, hun?"

Lifting his head, he said it clearer this time. "I can't go back."

"Do you mean tonight or like ever?"

"Ever."

"Okay," I nodded. There was something there, but we didn't need to discuss it here. "We'll figure it out. Come on, let's get home."

My acceptance had him relaxing, and I pulled him under my arm as we walked out. My wall companion was no longer there, so I hoped she finally got what she came for. Sax opened the door for us, continuing to show me the caring man he was. Smiling at him, he winked down at me, and I found myself blushing again. His shit-eating grin conveyed he knew precisely how he made me respond.

Once we were outside, I realized I didn't have a car here. "Shit, I'm going to need to call someone or get a taxi. I didn't drive."

"We'll give you a lift. Come on," Sax responded, leading us to a blacked-out SUV idling on the curb. Shrugging to Jude, I followed him to the car, happy we didn't have to wait.

Opening the door, I stepped up into the SUV, pausing mid-way with half my body in and the other half out of the door when I came face to face with Atticus. He appeared as shocked as I was to find one another there. It was the first sign of emotion I'd seen on his face as his eyes met mine.

"Mrs. Carter."

"Oh, hey, sorry. Sax said he could give us a lift home, but if that's not cool, we can wait for a ride."

"No. I mean, of course, that's fine."

"Thank you."

He nodded and went back to his phone, and I finally managed to grab a seat. It was the oddest SUVs, having two bench seats facing each other and a plexiglass divider between the back and front. Sitting across from Atticus, I buckled up and tried to be as professional as I could. Jude sat next to me, Sax joining Atticus on his side. Once we were all seated, it took off, and I wondered briefly how they knew when to go. It seemed like some kind of alpha male intuition was at play.

"Thank you for your help in there. I was clueless on what to do."

"It was my pleasure. Agent Clark owed me a favor anyway."

"Oh wow, that's generous of you." Heat rose up my neck, not sure how to respond to that. When I realized I hadn't told Sax my address, I turned to him, hoping he had some more of that magic to communicate to the driver. "Um, do you need, like, my address?" I was floundering all over myself in Atticus's presence.

Sax smiled at my question, probably knowing what was happening. "You're too cute, spitfire. No, we do not need your address."

"Okay, that's not creepy or anything," I muttered to myself before remembering Sax had dropped me off. It still didn't explain how Atticus' magic car knew.

Jude laughed at my comment, stifling it under his

breath, causing me to laugh with him. I think the night had finally caught up with me. Checking my phone, it was way past midnight. Tomorrow was going to be a long day.

"What were you doing out so late, Mrs. Carter? If you don't mind me asking?"

"Oh, um, well, I had kickboxing class, and then I decided to go to a club."

My answer had Sax and Atticus both looking at me, clearly more interested now.

"Which club?"

"Well, I didn't make it there, so it doesn't matter. I got Jude's call on the train, and after I wrestled my phone back from the asshole who tried to take it, I ran off the platform and made my way here."

I didn't know why I'd told them everything, but something about Atticus made me spill all my secrets. His gaze was unrelenting, and I had a deep desire to please him. My mention of the incident had them tensing before they started firing questions off at me.

"Which train?"

"What did he look like?"

"Was he alone?"

"What did he say?"

"Umm… hold up. You guys are making my head spin. I don't remember what train because I kind of zoned out. He had two other guys with him. He said a bunch of stuff I can't remember. Some comment about showing me how to use my mouth," I mumbled, blushing. "Um, he was kind of handsome. Had tattoos, dark hair, I dunno. It all happened so fast. He wouldn't give me my phone, and it pissed me off, so I twisted his balls and then ran off with my phone."

They hadn't expected the last part based on the opened mouth expressions across from me. Jude was the first to break the silence.

"That's badass, Loren!" he chuckled before cringing at his use of a cuss word in my presence.

Knocking his shoulder, I agreed with him. "Yeah, it kind of was badass, huh?"

"Definitely." He smiled, relieved I wasn't offended.

The two across from me sat stunned the rest of the way to my condo, no longer firing questions at me. I felt a little proud at having silenced them. A few minutes later, we pulled up to my building. Exiting the car, I stopped and turned before shutting the door.

"Thank you for your help. It meant a lot to me. Good night, fellas."

Kissing Sax on the cheek, I winked at Atticus before I shut the door. I happened to see Sax's knowing grin and what appeared to be a slight blush on Atticus' face. Smiling, I took Jude's arm in mine and led him up to my apartment. After a brief tour, we both headed to bed, exhaustion weighing us both down.

I hadn't made it to the club, but the darkness had been satiated for now. Lying in bed, I felt the last tendrils of it evaporate off my skin as I plunged my fingers into my pussy. I played Sax's words over in my head, imagining them coming to life and what it would've been like had he taken me in the small room.

Only this time, I found myself also picturing Atticus on the other side of the glass watching, stroking himself as Sax plunged his cock deep in me. My breasts bounced from the force, his muscles clenching with each thrust. Atticus' hand gliding over his hard cock, the cuff of his sleeve a contrast to his flushed skin. The vision of him in his suit, cock out, and stroking it did something to me.

Within seconds, I found myself climaxing and my body soaring as I fell into a boneless heap. A question began to plague my mind as I fell asleep, just who were Sax and Atticus? It was becoming apparent they were more than met the eye. The real question, though, was whether I cared at this point. Dreams of dangerous men in suits and forbidden desires swirled in my mind as I moved against my sheets, a wish on my breath that it was real.

THIRTY-NINE

LOREN

The banging on the door woke me up early Wednesday, and it brought the morning in with a bang, and not the good kind.

"I'm coming, geez," I grumbled, shuffling my feet as I made my way there. Jude groggily made his way out of the spare bedroom as I passed. His hair was all a mess, as he wiped sleep from his eyes.

"Who's here?" he mumbled, a yawn breaking the last of his words.

"No clue," I shrugged. "I don't get a lot of visitors."

A look passed over his face, and I couldn't decipher its meaning before coffee. Peeking out through the peephole, I exhaled in relief at the person standing there. Before I could open it, Jude braced his arm against the door, halting me.

"Maybe I should open it?"

"It's okay, sweetie. It's just my neighbor." I smiled reassuringly, and Jude relaxed before nodding. When I smiled encouragingly, he stepped back to allow me to open the door. He turned back to his room. His protective nature was sweet and had a smile spreading across my face. Unlocking the locks, I smiled bigger as Monroe came into view.

"Hey, *neighbor*. What can I do for you this morning?"

"Hey, Lo. Can I come in? There's something I need to talk to you about, well, a couple of things."

"Yeah, sure. Come in."

Pulling the door the rest of the way, Monroe entered, taking in my state of undress. When he heard a noise coming down the hall, he got a funny look on his face.

"Oh, I can come back later if you have company."

"Huh?" I asked eloquently, scrunching up my nose, unsure what he was implying.

Monroe started to reply, his mouth making one of those fish impressions where he struggled to find words. As he finally started to gather himself, Jude walked out from the bathroom, his hair a little more controlled. When he noticed Monroe, he gave a shy wave.

"Jude, there's coffee and cereal in the kitchen if you want anything. Whatever you can find is up for grabs. Make yourself at home, hun."

"Thanks, Loren." He smiled before heading in the direction of the kitchen.

Motioning Monroe to follow me into the living room, I sat on the couch and waited for him to start. When he didn't begin talking after a few minutes, I decided to probe him.

"Um, Monroe? Is everything okay? You were banging on my door awfully loud earlier for there not to be an emergency or something."

"Oh, yeah, that. Sorry, I'm just processing. I didn't mean to get all weird. Jude just surprised me."

"Yeah, me too. It was a bit of a last-minute emergency. He called me from the police station and had nowhere to go, so I took temporary custody."

"Does Mitzi know? The Center?"

"Shit, it was so late, I didn't even think about it. I'll handle it today."

"If you need any help with it, just let me know. I can even help if you need a lawyer or something." He blushed, almost as if he was embarrassed about being a lawyer or offering to help. I wasn't sure which.

"Thank you, I appreciate it. I don't think he's being charged with anything, but I'll keep that in mind. Is that all, though?"

"No, it's not. I don't know why I'm floundering. It's just that I felt I needed to tell you something."

"Well, I've been told I'm a good listener." I smiled, making a lame joke at my job. Apparently, it was what he needed to hear as he relaxed and sat back on the sofa next to me. Taking his hand in mine, I squeezed it and linked our fingers together, the gesture feeling comfortable.

"It's just my ex is making things difficult for me at the moment. She has nothing to stand on, but it won't mean she's going to stop. Brittni brought you up again when I picked Levi up before school today. I thought you should know you're on her radar. She's vicious and simple minded. "

Thinking for a moment, I turned his words over in

my head before responding. "I'm not sure what she could do to me, though. I have nothing to hide."

"Yeah, I basically told her the same thing. You know when we were at the art fair, and we ran into, um, yeah, well." He trailed off, and I swallowed the lump that appeared anytime I thought of him and nodded.

"Well, he was with Christina, Brittni's sister, so I guess it got back to her that way. Again, it's all hearsay shit, but I didn't want you to be blindsided with anything if she decided to push harder."

"Thank you. I appreciate that. It also means a lot you felt the need to tell me, you know." I grinned. "Things are still new and unsure between us, but I like that you're taking it seriously and being open. It tells me a lot about who you are as a person. You're a good man, Monroe."

Leaning up, I kissed him gently on the lips before pulling back. He seemed a little stunned at my move, and I wondered if I'd gone too far. As I moved back, a brilliant smile crossed his face before dropping.

"Uh, there's just one more thing."

Laughing, I nodded for him to continue. The fact I was having these conversations before I even had my coffee was kind of blowing my mind when I thought about it. A week ago, I was staring out the window, grief so heavy it was a coat, dampening everything in my life.

"This is about… Wells," he started, darting his eyes all over my face. Keeping my expression blank, I knew this had to be important. I wanted him to be able to express whatever he needed to without my emotions getting in the way. It was a skill you learn basically on your first day of graduate school—how to be the safe space to hold someone else's emotions.

"I told you the other night how he was my oldest friend, my best friend."

"Yes." I nodded encouragingly.

"When we were teens, I developed feelings for him. It started as one of those things where we messed around because it was convenient and easy," he admitted. "I don't know when it changed to more, but it did. I kept them to myself, thinking I was alone in it. I met Brittni at school, and we dated on and off for a couple of years."

Monroe swallowed, squeezing my hand more as he gathered himself. I turned more, keeping his hand in mine but now able to hold it with both of mine. Swiping my thumb across his palm, I attempted to soothe his anxiety with my touch. His soft smile made me feel on top of the world.

"There was a moment I thought he might say something, but when it didn't happen, I told myself to move on. I wanted the life I hadn't lived. The wife, the kid, and the picket fence," Monroe chuckled. "So, when Brittni and I got back together again, I decided to propose. She was the closest thing I'd felt to him, so I thought it was love, and it would grow once I'd let him go, you know. I finished law school, we got married, and we bought a house. When she got pregnant, it was like I finally had it all."

"But you weren't happy," I guessed. My words had him looking up, relief and appreciation in his eyes.

"No, I wasn't. How did you know?"

"I just do," I shrugged, not able to explain it. "What happened then?"

"Wells and I had drifted apart in my attempt to build the life I thought would make me happy. Time to time though we would still get together and catch up. He'd gotten his MBA and passed his series 7 test. Wells worked almost as much as I did. We both were trying to move up our corporate ladders, thinking it was the way. I was at a big firm, and I was the little guy inevitably ending up with all the shit cases. Anyway, not the point."

"It's cute when you ramble. Usually, I'm the one doing it," I admitted, smiling to help relax him. His responding chuckle made me feel like I'd succeeded. Butterflies erupted in my chest, my face flushing at the sound.

"We had a fight about something, and I didn't see him for a few years after that. It sucked because he was my best friend. At the end of the day, I didn't care about whatever we'd quarreled over. I just wanted him in my life. It was an empty one without him."

Monroe paused, the emotion heavy and I could hear his sadness. I never had a friend or a person I felt that strongly about. Even what I thought Brian and I had wasn't even close to the despair he was sharing. It made me want it too.

"I eventually moved up at work and became a junior partner. Levi started school, and we'd moved into a nicer house. I thought we were happy, or as happy as I imagined I could be. Everything was falling into place."

Clearing his throat, he picked up our hands, tracing

his own pattern over my hand now. The feeling was nice and I cherished the small gesture.

"The first time I found out she was cheating, I'd come home early from work, and I found them fucking in our bed. It was some guy I'd been golfing with. The worst part, though, I hadn't cared. I felt *relieved*."

"What did you do?"

"Nothing. I quietly backed up and left. I drove around the neighborhood thinking for an hour before I returned home. Then I acted like nothing was wrong. I started finding more and more men she slept with behind my back. It was easy to see if I looked. Late-night phone calls, random messages on her phone, new clothing, and gifts I hadn't bought her, several trips she took with the girls but never returned with a tan. I collected them almost as a penance."

Tilting my head, I looked at him quizzically, not understanding what he meant. "I don't understand."

"I thought I was being punished for loving Wells more than I loved her. It also made me feel like the better person in our relationship and gave me something to hold over her, a selfish indignation I used to fuel me to keep moving forward. After a while, it eased my own guilt."

"Why didn't you leave her?"

"Fear honestly. I was worried it would be worse on my own. Levi had a family this way, and her cheating meant I didn't have to try anymore. I was off the hook to pretend to be the doting husband I didn't feel in my gut. It was easy, sadly. I was used to the routine and the normalcy. It made sense for my job and the things I liked about our life."

"So what changed? How did you end up getting a divorce?"

Blowing out a breath, he inhaled deeply before meeting my eyes. "Wells, actually. It'd been about two years since I'd seen him and a year since I'd discovered Brittni's adultery. Levi was about five at this time. He'd called and asked if we could get together. At first, it was nice. He came over and met Levi. We started hanging out again, much to Brittni's chagrin, but she couldn't say anything. After that, we fell back easily into being best friends like we always had."

"I'm guessing something happened?"

"Yeah, you could say that," he grimaced. "I didn't know the struggles he was having at work at the time, but it makes sense now. One night he showed up spouting about how things were meant to be different, how he screwed up. I honestly thought he was drunk and losing it because nothing made sense. Finally, he broke down and told me the stress he was under. Once he had unburdened himself, he was like a different man."

"I'm having a hard time picturing that being the same Wells."

"Yeah, well, things have changed for him even more since then. It's not my place to say, it's his story, but he's not the person he outwardly presents."

"I'll have to take your word for it," I uttered in disbelief. But a part of me knew he was telling the truth. I'd seen glimpses of a different man, but they were so fleeting, it was hard to trust them.

"One weekend, I'd asked him to stay over since Brittni was away on one of her *girl's weekends*. I'd finally decided to file for divorce and wanted to share it with Wells. Before I could, though, he dropped a huge bomb on me. He disclosed all the shit he'd been going through at work and then confessed, he, uh," he paused, his blush rising. "He told me he loved me, was in love with me. He kissed me, and for one fleeting moment, everything was perfect bliss." Monroe's voice hitched, the joy replaced by pain. "Until it wasn't."

"Okay, you're officially the worst storyteller. Just tell me already, I'm dying here," I grumbled, my patience having worn thin for the good stuff. Chuckling low, Monroe gave me a wry smile.

"Sorry, Lo. It was during that perfect moment Brittni came home early. I guess her *guest* for the weekend got food poisoning or something. She walked in on us kissing. She started cussing and screaming, and of course, Wells bolted. The next day was hell for both of us. Brittni filed for divorce, claiming I cheated, and Wells, well he lost *everything*. For one moment, I felt like I had the world in the palm of my hand, and then it was as if life remembered it was me, and squeezed it until it became a deflated balloon. I was left empty and alone, a discarded party favor."

"That's horrible, Monroe. But what does it mean? Why are you telling me this?"

"Because I want to do things differently in my life this time around. I made the mistake of not putting value to what I had with him, and I hid it. Brittni is trying to use it against me now."

"That's moronic."

"Yeah, I know." He smiled, emboldened by my accusation toward Brittni. "But for whatever reason, she thinks people will care I'm bisexual. Jokes on her, though, because I kept evidence the whole year of her infidelity. I buried it last time to protect Levi, and I still got the divorce I wanted. I'd been heartbroken over Wells as it was, so I didn't have it in me to fight her."

"And now?"

"Now, if she tries to come at me, I'll take her down. I just don't want you to be collateral damage or to be blindsided by anything she might try to spring on you. I care about you, and I want things to keep moving, wherever that takes us." He smiled, a sense of relief on his face at sharing everything with me.

Part of me was glad he had disclosed his worries to me. It indicated a closeness developing between us and a level of trust. We were inviting each other into our worlds and sharing our troubles. There was just one thing bothering me.

"I just have one question," I hesitated, unsure how to ask it.

"Of course, Lo. Anything."

"What happens when Wells decides he loves you again. Where does that leave us?"

"Oh."

"*Yeah*, oh."

"I want to give you the answer you want to hear, but the truth is that I don't know. You're the first person outside of him I've felt this deep of a connection with. Whether it means anything in a month, a year, I don't know. I decided I wasn't going to live my life waiting for something that might never happen with him. Until the other night, I hadn't heard from him in over six months. Before that, a year, and then even longer. There's a deep history there, but there's also deep pain. There's a lot of things that need to happen before him and I could ever be anything."

"So, am I a consolation prize? The one waiting in the wings until he does redeem himself?"

"No, no, no, of course not," he panicked, sitting up. "Shit, I'm not explaining this well. Loren, I'm going to be real with you, okay?"

Nodding, I held my breath to what 'being real' meant, preparing myself for the inevitable pain.

"If Wells came to me today and said he was ready to finally be together after twenty years of dancing around it, I would without a doubt tell him yes. I won't deny that. I—"

"I wouldn't want you to. I just don't think I fit into this picture."

"You didn't let me finish."

Sighing, I waved my hand in a 'get on with it then' gesture, and sat back against the couch, wrapping my arms around me now. I couldn't touch him, not when he was breaking my heart a tiny bit.

"Loren, look at me, *please*?"

The anguish in his voice had me lifting my eyes to his. I hadn't expected it. I know I was being petty and closing myself off. He'd been open with me, and I was punishing him for it. But in that space, I couldn't hold his feelings anymore without letting mine leak out too. I had to protect myself now.

"You swept into my world like a beautiful breeze. Your brokenness calling to my own. I saw myself in you, and I felt a connection instantly. You make me excited to get out of bed in the morning just to get a glimpse of you in the hall. Our morning races to the elevator, our nonverbal fights over the corner spot, and the small glimpses of your heart when you think no one is looking had me smitten before we even shared words with one another. I didn't talk to you only to have a convenient fuck buddy across the hall. I didn't introduce you to Levi just to yank you into my life on a whim. I'm not telling you this now to push you away. I'm coming to you as a man with my heart in my hands, showing you all my scars and asking you to give me a chance."

Damn. The man had word game.

Tears edged in the corners of my eyes, his words piercing my heart with their honesty. I couldn't fault him for being upfront with me. Not once had he ever misrepresented himself. He'd taken a chance to be vulnerable in the hopes I'd see it for what it was. His truth. If more relationships started this way, I bet there would be less heartbreak.

"Okay."

"Okay?" Hope shined through Monroe's voice, his face a beautiful reflection of his heart. He was breathtaking and I'd never paid attention before. Monroe was like pure sunshine and it called to my darkness.

"Yeah, okay," I chuckled. "I can't say it as poetic, but I'd like to take a chance with you too."

"Thank you, Lo. I don't know what the future holds, but I know I'd like you to be in it. If that includes Wells as well, then I'd be the happiest person on the planet."

"You'd want to be with both of us? Not just with him?" I asked, a gasp clogging my throat at the possibility.

"Are you kidding me? That's every fantasy right there."

"You know, you might've led with that," I teased, playfully shoving his arm.

"Nah, it was perfect the way it was."

"Yeah, it kind of was."

Matching his smile, I leaned in and gently kissed him. He returned the kiss, his lips perfectly fitting mine. Sounds from the kitchen had me pulling back before I deepened it and found myself in a precarious situation with my teenage ward.

"My turn to be vulnerable."

His hand cupped my cheek, his fingers in my hair from our kiss. I hadn't noticed he'd moved; it had felt so natural. His thumb swiped a tear I hadn't known escaped, and I blinked to keep the rest at bay. He gently nodded, his focus seared on me.

"It wasn't fair of me to get upset about Wells. You guys have a history, and it makes sense. I just got a little jealous, sad I'd miss out on a guy like you. Yet here I am seeing other people and getting angry with you. I'm sorry."

"You have nothing to be sorry about, babe. You already told me, remember?"

"Yeah, it's just, I don't know, complicated. I don't even know where to start with it all."

"Start with what you're thinking and go from there."

"Okay, so, there are two guys I've kind of been out with…"

As we sat on the couch in one another's embrace, I shared the things on my heart I'd barely admitted to myself. When our stomachs growled an hour later, I realized the time, and we both decided to call off work. Monroe went across the hall and retrieved some clothes for Jude to borrow. He'd been so quiet after he left the kitchen, I'd forgotten he was here. I found him in the spare room, lying on his stomach, focused on his phone.

"Hey."

"Hey, I hope I didn't interrupt anything."

"Nope, you didn't." I braced myself in the doorway, trying to give him privacy. "I've decided to take the day off so I can help you figure out some things. Monroe's grabbing some clothes for you."

He sat up, worry crossing his face. "You don't have to do that."

"I know. I want to."

I found myself sticking out my tongue at him, laughing as I went to make eggs for Monroe and I. It was the only thing I wouldn't burn. Monroe ended up spending the day with us and helped me navigate the legal things I needed to do to help Jude. We went to the market to get groceries, my condo not having a lot to feed a teenager. The Lean Cuisines and moldy bread weren't part of a balanced diet for a boy, nor were they appetizing. I couldn't blame him, they weren't to me either, hence why they were still in the freezer.

I managed to buy him some clothing so he wouldn't have to keep wearing Monroe's. Jude was hesitant to accept anything, but the fact he currently had nothing helped. It was an accept it or go naked situation, and his concern for his modesty won out in the end.

By the end of the day, I had an epiphany, and with it, made a major decision. For the past two years, I'd been grieving the life I'd thought was perfect. The dreams for the future and life I was intended to have. But it was all shit. All of it.

Life wasn't meant to be perfect. The more chaotic my life became lately, the happier I was becoming. My whole life, I'd done it all wrong, and then when I had a redo I'd pushed everyone away. I should've been pulling them into my life. But perhaps, it was the people in my life now who made all the difference. Individuals that also knew pain, and understood the darkness, yet still chose to risk it.

Between five very different men, two crazy new girl-friends, and two teens, I learned the actual definition of living life, and it had nothing to do with perfection. In fact, it was quite the opposite. They were the true warriors.

"Hey, Jude?"

"Yeah," he responded distractedly as we made dinner later that evening.

"What would you think of moving in with me... *permanently*?"

My question hung in the air, my breath catching in

my throat as I waited for him to answer. He stopped mixing the bowl on the counter and slowly turned toward me. I held his gaze, trying not to let my own feelings get in the way or how upset I would feel if he said no. After the longest minute spent regarding me, he gave me an answer.

"I think I'd like that a lot."

Letting my emotions free, the tears started to fall and I pulled him into a hug, holding him tight to me. Monroe walked into the kitchen at that second, concern lifting his brow at our display of emotion.

"Everything okay?"

"Yeah, everything's great."

"If everything is great, why are you both crying?"

Looking down at Jude, I realized he also had tears streaming down his face, but I didn't want to embarrass him, so I ignored them. "Because I'm a sap, and Jude is indulging me, so I don't feel embarrassed."

"Okay. Well, what are you sap about?"

"I just asked if Jude wanted to move in."

"Oh," a smile broke out on Monroe's face, "well, what did he say?"

"Well, naturally, he said he had a lot of offers."

"Understandably so. He's a cool dude."

"So, he needed to weigh his options and make the best decision for himself."

"Sensible request," Monroe agreed, going along with my game. Jude couldn't hold his laughter back at this point, and tears of joy rolled down his face now.

"Yep, I agree. So, I told him he'd be doing me a favor, really. I'm kind of lonely in this big place by myself, and it would be nice to have someone around. And Jude being the nice young man he is, said that, of course, he'd help me out."

"Ah, well, that's kind of you, Jude."

"Yep, that's me. *Kind*."

His response had us all losing it, holding our bellies as we laughed. When we were able to calm down, we finished up dinner and sat around the table to eat it. It was the first meal I'd ever eaten here. As we all joked around the table telling funny stories, I realized how foreign it would've been a month ago.

"I'm stuffed. I don't know what it was about the dish, but it was the best meal I think I've ever had," Jude confessed.

Smiling at Monroe, we shared a look at being able to give him that.

"Well, it's simple. The special ingredient made it the best," Monroe provided.

"Special ingredient?" Jude and I both asked.

"Yeah, you don't know about the special ingredient?"

"No, I guess we don't. Are you going to tell us, or do we have to beg? I'm starting to think you really are the worst storyteller and only win your cases because you drag them out so long they give up."

Monroe laughed, only increasing my ire at his secret-keeping. At my glare, he finally gave in, holding his hands up.

"Okay, okay. The special ingredient was making it together. Any meal made with someone you care about always tastes better. It's a fact. Some chefs say it's love, others say it boils down to someone to double-check things and some even say that it's just more fun with another person. Take your pick." He shrugged. "But that's why it's the best meal because you had the special ingredient. Each other."

Monroe's words settled over the room, and I looked to Jude. He looked nervous like I might deny it. Grabbing his hand, I squeezed it and gave him a soft smile.

"That makes perfect sense to me. To special ingredients."

"To special ingredients," they both chorused. We raised our glasses, clinking them together, and I wrapped myself in this feeling. This was the life I'd wanted. One with belonging, connection, and trust.

Empowerment surged through me at the realization I'd made it happen for myself. The darkness inside of me receded back to the shadows, appeased for the time to let the light have its moment.

FORTY

ATTICUS

"Hey, Attie. Do you have a minute?"

Immy's voice filtered through my open office door, and I was thankful for the distraction. I still hadn't uncovered why the books were off, and it was slowly driving me insane. Glancing up at the sound of her voice, I smiled as I directed her to enter the rest of the way.

"What did you want to ask me?"

"How do you know I want to ask you something?" Immy giggled, a blush rising to her face.

The change I'd noticed in her over the past month had been remarkable. I wanted to simultaneously pat myself on the back for taking her to therapy and kick myself for not doing it sooner. If it was the last thing I did, I would ensure Immy had the chance at a happy life, whatever she wanted it to mean.

"Because if it were to complain about your tutor, you would've just walked in and started talking immediately. If it were advice, you'd ask Nicco, and if you needed to go somewhere, you'd just ask Sax to take you and then tell me later."

Immy giggled more at my answer, knowing I'd hit it on the head. "Okay, maybe you're right about that. I just don't want to bother you sometimes, so I try to limit my interruptions." She shrugged.

A realization hit me square in the chest at her words. Our father had been that way. Dayton didn't want interruptions and preferred not to be asked. I didn't want her associating any of his traits with me. I needed to make sure she understood it wasn't that way anymore.

"Immy, look at me." My tone had her looking up, an uneasiness now present.

"Yes, sir." The sir hit me in the chest, and I had to hold my growl in at seeing her light dim. Taking a breath, I calmed my heart and reminded myself it wasn't her I was angry with. Softening my tone, I attempted to reassure her.

"Sweetie, you can interrupt me whenever you want. You come first, always. I want you to know that. The family business is stressful and dangerous, but there is always time for you too. I don't want you to feel you can't ask me anything or come to me, okay?"

"Yeah, okay." Immy shrugged but lifted a small smile my way, and I knew it would be all I got today. It was a start.

"So, what's this question you felt was important enough then?" I teased, wanting to see some of the joy she had in her eyes when she entered.

"Oh, well, I was wondering if after my session today with Loren, if I um, could, maybe, if it was okay, to hang out with Jude."

"Wow, that was the most words I've ever heard

anyone say for one question," I joked, trying to bring some levity back to the situation. It seemed to work as she stuck her tongue out at me in response, causing me to chuckle.

"Well, can I?"

"Hmm. Where will this 'hanging out' take place? Will there be adults present?"

Immy's full teenager dramatics emerged in response as she rolled her eyes at my questions. "Like you would let me go anywhere alone to begin with," she sassed. "Besides *that* obvious answer, yes, I do believe Loren will be present. I don't know if you heard, but Jude's staying with her now."

"Oh, as in a more permanent arrangement?"

"Yeah, I think so. Jude's happy about it, and I'm happy for him. Loren's really nice, and it's a better fit for him. Which benefits me because I know you wouldn't have let me visit him where he was before."

"That you would be correct on," I chuckled. I knew she'd figure out we'd run a background check on him. It was standard in our life, and I wouldn't have let her keep talking to him if he hadn't been a good kid. Immy accepted this as part of our routine, and it helped ease some of the things I had to police about her life. She might not always like it, but she at least understood the why's of this life.

"*Soooo*, can I?"

"Immikins, I'm not your father, so you don't have to get permission from me to do things with your friends. I trust you to take the proper precautions and make the necessary arrangements to ensure your own safety. That being said, I do appreciate you letting me know as I worry about you, kid. You're my baby sister, and I always will." I paused, wanting what I'd said to sink in. She had to trust her own judgment again, and I hoped by showing her I did, she would.

"You're almost 18, which means I need to let you make your own choices for yourself. So, if you want to hang out with Jude, who I do approve of by the way, then you have my blessing. I worry about you, but you do make this parenting thing easy, Immikins."

"Thanks, Attie," she said, her voice soft. "You know, you haven't called me that since I was small." I didn't miss the affection leaking through, making me feel rewarded for my efforts.

"You'll always be small to me, Ims. Can this old brother of yours request a hug before you go?"

"Ugh, I guess. If I must," she groaned, smiling.

"You must."

Pulling her into my arms, I held her tight as I warred with my need to protect her and make her strong. Kissing the top of her head, I sent her off before I broke down or something equally embarrassing. Once she was gone, I dove back into the ledger, hoping something new would stick out. When it didn't, I slammed it shut and gathered everything as I headed out to the location for our family meeting.

I had the penthouse in the city I'd gotten after graduating, and we'd been living here primarily because of the ease of day-to-day dealings of this life, but our primary place was out in the suburbs. We gathered there for the critical things as security was easier to manage on a 100-

acre lot in a gated community. The house was where I spent most of my youth and Immy too. Which was also part of the reason we'd currently been at my place. The memories weren't as strong here for her.

"Sax? Are you ready to roll out?"

"Yeah, just getting Im's guard sorted."

Stopping in my tracks, I hung my head. Shit. This was one of those moments where it sucked to be boss. I wanted Sax with me, but despite my statements to Imogen earlier, I only trusted her because I knew Sax watched over her. I still didn't have my mole identified, and I didn't trust anyone else outside him and Nicco.

At that thought, an idea formed in my head. "Send Nicco."

"Wait, what?" Sax asked, a perplexed look on his face. "He's not trained as a guard, though. Are you sure?"

"Then someone else too, but I want Nicco there in the apartment with her. Loren won't understand an outsider, and since you can't go, he's the best solution as they seem to be dating or whatever. I don't want her to be out of sight despite trusting Loren. Someone could easily get to their apartment. Loren won't recognize the danger, and she'd let them right in. It's the best solution, and you know it."

Sax contemplated it for a second but eventually nodded, not seeing any fault with my logic. He dialed the number and had it arranged within thirty seconds. I often undervalued his skills because he was so efficient at getting things accomplished. Those two days I'd distanced myself, I gained a whole new level of appreciation for him.

"Nicco, man, hey, got a favor to ask you." I heard Sax chuckling at something Nicco said on the other end, and I could only imagine what my smart-mouth cousin had retorted back.

"Yeah, yeah. I know. I think you will like this one though, hear me out."

It was weird being on this end of a conversation and not hearing what the other person said. Typically, I guess I didn't stick around for this part, but I wanted to know the details since it was Nicco and Immy.

"I promise, man, okay, so our girl, Loren? Yeah, her foster kid and Ims have become friends," he paused, and I hated feeling left out of the conversation even when I had no right to feel it. "Yeah, good, okay. So, Immy wants to hang out with Jude, and we have a family meeting to head to. I know it will be a huge hardship for you, but as Loren doesn't know why we would insist on a guard inside, it would need to be someone she knows. Ergo, *you*." Sax grinned, laughing at something Nicco said.

"Okay, great. I'll tell Dakota to expect you. Ims has a session soon and will be done at 5 pm. Can you meet them at New Horizons, or will it be the condo?"

"Yeah, yeah, man. Okay, talk to you later."

"Everything good, then?"

"Yeah, he said you owe him another favor, but based on the shit he was saying to me, I think he owes you the favor," he groaned, shifting himself in his pants. Swallowing, I tried to ignore the thoughts that wanted to rise to the occasion. Loren was becoming more and more a part of our life in some way or another.

The other night, when Sax had told me he was going

out to meet her, I didn't even hesitate and left with him. I didn't want to admit to myself it was because I cared. She intrigued me, that was it.

So, why did the little wink she gave me at the end have me stroking one out when I got home? Denial was my middle name.

Ignoring my inner thoughts, I headed to the garage with Sax.

"Have you heard from everyone?"

"Yes, all will be in attendance. Do you think your uncle will try to make a play?"

It was the very same question that had plagued me for months.

"I don't know, and that's what bothers me. He's too clean, too careful. Either he's perfect and loyal to the family, or…"

"He's covering up his tracks," Sax finished.

"Yeah. Has Jasper uncovered anything yet?"

"He hasn't reported in today, so I'm hoping it's just because of the meeting."

"You know we can't hope in the mafia, Sax. *Shit*. Can you get confirmation on his whereabouts? We need to make sure we aren't walking into a trap."

"Shit, yeah. I'm on it."

As Sax began messaging people, I went over the info I had on the others again from the past thirty days. My uncle, Seth, for all intents and purposes, was clean. Lucca was on my side, as was Nicco. It was between Joel and Marcel and their divisions at this point. I needed to uncover the rat. *Today.* I was afraid too many of our futures depended on it, especially since I was still waiting to hear back from Darren Delgado.

It didn't bode well, whatever he thought I would accomplish for him. My father hadn't been in bed with them for fun. He needed them for something. Otherwise, he would've never dirtied himself with Darren. At least the father I knew wouldn't have. Nowadays, I'd started to realize I never knew him, not really.

By the time we pulled up to the estate, Sax had gotten confirmation from Jasper, alleviating one worry off our plate. I planned to do something risky during the meeting to see if I could snuff out the leak. I was convinced at this point it was one of the Capos. There was no other explanation.

"Good afternoon, Mr. Mascro."

Nodding at the butler, I kept my focus on the plan. I needed to be the stone-cold boss today. Heading into the Den of Secrets, I walked through the scanner that checked for weapons, bugs, and recording devices. None of it was allowed inside, and every member had to pass through before they were permitted admittance. It ensured our meetings were safe and unhackable.

Inside the room, there were no electronics, just a table and seven chairs. A device in the walls scrambled radio waves, disrupting listening devices from trying to pick up conversations. It was soundproof with only one entrance. The air vents were even separate from the rest of the house. The room was checked daily, and hourly on meeting days, at random intervals. It was the most secure and unhackable room. We took privacy that seriously.

It would be my best chance to illuminate the traitor. They wouldn't have an escape or be able to communicate with anyone to warn them. I just had to pull it off. All the grooming I'd had throughout my whole life would come down to this. When it mattered, did I have the stones to do what needed to be done? Even if they were 'family'?

For the sake of *my family*, yeah, I could.

Marcel and Lucca were already present when I entered. Their trusted guards, Jasper and Domino, stood against the wall. Each Capo could bring in one person they trusted with what was said in here. Again, it limited access to the information and provided a level of accountability to follow through with what was decided. At the end of the day, they all had to be loyal to me no matter who they served under.

Today, we would test that loyalty.

Opting not to take my seat, I stood behind my chair, leaning on it as I surveyed the room. I watched the two as they shifted in their seats, unease in their posture. It was an odd thing nowadays to be without your phone, but it gave me great insight into them when they couldn't hide. A minute later, we were joined by Uncle Seth and his son, Joel. Hugo and Victor followed the two, taking their places against the wall. When Seth had stepped up to be my underboss until Immy came of age, Joel had been promoted to Capo.

My cousin was a few years older than me but was someone I didn't particularly like. He'd always been envious of my position and felt he deserved it as much as I did. The thing was, he could've taken it, but he didn't have the gall to do it. Instead, he whined and complained about it. He was the obvious choice for the leak, yet it felt too convenient, but I wasn't going to rule him out just yet. Joel at least had plenty of motive to want to take over the family.

"Welcome, gentlemen. Shall we get started?" Not waiting for them to respond, I started, not needing their permission. "Lucca, report in."

As I listened to Lucca detail out the gambling side, I watched everyone else. I knew Sax would remember the essential facts with his crazy memory, so I could tune it out as I took in my family around the table as I paced.

"Crash's forfeit last week was a hit to our take. A lot of upset customers over that one. Nicco said he was taking care of it, so I left it alone."

That did interest me, and I made a note to ask Nicco about it later. Nothing else stood out from Lucca's report, so I moved on to Joel.

"Joel, report."

His posture stiffened, not liking my command, allowing his frustration to leak through his voice. He'd never survive as boss, his emotions too easily riled and known. But like a good soldier, Joel heeled and gave me the details on how the clubs were doing.

"Evolve is set to open this weekend. The soft opening went well, and I think it's going to be well received. Climax continues to be a winner, with numbers increasing nightly for Illusion and Verity. The blackmail material alone is setting us up for some prime paydays." Joel sat back, boasting about his perceived accomplishment despite having no real influence on the earnings.

While I didn't particularly appreciate how he talked

about the clubs, I couldn't find anything in his report that set off red flags. Continuing my jaunt around the table, I kept my hands behind my back and watched him when he didn't think I was looking. He seemed relaxed, so once he finished, I moved on to the last Capo.

"Marcel, report."

He hesitated, and I paused as I waited for him to report in. He swallowed, and when I looked at him, it wasn't me he was staring at nervously, but my uncle, Seth.

"Something I need to know about, *gentlemen*?" The steel was evident in my voice. I didn't like to be kept waiting or out of the loop on something. My prompt had Marcel finally beginning to speak.

"We've had some difficulties with a few shipments lately. Items have been going missing."

"And why am I only now hearing about this?" The rage was carefully contained, but I was feeling ready to let it out to play.

"I thought I could fix it before it would need to come to you."

Strolling to the back of his chair, I moved faster than he expected and slammed his head down onto the table. Getting down low by his ear, I let my words hang in the air for all to hear. "How did that work out for you, Marcel? *Hmm*? You're not the fucking boss. You don't get to make decisions. You don't think anything in this pea-size brain about what I do and do not need to know. Do I make myself clear?"

His whimpering made my heart race with adrenaline, and a sick part of me enjoyed feeding the monster within. Leaning down further, quieter this time for only him to hear, I whispered, "Now, do you want to tell me why you can't quit eye fucking my uncle, or should I kill you first and then ask him?"

Marcel let out another whimper, and I wondered how he'd ever made it up this high in the family. Most positions were handed down from family rank, but it wasn't the only way. Marcel wasn't a Mascro by blood, so he'd had to have worked to get to his status. Unless he was the patsy someone had put into place to give the illusion of power but was being puppeteered behind the scenes.

Things started to click in my mind as I thought through the possibilities. It made the most sense. It also explained why Jasper hadn't found anything. Marcel was too dumb to know what was really going on and, therefore, unable to slip up or leave anything for Jasper to uncover. Now, was it my father or my uncle who was pulling his strings?

He managed to whisper out one word, and I let go of the simpering fool, deciding to use another tactic. It was time to play the odds.

Nodding at Jasper, he came over and bound Marcel. It was clear to everyone he was a loose end. He would need to be dealt with in the only way the family knew how. But first, I needed to find the real culprit, and then I might be able to save his life.

"Such an interesting story, Marcel just admitted. Would anyone care to guess? Offer up their own version first for some leniency? Hmm?"

I kept moving, attempting to make them nervous and on edge as I came upon their chairs. Internally, I laughed at my words, knowing there wasn't such a thing as leniency in the mafia, but it had a nice ring to it. Focusing on the men at the table, I knew Sax would be watching the whole room and keeping my six. There were a few other guards who were loyal amongst us, filling me with confidence that no one would stab me in the back with a pencil. It was the closest thing to a weapon they'd have, nothing else allowed in this room.

"No volunteers? Interesting." I stopped and rubbed my chin in concentration. "Okay, I guess I'll get to talk today."

By this point, Marcel was bound in zip ties and duct-taped. He couldn't discount anything I said, making this even better for me to outsource. I started pacing again around the table, focusing on the men sitting there.

"For the past month, I've been trying to figure out who the leak was in our family. Someone helped the Grim Reaper, and someone was still stealing even after he'd been taken out. It couldn't be Dayton, right? He's dead. I shot him myself. So, it had to be someone still *here*. I poured and poured over the books, but I couldn't figure out how they were doing it. Something wasn't adding up, but everything was perfect. Now, someone remind me, what did I go to school for? Was it bull-shitting?"

"No, boss. You went to school for business. MBA, if I remember correctly."

"Excellent, Jasper. Thank you. Yes, my *mother fucking MBA*. And you know what my specialty was? Hmm? Let me help you out with this one. *Finance.* So, imagine my surprise when numbers are my specialty, yet I cannot find any accounting errors. None. Zilch. Nada. What do you think that means? Joel, care to field this one for me?"

"Um, that we're all really good at *math*?"

His cluelessness saved him, and I moved on to my next contestant on 'who screwed over my family'.

"Actually, *Joel*, that would be wrong. The opposite, in fact. You see, there's a certain percentage of error that is a given because people are involved. If it were all machines, then yes, I'd expect it to be perfect. But since the money is passed through many hands and many fronts, there's a small margin for discrepancies. It's natural and expected. So, why aren't there any errors?"

"Lucca, any guesses?"

"Because someone's stacking it?"

"Bingo, we have a winner. Wanna know your prize?"

I twirled around, zeroing in on my prey. I felt a bit manic at this point, the adrenaline buzzing through me, pushing me to make a big scene.

"Um, sure?"

"Well, Lucca, your prize is that you get to live today. So where does that leave us, folks?"

Leaning down on the table, I stared across it at my uncle. Disgust filled me with all the memories over the years of him helping me, and I couldn't trust any of it. *Not now.*

"Uncle, what do you have to say for yourself?"

"I don't know what you're implying, *nephew*. I haven't been involved in the business at all in the past six months. You know this."

He was good, and I almost bought it. The last piece of the puzzle would seal his fate, though. Flipping a switch under the table, I activated the blacklight before moving away from it.

"Well, that's easy to prove, Uncle, if you're as innocent as you say. Can everyone around the table please empty their pockets and put what they have on the table?"

Change, bills, wallets, and a few odds and ends clattered on the surface as the three people remaining emptied their pockets. Immediately, I knew who the culprit was. And once everyone had their pockets emptied, so did everyone else. Seth started to slow clap before he stood, no longer playing the idiot doting uncle.

"I'm impressed, Atticus. Genius move really to use the blacklight on the cash. I didn't give you enough credit, and that's my fault. It took your father much longer to figure it out. Of course, he chose to join in on my scheme, and together, we aligned ourselves with Delgado. I feel so bad about what happened to Immy. Tragic, really, but it's all part of this life. Shame she had to see her mother shot like that, but you're no stranger to deaths, either, are you?"

Locking down my emotions, I strained not to punch the lying bastard in the face. Thankfully, Sax had blocked the exit already, trapping him. So despite his guard, Victor, coming from the other direction, I was confident the rest of the men were loyal. This would be the determining point for Joel. Who did he follow when it mattered?

"How did you do it, Atticus? May I ask?"

He kept slowly moving, locking eyes with me, and I knew it was a ploy of some sort. I cast my eyes to Joel, and the look of hurt on his face showcased he hadn't known of his father's deceit. Now, it would depend on his actions.

"Easy enough, I slipped it in with every deposit. That way, I could see who was stealing from me. I hadn't expected you, though, Uncle."

"That's where you lack the creativity to think beyond this family. I'm expanding us and making us richer beyond belief—"

Before he could say anything else, Jasper had finally subdued his guard, allowing Sax to come up behind Seth and knock him out by activating his pressure point, not needing to hear any more of his evil monologue. I didn't want to give him time to escape or activate any failsafe plan. Once he was bound and gagged alongside Marcel, I turned to Joel.

"Time to decide, cousin. Who's side are you on?"

He looked back and forth between his father on the ground and me. I allowed it because it was an important choice, and he needed to be behind it completely, or no one would ever trust him in the family. I saw when his decision was made, and he turned to me.

"Family above all. I choose the family. My father is dead to me and will forthrightly be known as the traitor."

Nodding, I accepted his answer and indicated to the guards to take out the three who had made their choice. I'd deal with Marcel later, but it was obvious he wasn't fit to lead. Finally, taking a seat, we got to business. I nominated Jasper to take over Marcel's Capo role, and it was voted on unanimously.

I disclosed my meeting with Darren and how it appeared he was working outside his own father, and how we might use that against him. Lucca suggested scheduling something with the Rawles, as well, and we might be able to form an alliance to rally against Delgado.

I wasn't at that place yet, but I acknowledged the path as a possibility. I just hoped it wouldn't be necessary. Chicago hadn't seen a turf war in fifty years. I didn't want to start one now. Not if I had anything to do about it. The casualties from it would be devastating, and I couldn't guarantee we would all survive. It was a chance I couldn't take with Immy's life. Not now, not ever.

FORTY-ONE

LOREN

"I think I'm ready to talk about what happened… or at least part of it," Imogen announced after she took her seat on the couch.

A spark of pride filled me with her words. The moment I'd been waiting to seamlessly happen unfolded before me. It amazed me how organic therapy could be at times. Taking the time to thoroughly build rapport always paid dividends in the end. You could rush things and check off goals on a treatment plan, but if no change was made internally, it was only checkmarks at the end of the day, pointless and ornamental.

Looking at her, I could tell she'd been thinking about this outside our sessions. The fact she'd entered the room and immediately wanted to spill everything was a good sign. It was like once the decision had been made, it bubbled up to the surface and waited, ready to spill over unbidden. It acted like a dam. The wall held the powerful force back, protecting everyone. But as soon as the wall lifted, the water rushed out and over everything. If it wasn't done carefully, it would create wreckage in its wake, but it could be a powerful source of strength for the person if done well. The hardest part was getting people to this point and then making them peel it back slowly. Sometimes, ripping the bandage off wasn't the best philosophy and only made us more raw and vulnerable if the proper shields weren't in place.

Assessing Imogen, I thought about the first time I met her. Her hair had been in her face, and she barely made eye contact. Today, Imogen's hair was shiny and brushed back, her eyes clear. She wore light make up and sat upright, engaged in the conversation. Imogen no longer hid behind her hair or arms. In fact, she conveyed openness and trust.

Imogen's outfit was also different, revealing more of her personal style and fit her frame instead of falling off. She no longer needed to cover herself in layers for comfort or protection externally. She'd learned how to protect herself internally now through our sessions. Her smile was bright, and she seemed lighter. Imogen was eager to share her story, and I could see more of her personality peeking through. Imogen was a completely different girl from the one who came to me a month ago.

"I'm honored you feel ready to share with me. Can I ask what prompted this decision?"

Her face blushed a little, and she blew out a breath before she spoke. "Several things, I think. Like you suggested, I've mostly been working on my thoughts, and I realized I didn't want those things to control me anymore. By not talking about them, it's like I'm giving them the power. But maybe if I share them, then they'll be out of me, and I won't have to fight them alone."

"That's insightful, Imogen. I can tell by your words this has been weighing on you, and it's important for you to share your story, for you to drive the narrative now and not let it control you."

"Yeah, exactly. Jude said something too that clicked, and I realized I was ready, you know. Like, I'm sick and tired of thinking and feeling this way, of having his voice in my head. I want it to stop."

Her emotion was thick in her voice as she shared, and I could hear her strength with each word she spoke.

"Your resiliency is strong, Imogen. You can do this. You can say the words and not let them destroy you. You get to be the voice of your own narrative. No one else."

I waited as she digested my words. It was up to her to share the scars she bore, the pain she felt. Giving her an encouraging smile, I kept my own emotions at bay, so she had room to share whatever she needed to without feeling the need to censor herself.

Often in our lives, we diminished ourselves for fear the other person wouldn't be able to handle the horrors we've experienced, so we shielded them from the true depths of our trauma. Or even worse, our feelings and experiences were dismissed or minimized to make room for the other person to share their feelings, making it almost a competition to who experienced the worst things. Trauma wasn't a race, and each person experienced things differently.

To minimize their experience only taught the person their feelings didn't matter. It was a slippery slope people found themselves on when they attempted to empathize with someone but inadvertently made it about themselves instead. Or worse, it made them not want to share to begin with, because it wasn't safe.

Therapy wasn't that.

In this room, only her feelings mattered. I was a neutral entity, ready to hold her emotions alongside her and help safely navigate them. This was a judgment-free zone, open to sharing the things we held back. If more people understood that about therapy, then perhaps they wouldn't be as adverse to it. The long-held stereotype of lying on a couch while someone asked you, "how does that make you feel?" or, even worse, connecting it to some deep-seated Freudianism, was severely outdated.

"You can start where you feel like. I'm not going to check for accuracy or question what happened. You can tell me whatever you feel ready or comfortable to share. There's no pressure to do it all today either, okay?"

She nodded before taking a breath. Imogen's hands shook slightly now, and I yearned to reach out and hold them. My boundaries were slipping with her. She'd quickly become someone I cared deeply for and wanted to not only help, but comfort.

The scary thing was, I didn't care about the potential risks, or the dangerous waters I found myself wading in when it came to Imogen. That alone should have terrified me, that I was willing to compromise my ethical beliefs for a client. Except when I saw the hurting girl in front of me, they didn't seem as important.

Without thought, I reached over and held her hand in a comforting grip. I was relieved when she didn't tense or shrug me off. Instead, she squeezed it back and held on to me tightly as she began to talk.

"There are some things that won't make sense. My family doesn't make sense to people outside of it. But I've been raised to be strong, to be a leader, and to know what was important. *Family.* There are things I never questioned because it's the way it was. It didn't seem odd to me, and I accepted it as what was best. I'd always believed my father and was taught he had my best intentions in mind."

Imogen dropped her head as she spoke, speaking her story to my hand. She traced patterns on the top of it as she spoke, almost as if in a trance.

"When he told me he needed me for a deal, I didn't question it. I'm almost 18, and while Attie will be the one in charge, I was meant to be his... backup for the... family business."

She paused, hesitant over her words, almost as if she had to be careful to choose the ones she did. It struck me as odd, but it wasn't important right now. Her saying the words was all that mattered in this instant.

"When I got to the warehouse, I started to get nervous. I'd never been to something like that, and fear started to consume me. I refused to get out of the car at first, but then my mother was there standing in the doorway. When I saw her, I got out and took off running to her. She hugged me tight when I made it. I was so happy for those few seconds her arms were around me. It'd been a week since I'd seen her. She'd gone on some trip with my dad, but when he'd returned, she hadn't."

I watched her face as she spoke and I saw her scrunch up her nose at the realization. Sometimes, the streams of consciousness bring to light things a person hadn't known they remembered or thought about before. I had a feeling this was happening now with Imogen. I would leave that for her to work out later.

"Things went sideways once I was out of the car. When I pulled back from her hug, I realized my mom was crying and telling me she was sorry over and over. I stood there for a minute, not understanding. If I'd just pieced it together… maybe I could've run, or hit the person, or something. But I did *nothing*." Imogen turned to me, pleading with me to understand.

"Imogen, you are not responsible for whatever happened next. Neither is your mom, from what I can tell. The people or person who did this, they're responsible. You could've made different choices, yes. But it wouldn't have mattered in the end, and it might've even been worse. You are not to blame here, hun."

Imogen nodded, her lip quivering some as she sucked in her breath to continue.

"It's all kind of a blur after that. These men came up behind me and pushed us into the warehouse, tying my hands behind my back. Someone kicked me, and I fell to my knees. I remember the feeling of the concrete as I hit it. It ricocheted all the way up my body, and I could feel it in my teeth. The place smelled of stale urine and Cheetos. I remember thinking that was a weird thing to smell, but it's seared into my head."

She shook her head to clear whatever memory she'd just gotten trapped in before she continued.

"My dad was yelling at my mom, telling her to do something. I'd never seen him like that, and I remember being shocked by it. He called her some hateful names, each one hitting her in the chest almost like he shot her. By the time they were done fighting, I could see all the fight had drained out of her. I yelled and screamed for her not to give up, to fight, to just wait, but she was vacant, an empty shell. She stood there with a blank look in her eyes. I can't get it out of my head. She looked right at me and said, 'I love you, sweetheart. Be strong.' And then..." she paused, gathering herself. Her breath hitched, and I wondered if she'd hit the wall, unable to move past anymore today.

"Hey, it's okay. If you need to stop, we can," I offered.

Shaking her head, Imogen held my eyes as she said the next part, urging me to understand, to share in her pain.

"The sound was so loud as it cracked through the empty warehouse. I flinched at it, shutting my eyes tight. At first, I thought it had been for me, but when no pain came, I peeled my eyes open. I hadn't even felt the wetness that had sprayed onto me. But as I blinked, I felt the sticky liquid on my face. I couldn't wipe it since my hands were tied, but somehow, I knew. I *knew* it was her blood. She laid in front of me, her eyes open, unblinking as the blood pooled around her. I remember thinking it was darker than I thought it would be and how fast it spread. I didn't even know I was screaming until the sound returned, and my throat twas raw."

Imogen's tears streamed down her face as she recapped the horrors she'd witnessed. Her eyes had almost gone distant, removing the emotions as she told me this part. She was there, but she wasn't. Squeezing her hand, I tried to bring her back to the present. I didn't want her trapped in the past. Almost as if my squeeze was a shot, she jerked back to the present, focusing on me.

"Do you want to continue, or are you at your limit today?"

Imogen watched my face, searching for the answer. I kept it neutral, offering her whatever she needed. This wasn't about me; this was about her and what she was ready to process. I didn't want her to scar herself by thinking she needed to please me by sharing more.

"I think just a little more," she decided, and at my nod, Imogen continued.

"Time goes funny after that. People came and went from the place, and I guess, I was in a state of shock. My body did that freeze thing you told me about. It just locked down, and I was motionless as everything around me happened. At first, my captors seemed to prefer it to the crying and screaming. But eventually, they got annoyed and started doing things to me to get a response. I barely had food, minimal water, and had been tied to a bedpost they had in a separate little office. The mattress was disgusting, but it's where I stayed mostly. I was so gross by then, having little access to the bathroom or shower."

"Where was your father during this?" I asked.

"I didn't see him for a while after he'd shot my mom. It might've been hours or a few days, but one day, he was back, and he was happy. At first, I thought it was for me. Maybe I'd done what he needed me to do and was there to take me home now. But when he shook hands with the main guy and left without even glancing at me, I knew that wasn't the case. I'd been part of some… some deal instead. He wasn't coming back for me. I was truly alone with those monsters."

Not being able to take it anymore, I pulled her into my arms and held her. The move seemed to be the last thing holding her emotions at bay because as soon as I wrapped my arm around her, she fell into my chest and began to sob. Patting soothing strokes through her hair, I tried to offer her comfort the best way I could.

"It's over. You're not there anymore, sweet girl. You survived it, Imogen. You are strong, just like your mother told you to be."

Over and over, I shared those words with her trying to make them a mantra for her to sear into her brain. A knock at the door brought me out of the bubble we'd fallen into. Confused at the uncommon sound, I didn't know who could be at the door interrupting my session. I didn't immediately say anything as I sat there staring at it.

Imogen wiped her eyes and blew her nose on the tissue I gave her. Another knock sounded, and this time, she looked at me.

"It's probably for me. If you don't answer, they'll come in on their own," she chuckled in a depreciating way.

Getting up, I walked over to the door, wondering why they'd interrupt us. When I opened it, I hadn't expected to find Nicco on the other side.

"*Nicco*, um, what are you doing here? Never mind that, I'm busy at the moment. I'll talk—"

"It's okay, beautiful. I know now. I'm here for Immy. I

was just getting worried. It's thirty minutes past her session."

Looking at my watch, I realized he was correct. Sheepishly, I blushed. "Oops, I guess we lost track of time, Imogen. Do you care if this brute comes in? It seems he's worried."

"Yeah, better let him," she sighed, smiling. "He'll only get more annoying the more you make him wait." Imogen joined in on my game. It helped dislodge the emotions we'd shared by putting Nicco on the spot instead.

"Hey, I'm not that bad," Nicco defended, coming up behind me, putting his arms around my waist, pulling me into him. "Besides, I think you like it when I'm a brute," he purred into my ear. I tried to remind my body I was at work and in the presence of a client. The flush of my skin and the goosebumps erupting disagreed with my plan.

I watched as Imogen looked at me in a new light, and I realized she didn't know I was seeing Nicco. Pulling away from his embrace, I stepped closer to Imogen, wanting to make sure she was okay with everything. Grasping her hands, I peered into her eyes before I spoke. "Are you okay with how we ended?"

"Yeah, I'm good. Thanks for checking, though."

"Of course, Imogen. You're my concern, and I want you to be in a good place when you leave. We can pick it back up in our next session if you want, or we can even take a break and work on some thoughts. It's your choice. You're the guide here."

"I'd like that. Thank you, Loren. Um, so off-topic, but how do you two know one another? Hmm?

"Oh, well." I blushed. "We met a couple of weeks ago and are dating. I didn't realize you guys knew each other. Is this okay?"

"Ah, so you must be the girl he won't shut up about."

"Yeah?"

"Yeah," she teased, "and I approve. I'd been holding out hope for Attie, but he's a bit of a boring bear. Nicco's great, though. I like this a lot, actually."

Hugging her, I figured I'd already broken most of my boundaries at this point. What was one more hug? When we pulled back, she had a sheepish look on her face now.

"Um, did Jude talk to you about us hanging out tonight?"

"Hmm, it seems you already know he's living with me. I'm guessing you guys have kept talking since our lunch a week ago?"

"Yeah. We're just friends, though," she quickly added. "We oddly have a lot in common."

Thinking about that, I realized, based on what I knew of his past, it was sadly accurate. I couldn't help but be glad they'd met each other, though. Another line of my boundaries was erased, and I realized I was practically boundary-less at this point. Again, I should've been more concerned about it, but I wasn't.

"What's this about hanging out?" I asked, stepping back now we weren't talking about the session.

"Oh, well, he asked if I wanted to maybe hang out tonight. I assumed he checked with you. Is that not okay?"

I thought for a moment and knew we hadn't had a conversation yet on the rules, something I would need to correct. It wasn't a bad thing, but it was tricky with her being my client. Of course, Jude didn't know that since we'd introduce her as a friend. When I put it into their perspective, I couldn't fault all the parties involved. They didn't know the difficulty it created for me, and at this point, I'd already entered the bubble, might as well erase that last line.

"Of course, it's fine. We haven't had a conversation as everything happened so quickly the other night. I'm supposed to have kickboxing tonight, or at least, I think I do. I'll just need to check. I'm sorry, my mind is all over the place. What's the plan?" I laughed when I realized I was oversharing and not making sense.

"I think that's where I come in, beautiful," Nicco offered, walking over to us again. Smiling at him, I wanted to kiss him.

"So, how is it that you're dating Loren?" Imogen challenged him. "Out of all the women in the city, you had to pick my therapist?" she teased, already knowing the answer. I could see their bond in how they regarded one another.

"To be fair, squirt, I didn't know she was your therapist until this afternoon when Sax asked me to pick you up, so there." He stuck his tongue out of her, and it was fun to watch their relationship. "I even got upset with Loren when I realized she knew Sax and Mas. I thought she was playing me or something," Nicco confessed.

"Yeah, he was a real turd, but he made up for it." I grinned, remembering the mind-blowing orgasm he'd given me on his desk. The heated look he returned told me he was replaying the same thing.

"Okay, *gross*," squealed Imogen, causing us both to break our heated look.

Embarrassment heated my cheeks as I sat down at my desk, needing to finish up my notes and trying to distract myself from the desire. Checking my phone, I sent Jude a text while the other two joked with one another.

ME: Hey, I heard we have a guest tonight?
Jude: Um, yeah. Sorry, I forgot to clear it with you. Is it okay?
ME: Yes, it's okay. I think we should probably sit down, though, and go over some guidelines just for the future. I'm not trying to control you or anything, but some reference for us both would be helpful. It's my first time being a foster mom, after all.
Jude: You're already better at it than any I've had before.
Jude: I'm cool with talking about things. It probably helps my anxiety, too, so I know what I can and can't do.
ME: Ah, look at us having our first little family conversation.
Jude: Gag.
Jude: Actually, it was nice. I liked it.
Jude: This I mean.
Jude: Crap, now I sound like a weirdo.
ME: No, you don't. I get what you mean.

ME: So are there plans made, or do we need to sort them for this hang-out thing?
Jude: Plans? Umm… What kind of plans?
ME: Food? Drinks? Activity?
Jude: Shit, I have nothing.
Jude: Crap, sorry, I didn't mean to cuss.
ME: Jude, you use whatever language you like to express yourself. Freedom of speech and all that. Just don't use it *at* me, if you get what I'm saying.
Jude: Uh, yeah. I think so. Don't call you the b-word, basically?
ME: Precisely. Okay, how about I talk with them and let you know the plan?
Jude: Them?
ME: Nicco is with Imogen.
Jude: Oh, who is this, Nicco? Do I need to be worried?
ME: Well, I believe he's 29 and her cousin. So no. Unless you were asking in regards to me?
Jude: I wasn't, but now I am. Do I need to pull out my stern, disapproving face?
ME: Ha! No, Nicco and I are dating. So you can reign in your look for later.
Jude: I thought you were dating Monroe?
ME: I am. It's complicated. Can we talk about this later? Put it on the agenda for shit we need to discuss.
Jude: Ha, yes, definitely. I feel like I need to step up and make sure these guys are worthy now.
ME: You're hilarious. Okay, I'll let you know what's decided.

Jude: Thanks, Loren. Sorry I didn't ask ahead of time. I'm kind of used to doing my own thing, and no one cares what it is. As long as I stay out of trouble and I'm there when the inspection occurs, so they get their check, they don't want to know.
ME: I know, bud, but it's not that way anymore.
Jude: Yeah. I see that. Sorry, I forgot for a minute.
ME: It's a learning curve. We'll both mess up, so no fretting. We just have to make sure we talk about it and fix whatever it is we need to. We're in this together, remember?
Jude: Together.
ME: Okay, weirdo, I'll text you in a min.
Jude: Takes one to know one.

Laughing, I looked up to find both Nicco and Imogen watching me.

"Oh, sorry. Just having a conversation with Jude about what was going on. Nicco, he wants to give you the third degree to make sure you're worthy," I chuckled.

"I am so there for this!" Imogen exclaimed.

"Bring it! I will prove to whoever I have to, gorgeous, that I'm 100% right for you."

At his use of gorgeous, the other night flashed in my head and the sexy, dangerous guy who had said it to me. My face must've dropped because I found Nicco turning my chair a moment later, concern in his eyes as he stared at me.

"Hey, I was just joking. You okay?"

"Yeah, sorry. It was just something you said triggered a memory from the other night. A man I met on the train stole my phone and wouldn't give it back to me. He called me gorgeous, and yeah, it was a whole thing. But it's not important. So, I need to finish up some things here before I can leave. How about I task you both with figuring out the plan for this evening, whether that means ordering food or heading out? I'm game with whatever."

"Yeah, we can do that. Are you sure you're okay?"

Softness etched his skin, and I got lost for a second in his eyes. Nicco had the most dynamic blue eyes. They always captured me in their intensity, and if I wasn't careful, I would become lost in them. I could only nod, at a loss for words. Nicco smiled, knowing I'd fallen into his trap, and kissed me gently before walking out and pulling Imogen with him. She was buried in her phone, probably to Jude, so she walked along with him effortlessly.

Finishing up my note for the session, I sent a quick text off to Wells about our session.

ME: I can't make the session tonight. Something's come up. I'll see you Tuesday.

I hadn't expected him to respond so quickly. I was putting my phone away when I felt the phone buzz with a response. Looking at the screen, a scowl crossed my face at his terse reply. Tossing it back into my bag, I decided to deal with him later.

Surly: You know the rules, kitten. You miss, you still pay. I should've figured you couldn't hack it

for long. Miss one more, and you might as well
not even bother coming at all.

New Horizons was dark as I walked through.
Everyone else had left for the evening already. My
session running over had hindered anyone from saying
goodbye, and I guess how Nicco had gotten past Doris
too. Stepping into the lobby, I found Nicco and Imogen,
along with another burly dude standing there in a deep
conversation.

"Did we decide what we're doing?" I ignored the
other man, figuring they'd introduce him to me if it was
important. Nicco turned, a smile on his face.

"How do you feel about sushi?" Based on Imogen's
bounce, she was very excited about this plan.

"I could do sushi. Do we know if Jude likes it,
though?"

At my question, Imogen frowned and then pulled out
her phone, sending off a quick text. A second later, she
popped her head up, a massive smile on her face.

"He's never had it, but is wanting to try."

"Awesome, so how are we getting to the restaurant?
Or are we picking it up?"

They both looked at each other, then at the other man,
neither with an answer as they all kept hoping it would
magically come to them. Pulling out my phone, I sent a
text to see if Nat was available.

ME: Hey, girl. Are you free?
Nat: For you? Always!
ME: You're the best. Can you stop by my apart-

ment and pick up my foster kid, Jude? And then bring him to Sushi Roll?
Nat: Since when do you have a foster kid?
ME: Um, two days ago? It's a long story. Drinks soon, and I can update you?
Nat: Oh, that sounds like fun. I'm in.
Nat: I'm two mins out from your place.
ME: Okay, 6ft-ish teenager, brown hair, answers to Jude
Nat: That could be 1/2 of Chicago!

ME: I have a car coming to pick you up. Silver SUV. Nat is her name. She's a friend. She'll bring you to the restaurant. Two minutes out.
Jude: Okay, thank you. Are, like, jeans and that shirt we got yesterday okay to wear?
ME: That would be perfect to wear. Bet you're glad I made you get it now, huh?
Jude: haha… but yeah.

ME: Okay, he will be down in a second. I'll send the address to the restaurant.
Nat: I can't believe you just ignored me!
ME: You'll be fine. Ask him for a password. I want to see if he panics.
Nat: That's mean, but I can get behind it.

"Okay, if I can ride with you guys, Jude will meet us at the restaurant. The Uber is picking him up as we speak. I just need the address," I stated before I looked up from my phone. All three of them had turned to me with matching locks of shock on their faces.

"What?"

"Um, beautiful, has anyone told you today how amazing you are?"

"No, they haven't, actually."

"Well, you are. Absolutely, you can ride with me. I'm on the bike, though, but Immy has her driver and can meet us at the restaurant."

"Yep!" Immy agreed, glancing at her phone. "Oh, wait. Jude's asking about a password for the car?"

Laughing, I pulled out my phone and sent Jude a text before heading out with Nicco once I'd locked the last door.

ME: Special ingredient. The password is our special ingredient.

FORTY-TWO

NICCO

"Have you ever ridden on a bike?" I asked Loren as we rounded the corner of her building.

"Um, no," she cringed.

Pulling her by the lapels of her coat, I held her body against mine. I loved the sound of her gasp as she collided with me. I had to remind myself we were meeting Immy. Not to mention, I was supposed to be watching her. Otherwise, I might get it in my head to head back into her office for some one-on-one couch time. I think I had a different purpose for it than she did, though.

"Oh, this will be fun, beautiful." I grinned wide at the thought of her legs wrapped around me. My mind had to slap that down too. Loren made the naughty thoughts rise up, well lots of things rise up, if the hard cock against my leg was any indication. She made it easy to forget the baby cousin factor. Damn, Immy was majorly ruining my game. It had gotten me out of a family meeting, though, and I got to spend it with her and Loren. It was still a winner, even if it had to be more PG-13 and not the X-rated version I had in my mind.

Thankfully, Immy had been willing to take Loren's bag with her, so it helped her not be encumbered by things. Straddling the bike, I started it and released the kickstand as I waited for her to climb on. Loren tentatively put her leg over the back and placed her arms around me. Grabbing them, I pulled them tighter to me, needing her to grip harder. Handing her a helmet, I showed her how to tighten the strap. Using the intercom, I directed her on how to position herself.

"You're going to want to hold on tight, beautiful. Squeeze your legs to mine as well, and lean with me."

"Okay."

"Don't worry. I got you."

Loren braced her arms more securely around me before placing her head against my back. I sat for a moment to take in this perfect moment. The bike rumbling between my thighs and my girl's arms wrapped tightly around me. It was the second-best place I could picture her. Though Loren naked in my bed or on my tattoo table were closely tied for first.

Pushing off, I navigated the streets to the restaurant. Immy and I had agreed it would be the best place. I needed to check on it anyway, and we knew it was safe with our guards posted. Her being out in public without Sax or Mas was a risk, but I didn't want her to feel like she couldn't still live her life. This was a big step for her. I could tell how much it meant to her that she got to do this, and I wanted to make it happen for her.

We arrived at the restaurant fifteen minutes later, and I pulled around the back to park. The SUV idled there waiting for us. Stepping off, I put my helmet on the handles and helped Loren take hers off. She was all smiles as she placed one leg over the seat and stood.

"Does that smile mean you enjoyed it?"

"It was amazing! Please, tell me you'll teach me?" Loren pleaded, pouty lip and all.

Pulling her close, I kissed her quickly before heading to the SUV. Knocking on the window, I stepped back so the door could open.

"If you're going to be kissing her, I'm going to need a barf bag."

"Listen here, MoMo, I'll have you know that kissing is perfectly healthy…."

As I began to explain, she plugged her ears and started running away from me, screaming, "La la, I can't hear you."

Loren caught up to me and took the hand I offered for her. Raising my eyebrows, I tried to gauge how she was feeling. Once Sax had told me the real reason Immy and Loren knew one another, I'd felt like a complete ass. All the fantastic things Immy had said about her too, and I hadn't even realized it was the woman I'd become obsessed with.

I knew this had to be hard for her, but she seemed to be handling it, so I accepted it and followed the two guards and Immy into the restaurant.

"Why are we entering this way? And does she always have so many guards around her?"

I'd been surprised Loren hadn't asked more questions yet, so I was prepared when she finally did. "Well, this restaurant is in my family, and I'm kind of overseeing it for my cousin. So, it's an owner perk, not having to wait in line. I'll let the hostess know to expect Jude, though."

"Huh, that's kind of cool, and thanks, I was about to ask that." She smiled up at me, and I was momentarily stunned as I stared down at her, transfixed by her beauty. Loren had always been a beautiful woman, but over the past few weeks, I'd started to see her shine in new ways, and now I felt like I finally saw her. The person she was under it all. *She took my breath away.*

"Everything okay?"

Stumbling, I stopped to gather my bearings and hadn't realized we'd stopped until her question.

"Yeah, beautiful. Everything's wonderful. Come on. I'm starving."

Pulling her along, the grin on my face was genuine and had to match hers. Immy and Dakota were waiting just inside. Immy rolled her eyes at me, but her smile gave away her true feelings on the matter. She was happy for me.

We followed the maître d' into the restaurant and headed for our private room. We hadn't done much remodeling to the restaurant when we took it over. Mas only insisted on a private room for us. I was suddenly glad about it.

"There will be one more to our party coming from the front. Ask him for the password," Immy directed to our escort, a mischievous smile playing on her lips.

"Poor Jude, I don't know if he's prepared for us," Loren chuckled. Immy shrugged her shoulders, clearly amused with whatever game they were playing.

Pulling out Loren's chair, I handed her coat off to the attendant, and they hung it up against the wall. Immy and I handed ours as well before taking our seats. Waiters began bringing in menus, drinks, and appetizers so quickly, we didn't even have time to talk to one another. When they finished, Immy's phone went off, followed by her laughter.

"Oh my God," she chuckled. "He told them it was 'Imogen's a nuisance', and now they won't let him pass. I'll be right back. Gotta go rescue the dweeb."

I nodded discreetly to take Dakota with her, and she accepted as she stepped out of the doors.

"I didn't realize how close they'd become," Loren admitted.

"I didn't realize it was the same Jude. She talked about a new friend she made a week ago, and I didn't put two and two together even after Mas mentioned it. I was so focused on thinking I was being played. I'm sorry again about that. It's nice to see her smile again. It felt as if she wasn't ever going to shed the darkness," I confessed to Loren. She made it feel safe to disclose, and I knew she had to know some of the story, so it wasn't as if she'd ask questions. Her reassuring smile back told me I'd been right.

Laughter preceded the duo, and I was happy to finally meet the kid who'd wormed his way into both of my girls' hearts. Standing, I tried to give my best badass face as they approached the table. Loren stood and hugged him, and I watched the way he melted into her embrace. Immy gave me a look when she noticed what I was doing, but I ignored her, prepared to give my best disapproving look.

When Jude stepped back from Loren, I wasn't prepared for him to start giving me the third degree instead.

"What are your intentions with Loren? Do you treat her well? Why should I approve of you?"

Momentarily stunned, my jaw dropped open, and I stood stock-still as I regarded the kid. Loren and Immy broke out into chuckles, but Jude remained stoic, arms crossed as he took my measure.

"Um, well. I care for her a lot, and I treat her like a queen. Wait, why do I need your approval? Shouldn't you be trying to get mine?" Scratching my head, I sat back down, not sure where I stood now. Was I not scary anymore? Had I lost my street cred? Were my tattoos not intimidating enough?

At my confusion, the three of them broke out into more giggles, and after pouting like an insolent child for a minute, I joined them, realizing I'd been played.

"Okay, kid. I'll give you props for the reverse psychology there. You threw me off my game. I'm Nicco, by the way."

Reaching over, I offered him my hand and was glad when he took it. Weirdly, I did still feel a little like I was trying to seek his approval. It was the weirdest thing I'd ever felt, but perhaps, it was because I'd never dated anyone long enough to seek approval from their family and friends.

"We've got to try this! It's new, and the chef was telling me about it. Plus, as a newbie sushi connoisseur, you need to try these, and oh, what about this?"

Immy excitedly professed, bouncing in her seat as she went back and forth over the menu with Jude. I noticed he stared at her with stars in his eyes, and I knew that while they might be only friends at the moment, it probably wasn't staying that status for long. Not if the side looks she gave Jude when he wasn't looking were indicators of her feelings.

"Let's just order a little of everything, and then we can all try it," Loren suggested.

"Sensible. I'm game," I agreed, closing the menu.

"Oh, let me order! Please!"

Nodding to let Immy order, I kept studying her and was amazed by the changes since I'd last hung out with her. Pulling Loren close, I whispered in her ear, "I know you can't say anything, but whatever you've done for Immy, it's working. So, *thank you*. The difference in her is astronomical."

"I can't take the credit for that. Immy's done all the work. She's an amazing kid and so strong. I think having all you strong men in her life has helped her be. It's not going to be easy or smooth the rest of it away, but she made a big step today."

"Well, you can say all day long how you didn't do anything, beautiful. But I know you did. Just being your amazing self was enough."

"You're just saying that because you want to spend more time with my amazing self… *naked*."

"Oh, no doubt I do. But I'm not saying it for that reason. What's that thing you're always saying? Don't dismiss my compliments? Accept it. Deal?"

Loren turned her head, our noses practically touching as she searched my eyes for something before responding. "Deal."

Kissing her softly, I pulled back to the sounds of gagging from across the table. Smirking, I threw a piece of the garnish at Immy, causing her to shriek and use Jude to hide behind. The poor boy's ears turned bright red at her touch, but he looked pleased to shield her. I wondered if Loren had picked up on this budding relationship yet. While I trusted them, we would need to watch them. Immy's life wasn't easy, and anyone she brought into it would have to understand the risk.

The sinking realization I wasn't being fair to Loren hit me square in the chest. Sax's words from earlier echoed in my mind, *our girl*. Had he been referring to Loren? At first, I'd assumed he meant Immy, but replaying it now, and it felt more connected to Loren. I'd noticed their spark the other week at the fight. I'd told Loren I wanted her to explore, to be able to live and do things she'd never been able to with her ex.

Part of myself was screaming, idiot! The other part knew it had been the wiser choice, the better option. I needed to accept my feelings and let her do this. I didn't want to be like her ex and restrict her, and while I felt our connection was growing, this life was dangerous, and who knew if I would even be around ten years down the road. I was looking for a way out of the family, but it wasn't a guarantee I'd be granted it.

I couldn't promise her anything at the moment. The reality of the statement sat heavy in my chest. Maybe I was only kidding myself. Was I only setting myself up for a potential heartbreak? No, this was the best course of action. Casual and open. It was the least amount of risk with the highest level of reward. It meant I needed to guard my heart and make sure I wasn't cashing checks for feelings I couldn't afford to repay later.

The waiters placed the food on the table, effectively breaking the reverie I'd fallen into. I looked around the room and noticed Dakota was still inside. He nodded as I glanced over, and I returned it. They were good at their job. You forgot they were there the majority of the time. Taking my arm off the back of Loren's chair, I felt myself start to withdraw inwardly.

It would be for the best to protect us both. She needed the room to explore, and I needed to protect her from a life that was dark and dangerous. Loren was too pure for this life. She could have dreams, and a future not built on the backs of others or the hope of an impossible escape. Immy noticed my change in demeanor and gave me a worried look. She understood, but I think her teenage optimism would always hope for happily ever afters, even for bad guys like me.

"Oh my goodness, this is amazing!" Loren exclaimed, happily eating the sushi, unaware of the turmoil I faced. I watched silently as they taught Jude how to hold his chopsticks and how to make the perfect wasabi-soy bite.

It was bittersweet to be here. I got a glimpse of what having a family could feel like, what having a future with this amazing woman would be like. Only to have to censor myself, water down my past, or ignore the guards to remember what was really at play here.

This wasn't a life for love, and I was the fool headed there in the fast lane with no airbag.

"Nic, do you want to join us for games, or do you have to go to the shop?"

Immy's question broke through my morose thoughts, and I blinked at her as I tried to comprehend what she was asking. Glancing around the table, I realized it was just the two of us.

"Where did they go?"

"They went to the restroom. Nic, what's going on? I feel like you've been on autopilot for the past half hour. Everything okay?"

"Yeah, it's fine. Just remembering how dangerous life is for us. Sometimes, it's hard being in the family."

Immy reached over and took my hand, understanding etched on her face. "Life is hard regardless of who your family is, Nic. If you don't surround yourself with the people you care about, you're just punishing yourself. Besides, what fun is being the mafioso if you can't protect the ones that make your life better?"

Her words struck me in the chest, and I realized how right she was. I didn't want her to know she'd just schooled me, so I shrugged nonchalantly, taking to heart what she said. I sometimes forgot, despite her only being seventeen, how mature she was. She'd been sheltered, yes, but she also knew a reality most kids her age didn't.

A waiter walked over with the tab just as Loren and Jude entered back into the room. Opening the black portfolio, I stared, temporarily stunned at what I saw. I'd expected to see a receipt to sign, but instead, a message sat inside.

> *I gave you one warning. This is two. You don't want to make it to three.*
>
> *-D*

When I looked up to try to gauge the threat, a loud boom sounded throughout the room, throwing me back. My chair fell backward with tremendous force smacking my head forcibly into the floor. The heat rolled in next, followed by the sound as I started to come to. Through the fog in my head, I tried to piece together what was happening.

Hands braced my face as someone slapped my cheek to get my attention.

"Nic, wake up! Nic!"

"MoMo? Ow. Why do you keep slapping me?"

"Nic! There's no time to explain. We have to go. Now, come on. *We have to go,*" she screamed.

Immy's tears hit my face as I became aware. Sitting up quickly, I gathered her in my arms and took off for a run toward the exit. When I made it out the back, a sound drew my attention, and for a second, I turned. Deep espresso brown eyes hit mine, and it felt like I'd been shot in the gut. I started to turn back toward her when my arm was pulled in the other direction. Fighting against the force, I attempted to go to her, but the hit to the head had disoriented me, and I couldn't fight the arms off that wrapped around my middle and shoved me into a waiting car.

"NO! Let me go. I need to go to her. Stop the car! You can't leave them!" I screamed it over and over, but there was no response. No one paid any attention to my command.

Immy was curled up in a ball in the other corner of the car, and tears streamed down her face as she rocked. Flipping back, I watched out the rearview the chaos unfolding before glancing around the car to identify who I was with and hoping I hadn't been abducted by one of the other families. Looking to the front, I recognized another guard. His name wasn't coming to my mind at the moment, but I knew he was family.

"Where's Dakota? Where are you taking us? Why wouldn't you stop? Our friends are still there, *goddammit*!"

Each question was met with silence. Slapping the back of the seat in front of me, I tried to get a reaction, but no one answered me. They continued to drive further and further away from the restaurant in silence. Immy jerked her head up at my command, her fear clear on her face. When I realized I wouldn't get anywhere with the men up front, I gathered her in my arms and rocked her while she cried.

While I wanted to believe her words earlier, the truth was, this only proved how dangerous our life was. I didn't know how Loren would forgive me for leaving her there, but maybe it was better this way. She could hate me now, but she would still be alive. At least, I hoped she was.

I cared enough for her at this point to be able to live with her hating me. It wasn't until we pulled up to the estate I remembered the note.

The question was, who were they threatening?

FORTY-THREE

LOREN

"Thanks for waiting for me. Did you enjoy the sushi?"

It felt like everything stopped in that moment, the second between when I asked him a mundane question, and everything changed. In slow motion, I watched as his mouth opened to respond and then the sound was sucked out like a vacuum as a loud boom exploded behind me.

Pain surged through my body as I was knocked forward by the force. Heat seared my skin as I felt the flames erupt in a blaze from the front of the restaurant. I'd somehow managed to cover Jude with my body as the debris from the explosion rained down around us. Blood dripped down my face, a wet stickiness blinding my eyesight in a red haze. I felt the blood dripping down my leg as well, but I couldn't move my arm to check it.

Jude laid dazed below me, the fall having knocked him out. He started to rouse as the noise returned to me. I could hear people screaming and crying from every direction. Car alarms beeped in the distance, and water gushed from a pipe nearby. Debris continued to fall around us from above, but it didn't appear the fire had spread. I couldn't make out where anyone else was. Nicco and Imogen were lost in the mess, but I knew they had to be close to the back wall.

"Jude, can you hear me? *Jude*?"

"Hm?" He blinked, looking at me. "Loren?"

"Yeah, can you sit up? We probably need to move so this ceiling doesn't crash around us. Are you injured?"

"I don't know. I don't think anything major at least."

"Okay, let's try to move, okay. I'll move off you, and then you try to sit up."

"Okay."

"Ready, and go."

I rolled off him as my body screamed at me in pain, and I laid on the floor for a moment, gathering my strength. My new position provided me with a view of the restaurant's back entrance, and I could see guests running around as they tried to escape the wreckage. Dark hair and tattoos caught my attention, and when I looked up at the person, I realized it was Nicco.

He was carrying Imogen and looked dazed as he tried to find his way out of the restaurant. He turned, his eyes catching mine, and time stopped again. Nicco stared at me for a while, and it felt like he looked right through me. Pain separate from my injuries pierced me, and I held his eyes, praying for him to see me, not to leave me. Across the distance, almost as if my silent pleas traveled to him, he halted, recognition in his gaze as he started for me.

Nicco took one step when someone took Imogen

from his arms, and another grabbed him around the waist, pulling him back with him. I watched as Nicco fought them off as best he could with his injuries, but eventually, he was pulled back against a chest and dragged out the door. As he disappeared from my view, the arm I hadn't realized was outstretched to him fell to the ground in despair. Pain raced up my arm as I laid there, both from the action and reality of being left behind.

My screams to return made no difference, as they kept dying on my tongue. "Nic, Nic… " Until eventually, my throat filled with liquid fire, and I could no longer bear the agony. The pain became too much, and I succumbed to the darkness calling my name.

BEEPING ECHOED IN MY EAR, but as I tried to move, my body cried out in anguish. Whimpers left me unbidden, and I reached for someone, anyone, to comfort me. A hand gripped mine, and I settled at the connection. I realized my eyes were closed when everything around me stayed black. My fear made me hesitant to face reality, scared at what I might find out there, or even worse, *not find*. When I felt the squeeze of my hand again, I slowly blinked my eyes open, deciding to brave my surroundings.

I could hide all I wanted from things, but they always found you in the end.

"Loren? Can you hear me, babe?"

At the sound, I located the voice and blinked to

ensure I saw things accurately. Did I hit my head harder than I realized? Reaching my hand up to check my head, I found my right hand was in a cast up to my elbow. Memories of my arm hurting and debris falling around me returned, and I connected the dots to the injury. As I sifted through the memories, my condition began to make sense and explained the pain level I felt.

"Loren, sugar? Are you okay? Do you want the doctor?"

Blinking again at the voice, I tried to recall how I ended up in this hospital room. "Doctor?" I finally managed to ask, my throat sore and raw.

"Of course. I'll be right back, babe."

Once I was alone, I took in my surroundings. Cards, flowers, and stuffed animals littered my room in an alarming amount. There was barely any space left from all the things occupying it. I didn't understand anything. Nothing was making sense. It was like I woke up in some weird alternative dimension. I was beginning to believe the twilight zone was even real at this rate.

The doctor entered a few minutes later, and a relieved breath left me. Finally, perhaps I could put the pieces to this weird puzzle together.

"Doctor!" I croaked out, my voice hollow and soft.

"Ah, Mrs. Carter, you're awake. You gave us all quite a scare there. I'll have the nurse bring you some ice chips for your throat. How does that sound?"

Nodding, I hoped he'd get on with giving me the information I wanted and not bore me with this pleasantries crap. I needed to figure out what was happening. I needed… Jude!

"Jude?" I whispered, the doctor giving me an odd look at the name. He flipped through my chart, but it didn't seem he knew who I was talking about. Oh no, this wasn't good.

"What happened?" I asked instead, hoping to get as much information as possible before the voice returned.

"Ah, yes, let me go over your injuries, shall I?" He started, relieved to have something he knew to discuss. Flipping back to the front, he began to read off the information. "You arrived in the ER with a right distal radius fracture and minor burns on your legs and arms along with bruising. As they assessed you, you started to code and had to be taken into immediate surgery. You had swelling in the brain from a contusion on the right frontal lobe. To reduce the swelling, you were placed in a medically induced coma. They were able to repair your wrist and reduce the swelling over time. Your throat is raw from the breathing tube they only removed this morning." He stopped, looking up at me finally after his spiel. "I'm sure you have a lot of questions."

I wanted to laugh at his blasé attitude, reading off my trauma with as little regard as one reads a fucking recipe. To minimize my feelings down to mere questions felt inaccurate because they plagued me. I just couldn't bring myself to voice them as I processed his information.

I'd been in a coma and almost died.

It was sobering to absorb the information. Maybe the brain trauma explained the hallucination I had when I awoke? No one had returned yet, so perhaps it was possible, and their presence was only a figment of my imagination.

While I assessed the information in my head, the door opened, and the voice returned with some ice chips crushing all my hopeful conclusions.

"Here you go, babe. This will help."

Staring at the figure, I blinked and tried to erase them from my sight. It didn't work. Squeezing my eyes tight, I tried again to restart this apparent nightmare. When I opened them again, it was, unfortunately, the same scene I left. Glaring daggers at the doctor, I attempted to ignore the voice, hoping they'd get the hint and go away. The doctor continued to go over something in my chart but must've felt my eyes on him, lifting his to mine a moment later.

"If you're having trouble remembering, it's normal. We don't know yet the extent it might have on your brain, short-term or long-term. Did you think of a question yet?"

"Yeah," I croaked, taking an ice chip and sucking it down before I tried again. "The first is, what the hell is my ex-husband doing here?"

My question startled both men in the room, and looks of shock appeared on their faces. Perhaps it was the cursing, but more than likely, it was the nature of the question. Brian's mouth gaped as he stared at me like he'd seen a stranger. The doctor looked uncomfortable and shifted on his feet as he tried to find the answer in the chart, he clutched to his chest.

"Loren!" my mother exclaimed, walking into the room.

"Fucking great! It just keeps getting better," I whispered. However, it must've been loud enough if my mother's outrage was any indication.

"Doctor, is this a symptom of brain trauma?" Brian asked aloud, looking back and forth from me and the doc. The doctor swallowed, clearly uncomfortable with the level of tension in the room.

"It's *possible*. We'd have to do more tests to be certain. Excuse me while I grab the nurse, and we can see about getting those scheduled."

At that, the little man escaped the room and the building tension. I wanted to be angry with him for leaving, but I couldn't blame him in the end. I didn't want to be in this room either with those two, but I had no way of escaping, unlike him.

Sighing, I closed my eyes and wished them away. This whole hospital stay gave me the courage to be my true self. I didn't have enough energy to fake anything today. As the kids said in sessions, I had *zero fucks left to give.*

"Loren! My stars! I can't believe this is how you treat us. Don't you know how worried we've all been? I swear, you purposefully do these things…."

My mother droned on, but I tuned her out, tired of her bullshit altogether. She didn't care about me, only how it made her look. It was the harsh reality of Jacqueline Hanover.

"Can it, Mom. You're giving me a headache."

Rubbing my temples, I was thankful when she did shut up, taking my words to heart. Even with my eyes closed, her ire radiated as she huffed and sat angrily in a chair. I could feel her irritation and disappointment directed at me with my eyes closed.

"Brian, why are *you* here?" I sighed, exhaustion weighing heavy on me.

"You're asking why *I'm* here? Loren, you almost died!"

"*And*?" Rolling my eyes, I leveled him with a look of disdain. "You're not my husband anymore. In fact, it's been official for a whole year now. So again, why are you here?"

"How can you be so callous? They called me when you were brought in. I guess I'm still your emergency contact through insurance," he finally admitted.

"You could've easily told them the truth. I don't want you here. *Please,* just leave."

"You want me to leave? After being by your side for days, you want me just to leave?" Brian shouted at me, incredulity heavy in each word.

The volume of his voice made me wince as I started to feel a sharp pain in my head. Part of his rant filtered through, and I focused on what he'd just said. *Days.*

"Wait, how long have I been here?"

I opened my eyes, needing to see them when they answered. They looked at one another, uncertainty plaguing their features, before returning their gazes to me.

"You've been here almost a week."

"A week…"

My breath caught in my throat, and anxiety began to rise as the heart monitor beeped incessantly. Somewhere, in the back of my mind, I knew it was because of a panic attack, but all I could focus on was how long it had been. Almost *a week.*

A nurse entered a few seconds later and inserted something into my IV. Consciousness and voices floated around me, and I soon found myself back in a peaceful state of darkness. It was calm and soothing as I drifted along, and I decided to hide here for a while. I'd thought facing things was the wiser choice, but when my present was worse than my nightmare, what was the point?

In the dark recesses of my mind, I fell into the arms of sexy men with delicious voices and steamy words that made me forget everything else. Their faces swirled around me, and in my dream, I didn't have to choose. I was cherished by them all, and jealousy didn't exist in the land of make believe. I indulged in their embraces and forgot about everything outside of me that brought me pain.

Consciousness flitted in and out, and my subconsciousness screamed at me to wake up, to stop hiding, and to *remember*. I didn't know what I was supposed to remember. I just knew it was better here in this place where I didn't have to worry or think. Here, I was free.

Though something about that didn't feel right, and after a while, I couldn't ignore it any longer. The despair and heartache were too much, and I wouldn't let myself hide. This time when I woke, I was prepared for what awaited me. Thankfully, my room appeared empty, and I prayed my last guests had taken the hint and left.

The faint smell of my mother's perfume that still lingered in the air didn't give me a lot of confidence.

I stared at the ceiling for a while, thinking through everything this time, trying to gather myself so I wasn't as disoriented. I knew I had a brain injury and a broken wrist. There were some other injuries as well, but I couldn't recall them. Based on my body, it felt bruised and battered, but nothing else felt broken. I couldn't feel any other casts, at least.

A nurse entered a while later, surprised to find me awake, her startled gasp drawing my attention.

"Mrs. Carter! How are you? Do you need anything?"

I assumed my voice was still raw, the ache still notice-able in my throat, so I'd been thinking over what I could use my limited words for. "Phone?"

"I'm sorry, Mrs. Carter. There wasn't one on you or with your possessions. It was probably damaged in the explosion. Can I bring you anything else? Do you have someone you want me to call?"

Her question brought an idea to me. Nodding, I mimed writing, and she seemed to understand as she quickly exited the room and returned a second later with ice chips and a paper pad. This woman was a Goddess. Clipping the pen from her scrub top, she handed them to me.

It was challenging to write with my left hand, but I managed to get out two words before giving up.

Ignite. Mitzi.

The nurse glanced at the two words before looking at me in question. "I don't understand. Is Ignite a code word?"

I shook my head no, and she thought about it more, asking me several in a row this time. "Is it what happened? A person? A place?"

At my nod of approval, a smile broke on her face, excited to figure out my clue. She pulled out her phone and started to google the word. She showed me the list as she began to scroll through it.

Ignite Gaming

Ignite Chicago Walk

Ignite Talks

Ignite Youth Center, Non-For Profit

At the center, I eagerly pointed at it, wanting her to click on it.

"This is the place you want me to call and ask for, Mitzi?" she clarified. At my nod again, she smiled and clicked on the number listed on the website. It felt as if I'd waited a hundred years for the phone to ring and connect.

"Hello, yes, I was wondering if I could speak with Mitzi? Uh-huh, I see. I have a patient here that's needing to get in contact with her. Do you have a different number I could reach her at? Yes, I understand. Can I give you my number and you have her call me? It's in regards to Loren Carter. Yes, thank you for your assistance," she stated before hanging up the phone. "*Well*, she was a delight."

Her comment caused a laugh to bubble up in agreement. The front desk girl was a nightmare. I prayed Mitzi would get my message. It was my best chance at finding what happened to Jude. I didn't have a good feeling, and I didn't want him to suffer any longer than necessary. He was my first priority at the moment. Everything else could wait.

"I need to make my rounds, but if she gives the message," she stopped, glancing down at the vibrating phone. "Well, I guess she's more helpful than she sounds," she mumbled before answering. "Hello, this is April. Yes, is this Mitzi? Oh, wonderful. I wasn't sure if you would get the message. I'm a nurse at Chicago Hospital, and a patient of mine requested to get in touch with you. Yes, Loren Carter. She isn't able to speak, but she might be able to get a few words out. Would you like to talk to her? Okay, I'll put her on."

She handed me the phone, and I eagerly brought it to my ear, "Hello?" I croaked. The nurse brought up some water, and after a good drink, it felt better.

"Loren? Oh, my sweet girl. It's so good to hear from you. I've been so worried. How are you? Do you need anything? How can I help?"

"Slow… down…" I managed before I needed to take another drink.

"Sorry, I'll be patient."

"Jude?" I asked, hope in my voice.

"I'm so sorry, Loren. I tried to keep him out of the group home, but the state didn't want to wait with your placement being new and the paperwork still being processed. What can I do to help?"

"'Is he… okay?"

"Oh, yes, sweetie. He's fine. A few bruises and scrapes, but you were the real hero, it sounds like. You kept anything major from hitting him. He was so brave by your side and refused to leave when CPS showed up. I had to persuade him it would be best for now."

"Mon… roe?"

"I haven't seen him around the center, but do you want me to give him a call?"

"Yes, please. Tell him, hospital."

"Of course, Loren. Hand me back to the nurse, and I'll get the rest of the info. I'm just so glad you're okay. We'll send cards from the kids and flowers now that we know where you are. We've been so worried, so it's good to hear your voice."

"Thank you."

Handing the phone back, I watched as the nurse told Mitzi the room number and visiting hours. Smiling, I fell back to sleep, feeling relieved and hopeful for once.

I AWOKE a few hours later to shouting, and it took me a minute to register what was going on as the voices grew louder and louder.

"Who the hell are *you*? Get your hands off my wife!"

"No, I don't think I will since I was asked to be here by *Loren*. I also know she's your *ex-wife*, and I doubt she wants you here."

When I realized it was Monroe, my heart leaped, and I fought to open my eyes to find him. Focusing on the sounds in the room, I found him at the foot of my bed, refusing to budge as Brian attempted to intimidate him. It took me a minute to work out my hand was being held by someone who wasn't Monroe since he wasn't anywhere near me. Twisting my head slowly, my eyes zeroed in on dark pools of whiskey full of demons. Wells regarded me carefully, assessing my face almost to gauge how I would react to his presence.

"You seem disappointed?" I wheezed. Wells' smile lifted at the words. I think he needed to hear my snark to know I was okay, or perhaps he expected me to yell at him.

"Nah, *kitten*. I was just wondering if they removed that big stick you had up your ass." He smirked.

"Me? You're the one with the stick, asshole. Why do I like you again? You're a pain in my ass. Wait, that's right. *I don't like you.*"

"Nope, you said you did, so you can't take it back now."

Wells smiled, and it changed his face so much, I no longer had the heart to fight with him over it. It would be a tragedy to make him lose his smile.

"Lo! You're awake. How are you feeling?"

Monroe rushed over to my side, compassion and worry warring on his face. Brian stood rooted at the end of the bed, but I hoped if I ignored him, he would disappear again. It seemed to have worked the last time at least, so it was worth a try.

"Hey." I smiled. It was nice to wake up this time and see people I wanted instead of the ones who made my life hell.

"Loren! They need to leave right now! I'm not going to stand for this. Your slut ways are over. You'll be moving back with me. I've had enough of this."

A growl resonated next to me as Wells stood and

walked over to Brian. I could see his fighting persona, Crash, peeking through now. He looked menacing and scary as he approached. Brian backed up at his movements, swallowing as he took in the hulking man in front of him.

"Actually, *Brian*, you can leave. We're divorced, and I plan to stay that way. I'd say thanks for coming, but since I didn't ask you to and was asleep, I don't feel you're owed one. So, *bye*."

Brian looked shocked at my command, appalled at my words, and I realized he'd never seen this side of me before. I'd always been the meek wife who adored her husband and would do anything he said. I've never spoken back to him before, always agreeing with him. His face started to turn purple with rage, and Wells moved closer. Each step he took, Brian took one back, and Wells managed to push him to the door. I tried not to laugh as he stumbled and almost fell over. Not liking his odds, Brian finally got the picture and stalked out in a huff.

"Thank God. I woke up with him here and thought I'd dreamt the past two years and was still married to the asshole."

"That does sound like a nightmare," Monroe agreed, squeezing my hand.

Nodding, I started to drift off again when I remembered Monroe could give me the answer about Jude. Peeking open my eyes, I grabbed his hand to get his attention.

"Jude?" I asked, fear in my voice.

"Funny you should ask." He grinned. A few seconds

later, the door opened, and in walked my shaggy-haired, goofy-looking teenager. At the sight of me awake in the bed, he ran toward me and started to hug me but stopped himself when he took in my injuries.

"You better get over here and give me a hug, weirdo," I ordered.

Not hesitating this time, he pulled me into a tight embrace. It hurt at the movement, but it was worth it. Once I settled into his arms, everything felt right in my life again. After a few minutes, I pulled back, wiping the tears from both of our faces.

"I'm so sorry, kid. I didn't think about having a contingency plan in place. I told you I'd keep you safe, and then this happens, and you're yanked all over the place again. I..."

"Stop, it's not your fault. You saved me, Loren. I felt so scared and then when I had to leave you I worried you'd be alone. I hated it, but Mitzi told me it would be better for you, so I agreed. I regretted it each day I didn't hear any news, but I kept hoping. I had to."

"Hopefully, that won't happen again. I'm sorry I didn't think about it sooner, Loren. When I couldn't get a hold of you, I started to get worried. Then I heard about the explosion on the news, but when I called the hospitals, they wouldn't release any information to me," Monroe admitted.

"It's okay, you guys. It doesn't matter anymore. You're here now. Thank you. Even you, *Surly*."

"I'm just here because I didn't have anything better to do, and I was tired of hearing that one whine about how he missed you. Don't let it go to your head, kitten."

"Yeah, *okay*," I snarked back, making everyone, including Wells, break out into laughter.

"So when you say it won't happen again, what does that mean?" Jude asked Monroe, picking up on something I'd missed.

"Well, I submitted paperwork today to fast track your case, and I added me as your emergency placement until Loren is out of the hospital."

"Really?" Tears came to my eyes at his thoughtfulness. Monroe was too good.

"*Really.*"

"Thank you," I mouthed, no longer able to get the words out as the emotion leaked out of me in full force.

"Well, it's getting too touchy-feely in here. I'm going for a walk. Text me when you're ready to go, Monroe," Wells said but hesitated at the door, looking back. "Glad you're not dead, kitten. I expect to see you in Windy City as soon as you can, though. No wussing out on me."

Rolling my eyes at Wells as he left, I sighed in relief at finally getting ahold of someone I cared about.

"So, what's up with that?" I asked Monroe. He shook his head, giving me a look I hoped meant he'd explain more later. "Well, what happened after the explosion? I don't remember much," I admitted to Jude.

"It's kind of a blur for me too. I remember you saying something and then the noise, you pushing yourself in front of me and covering me as we fell. After that, it's all a haze. We came to the ER, and I stayed as long as possible until they forced me to leave. Since then, I've been waiting to hear something. My phone was destroyed, so I've had no way to get ahold of anyone. I haven't even heard from Immy."

The mention of Immy had me remembering Nicco and how they'd been dragged out of the restaurant. Clearing my head, I pushed it aside for now. I'd have to find a way to reach them when we were out of here, but for now, the two people in the room were who mattered. Holding both their hands, I relaxed into their hold and comfort. This time when I fell into oblivion, it was with two anchors securing me to them.

FORTY-FOUR

ATTICUS

Nicco slammed my door, the force causing it to slam against the wall as he entered the office. His anger was a living, breathing thing these days. I knew he was upset about the lockdown, but we couldn't risk being out in public at the moment.

"*Cousin*, what can I do for you this fine morning?"

"You know what I *fucking* want, Mas. Don't start playing dumb now, man. It doesn't suit you."

Sighing, I hung my head as I rubbed my temples. My headache didn't look to be leaving me anytime soon. The past week had been an utter shit show of epic proportions.

As soon as I'd dealt with Uncle Seth's treachery, I'd gotten word about the explosion at the restaurant. I hadn't known at the time that Immy had been there. I was livid when I'd been informed. A level of fear I hadn't known hit me square in the chest. It didn't dissipate until I saw her safe in the house.

Implementing the lockdown protocol was standard, and the guards had extracted Imogen and Nicco and brought them to the estate. It was standard procedure for any time an attack against the family occurred. Nicco and Immy both knew this, yet they couldn't think clearly about the situation, too twisted up in romantic entanglements to understand the bigger picture. It was another example of why love was a myth in the mafia.

"Nicco, you know the rules and the procedures. It's been drilled into all of us since we could understand words. Don't make me into the bad guy here. I'm doing what's necessary to keep our family safe."

"Yeah, well, what if there are other people just as important? Huh? What if there is more to life than *family*?" he sneered.

Slamming my hands down on the desk, I rose slowly, my own rage now showing. "You forget your place, Nicco. I've allowed you to storm the mansion in a fit of fury this past week because I understood you were upset. I, however, will not tolerate dissension. Especially not now when we're up against outside threats. Do you think I don't care? I'm not a heartless bastard! Fucking cool your heels, or I'll have you sidelined myself."

The eerie calm that came over me as I spoke to him settled my own frayed nerves. I'd tried to be patient, knowing they both were upset and worried. My patience had run thin, though, and I needed them both to fall back in line. Nicco glared at me, but he kept his mouth shut. It was a start.

"Things are going on that you're not aware of. I've kept you out of them for your own protection and to honor your wishes. I know you want out, Nicco. I know this isn't the life you envision for yourself."

Nicco's face would've been comical if I wasn't so pissed at him. He quickly schooled his features as he attempted to hide the effect my words had on him. Nicco was an idiot if he thought I didn't know what was going on in the family. I might seem nicer than Dayton, "the Grim Reaper" on the outside, but my father had groomed me from birth to run this empire one day. That type of training left a mark on one's soul.

So while I wanted things to change and be a better environment for our family moving forward, it didn't negate the ruthless killer I was underneath. At the end of the day, I was the boss of this family, and I intended to keep us all safe regardless of what I had to do. It was the weight I had to bear alone.

"Did you think I didn't know about your classes? That you bought the shop and started that foundation? I know you're smarter than that, cous. Don't play dumb now. You've been shouting at me for days. Who knew all I needed to shut you up was reveal I knew your secret."

Sitting back down, I waited for him to gather himself. His jaw ticked as he thought things over. I watched as he clenched and unclenched his fists, his breathing unsteady. Finally, Nicco seemed to have gathered himself enough and took a seat in front of my desk.

"So, what now? Now that you know, I mean?"

Leaning back, I was the picture of calm reassurance as I regarded him. This was the moment I'd been waiting for with Nicco. The chance to either fully bring him in or push him firmly over the edge. I didn't want this life for him if he genuinely despised it. I needed him, but I'd let him make his own decision, even if that was to walk.

This was how I'd be different from Dayton. Family was everything, but you had to want it. It couldn't be forced.

"I'm going to give you a choice. After this conversation, you can fully walk away, no strings or repercussions from the family, or..." I drifted off, waiting to see if he'd take the bait.

"Or what?" he huffed, clearly annoyed now as he leaned back, crossing his arms.

"Or you fully commit to the family and this life. You take Immy's place as the Underboss."

The tension in the room was thick as he glowered at me. His eyes had shone in surprise at my request, but he gave nothing else away. After a few minutes, he broke the silence with a question.

"I don't know how you expect a conversation to change a decision I've had for years, but go ahead, see if you can change my mind."

Disbelief weighed heavy in his words, and he settled back in the chair. Nicco thought he would be walking out of this office a free man to pursue his goals and finally get Loren. Except I knew differently. After he heard what I had to share, it would be the tipping point for him to commit. If it didn't, nothing else would.

"The note you said you got before the explosion. Who do you think it was about?"

"I don't know. I thought it was odd, but I guess," he paused, blowing out a breath as he weighed his words. "I guess I thought it was concerning Immy."

"It's a fair guess, but this time, I believe it didn't only concern her. I have no doubt that Darren left it vague to include both of them."

"*Them*?" Nicco sat up straighter, a look of worry etched in his brow.

Opening my desk drawer, I pulled out the manila envelope I'd gotten the week prior. Nicco would need to choose if he was ready to see the contents or not. Pushing it across the surface, I left it in front of him. With shaky hands, he picked it up and slid out the 8x10 photo from inside. He stared at it for a while, the color draining from his face, his eyes memorizing every detail before swallowing and putting it back in the envelope.

"Tell me everything."

"I GOT your message to Crash. He's agreed to meet, but only if we come to him. He'll be free in an hour," Nicco reported a few hours later.

His anger had shifted from me to the Delgados after I filled him in on the whole picture. Their collaboration with Dayton, or Darren's involvement at least, and what it entailed. I was beginning to expect Austin Delgado, the current boss, had no clue what his son was running in his own family. Add in the suspicion that no one had seen Austin for months. I'd begun to wonder if he was even still alive.

The agreement with Dayton regarding Immy made me suspect an arranged marriage alliance had occurred. With this threat against Loren and this job they wanted us to do, Nicco began to think differently about things. The danger to her life was clear after the explosion, and it was only my reassurance that I had a guard posted along with a nurse who was a friend of the family watching her that finally settled him.

I was beginning to believe my cousin had stronger feelings for Loren than even he knew. Sax, too, for that matter. He'd been almost as bad as Nicco. Reigning in that brute had taken effort, but unlike Nicco, Sax understood the risks and knew the score. Once his need to protect her had been satiated, he could think clearly and knew his presence there would only raise questions. Questions we didn't want to answer or bring to light.

I hated holding them here and keeping her from them. I didn't want to punish Loren, but there wasn't any other way to keep her safe. At least not yet. Immy had regressed into her shell and was avoiding me. She refused to talk to me until I gave her phone back. It was a risk I couldn't take at the moment, so as much as it pained me, my sister ignoring me was the better option, even if that meant she saw me as the enemy.

Focusing back on Nicco, I shut my ledger and stood up from the desk. Rounding it, I grabbed my suit jacket and headed out of the office. Sax waited with Nicco in the hallway, and we all walked toward the garage together. Sax might've accepted his distance from Loren, but he'd been quieter than usual this past week, and I had to guess it was from not seeing her. I tried not to take it personally, but it seemed to weigh on me more and more each day.

The worst part was that Sax knew there wasn't any other option. He was just pissed about it.

Immy intercepted us before we made it to the garage, and I didn't have it in me to deal with her teenage attitude today. Her arms were crossed, and her expression fierce as she blocked our path. It was the strongest I'd seen her in a few days, so while I was annoyed at being delayed, internally, I was glad to see some life returning to her.

"Immy, we don't have time. Please, move."

"No!" Immy screamed, and before I could blink, I felt her palm striking me across the face.

I stood motionless, shocked she'd slapped me. Immy must've felt the same because she stood frozen with her hand in the air. Sax and Nicco stood stock still, watching me to see what I would do. When I didn't retaliate, Immy began to speak again. This time with a lot less sass but determination all the same.

"You're going to tell me what's going on and let me get in touch with Loren or Jude. This isn't fair to them, Attie! I need to know if they're okay."

"You know what isn't fair, Immy? I'm having to stop and have this conversation with you while I'm doing everything I can to save your little boyfriend and therapist, and yet, all you give me is attitude. So, how about you trust me and move out of my way before people are unnecessarily killed? Can you do that? You can be mad at me later."

Immy's lip wobbled, the harshness in my tone uncommon, but I couldn't use kid gloves on her anymore. If she was willing to strike the boss to get her point across, she wasn't the delicate flower I'd cast her as since the incident. We would all need to accept it, and it meant starting with treating her like a full member of this family.

She'd crossed a line by slapping me, and that resulted in a consequence. I'd have to be creative with how I went about it. Nothing would ever cause me to strike her, and our usual form of consequences wouldn't work on her anyway. Immy had taken steps toward a life I didn't know if she wanted, but if she insisted on walking down this path, I would have to be ready and make sure she was as well. First, though, I needed to eradicate the cancer that was Delgado.

Immy moved out of our way and allowed us to pass. I didn't say anything else to her, knowing it would only be a distraction at this point. She would know what was waiting for her when I returned. That would be torture enough for the moment. Nodding to the guard at the door, I wanted to make sure she didn't try to leave. That would be a problem I didn't have time for today.

Before we exited the house, I heard her quiet words whispered into the air, "I'm sorry, Attie…. *please.*"

Her plea gutted something in me, and I wanted nothing more than to be able to fix this for her, to give her what she wanted. I paused in the doorway as I debated, but unfortunately, the best solution might not be the one she wanted. I had to be the man who made that call. So, I didn't acknowledge I heard her words. I couldn't. Instead, I wrapped them safely around my heart and focused on protecting the family.

It was the only thing I could do. The one thing I'd been born to do, and the only promise I could make her. *Family above all.* The scary part was, I wasn't sure who fit into the category anymore. My life was changing all around me, and with it, my worldview. I prayed we'd all be left standing in the end.

"YOU SURE CRASH LIVES OUT HERE?" Sax asked Nicco for the third time. When Nicco didn't answer but merely rolled his eyes, Sax huffed but went back to looking out the window.

We were way outside of Chicago and headed down an unpopulated road. There hadn't been another house for a couple of miles now. I wasn't sure if we were headed to a possible solution or a trap resulting in our deaths. It was hard to know at the minute.

The SUV full of guards stopped ahead of us and turned down a gravel road. Our car followed, as did the one behind us. The three-car parade proceeded to make its way down the long gravel road spitting up dust as we went. I felt bad for whoever had to wash these later.

A house came into view finally, and it was, quite frankly, a dump. It might've been nice at one time, but years of poor maintenance had deteriorated it. If what our sources had found was true, it made sense he lived in such disrepair. The guy was penniless with a mountain of debt on his shoulders.

Dogs barking could be heard as we neared, and as we rolled to a stop, Crash walked out the door, holding a menacing dog by the collar.

"I thought you said he was agreeable to this meeting?" I questioned Nicco as I kept my gaze focused on the mysterious fighter.

"He is. I think he's holding the dog more for you than himself. He's a dog trainer or something. I imagine he's holding the dog back and not using it as a threat, but that's just a guess." Nicco shrugged. He'd been quiet since I'd filled him in on everything dating back almost twenty years. He hadn't remembered Jaz since he was only about eleven at the time, but once he'd heard the whole story, Nicco had jumped all in, as I believed he would.

Based on his reaction to the photo, I think Nicco's priorities had already shifted more than he realized. I hated taking away the normal life he'd dreamed of, and I hoped I'd be able to give it to him someday. But now it was war, and I needed him. We needed people we trusted and who knew the costs. I understood what he'd sacrificed to join me. Now, I had to prove it had been worth it. Loren would be a weakness for him unless I could make it a strength.

I was still working out the how on that one.

Stepping out of the car, the three of us observed our surroundings, training kicking in as we all fell into our roles. The guards were stationed around the property and watched our back as we approached the fighter and his dog.

"Crash, thank you for agreeing to meet with us. I take it you know who my cousin is?" Nicco asked, taking the reins for the moment as I assessed him.

The man gave very little away, and I was impressed with his level of control. Not a lot of people could shield their emotions enough to hide what they felt. Taking in his background, though, growing up in foster care and group homes, I could guess it had been a skill honed as a need of survival.

"I do," Crash responded flatly.

He let go of the dog, who sat back on his haunches, quietly observing us. The dog watched calmly, with no sign of aggression. I felt reassured at the sight but had to assume it was a tactic. Why else would he bring out a scary-ass dog if not to intimidate us a little?

"Crash, or might I call you by your given name, Mr. Young?"

"Whatever you want to call me is your choice."

Attitude rolled off the man in waves, and I had to swallow the urge to put him in his place. He wasn't a made man, he wasn't bound to the hierarchy, and I needed him on our side. Squelching the urge to put him on his knees at his obstinance, I gritted my teeth and swallowed.

"Mr. Young, it's come to my attention you have an issue with the Delgados. Particularly that you owe them a sum of money. Would you say that's correct, Mr. Young?"

"That's one way to look at it."

"How would you phrase it then?"

"For starters, I don't owe them anything. They set me up to take the fall for some Ponzi scheme they had going on. I didn't realize it until too late. I lost everything because of those assholes and my stupid pride for thinking I could outsmart them. So yeah, they say I 'owe them money' because they lost it in the stock markets, but it wasn't their money to begin with. So, I'd say we disagree on the definition of 'owing' a person," he seethed.

The anger rolling off him now was palpable, and the change from the cold, emotionless man a moment ago was astounding. Nicco was right. He was perfect for what we needed.

"So you wouldn't say you have any *loyalty* to them?"

"Fuck no. I'm doing everything I can to stay above water and pay them off. They still want it faster than I get it and decided to beat me up to send a message. There are no good feelings between us."

"Then I think I might have a solution for you, Mr. Young. In agreement with this, we would pay off all your debts and set you up with whatever you need to get back on your feet. You wouldn't owe us anything outside the job. That I can promise."

"Yeah, right, you guys are all the same, or you'll have me doing something worse. I barely escaped prison. I'm not falling into this trap. You can leave now." He rolled his eyes, turning to leave us, done with this conversation.

"I think you might want to hear him out, Crash," Nicco interjected. "It involves the bombing and a certain brunette that likes to punch you in the balls."

Internally, I chuckled at Nicco's statement, making me like Mrs. Carter a little more. Mr. Young stopped in his tracks, his body going rigid at Nicco's claim. Slowly, he turned, an odd look of determination on his face now.

"What is it you want me to do?"

It seems Mrs. Carter was turning out to be the best persuading chip I had. Whatever strange pull she managed to have over all of us was going to save her life.

Because as beautiful as she was, as helpful to Immy as she'd been, as enchanted as I'd become by her... in the end, she was a liability.

And liabilities left you dead in our world.

For her sake, I hoped her power to persuade men to fight in her name lasted longer than her lipstick.

A war was brewing in Chicago, and we were all pieces on the board. The dangerous truth was, I didn't know who was behind it all, the true grandmaster of the game. Worse, I wasn't even confident I knew all the players, yet.

I'd like to think I was the king in this scenario, but the truth I was too scared to admit to myself, the lie I was willing to swallow down whole, my dark confession I hid from everyone... I was only a pawn.

The truth might set you free, but it could also condemn you to a fate worse than death. When no one respected you, a gentle breeze would blow over your kingdom, crumbling it to the ground.

As we walked into a house that was falling apart, I lied to myself that I had everything under control. I lied to myself that this would work. I lied to myself that I didn't care what happened to Loren. But mostly, I lied to myself that I wasn't scared of losing everything and everyone.

I'd been told my whole life the only thing that mattered was the family. That might've been the biggest lie of all.

The danger with lies was, if you told them well enough, you started to believe them.

EPILOGUE

LOREN

It'd been over a month since the explosion, and my body still felt sore all over. I'd begun to wonder if I'd ever remember what it felt like not to hurt every time I moved. My cast was supposed to be coming off in a few days, and I had passed all my tests for brain functions. I'd been so fortunate in that respect.

There were still some pockets of things that I'd lost, and sometimes, it took me longer to recall something. I'd also noticed some shift in my creativity, my spark for photography now diminished. I'd kept that bit of info to myself, scared to admit there had been repercussions. Pretending had become such a habit for me, it was hard to break it when I needed to.

Today was my first day back to work, and I was only seeing a few clients. I didn't have the complete function of my wrist yet, so I'd been placed on part-time. I could at least type to some degree, even if it did take me twice as long. It was more readable than trying to write with my left hand.

Monroe had been successful in taking temporary

custody over Jude until I'd been released from the hospital. With a nurse's aid the first week I was home, we managed everything together. Jude had been a blessing to me during this time, and I felt like he'd kept me from falling back into that pit of despair I was so familiar with.

We'd bonded over the past weeks, spending time together watching movies and binge-watching TV shows on Netflix. Sometimes Levi and Monroe would join us, and it felt like a regular family unit during those moments.

I never did recover my phone and ended up getting new ones for both Jude and me. Neither of us could get a hold of Immy, and the number she had on her paperwork appeared to be a fake one. All the questions and curiosities I had about that family kept building and building, and I wasn't sure I could handle the answers anymore.

Wells had randomly disappeared again, and while I felt terrible for Monroe, I trusted him when he said it was Wells's pattern and not to worry. I dropped it for his sake, but deep down, I was pissed all over again at Surly. He couldn't keep doing this to people and expecting them to be there every time.

Nicco and Sax hadn't been in touch either. It stung the first couple of weeks, but I had finally started to move past it. Monroe and Jude had been a big help in that aspect. Nat and Cami even came over for the girl's night I promised and helped me girly it up. It had been good to laugh and enjoy time with them while Monroe took Jude on a 'dude adventure'. Whatever the hell that meant.

They'd both been quiet about Nicco, and even though I was dying to ask, I didn't. Our friendship was separate, and I didn't want to use them that way. After the initial question of whether they'd heard from him, I quit putting them in the position of having to lie to me. It was apparent they knew something, but it was obvious they couldn't tell me or had been asked not to. I would respect it. I wanted to, at least for the sake of their friendship. They were the first two girls I'd ever really connected with before, and I didn't want to ruin that over a man or two.

Besides, at the end of the day, both Sax and Nicco knew where to find me. My number might be different, but they knew how to track me down, both at work and home. If they didn't want me to find them, I wasn't going to look anymore. I conveniently pushed aside the trip I'd made to Nicco's apartment and tattoo shop, and the scene I caused, to the far recesses. It was part of my moment of insanity, and it was best to ignore that week. At least, it was what I tried to do.

Preparing for my first session, I noticed I had a text from Monroe. He'd been helping me get custody of Jude officially, so I assumed it was an update on the case. Otherwise, I would've waited until my break to check, but I was anxious to see if there had been any updates.

Monroe: Brittni did it. She found a judge willing to grant her temporary custody. She's taking Levi from me. I've just left court. I need to get on top of this. I won't be able to make it to dinner tonight.

Me: Of course. I'm so sorry, Monroe. Let me know if there is anything I can do. I'm here for you.
Monroe: I think we should take some time. I need to focus on this for the moment. I'll be consumed with it. I need to focus on getting my son back right now.

His words sliced through me, and I had to reign in my emotions not to start crying in the middle of my office. The message blinked on my computer, alerting me my client was here. Storing my phone away, I messaged Doris I was ready. They had worked out a new system to bring me my clients, so I wasn't walking as much. It was one of the stipulations from the doctor to return.

I hated being treated differently, but I'd been so bored, I would have agreed to almost anything to return to work. A moment later, the door opened, and she smiled before stepping back to let the client in. I was shocked for a moment when a man entered, not used to seeing them in my office for therapy.

Putting my game face on, I shoved down my feelings about Monroe and focused on this client. I smiled in greeting as he entered and chose a place to sit. Once he was situated, I began the session.

"Hello, I'm Loren. It's nice to meet you. I'm sorry to say I'm a little shocked to see you, though, as I typically only see teens and adult women. Which you obviously are neither," I laughed, but when the client didn't join me, I quickly blanked my expression, realizing I might be more out of practice than I realized.

"Well, can you tell me why you're here and your name?"

"Of course, Mrs. Carter. I do apologize, but I insisted to the wonderful Doris that I had to see you. It was imperative I had you as my therapist. I was recommended to you by a friend, and how much you helped them, so you see, if I was going to come to therapy, then I had to see *you*," he rambled in a somewhat manic nature while maintaining his manners.

It was an odd combination and had me feeling a little on edge. Perhaps, returning to work had been premature. Trying to reassure him, and myself, I offered him a kind smile as I started on his intake form.

"Well, I'm glad you felt you could come in, and hopefully, I'll be a good fit for you. So, let's get started. Can you tell me your name?"

"Oh, yes, my apologies, Mrs. Carter. My name is Dayton Mascro."

To Be Continued in Dangerous Lies

If you made it this far, I just want to say thank you for reading Loren's emotional story. I think as women, we can all relate to at least some aspect of her, or at least that is my hope, that she would resonate with you. Depression can overtake us and even when you know how to deal with things, it can sneak up on you out of nowhere. Many times, we feel like we have to manage it all with a smile. Well, I don't know about you, but smiling gets exhausting after awhile.

Life is hard, but it doesn't have to be all it is. Loren slowly begins to trust herself, make her own decisions, and figure out who she wants to be. I don't know about you, but that resonated with me to my core. I hope you found something to connect with her, or even with the men who are all just as broken in different ways.

If you've read my books before, you know I focus a lot on mental health, trauma, and deep emotions, but especially women overcoming difficult things and finding their strength. This book is no exception and I think you will find Loren does that in her own way.

This book has been the most raw and vulnerable piece I've written yet. It has been healing in a way I hadn't anticipated, but it's also slightly terrifying in a whole different way. I'm going to do my best to avoid reviews in order to protect my emotional well being, but that being said, if you loved the book or it impacted you,

I would love to hear from you. Send me a message on social media, or email and let me know what you thought.

And well, if you didn't love it, and you reach out to me to tell me why, be mindful you just might end up in a book someday. You don't have to like this book, I know everyone won't, but it doesn't mean you need to point it out to me. Be a decent person.

Book 2 will be out shortly, so that cliffhanger won't leave you hanging for long. In the meantime, if you haven't read the Council Series or Pride, they are all on KU. I also have an angsty duet releasing in a few weeks that will be free if you sign up for my newsletter.

ACKNOWLEDGEMENTS

As always, this book was made possible with a lot of love and edits. I'm switching it up this time and shouting out to my husband first. You don't get half the things I'm doing, or what most of it means, but you pretend to be interested, and I love that. This book is for you as well, and our healing journey to hope.

Emma, you were the first person to read this story and encouraged me to keep writing it. Thank you for the love of these characters and encouragement when I was scared to let it out of my sight.

Marla, you rallied along with me after the first draft giving me all the encouragement I needed to keep pushing these characters. Your love for Atticus was quick and I think you love him the most.

To Cat, Tory, and Becki, you three gave it the extra love and care it needed before I sent it off, helping me refine those characters and find the perfect balance. Thank you for your invaluable feedback and willingness to read it so quickly. You guys were the first to shout at me for the ending. Sorry, guys!

To Dani for making it perfect and being a cheerleader for these characters! I'm so glad to have found you.

To my beta babes, sorry to have broken you. Shawna, Kayla, Megan, and Michelle, you gave me the last bit of encouragement I needed to know this book was ready for the masses. Your willingness to answer all my burning questions and be a sounding board for things is what makes you all the best!

To my arc and street team, thank you all to the new readers and the ones who have been with me from the very beginning, you all rock! Your voraciousness for this book has been the boost I needed! Thank you! Thank you!

Dark Confessions

(Dark Contemporary Mafia RH)

Dangerous Truths

Dangerous Lies *Winter 2021

Dangerous Vows *Early 2022

Book 4-TBD *Spring 2022

The Council Series

(Completed contemporary sports RH series)

Damaged Dreams

Shattered Secrets

Fractured Futures

(Council Christmas Novella-Title TBD)

Christmas Wishes : A Christmas Anthology

12/10/21 Preorder the ebook for 0.99 cents

The Order

(Council Spinoff- contemporary spy-esque RH)

Stiletto Sins *Summer 2022

Sinners Fairytales

(Dark Contemporary shared world standalone)

Pride

Tattooed Hearts Duet

(Contemporary Romantic Suspense RH)

Riddled Deceit *free if sign up for newsletter

Smudged Lines *October live release

Kris Butler writes under a pen name to have some separation from her everyday life. Never expecting to write a book, she was surprised when an author friend encouraged her to give it a try and how much she enjoyed it. Having an extensive background in mental health, Kris hopes to normalize mental health issues and the importance of talking about them with her characters and books. Kris is a southern girl at heart but lives with her husband and adorable furbaby somewhere in the Midwest. Kris is an avid fan of Reverse Harem and hopes to add a quirky and new perspective to the emerging genre. If you enjoyed her book, please consider leaving a review. You can contact her the following ways and follow Kris's journey as a new author on social media.